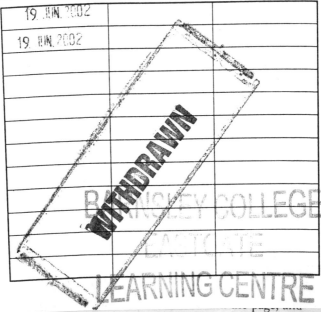
the writing is good enough to ensure that we do . . . a challenging, thought-provoking book.'   PENNY FOX, *Glasgow Herald*

'A vivid, magnetic novel . . . a mix of the story of Marilyn Monroe and the perceptions of Alice Walker, in a gritty, readable style

2796

that gives us Hollywood and ethnic America from a unique angle.
Marsha Hunt is not afraid to face the unfaceable.'

MICHELENE WANDOR, *Ham & High*

'Gripping, poignant and brilliantly written ... Marsha Hunt is
hailed by critics as a writer at the height of her powers and here
that praise is completely justified.'

JENNY PARKIN, *Huddersfield Daily Examiner*

From the Irish Reviews:

'A tautly written page-turner, *Like Venus Fading* tells the story
of Irene O'Brien, a child from the slums of 1920s New Jersey
who becomes America's first black screen goddess, but at a terrible
cost.'

LIAM FAY, *Sunday Times*

'A powerful, horrifying story ... But the tale is so sweetly told it
seduces the reader into paying full attention to the subtleties of
its flavour.'

DJINN GALLAGHER, *Sunday Independent*

'A vividly written tale of abuse, identity, endurance and
resurrection.'

DONAL O'DONOGHUE, *RTE Guide*

'Hunt is a breathtaking writer and her story of Irene O'Brien, a
poor little black girl from the South who finds triumph and
tragedy in Hollywood, is stunningly well told ... a wonderfully
vivid, imaginative, memorable book.'

MADELEINE KEANE, *Image*

Also by Marsha Hunt

REAL LIFE
JOY
FREE
REPOSSESSING ERNESTINE

MARSHA HUNT

Like Venus Fading

Flamingo
An Imprint of HarperCollins*Publishers*

Flamingo
An Imprint of HarperCollins*Publishers*
77–85 Fulham Palace Road,
Hammersmith, London W6 8JB

Published by Flamingo 1999
9 8 7 6 5 4 3 2 1

First published in Great Britain by
Flamingo 1998

Author photograph © Trevor Leighton

ISBN 0 00 655099 1

Set in PostScript Linotype Electra and Monotype Photina by
Rowland Phototypesetting Ltd, Bury St Edmunds, Suffolk

Printed and bound in Great Britain by
Clays Ltd, St Ives plc

Contents

For Alan

'And her joy was nearly like sorrow.'

JOHN STEINBECK
The Grapes of Wrath

The End

Los Angeles. 6 September 1965. Sweltering.

There's a dull stench. I think it's the garbage. But it's me.

The sun feels hot. Is it afternoon? No birds sing.

Why can I hear but not see?

The two ambulance men mistake me for dead.

The one popping chewing gum jabs my right nipple. 'This can't be *the* Irene O'Brien,' he says. 'Irene's got bigger titties.'

I try to scream but nothing comes out.

The gum chewer coughs. 'Wouldn't no movie star be livin' here.'

Tell me about it. Thanks to bankruptcy, my puny, one-bedroom apartment was on the wrong side of Sunset.

'Let's dump her at the hospital and drop by the Fat Burger.'

'This here's a morgue job,' says the one with the deep voice.

'Where's the body bag?'

'You left it downstairs. Throw a sheet over her. Fuck rules.'

I imagine that I am lying face up. But a newspaper picture I later saw showed me curled on my side on the kitchen floor. Stark naked. Which had never been my style. I always sleep in nightgowns and had put one on the night of 5 September before crawling into bed with a nightcap.

The gum chewer says, 'Spooky that her hair's all over the floor.'

I try to scream again but can't get my lips to move.

'Irene O'Brien. She was a credit to the race till she started fucking honkies.'

'Shit . . . you ain't had nothing but white pussy since I known you. Grab the stretcher.'

1

'Stub out that cigarette,' says the deep voice. 'You droppin' ashes on her head.'

As they lift my body, a siren blares with the sound getting closer until it halts abruptly outside my building.

The gum chewer says, 'Check the window. Ain't no coincidence that two ambulances get called out to the same corner at the same time.'

'Betcha Claudeen at the office double-booked again. See her butt in that tight skirt today? She can call out ten ambulances.'

Suddenly from down in the street there is loud raucous laughter. The gum chewer says, 'That's Bobby Lee out there clowning. Don't nobody else laugh that loud. . . He's on duty with tired-ass Charlie Adams.'

'Yell down and say we're on the case.'

'No wait. Let Charlie dump her at the morgue, so Bobby can eat with us.'

My neighbourhood was normally as quiet as a suburb. All white till I moved in. I figured the young professionals were peering from their windows. Blue eyes alarmed.

Then the poodle in 2c started barking.

It's hard to believe that happened almost thirty-five years ago. Here it is, 1998, and who'd believe I'm still kicking?

Tired-ass Charlie Adams.

What would have happened had he not come along? I can still see him drawing on a joint and saying 'Now is won spelt backwards. This minute, this second. That's what matters. The past is memories and bullshit.'

Since he was destined to die young, Charlie should probably have been a musician. He would have made a great Mingus or a Thelonious chasing his angst back and forth through a melody.

On the surface he came across as a draft dodging militant, a college boy with half-baked philosophies. But like Mother used to say, 'The good Lord comes in many guises.'

*   *   *

Just yesterday in a Berkeley bookstore, I heard somebody mention Irene O'Brien and the sales assistant quipped, 'Killed herself back in the sixties.'

It was all I could do not to tap him on the shoulder and say, 'No, I even messed that up.'

Charlie gave me the best advice when he said don't look back. Yet sometimes when I sit out on this roof like tonight, it's hard not to remember the things I made myself forget. Memories are so elusive. A bit like the stars when I'm painting them at dawn. Clear as day one minute, then I turn my back and they're gone.

PART I

Irene Matthews

1

People refer to '29 as the start of the Depression, but it's firm in my memory as the year Mack O'Brien got arrested for killing his wife.

I guess I was Mack's bit on the side, though I was only six and he was forty-five. Had I been older, I might have realized that his wife suspected he was up to no good, because twice that October I'd stood outside their corner store and heard Mrs O'Brien drill him. Once she'd yelled, 'I know what you're up to!' But she didn't really raise hell until he slipped two free pork chops to Hortense Alvarez, our neighbour down the hall, whom Mother accused of flaunting her large bosom.

I don't tell my age, but it's relevant that I was born 11 November 1922, because that same day four years earlier, World War I had ended. So most neighbourhoods held their annual block parties around my birthday. Whole streets decorated. Red, white and blue streamers, our Stars and Stripes billowing on flagpoles. Victory blowing in the wind and we kids bragging that we'd won that war. Patriotism was powerful back then.

Miss Hortense, as my sister Lilian and I called her, lived in a room above Mack's grocery like we did. But whereas ours was L-shaped and overlooked Buchanan Street, Miss Hortense lived at the back near the toilet. She had two windows like ours, but hers glimpsed Philadelphia's skyline on the opposite side of the Delaware River.

Mother rented our room from Mack. Two dollars a week, I think she paid. She kept it spick-and-span and considered that corner of Camden, New Jersey to be her slice of paradise, because growing up like she did in a Mississippi backwater, any place north of the Mason-Dixon Line was heaven.

Miss Hortense, who I idolized, was from Rosarita Beach, Mexico, having come to Camden via Los Angeles. She'd done some walk-ons on the silent screen which Mother said gave her airs.

I adored Hortense and she used to half tolerate me running up to greet her in the street. Occasionally she'd even let me hold her hand. 'Irene,' she'd say, 'you got sense, and if you don't get fat like your mother, you gonna be a pretty woman. Finish the school, then go straight away to California. You could be a maid to one of them big, big stars.'

I can remember daydreaming about how I'd become a maid in a uniform like a pretty brown-skinned one I'd once seen on the silent screen. No Aunt Jemima in a head-rag but a credit to the race.

Lilian used to believe that living above Mack's had been the best time of our lives. But after I became a name, I slipped back to our old neighbourhood to discover that our corner of Prince and Buchanan had nothing to recommend it. Rows of poky, brick-faced, two- and three-storey houses with little two-by-four windows. Dusty sidewalks littered with rubbish. Kids looking like they didn't have homes and old people sitting on stoops brushing away the flies.

Mother had been so grateful because the area had a handful of Negro families dotted amongst the poor whites: new immigrants who probably didn't understand about segregation.

Camden, New Jersey. Connected to Philly by the Delaware River Bridge which I'd thought was majestic. The nuns had me believing that bridge was the hub of the universe.

Lil and me with Mother.

It's hard to believe that we three once shared a bed, a pile of newspapers padded with blankets. Covered with a blue and pink floral bedspread in summer and our coats in winter. No lamp or side table.

I thought we were rich because the Herzfelds that Mother worked for had loaned her their old Motorola radio. To start, it needed a hard whack and had a loud, annoying hum. But even that became as much comfort to me as the crooners crackling from it. Rudi Vallee, Vaughn DeLeath, The Rhythm Boys . . . Lil and I used to

8

stand side by side, shoulders touching, straining to imitate their old-timey harmonies.

We ate and did homework at a square pine table in a corner. We had three wooden chairs and I'd sit there with my copybooks gazing out that window.

I was content. Especially when Lilian and I sat opposite each other devouring goodies Mother brought from work. The Herzfelds employed her at four dollars a week plus leftovers, and we ate so well from their table that we hardly spent much in Mack's.

I remember being six like it was yesterday.

I see myself standing by the head of Miss Hortense's bed one Saturday morning in my red and white polka-dot dress. A flimsy little seersucker that Mrs Herzfeld had given to Mother because it had peach stains down the front.

Each Saturday while Miss Hortense was at ten o'clock mass, Lilian and I cleaned her room and changed the bedclothes.

That particular Saturday, although it was still summertime, she'd gone out wearing her black velvet cloak. Not that we dared question why, because kids asked nothing back then.

Miss Hortense made some remark about being chilly, but we were having a heatwave. Through the hole in her floorboards we could hear the ice man complaining to Mack that it was so hot that his blocks of ice were melting faster than he could deliver them. Hortense's was directly above Mack's storeroom and as Lilian and I folded the dirty sheet, we could hear the white voices mingling and Mack intermittently whistling, 'It's a Long Way to Tipperary' and 'Smile'.

Called himself Irish but was New Jersey born like me.

Miss Hortense's room was stuffy as a closet that Saturday in '29 and I recall just how Lil and I stood either end of the ray of sunlight, struggling to fold Hortense's sheet without letting it touch the floor.

Mother had gone to work at 6 AM, because Mrs Herzfeld was holding her nephew's bar mitzvah. This meant extra hours for Mother and the likelihood of kosher treats that night for us.

9

I was practically nursed on pickled herrings and potato latkes and still get cravings for strudel, thanks to the Herzfelds' preferences. And their lemon cake! It makes my mouth water just to think about it, although it was the one dessert that Mrs Herzfeld was stingy with. Mother always came home with crumbs instead of slices.

My sister and I actually preferred those odd Saturdays when Mother left at dawn, because we didn't have to wash first thing and heard at least two radio shows before doing chores for Miss Hortense.

Lilian, being devout in those days, always reminded me to be thankful for Mr Herzfeld's old set which was plugged into the light socket in the middle of our room. We never minded walking around it. Being small for our age, the radio was taller than us.

The day that Miss Hortense went out in her velvet cloak, we had listened to *Storybook Hour* when we got up.

Our Saturday-morning job made me feel grown up, although Mother kept the proceeds, and we never expected otherwise. But had I known that those were as much of the halcyon days as I was going to get until I turned nearly forty-three, I might have been upset that I wasn't in the street playing hopscotch or bouncing a ball.

Had we known that all we took for granted would soon fade, we might have savoured each second and not killed the flies that plagued us. Lilian probably wouldn't have slapped me for accidentally ripping the arm off her paper doll, and I might have appreciated the boiled eggs Mother had left for breakfast. Maybe Mack would even have forgiven the ice man for bringing his order two days late.

Mack and Mrs O'Brien owned our building and another identical to it a block east of Prince. But they lived over on Hanover which had trees and neat A-frame houses with porches, front lawns and hedges, and a few families even had cars.

Mrs O'Brien only had part-time help and their neighbourhood wasn't as fancy as the Herzfelds', who not only employed Mother full time but needed a Saturday yardman as well.

Mother used to say, 'Mis' Herzfeld cares more about them flower beds than them four girls.'

Mack and Mrs O'Brien were childless and had inherited their properties from her father, Tommy Sullivan, who'd died in '25.

Even our priest, Father Connolly, complained about the store.

In their dirty window display, sun-bleached Corn Flakes boxes leaned this way and that. Dead flies and soot had been collecting around them for so long that Mother had finally said, 'Lemme clean your window for free.'

Of course, Mrs O'Brien had snubbed the offer like she'd always snubbed Mother, who nevertheless grinned and fawned. Petrified that we'd be evicted.

Mother died a little every time she saw Mrs O'Brien. Both Mack and his wife got a kick out of seeing Mother crawl when she was as little as a dime short with the rent. So, little though I was, I tried to do my share to keep Mack happy. At least that's why I tell myself I let him feel in my bloomers.

To any fool who'd listen, and it was most often me, Mack would explain that he was a butcher by trade and was saving to buy a real butcher's shop, kitted out with a walk-in cold store, chopping blocks, hanging rails and dark green awning. He'd describe how he was going to unwind this awning that would shade his name painted in a semi-circle on the window. He even talked about getting one of the fancy meat grinders which I told him that I'd seen in the kosher butcher where Mother shopped for the Herzfelds.

I used to stand in Mack's watching him scratch his behind and listen to his big talk. 'Irene,' he'd say, 'you'll sweep my floor and be delivery girl. But you've got to get bigger before you can clean butcher's knives.' I used to daydream of wearing a blood-stained butcher's apron and despaired that this wouldn't happen after Mack was accused of murdering Mrs O'Brien.

While he supposedly ran the store, her sole duty was to arrive in her fox-fur stole to empty the cash register after a day of lounging at home. She used to mosey in at five during winter and six in summer when Mack stayed open longer.

The kids in the neighbourhood called her Humpty Dumpty but she wasn't exactly egg-shaped. She had thick, reddish-brown hair, the same colour as her stole, and might have been attractive had her teeth not been rotten.

Mack said she'd kill me if I told anybody what we did in his storeroom, but I might have told anyway had Mrs O'Brien lived longer, because I was a blabbermouth.

How was I to know that his game in the dark was wrong?

I actually thought I was the one who would go to hell for not sharing the measly caramels he gave me with Lilian.

At six, I missed the plot.

For instance, I couldn't figure out why Mrs O'Brien got so upset because Mack gave Miss Hortense two free chops. I couldn't understand how they had caused so much havoc. Especially since I had collected and delivered them. But now, I understand that it matters to a wife if her man is giving things to another woman. Particularly one as pretty as Hortense was.

Right up to the Second World War, amongst the clippings which mother saved about Lilian and me, she kept the headlines of the *Philadelphia Inquirer* which had featured Mack's trial. I finally convinced her to throw it out by claiming that the picture didn't do him justice. I said, 'Mother, he looks terrible with those little teeth and big gums.' He wasn't wearing his glasses or calico apron which he double tied around his belly . . . And his straw boater had slid back exposing his bald head.

Me and Mack . . . whose vile breath reeked of garlic salami.

He did more than anybody realized to prepare me for the Hollywood relays. Who could have trained me better to endure the humiliations of fat-bellied old men who belched and farted as they reached inside me, searching for what they'd lost? Still, it disturbs me less for myself than for the world to think that all those years ago, when people still supposedly had some morals, a forty-five-year-old with a wife needed to sneak into the shadows of a nasty storeroom to slide his finger between the bony legs of a six-year-old.

But what really stings me is suspecting that Mother knew.

Before the War, she used to reminisce about Camden with an air of innocence and say, 'I keep meaning to find out what happened to Mack. He stayed locked up all those years and then they decided that he didn't do it. But during the summer of 1930 before I was eight, when Mother moved us to Los Angeles, I had already eased him out of my mind.

Forgot him. Forgot his storeroom. Became the Olympic champion of blotting ugliness from my mind. 'What You Can't Forgive, Forget' became my motto.

Yes, so I forgot Mack, like I forgot Daddy.

Denial was my partner in crime, whereas my sister, Lil, is probably still recovering from the shock of Pearl Harbor. Still contemplating who she could have been or should have been . . . The queen of 'If Only . . .'

Had I stopped to look back, to examine the hurts and debris I left behind, I doubt that I would have had the courage to carry on. But suddenly tonight I finally feel safe.

Nothing soothes me like being out in this night air listening to the wind rustle the pines while I'm under this canopy of stars. If I close my eyes, it could be the ocean I hear, waves crashing against rocks. I can sit out here on this roof garden with the dark surrounding me and the dog snoring at my feet and I am not lost.

The way Venus is juxtaposed to the moon and Orion is outshining the Big Dipper makes me feel brave enough to recall what I've buried in the cellars of my mind.

In a few hours, Daylight Saving begins, and tomorrow's Palm Sunday, the day Christ entered Jerusalem victorious. Is that really why I got off so easy? Because he died for my sins?

2

Hortense Alvarez couldn't have been more than a bit player during the silents . . . Not with her dark complexion . . . Yet the photograph she had of herself in a group with Charlie Chaplin in his tramp outfit made Lilian and me take her for a movie star.

I now realize that that picture had just been a location shot, but as a kid I imagined that Miss Hortense and Chaplin were really connected. And since he was featured on posters outside the Biograph, I thought he was more important than the President. It filled my head with fantasies, and I secretly expected him to come knocking for Miss Hortense any day.

Mother used to say, 'Hortense ain't all that to look at, even with her fox stole slung over that velvet dress to draw attention to her bosom. She tiptoes round like she thinks she white, but a Mexican ain't nothing.'

To brush against Miss Hortense's black velvet dress was like brushing against mink and hearing her warble 'Ave Maria' behind her closed door added something exotic to our otherwise dismal treks to the toilet where the only excitement was to sometimes get a splinter in my foot.

Her old kerosene burner was the sole object in her room which I didn't wish was mine. It smelled like burning hair and sat near the window above a bucket of water she kept to rinse her china cup and saucer which she drained of watery weak coffee or strong green tea several times a day.

Some Saturdays when we cleaned her room Miss Hortense would dawdle for a few minutes and speak to Lil and me in that broken English. But I saw her as mysterious and magical rather than a stuck-up, independent spinster which is how Mother sometimes described her . . . And she alone may have inspired Mother's sideways assault on Hollywood, because she said that if Hortense could get into movies, anybody could.

Lil and I knew what was in her bureau, because on Saturdays we handled her most intimate things.

I had watched Lilian giggle until tears ran down her cheeks the first time we found Miss Hortense's corset.

But no letters ever arrived for Hortense and her past remained her own. Except for the picture with Chaplin, which she probably left out for a reason.

We believed that she had no friends other than Father Connolly who would climb the stairs to reach her even when he said his arthritis had him too stiff to bend his knees.

It was shocking to hear his laughter behind her door, because when he served at the altar, or when he limped down the halls of St Anthony's Elementary School, I imagined that to be joyless was part of a priest's calling. But in Miss Hortense's room his laugh would erupt like a volcano. Like a blast of dynamite that was sparked by her giggle which was silvery. As delicate as my glass chime in a night breeze.

The Mexican señorita and the old Irish priest.

Far from home in Camden, New Jersey.

With the view of the skyscrapers in Philadelphia to remind them that there was a lot more to life than what was on offer at that corner of Buchanan and Prince.

Father Connolly's green eyes must have often fallen on that photograph of Miss Hortense dressed in a frilly white blouse and ankle-length skirt in that group shot with Charlie Chaplin. And she must have told him like she'd told us, 'Tell no-one.' And maybe like Lilian and I, he carried it to the window to examine it better, as frustrated as we'd been that the sepia image of those seven people standing in a line wasn't sharp enough. Five men and two women on a studio lot in Hollywood. No fancy scenery. No trees. No animals. No props. Just six white faces and Hortense Alvarez. Right there in that line with the great Charlie Chaplin.

Mother always wondered what Hortense was living on and interrogated me, because Lilian was more interested in her catechism.

Mother's questions usually came when my back was to her while she greased and braided my hair; my thin, kinky braids which to my great dismay barely reached my shoulders.

I'd grit my teeth, anticipating Mother's yanks with the comb. Her breath warm against the back of my ear.

'Irene, now where's she getting the money to dye her hair? Couldn't nobody's hair be that black. It ain't natural ... And what about all that to-ing and fro-ing to church? Father Connolly wouldn't be slipping by here if she wasn't putting something in that collection box every day.'

Who could blame Mother for her agitations?

Mother was fat and Miss Hortense was thin.

Hortense dozed under her satin quilt while Mother rushed to work six days a week in all kinds of weather and got neither holiday nor holiday pay.

While Hortense spent as much time in quiet prayer as a nun, Ruthie Mae Matthews, who was a very old twenty-five, worked hard to feed us from the Herzfelds' table.

Some great artist should have painted Miss Hortense kneeling in the back pew at St Anthony's. Her jet hair as thick as a horse's tail was always covered by a white lace mantilla which had belonged to her grandmother.

Along with high mass on Sunday, with its incense and candlelight and the Latin chants, she was the pomp and show business in my life, and considering that we hardly had furniture and slept on stacks of newspapers which Mother cleverly arranged like a low mattress, it's a wonder that Lilian and I knew how to make Miss Hortense's bed.

But we loved handling the satin quilt with the matching pillow case and polishing her dresser which meant that one of us got to lift the white kid gloves with the pearl buttons which rested upon it. My sister and I wouldn't have handled Miss Hortense's things with greater care had she been Mary Pickford.

I understood why Father Connolly sought her company and Mack gave her those pork chops.

Several times she visited our room to listen to the radio, but she didn't speak enough English to appreciate the seven-o'clock comedy hour, so Mother would tune into some music.

Miss Hortense always arrived with her own chair and a Chesterfield cigarette for Mother, although neither of them smoked. Mother would slip the cigarette into a cigar box where she kept our baptismal papers, and the four of us would arrange our chairs around Mr Herzfeld's radio, sitting as attentively as an audience at a piano recital.

The music we listened to was invariably interrupted by loud crackling, because reception was poor at night, but it didn't faze us. And if there was a piece of strudel to split between us, Miss Hortense would only accept the smallest piece which she'd nibble and say, 'We have a party.'

Mother's eyes bulged with shock and envy the evening that Miss Hortense told us as she was leaving, that she was going to be taking singing lessons in Philadelphia. Mother yelped, 'Singing lessons!' as though she had been asked to pay for them.

Miss Hortense had her hand on the radio console which was so warm it added to the heat of that summer's night, while the sounds of boys playing stickball below in the street drifted up through our open windows.

Lifting her tiny foot to adjust the ankle strap of her high heel, she said, 'I went to see about English lessons, but I can take singing lessons for less.'

My heart leapt and I thought that I was in the presence of a saint. I could see her on posters and imagine her on advertisements draped in furs.

For all the nonsense which will be remembered as my life, who will ever know the impact that Hortense Alvarez made. It's now conceivable to me that Father Connolly was in love with her. After all, he was only a man and men of all persuasions fall in love, though priests aren't meant to. So at six, before I had enough savvy to shade the grey into black and white situations, I would have called his sin love, but now I'd see it as human nature taking control.

3

Hortense.

Mack.

In my child's world, they were family. And I was as hungry for the caramels he would slip me as he was for the sordid pleasures he took for them.

That first time he touched me must have been some weeks before the stock market crashed. At the end of summer. When the nights still twinkled from the fluorescent lightning bugs that Lil and I used to catch, and the mornings brought a few hours of dry relief to those last, long, humid days.

Trying to keep up with Lilian, wanting to learn to whistle because she could, is what I partly think led me to his store that afternoon.

For as long as I can remember, I struggled to keep up with Lilian. That's how I got old before my time. Desperate to do everything that she could. At six I was struggling to be eight and a half like her.

All that summer, Mother had been talking about us being the angels in St Anthony's big Christmas pageant. It was months away, but she was always looking for ways to impress Mrs Herzfeld, whose four girls all did well at school. But it was Miss Hortense who came up with the cockamamie idea that we should learn to whistle 'Silent Night' instead of singing it. Mother got as excited as a kid about that. So by the time the fall term began, whistling at the Christmas pageant was all that I could think about.

And there was autumn, that foolhardy autumn, rushing into a head-on crash with the Depression.

The elm beside the church was shedding leaves by late September and Mother was dressing us each morning in the high socks handed down by Mrs Herzfeld. But they were too big to stay up on my bony legs.

Socks. Were they part of the reason I ended up alone that rainy afternoon in Mack's?

Lilian was off school that day with what Mother feared was mumps, and I walked home from school amongst a gang of the other kids.

Although my socks kept slipping down into my shoes, I was scared to bend over and pull them up, in case one of the boys teased me about my legs. So when I felt a drop of rain on my forehead, my socks were clumped around my ankles. As it suddenly pelted down the other children ran, but my socks slowed my pace.

It felt good to be in the rain as I dawdled home. I remember taking a deep breath and pretending that I was exhaling cigarette smoke.

I felt grown. Bold. Out there on my own . . . Six years old . . .

When I passed a robin on a water hydrant who seemed to be whistling at me, I tried whistling back, puffed out my cheeks and blew, but all that came forth was my breath.

I'd often heard Mack whistle through the broken floorboards in Miss Hortense's room, so, sticking my copybook under the sweater of my uniform, I headed straight for his store like somebody with a mission.

Mother was at work, my sister was in bed, and with my socks around my ankles, what immediately came to mind was Mother's daily 'Don't you girls go talking to strangers.' But Mack O'Brien was no stranger. He was the man she gave the rent to. The landlord who could make her bottom lip tremble over a dime.

Did I decide to ask him for a whistling lesson to satisfy my mother's pitiful ambition to brag to Mrs Herzfeld that we had been chosen for the Catholic Christmas pageant?

Did I head for that store to tempt that man, or did evil coax me to slip there alone? I was quiet and shy, maybe even a little mousey

19

and normally took pride in following rules and doing exactly as I was told. But to blame myself is easier than blaming Mother. Yet I have a vague recollection that she'd told me to stop by Mack's after school.

I recall what I did but never remember exactly why. Just like that night before I was found on the kitchen floor ... I can pull the oddest details out of the hat but am hazy about the crucial facts.

It's possible that what I remember as a perfumed downpour in '29 was just another Jersey drizzle. Maybe I'm trying to make something monumental of a bad luck day.

A small bell attached to Mack's door jingled when it opened or closed. Tinkled like a Christmas bell. It was the only nice thing in the store apart from the silver cash register which Mrs O'Brien bragged was antique. As the bell jangled above my head, I was greeted by the smell of his open jar of striped candy canes wafting from the counter, mingling with the scent of rotting bananas.

I couldn't have felt more anxious had I gone in there to steal. My heart was throbbing. Nose started running. Legs felt shaky ... I was like somebody experiencing a heavy dose of stage fright.

Mack's tap was dripping in the back room and rain was spitting on his display window. Somebody had drawn an 'eight' in the dust on an empty bottom shelf and my own fingers nervously rubbed the rough cover of my yellow copybook.

Mack was seated behind his marble counter. With an elbow resting on the till, he was grumbling loudly to himself about shank.

Of course he was crazy, but I didn't know it. Back then I thought storekeepers were mini-gods, along with priests and police-men.

Mother thought Mack was good with kids, because he would tease Lilian about her braids sticking out or he'd jibe Willie Ruttles about the racket Willie's scooter made on the cobblestones. But when I walked in out of the rain that day, Mack didn't acknowledge me.

I stood in the doorway staring at him, recalling how Father Connolly had said that when Mack's father-in-law, Tommy Sullivan, had had the store, there was no cleaner grocery in Camden. Father and Tommy had been schoolboys together in some Irish fishing village and had moved to the States around the same time. Father would say in his sing-songy way, 'Tommy was a fair landlord and the finest grocer to come out of County Mayo. Even before I took over his parish, he gave more than a tenth of his income to the Sisters of St Anthony's.'

I stood with my mouth open, thinking of how to ask Mack to show me how to whistle, but what came out was, 'What's a shank, Mr Mack?'

Peering at me from behind the cash register with his hairy hands planted either side of the counter, he rose to answer my question. His glasses magnified his sunken eyes. 'A shank, Irene? That same word stumped me on my first day apprenticed to a butcher on Rathbone Street. I was just a kid.'

It always pleased me that he knew my name.

As he spoke I inched further into the store which not only smelled of rotting bananas, but of the pickle barrel and those peppermints.

The stench in Mack's was a constant source of speculation between my mother and Miss Hortense, because Mack didn't sell bananas any more than he sold fresh meat. Miss Hortense was sure that the rotten banana smell was Tommy Sullivan, trying to materialize after Mrs O'Brien left the store door ajar to admit her father's spirit on All Souls' Day. Mother thought it was a rat decaying under the counter.

With the blind half drawn, it was hard to see the dust on the shelves of canned goods. It also made it harder to spot the cobwebs which hung like cheesecloth above the door that led to the storeroom.

The only thing he wiped was the counter which he swabbed occasionally with a grimy rag. Otherwise, he expected the stock and shelves to mind themselves.

The old feather duster, which never left its hook by the double doors, had belonged to his father-in-law. Like the broom propped in the alcove against a jumble of wooden clothes pegs, tapered candles, tins of rat poison, boxes of nails and Dutch Boy cleanser. Leftovers from the days when Mrs O'Brien's father had sold hardware as well as food.

The sawdust on the floor, caked with dirt and dust, made Miss Hortense sneeze. So, often when she had needed something, I was sent with her shopping list scribbled on a torn piece of brown paper bag. Those regular trips down our dim, narrow staircase and out the door which was ten steps from Mack's gave me the same odd feeling that I had in his store that afternoon as the rain fell.

When Mack explained what a shank was, it must have been mid or late September. Hardly a matter of weeks between my request for a whistling lesson and the end of Mrs O'Brien's life; between hope for the future and the Depression.

He pointed to my exposed shin saying, 'That's your shank and if you come closer, you can feel mine.'

Mack drew up his pants leg. His ghostly skin looked so white to me. And hairy. I couldn't have been more interested had he offered to let me stroke a live mink. I touched the orange fuzzy hairs with my index finger and allowed him to run his thumb along mine while he quizzed me about school.

I said, 'I'm the youngest girl in Sister Elizabeth's class.'

Mack teased, 'Does that make you ten?'

'I'm six ... seven on 11 November. On Armistice Day.'

He pulled up my socks. '11 November?' he said. 'So that's how come there's a parade downtown! It's your birthday!'

I didn't expect to be lifted up, but I liked seeing the store at that height. Up with the cans of potted meat that I had seen him take down for Miss Hortense whenever I'd come as errand girl. His thick fingers curled around my thighs, but I was embarrassed to ask him to put me down. He hugged me so close that my instinct told me to wriggle free.

So close that the only air left to breathe was heavy with his smelly breath ... When he finally put me down, some sweat from his forehead was on my leg but I didn't dare wipe it and just clung to my copybook.

He patted me on the behind and said, 'When Ruthie gets home, tell her Mack said everything's okay.'

He'd been smart to treat me to a caramel. Unlike a mint, it left no scent of our encounter on my breath.

That September of '29 turned out to be the last time Mother paid him rent. I recall standing with her in his store and she was holding my hand. Mack's voice was high pitched and he had a habit of starting a sentence without finishing it, but whenever he spoke to her, she'd get so anxious, she'd finish them for him. I remember him saying 'Your Irene . . .' and leaving my name to dangle in the stinky air.

Mother clutched my hand tighter and pulled me nearer and her normally lazy speech was punctuated by a note of alarm. 'She ain't but six! She's my baby!' Then she fell silent, head bowed like an obedient child. And while I looked from her to him I felt something was wrong but I knew better than to ask what.

While Mack was telling her that he loved to sit me on his lap and recall his days in Patterson as a butcher's apprentice, Mother's palm grew sweaty. 'She don't fidget,' he'd said, 'and asks intelligent questions.'

Of course I used to sit still while his dinky grew hard under the weight of my behind.

Was it in ignorance that Mother imagined that I would have no aversion to Mack's breath or the way that he would sit me too squarely on his lap? Not on one knee but drawn back against his blubbery belly so that all I could think about was his belt buckle pressing against my spine.

That afternoon, Mack closed the shop after his wife had emptied the cash register and drove home, leaving him to pull the blind down before slamming the door on the dust, the food, the odours and those caramels which were flat and round with a vein of white sugar running through them.

Were we playing out our part in the great scheme of things?

Maybe, like Charlie used to say, we're all just dominoes . . . maybe Mack had to do what he did to twist me towards becoming what I became.

Anyway, sitting out here tonight I'd be lying if I claimed that I ever lost sleep over him.

4

When the O'Malleys opened a grocery store two blocks away, across from the Italian bakery, people like Mother still bought a few items on credit from Mack but O'Malley's attracted the neighbourhood's Irish customers.

So, while I waited impatiently for my seventh birthday, praying for the days to gallop by, Mack, with business lagging, would lure me with caramels to his storeroom every time I played Miss Hortense's errand girl.

Worried that Lilian might spot candy juice in the corners of my mouth, I'd stand at the bottom of the stairs to gobble that caramel before running back up with Miss Hortense's items.

Mack told me about his plan to give away items to customers spending over fifty cents, and though I couldn't read the sign when he placed it amongst the dead flies and the faded Corn Flakes boxes, I knew it said something about his offer.

When Mother received a free bar of Sunlight soap, I expected Miss Hortense to receive something better. A can of condensed cream or even a tin of kerosene. Some lanolin or a bottle of Karo Syrup, because she was a regular, thanks to me. But Mother was speechless when she heard that Miss Hortense had received two pork chops.

And what upset Mother most was who told her the news.

She had arrived home early from work that evening, hanging her coat on the back of the door as the six o'clock whistle blew.

I helped her slip off her shoes which she always removed before her hat. Lilian and I knew better than to try and talk to her till she'd had her cup of sweet tea, but we also knew when she switched on the radio and hummed along with a tune that she was in a good mood.

The afternoon's rain had sweetened the evening air and the sunset was dark apricot. While Lilian studied her catechism, I slid my chair nearer the radio. Mother hadn't noticed that my hair was still damp, because earlier I'd gone to the butcher for Mack. I was eager to explain, though she looked too tired for details, and I prayed that we could get through the evening without her noticing that my shoes had got wet.

Mother still had her hat on when Mrs O'Brien rapped at our door. 'Ruthie, I want you out!' she yelled like someone might yell 'Fire!'. Within that second our peaceful lives felt as overturned as dirty clothes tossed from a laundry basket. Mrs O'Brien had never been to our room before and to hear her snap at my mother from the doorway made me wish for my funeral. Casket. Hearse. Mourners. Death seemed easiest.

Though I'd told no one about my visits to Mack's storeroom, I sensed from his wife's violent rap on our door that he must have. My ears started ringing and I thought I would vomit as my lips quivered, my mouth went dry, and my knees seemed to buckle under me.

Today kids have rights, but in those days white people could do anything to coloured children, and I burst into tears, believing that I would be jailed or killed and damned to Lucifer's cauldrons by every caramel that Mack had given me.

Whenever I cried, whatever the circumstances, I have to admit that Lilian used to rush to console me. So while Mother stood at the door face to face with Mrs O'Brien, Lilian's solidarity made me feel all the more guilty as she whispered, 'Don't cry . . . Don't cry . . . That old witch can't hurt Mother!'

I sobbed louder, staining my sister's red sweater with tears and needing the toilet so badly that I was ready to pee myself.

'Hush up, Irene!' my mother yelled over her shoulder. Her being much wider than Mrs O'Brien, all that I could see of Mack's wife in the doorway was the feather in her hat as her voice spat out an ultimatum that threw a pall over our room. 'Out!' shouted Mrs O'Brien, 'I want you out of here before Thanksgiving.'

From the way that Mother stood with her shoulders drooping, her large arms folded in front of her and her flat feet planted too firmly on the floorboards, it was obvious that she was too weary to face an assault. There was a litany of reasons why she might have looked so beaten. Perhaps the Herzfeld girls had been bickering with each other all day or Mr Herzfeld had complained again about Mother's cooking.

Miss Hortense said her rosary before night fell, and nothing could disturb her religious meditations. Not even the sound of Mrs O'Brien yelling, 'Not only did Irene collect those chops from the butcher, but she delivered them to that snotty little hussy down the hall!'

A surge went through me as I was restored from darkness to light, realizing that Mrs O'Brien had only come to complain about my trip to the butcher for Mack.

Lilian held me tighter and I found enough confidence to explain that when Miss Hortense had sent me to Mack's to buy crackers earlier, he'd sent me over to Enright's Butcher's for her gift.

I was too terrified of my mother's reaction to mention that I'd gone in the rain and I was also afraid that Mrs O'Brien might guess that the free caramel Mack had given me wasn't the first I'd swallowed.

When I'd set off, the distance had been less worrying than the big street I had to cross and the drunks that I expected to encounter on the way. But what made me certain that I could survive the long walk was that that morning before school I'd stuck what I believed to be a lucky penny in my shoe. My mind focused upon it as I made my way to the butcher's, hopping and skipping to quell my fear as I was pelted by rain.

I can still remember the feel of the penny against the ball of my right foot as I skipped along. It must have been about four in the afternoon. There were no children out and clouds filled the sky. While I thought about the penny, the story of a chick named Henny Penny snuck into my mind. Having heard the story on the radio and seen an illustration of Henny Penny in a storybook at school, I suddenly felt that I was that yellow chick who had run around the farmyard to alert the animals that the sky was falling as a black cloud pursued him. A line from the story repeated in my head: 'The sky is falling ... the sky is falling ...'

When I rounded a corner and spotted Enright's, I saw it as shelter and ran in, more to seek safety than to do that errand for Mack.

Drenched and panting, I clutched his note so tightly that my fingers ached.

I'm not one for gasping. Hell, I didn't gasp when I heard that I was up for that Oscar ... nor when the doctor confirmed that there was something wrong with my little Nadine. But I definitely gasped that afternoon in Enright's ... Sucking my breath in hard at the sight of Mrs O'Brien standing there in a raincoat waiting to be served. Two women were ahead of her who both turned to look down at me when she snapped, 'Mercy, Irene! Trust your mother to send you out in this storm.'

It was Mrs O'Brien's sugary voice, reserved for Mack's Irish customers. I wouldn't have believed that she was addressing me had I not heard my name.

She'd called me *I*-rene with the stress on the 'I', but I-*reen* is correct.

And without meaning to, I actually looked into her eyes.

They were blue. A clear aquamarine. They sparked anger that went way, way back. Somewhere deep.

Mack's wife. Nola O'Brien. More important to him than I was.

She spoke so loudly that the butcher and his boy and the two female customers heard her. 'Your mother has owed me fifty cents since the first of the month. I knew she was lying when she claimed she didn't have it, and it'd better not be my money she's wasting on meat.'

Her husband had on several occasions fingered me in his dank storeroom, but I had yet to figure out that I had good reason to be fighting mad at her for that. All I knew was that Mrs O'Brien was calling Mother a liar, and insulting somebody's mother in those days was a battle cry.

Scared to raise my head, with my eyes glued to Mrs O'Brien's galoshes and my heart pounding, I found the gumption to say, 'Leave my Mother alone!' Coward that I was, I probably only said it above a whisper, but somebody heard, an old craggy woman in a headscarf who whacked me on the head with the handle of her umbrella saying, 'No-account little niggers make you forget yourself.' When my arms flew to protect my head, I dropped Mack's note and, wet and wounded, I howled like a baby.

To be honest, I really thought I had no right to be in Enright's, because he was a white butcher and his customers were white.

Mrs O'Brien leered over me like she'd been smelling my scent on her husband's fingertips. As I bent to pick up Mack's note which had fallen by her foot, she kicked my hand away and reached down herself.

Her eyes flashed like a cat ready to take on a dog, and I was too terrified to swallow.

When she snorted, 'Kidneys!' only a crack of lightning could have made me jump more.

Before I could run Mrs O'Brien grabbed me, thrusting me violently towards the meat chopping block. Then she snapped, 'Mr Enright, give this child a couple pork chops. With the kidneys, and don't give her your best.' My pulse was pounding in my ears and I was gulping big sobs.

I blubbered half the way home, but the rain had stopped and when I spotted a rainbow, I forgot that I'd been hit. I'd heard about rainbows and seen them in storybooks but had never seen one for real and the sight now filled me with overwhelming glee. Of course this sudden mood switch, this inability to hold onto torment, is a sign of a weak character, a failing that Mother always said came from my father.

Any normal child would have probably delivered the chops to Miss Hortense in tears, devastated and confused, but I skipped into Mack's, collected the soda crackers that Miss Hortense had originally sent me for and popped that caramel in my mouth before hearing the bell tinkle as I shut the door. I had completely forgotten that I'd seen his wife.

Two hours later, when Mrs O'Brien was shouting at our door,

Mother blocking my view, I couldn't see the way Mrs O'Brien brandished Mack's note.

For such a skimpy piece of paper with so little on it, it carried an uncommon weight and was to be brandished again by Mack's lawyer. The newspaper report claimed that Mrs O'Brien mistook the note as evidence that Mack was involved in an illicit, sordid relationship with a coloured maid from Los Angeles named Hortense Alvarez.

Coloured being the operative word.

But the newspapers always mash up the facts and Mexicans do have some colour.

5

I don't know why Mother and Lil weren't enough family for me.

I don't know why I made so much of Miss Hortense.

But I don't want to recall what should have been, I want to look at what was ... And Miss Hortense filled a need that I must have had, a need to have a fancy woman to muse upon. Maybe that's all goddesses have ever been. Did I come into this world incomplete until I could connect with a woman whose beauty seemed beyond reach? Although my mother had some virtues, fancy wasn't one. Nor did I expect it to be.

Even her name, Ruthie Mae Matthews, conjures up the image of somebody who puts hands to the plough (and her maiden name, Ruthie Mae Higgins, even more so).

Mother was fifteen when she ran away from her home in Mississippi, and Daddy was a Pullman porter on the train she caught. It turned out that he had two ways of trapping naïve country girls: some got his compliments, others his lemon drops. But Ruthie Mae Higgins sampled both.

At that green age she could milk a cow, slaughter a hog and beat grown men picking a bale of cotton. But that is as much of her early life as she ever mentioned after she caught Daddy's train whistling its way towards Chicago.

I never met him and Mother rarely talked about him except to brag to other women that he was a Creole with hazel eyes who looked trim but broad-shouldered in his starched white porter's jacket. She spied him first while she was seated alone in the crowded coloured section.

She didn't explain why she let a stranger old enough to be her

31

father lure her to Philadelphia, but I guess she was open to any offer and his of a job taking care of his ancient aunt Lucy was all the coaxing Mother needed.

John Randolph Matthews.

He had women in half the cities that the trains stopped in, so I still can't decide if it was immoral that he married Mother even after she fell pregnant. For some reason, he moved her to Camden before she started showing and then stayed gone, apart from an occasional reappearance. So between having Lilian, a stillbirth and then producing me, Mother started to take in ironing. That's how she met the Herzfelds. Then, when Daddy disappeared altogether, they offered additional hours until gradually she cooked and cleaned for them full time.

An orphan would have had more to say about their childhood than Mother revealed about hers, and in later years, anyone would have thought that she'd been born a Herzfeld. They represented safety and salvation and I wonder if domestics like her felt that they had two homes, two families ... In Mother's case, I imagined she endured life with us but lived with them. Under the Herzfelds' roof from sun-up to sun-down, Mother must have felt kind of rich. Until she entered their back door, donned her fresh apron and gave the milkman his order, she was a Miss Nobody. Or worse, a 'coloured' Miss Nobody with no husband.

The Herzfelds were the nearest Mother got to owning a house, a car and three radios. She presumed they were nearly royalty because their eldest took violin lessons, and the fact that they *knew* people who could afford a night out in New York to catch a vaudeville show made my mother think that *our* future was secure.

When she scrubbed the ring of dirt away after Mrs Herzfeld's bath or scraped the mud off Mr Herzfeld's shoes, Ruthie Mae Matthews felt as significant as a clock's hands. Because her 'white folks' gave her status even though they didn't pay much.

The night that Mrs O'Brien gave Mother notice, created a sudden trauma in our lives, so of course my sister and I eavesdropped from behind our door when Mother went to Hortense's to tell her the news.

'Hortense, you gonna let her call you a Comanche nigger and husband stealer! Whatch'you gonna do, girl!'

Surprisingly, Miss Hortense merely decided to pack her things and go; it happened so fast that I had no time to adjust to the idea of losing her. With childish glee, two nights later, I watched her and Mother remove Hortense's bed, bedding, dresser and chair to our place. But when, the following morning, she pulled the door of her room to for the last time my eyes were wells of tears.

'Smile Irene!' She was chirpy. 'Things will get better for you.'

Lilian refused to stand out in the cold morning air to wave Hortense goodbye with me, but I was not on that sidewalk alone. Was it a mere coincidence that Father Connolly happened by as the ice man arrived to taxi her with her trunk to the ferry?

I can still see her smiling down at me, her cheeks rouged. 'You could work for the stars, Irene,' she said, before patting the ice man's old pony.

6

Miss Hortense wasn't just the glitter in our drab lives – some deity who merely slipped off to Mass each morning in hose washed each night and dried on the cord above the bath – sometimes she explained things to me in her baby English. And that's what I missed most that chaotic October after she left.

Though people on our block gossiped about daily headlines, front-page news passed us by until the stock market crashed and the banks failed.

They called that Black Tuesday. That was the day when sane men leapt from windows and workers lost hope, the day the poor got poorer, and people with their savings invested in stock went broke. But it was the following day which brought our corner to a standstill because Mack was arrested for Mrs O'Brien's murder. Being six, I imagined that it was the O'Brien murder which threw the entire world into chaos.

I recall Mack's arrest like it happened yesterday. Being late October a chill had sunk its teeth into the afternoon and Lil and I took our time walking home from school. As we approached our corner, we saw a police car pull up outside the store and before we could reach it, a crowd had gathered. Kids and grownups, some strange, some familiar, appeared from nowhere and Lil and I got pinned in our doorway. Taller kids blocked our view and adult voices floated back over our heads. Even Mr Lucas, the arthritic janitor from St Anthony's, hobbled up the street to join the excitement, pushing his way to the front where the big boys made silly jokes. When one kid yelled, 'Won't be no singing in Sing Sing for Mack,' Jet the local drunk who'd been banned from Mack's store cheered.

Then one girl asked if the store had been robbed, but the old Polish woman who worked for a man who lived opposite the O'Brien's claimed that Mack's wife had been stabbed to death outside her kitchen door.

For some reason a swell of laughter went up from the crowd before she added, 'Cops been over our way asking questions.'

Every night that Mother had come in from work and counted the days we had till Thanksgiving to find a new home, I had prayed that something bad would happen to Mrs O'Brien. But it scared me to hear that she'd been murdered, because what if my mother had done it? My heart was pounding like a tomtom when the police drove Mack off in handcuffs; as that old janitor shouted, 'Everybody's gone loco, including the President!'

It was dusk before Mother's footsteps plodded up our creaking staircase and before she could turn her key in the door, Lilian opened it. But Mother already knew about Mrs O'Brien and she couldn't kick her shoes off fast enough to cut a step of Charleston, the weight of her round body causing the windows to rattle. When she kissed Lilian's crucifix, I felt surer of her guilt, despite her asking us a few times, 'Do folks think he did it or not?'

My sister christened that day Killer Wednesday and suddenly kids at school were also calling it that. But I personally made no reference to Mack or Mrs O'Brien as I was sure somehow that some nun would spot my guilt. Smell caramels on my breath. But what I imagined that I was guilty of I can't say.

The Crash couldn't erase the holy days which followed Hallowe'en, but Mack's disappearance shrouded them for me, especially after some official boarded up the store windows and pasted a NO TRES-PASSING sign on the door underwritten with small print, big words that even Lilian couldn't pronounce.

To see grown people sitting on the sidewalk with their heads in their hands or hear women weeping during mass as the days trundled along had me thinking that Mrs O'Brien had many mourners. And when Mrs Carrington, the neighbourhood widow, started wandering up and down our street moaning, 'God wouldn't do this,' it never occurred to me that they were under duress because of the Crash.

Since nobody collected our rent after Mack's arrest, Mother felt like she was winning, until the bank foreclosed on Mr Herzfeld. She couldn't believe that her White Hope had been ambushed by Wall Street. Then a few days later, the Herzfelds let Mother go: the evening Mrs Herzfeld announced, 'We won't be needing you any more', my mother's world collapsed.

Initially, I think she enjoyed waking late and seeing Lil and me off to school. She certainly never burdened us with worries, although she must have been desperate. Yet by some act of faith she produced a cake with a candle for my seventh birthday.

Those November afternoons my sister and I would get in from school to find Mother seated at the window spying on neighbours she knew by sight but not name. She said what made it worth working at the Baptist church for no money was that she met other women who'd lost jobs.

But mother missed the Herzfelds. Probably missed the sight of their cosy fire that she complained about having to clean, and probably missed the luxury of their fancy bathroom and their kitchen which she said had too many gadgets.

Mother pretended that she was glad when Mr Herzfeld collected his Motorola, because Hortense's things took up so much space, but entertaining ourselves without it was hard.

In spite of these sudden changes, our room looked almost fancy with Miss Hortense's bed in it, especially after that big pile of newspapers had gone to the rag and bone man.

By Thanksgiving Mother had somehow started slipping to the Herzfelds' at daybreak to do their laundry and cook for a paltry few leftovers, but thankfully Mr Herzfeld had the grace to stop her visits. He sent her home with two apples, a slice of stale pumpernickel and an egg, wrapped in her blue apron.

The next day I nibbled my apple segment under a December sky as bright as Mother's apron.

That sliver of apple tasted sublime.

There are fewer glowing moments in my childhood than Lilian liked to record, but I don't pretend that I was in a perpetual state of gloom. I had a child's ability to assume that clouds drifted away.

In fact, Mrs O'Brien's murder may have had a positive effect, because I probably imagined that the baddies sometimes get it in the end.

Christmas that year turned out to be one of my happiest, happier even than the Christmas after my marriage, because the postman had arrived in the snow on 24 December with a two-by-ten-inch parcel. Having never received mail, I couldn't believe that a package arrived with my name and Lilian's crudely printed on the brown paper wrapping. To tell the truth that meant more to me than the two wooden flutes we found inside, with the small tag signed, 'from Saint Nicholas'.

Lilian thought it was from Daddy, but Mother said, 'That's ain't Mr Matthews' writing. That's from Hortense, and I can't understand why she didn't write nothing about when she's coming for her furniture.' I smiled for two whole days.

7

Mother rarely smiled after the new decade got under way and any small sound in the room seemed to annoy her. It never crossed my mind until now that she was not only worried and bored but irritable from a lack of food.

The mere sight of Lil and me must have reminded Mother that we needed food when she could no longer rely on credit at Mack's for a pound of sugar or a can of sardines.

She stayed out, walking around Camden to seek comfort from the faces of other jobless people whose miseries mirrored hers. After dark, she'd slip home and hardly look at us before unlacing her shoes and saying, 'Why ain't you two in bed!'

This was less punishing because we were using Hortense's things, Lilian and I curling up under that pink satin comforter like kittens, and if we were allowed to whisper, Lil would teach me a difficult prayer or relate details from her first Holy Communion ceremony. She had worn a short veil along with a hand-me-down dress, socks, and shoes that had once been part of Mabel Herzfeld's summer wardrobe.

From the moment that I had seen Lilian when she was seven in a veil, I couldn't wait for my turn.

'Patience, Irene,' Mother had chided. 'Your communion's in 1930, and you'll look as pretty in that dress as Lilian. It'll only need starch and an iron.' But seeing me eye that white ensemble too often, Mother put it away in a cardboard box, after returning the veil, on loan from St Anthony's. I knew better than to mention the words Holy Communion again but I continued to dream about mine, sitting in that short section of our L-shaped room where

Mother undid crocheted doilies so that she had some thread to crochet again.

Without the Herzfelds, Mother was lost. She'd dust Miss Hortense's dresser till it shone like glass and wash our few clothes so often that the bathroom looked like a washhouse.

Being winter, Lilian and I retreated to church and school, where the nuns' stern white faces and monotonous, subdued voices kept control. Sweeping through school in their black habits, they monitored our every move.

Lilian and I were Catholics because Daddy had been, and while Mother was Methodist, non-practising in those days, she kept us at St Anthony's in case he ever came back.

Some church life in Camden during those harsh times would have done her some good. She faked an interest in getting herself baptised whenever she bumped into Father Connolly, but Mother refused to study the catechism and saw no point in a Pope. However, she was proud that we were Catholics for some reason.

Lilian got her best grades in religion and loved going to confession. She even set up an altar in our room using an orange crate that Mack had given her which she draped with a yard of blue velvet donated by Miss Hortense and a replica of the Virgin Mary won in the third-grade spelling bee. Lil's altar even had a red novena candle on it got from goodness knows where. It sat on a doily that Mother had crocheted, but since Mother was afraid of fires, the candle was never lit. Wanting to contribute something, I gave Lilian a tiny white feather I'd found in church. It had probably fallen off some lady's hat. It lay upon the little white Spanish missal which Hortense had left behind.

Lilian's eyes, as dark and round as mother's, would study that altar until she looked mesmerized. Mother should have noticed that Lilian was going overboard. But maybe she couldn't think beyond our next bowl of grits.

I used to blush when people back then confused my sister and me, because Lilian's hair was longer and her skin was shades paler than mine so I considered her pretty.

We both got Daddy's nose and Mother's lips, but any fool would have envied my sister her hair, which reached below her shoulders. It irritated Lilian when I reached her size because people mistook us for twins, although looking alike was a bonus when we started singing together.

She'd say, 'Irene, how come you're as tall as me?'

But the truth is that I was never tall, Lilian was just short.

It was during our last six months in Camden that I seemed to shoot up. My skin itched like I was growing out of it and Mother would get vexed with me scratching and say, 'Irene, can't you set still? I don't for the life of me know how you got like your Daddy.' So I'd creep out to play, but downstairs, all I wanted to do was sit in the doorway of Mack's store and watch the people passing. They rarely smiled back in '30, because there was nothing to smile about.

The Depression was a snowfall in summer. It fell upon the rich and poor, and froze stout hearts overnight.

8

Mother said we were lucky to get hominy grits for breakfast, lunch and dinner, and she couldn't afford an omnibus across town. We saw whole families out begging on Wells Avenue and I always went to bed thinking, 'Will we be next?'

Lilian used to kneel before her altar and say the rosary with such intensity, believing that could save the world, and one night she told Mother that she wanted to become a Sister of Mercy so that she could help all the beggars. Mother laughed like Lil had told a joke. 'Things gonna work out. You watch . . . one of these mornings you, me and Reenie gonna take off for Sippy. I'm thinking about heading for Mamie's, if she'll still have me.'

I was working in my copybook and was alarmed by my sister's violent response. She yelled, 'I'll never go back to Sippy!'

Sippy was Mississippi and Lil had always avoided talking about it, but I gathered that something bad had happened there when Mother had taken us to visit her friend Mamie and Mamie's brother Buster when I was two and a half and my sister was five.

Lil was normally a quiet child so it unnerved me to hear her scream, 'You promised we'd never go back to Buster's.'

Mother's nostrils flared and I knew she was losing her patience. 'It ain't Buster's no more. It's Mamie's, and you'll go where I tell you to!'

That was the early spring of 1930 and I might have jumped to my sister's defence had I known that this so called 'aunt' would try to build her nest in our lives.

While Lil and I were at school on the last day of April, Mother sold Miss Hortense's things without warning us. To return

41

home to find the sun lighting bare floorboards was shocking.

The place where we normally sat to do our homework, warmed by the afternoon light, was empty, and our voices echoing disturbed me more than my sister's tears. Lilian drew the school books she was carrying to her chest as if to shield her heart from the bleakness. The room was empty apart from a trunk we'd never seen before and Lilian's altar upon which Mother had lit the novena candle.

Despite the heavy rings under her eyes Mother looked self-satisfied, producing some dollars from her pocketbook, saying, 'Good thing I kept Hortense's dresser polished . . . It fetched way more than the bed, so I got enough for tickets and then some.'

'Stealing,' I said under my breath, staring in horror at the spot where Hortense's bed had been.

'We're moving, huh?' Lil asked, probably hoping that Mother had landed a job with Mrs Herzfeld's cousin in Philadelphia.

'Sippy,' said Mother.

That nasal Jersey twang of Lilian's bounced from wall to wall. 'What about catechism? What about school!'

'We can't set 'round here waitin' to die!' Mother snarled, rushing to lower the open window so our voices wouldn't peal into the streets. 'Do y'all know how tired I am. Holes in my shoes, my pockets. Next there'll be a hole in my head!' She was twenty-five and had lost so much weight from our hominy grits diet that her dress hung inches too long and was practically touching the floor.

My sister screamed again, 'But you promised we'd never go back. And I won't! Not ever!'

I had been too young to understand anything during that first trip to Mississippi in 1925, but it was easy enough over the years to piece together the tragedy. I heard Mother's version, Lil's and, of course, Mamie McMichael's, who eventually accompanied my sister and I when we sang as a duet. But not one of them could be counted on to tell the truth . . .

The story began with Mother meeting Mamie in Camden when Mother was pregnant with Lilian and Daddy'd started his long disappearing acts. Visiting a little storefront church for solace, Mother had met Mamie, who was fifteen years her senior and was the guest pianist, on a visiting exchange from Mississippi.

When Daddy discovered that Mamie had coaxed Mother to recite Bible tracts, he accused them both of being bull dykes and forbade Mother to attend any church that wasn't Catholic.

Mother obeyed but happened to bump into Mamie five years later in '25 when Daddy was gone again. Mamie'd warned, 'Bad men get worse. Leave him and take them kids back to Mississippi.'

Mamie had such a soft spot for Mother she assured her that she could earn pocket money there, giving Bible recitations in small churches where Mamie and her brother Buster played. She even paid for Mother's train journey and ours.

In the many versions of this story I've heard, I've never found out where Mamie was that day Buster collected us from the station. He arrived with the mule and cart they normally used to transport their piano and Lil, like any five-year-old, was over herself with excitement.

Buster was a handsome, young World-War-I veteran. Dark skinned like Mamie, but way better looking. He bragged about his army experience, but resented that the local reserve board had refused him a disability pension for the headaches he'd suffered from being gassed in France while digging latrines.

The ten acres he shared with Mamie were on the north side of a big cotton plantation, worked by tenants so poor they considered Buster and Mamie to be rich. But the farm was paltry – chickens, turkeys, guinea fowl and a few hogs and goats in pens. Yet Buster expected to impress Mother with the two-room house and outdoor toilet which he'd built to resemble a proper A-frame house.

With Lilian perched on his shoulder when he showed it to Mother who had me in her arms, he teased, 'Y'all's behind-the-chairs won't set on no finer commode than that from here to Little Rock.'

It was a little shotgun house with the kitchen cluttered with pots, pans, sheet music and war mementoes, including a gas mask. Mother recalled how ashamed she was that we ate like we were starving, gobbling his peach preserves and government-surplus peanut butter after eating half of the fat back and greens which had been simmering on the stove. So when Buster promised Lil pancakes and sorghum syrup for breakfast, Mother said, 'You better stop or I won't never get her back up Jersey way.'

Next thing, Buster sat himself at the piano and created a song, a ragtime thing with some made-up lyrics about not letting Lil go back to Jersey.

Mother said everything in the kitchen was swinging and she got Lilian to dance, because Lil could always cut a shimmy.

We must have all been having a ball in that Delta heat until I strained to fill my diaper and Mother rushed me to the outhouse. While she held me over the toilet, a car rolled into the yard and backfired. Mother thought nothing about it, beyond wondering who Buster and Mamie knew who could afford an automobile. But it soon drove off again and next she heard Lilian calling. When Mother made her way to the front yard with me trailing behind, she found Lil standing over Buster who was sprawled motionless on the ground. His face and hair were covered in dust and blood and Lil was shooing the flies off him. Mother used to say, 'What was I meant to do? I was young and stupid and there he was on the ground with his eyes swole like two baseballs and blood streaming from his nose and mouth. I thought he was dead.'

Of course she started bellowing, because she never could cope with the sight of blood, and when she bellowed, Lilian joined her and then I started.

She didn't know if she'd walked into some kind of feud, but the whole scene petrified her, and there were no neighbours for miles. So grabbing us kids she ran in the house, shouting at my sister, 'Did you see what happened? Who done it!' But Lilian was crying hysterically by then and couldn't get a word out.

No phones. No neighbours. No real knowledge of Mamie or her brother. She was in a completely strange place with two little children, and a man she'd just met was in a heap on the ground. Mother was frantic that the culprits would return while Buster was laying out in his front yard with his chin split open and flies settling on his bloodied face.

44

She didn't even know where the water pump was to get water to clean his wounds, so she tied me to a chair with an apron she'd spotted and grabbed the pot of greens. Lilian followed her back outside where one of the roosters was pecking at Buster's trouser leg. Using the pot liquor and one of my diapers to wipe some of the blood from his face, all Mother could do was cry and say, 'You'll be all right. Just tell me what happened.' He never spoke.

Lil was just learning to count that summer and wasn't able to say whether Buster had been attacked by three or four, men or boys. All she knew is that while Mother had me in the outhouse, some white men had driven up and called Buster to the porch. He had told her to stay in the house so she'd watched from the door.

What had she seen? Did Buster resist being beaten and kicked to the ground? Who did what? Were words exchanged? At five years old Lil had no clear answers. 'One hit him with the stick and the others were kicking him,' she'd cried. The tyre mark across his shirt suggested that the car may have driven over him.

Mother couldn't move him so she placed an apron she found in the house over his face to keep the flies off it and made a promise to Lil: 'Let the Good Lord get us back to Jersey and we'll never come to Mississippi again.'

When Mamie arrived in the late afternoon to find her brother unconscious in the yard, she hardly seemed surprised. 'He pestered them bosses over at the reserve board for his disability pension and when they turned him down, he started putting it around that he was gonna write to Washington.' Mamie was a big woman, tall, broad and heavy hipped. Not the sort to back off a fight, but she sat on the porch and removed her hat and earrings and slung them on the ground.

Mother said Mamie had then pumped Lilian with questions that no child of five could have managed, like what kind of car had come and what ages were the men.

In later years, whenever my sister wanted sympathy, she used to tell the Buster McMichael story. But she was thin on facts.

When he died that evening, without regaining consciousness,

Mamie'd said, 'I hope his uniform still fits, cause he'd want to be buried in it.'

Five years later in our room above Mack's, Mother said, 'You're going to Sippy, Lil, like it or not.'

So that's where we headed with the proceeds from the sale of Miss Hortense's furniture. May 1, 1930. And my sister thought our lives were ending. In some ways they were.

We took the bus south and although Mother tried to look happy and tell us that living with Mamie was going to be good for us, I faced the prospect with as much dread as my sister, because she was the leader then. Lilian was going to turn ten that June and kept reminding me that I was going to miss my Holy Communion.

'Can't I take it in "Sippy"?' I asked Mother when we settled on the bus.

But Lilian pinched me to be quiet.

On the bus one woman talked about President Hoover as though he were God or a magician, but nobody could fix what had taken years to happen.

Our driver between North and South Carolina was one of those men born heartless or else his generosity had been stretched to the limit.

It was getting dark when he tried to get rid of a dirty, blond, sunburnt woman who boarded the bus at a deserted stop with four children and no tickets. He expected some of his passengers to help him, but everybody just sat there tight lipped. The grown ups were watchful, knowing they could be in her shoes.

The woman, whose old-fashioned straw sun bonnet shadowed her sunken cheeks, pleaded in a flat, southern drawl. 'We gotta get to Knoxville.'

With one arm, she cradled a baby on her hip, while her bow-legged toddler clung to the frayed hem of her floral dress. His dirty diaper was around his knees, and mucus streamed from his nose. Her two eldest boys, probably younger than I was, had struggled to climb on board with a burlap sack the size of a pillow case. The small cardboard suitcase in her free hand was more worn out looking

46

than Mother's big carpet bag which had a piece of clothesline for a handle.

When a pot fell out of their burlap, making a racket as it clanged down the bus steps, the driver threatened to push the five of them off. Though I didn't know where or how it would come, my every muscle was braced, anticipating violence.

Mother poked Lilian in the side and mouthed, 'White trash,' which made my sister and I smile for the first time in two days.

We were one of only three coloured families uneasily parked at the back of the bus. Scared to even whisper, because to remain invisible was the nearest thing we had to self-defence. Mother admitted years later that she'd been afraid that the driver was going to tell the woman that she could have our seats and that we'd be the ones turfed off.

During that journey I got my first glimpse of the way that twilight gradually blackens green hills. I still had the childish audacity to feel occasional pangs of joy at the sight of a baby lamb with its mother. I saw the silhouettes of herds of horses and cows as darkness fell. What I couldn't see was that my childhood was nearing its end.

As the bus bumped along, Mother's head bobbed in sleep. She was leaving Camden behind, but Lilian and I took it with us. I worried from time to time whether Mack would somehow tell her about the caramels.

I kept thinking about the previous morning when I'd sat at my desk in St Anthony's, fidgeting with the empty inkwell and a girl told Sister Elizabeth that she'd dreamt that Mack had cut off Sister Octavia's head. Then the Italian boy who had arrived in the middle of the term from New York raised his hand to say that he had had a nightmare too. But none of them could have been as scared as I was, expecting each night to be strangled in my sleep by Mrs O'Brien's ghost.

9

Mississippi was the crud between my toes from walking barefoot on the dry, crusty soil. And Mississippi was learning to stand back far enough when the man made soap by adding lye to the hog grease. 'Stand back, gal,' he'd say, 'If this lye catches you, it'll burn so bad you wish you was in hell.' Mississippi was also Mother's coy laughter when a ninety-year-old from Mamie's church patted her behind and told her, 'You're the juiciest Lucy I seen outside Biloxi.' And Mississippi was the wasted hope that Mother could make enough to feed us, by giving recitations up and down the Delta.

She had been gone too long to appreciate flattery from a hard-working cotton picker and she felt superior to the sharecroppers who raised their broken straw hats to her whenever she crossed their tenant farms. She had thought that she was back to stay, but when women at the small churches where she'd recite would complain about the white families they served, Mother would describe the Herzfelds as saints and brag about their mahogany highboy heavy with crystal and silver, like somebody homesick.

Once Mamie heard Mother say, 'Jews. I'd work for 'em any day, rather than these Mississippi crackers.' Mamie scoffed, 'Ruthie, there ain't no Jews 'round here. And nobody cares that you was Jew-rich up Jersey way. If you want coloured folk to give you a dime at prayer meetings, keep that Jew talk to yourself.'

Mamie McMichael was dangerous.

She talked a lot about God but she was more fixated by money and getting back what she thought she was owed by the local whites.

On moral grounds Lilian refused to eat the chicken that Mamie stole from the cotton planter near her farm. Mamie scolded after beating my sister, 'That bastard *owes* me. Since I was a bitty thing, he been fixing the scales that weighs cotton that my folks bent over 'til they couldn't stand up. But them ole nuns didn't teach you 'bout that.'

Lilian still said her rosary every night, kneeling before her small altar set up in Mamie's kitchen. Arranged with the same items that she'd had in our room above Mack's, it made Mamie's place more like home, although Mother had burned the novena candle down to nothing the night before we'd left Camden.

Had Mother not whispered to Mamie about 'the landlord and his wife', I might have forgotten about Mack altogether, because there was a lot to discover in Bofield, and Mamie's home-made peanut brittle was as satisfying as caramels. Some mornings before the sun became a hot poker, I'd wander off alone to look for rabbits or search for grasshoppers in the tall, scorched crabgrass. Even lugging buckets of water from the pump to the kitchen seemed like fun as long as Mother didn't make me do it. But during those three and a half months that Mamie's ten acres became my wonderland, I was most awed by the way her fingers produced songs on the piano. She'd ask Mother to sing along. 'Ruthie,' she'd beg, 'anybody that can recite like you, got to have *some* music in 'em. Let's hear the chorus of "Gracious Lord",' she'd say and bang out a minor chord.

Mother found every excuse from 'Woke up with a frog in my throat' to 'I can't waste time singing when I've got passages to learn.'

Her recitations were more popular with me that Mississippi summer than anybody, apart from that ninety-year-old man whose name I never knew but who turned up to sniff around Mother in the yard like a mangy old Tom cat. Her figure was filling out again from Mamie's fatback, beans and rice. Listening to my mother learn her Bible passages was better than radio, because she'd let me interrupt. She didn't know the meaning of every verse she recited, but she chose the easiest pieces which she'd practise aloud on the porch while I fought back the blue flies and picked at the scabs I got from scratching my mosquito bites.

I heard Mother practising her pieces so often that I knew some and could mouth the words with her. My favourite was the story of

49

Hannah asking the Lord for a son. First chapter of the Book of Samuel. Mother repeated it so often it hypnotized me like a Latin mass. Mother's bible stories were easier for me to follow than the catechism at St Anthony's.

If the sun wasn't too high or the mosquitoes too hungry on Mamie's porch, Mother would let me climb onto her lap and make requests. 'Do the one about Hannah.' If she hadn't already, she'd clear her throat and swim fearlessly into the verse with a power that she displayed at no other time. It was like sitting on a mountain that speaks. 'There was a certain man of Ramathaimzophim of the hill of the country of Ephraim whose name was Elkanah, the son of Jeroham, son of Elihu, son of Tohu, son of Zuph, an Ephramite . . .' She could lower her voice until the syllables swayed back and forth with the ease of a porch glider; slow, so slowly the cadences would rise and fall. Forward then backward, high, then low, carving a road into my psyche like the radio jingles did. 'Whose name was Elka-nah, the son of Jero-ham, son of Eli-hu, son of Tohu.'

Mother's voice was as round as her belly, as soft as her lap, as smooth as her hair when greased and straightened with tongs. So I was often lulled to sleep by her reciting the story of Hannah as I had been in the days when Lilian was learning to recite Hail Holy Queen. Repeating the lines over and over, Lil would entrance me with the phrase 'Poor banished children of Eve'.

During those mornings when I trekked through the open fields alone, I would often repeat Mother's verses, and once Lilian heard and challenged me in Mamie's front yard: we were to see who could say all the names in Hannah's story, and the winner could tickle the loser to death. But we never got that far because Mamie, in the yard feeding the turkeys, heard us. She yelled, 'C'mere, Reenie.' I thought I was in trouble for making fun of the way Mother recited 'Elka-nah, the son of Jero-ham' and the rest. But Mamie said, 'Come on in and do that again.' When she grabbed my arm to pull me into the kitchen, I looked less frightened than Lilian who was terrified of her.

Mamie's gruffness was straightforward, but unlike Mother she would slap us without warning. So when she sat at the kitchen table and told me to stand by the stove, I didn't know what to expect. I hoped that my Mother would rescue me but suspected that she was out back picking runner beans.

I began meekly and Mamie snapped, 'Speak up!'

'There was a man of Ramathaimzophim of the hill of the country of Ephraim . . .'

'Do it like your mama does . . . Go 'head . . . like you did in my yard.'

I knew where Mother paused for effect and recited as she did. And Mamie applauded and laughed until tears streamed down her dark cheeks and glistened on that black mole beside her nose. The more I recited, the more she laughed and her frolicking spilled into the yard until Lilian stuck her head in the screen door. 'Set down,' Mamie told her.

I was a show-off but everything I did my sister tried to do better, and that afternoon was no different. Competition was fierce but whereas Lilian knew the words, I knew Mother's phrasing.

Mamie McMichael had an instinct for what would please a crowd. To her everyone, kids, grown-ups, old people, was a potential audience. I've seen her arrive at a church for the first time, ask some deacons to help bring her piano from the rig, and proceed to organize the service. Merely after eyeing a congregation, Mamie would whisper something like, 'Ruthie, do "Punishment and Blasphemy" or "Hezekiah's Prayer".' Once I heard her warn in a church, 'Whatever you do, don't do no Proverbs, 'cause this minister *only* knows Psalms and Proverbs, so these folks can't take 'em from nobody else.'

When Mamie took Mother aside after hearing Lil and I do some of Mother's verses, Mamie said, 'Mark my words, them children could make us rich.'

The nuns had trained us well to learn by rote and the radio had taught us to listen. Mamie was impressed that we learned Bible verses and the little hymns she taught us so quickly. We'd stand at her piano and try the odd harmony and she'd get excited. 'Ruthie,' she'd tell Mother, 'folks will love these girls at church. All you have to do is press their hair and get some ribbons.'

Mother beamed like a natural-born stage mother but said, 'They too young to hot-comb their hair.'

As it turned out, performing in those small churches was no different from standing before a cluster of parents at a St Anthony's pageant. My sister and I wore enormous red bows in our hair but Lil made me refuse to wear her white Holy Communion dress. 'Suppose it gets ruined,' she'd whispered so that Mother couldn't hear. 'You'd have nothing for your Communion.'

Of course, I hadn't forgotten that I'd missed mine. In fact it's what troubled me most nights. That and Mother selling Hortense's things . . .

If Lilian kept the torch of our Roman faith burning, Mamie McMichael kindled another flame. She kept us thinking about our presence before a crowd. How to smile and charm and to test our new-found skill, was like a fix. We learned to pick out eyes in the churches and work to them. We learned to modulate our voices and sell songs, even if they were only children's hymns, and the buzz of getting ready for our performances was more fun than any game of chase or 'Simon Says'. Performing is a vanity, but Mamie taught us that it was righteous. Being examined and admired and then getting paid by a 'little collection from the congregation' hit my sister like an addiction. Maybe that's why she turned to drink after we split in '42 and she couldn't get a singing job.

Sure, Mamie gets some credit for my success, but it was the dollar signs rather than God that interested her. Yet tonight I'd give anything to hear her play that version of 'Boogie Woogie Bugle Boy' that she'd arranged for Lil and me. Nobody could play it like Mamie McMichael.

It was soon after Mamie's mule had to be shot when Mother announced that we were moving to Los Angeles, and Lil and I were speechless, because California hadn't been mentioned since it fell from Miss Hortense's lips. But after our two short months of performing in churches, Mamie had devised a plan which meant moving west, and while the details were never shared with us, we were about to live them.

We were luckier to get out of Mississippi than I realized, because for decades to come what had happened to Buster would be nothing out of the ordinary. In fact when Mamie would down a glass of sweet Mogen David wine once in a while, she'd reminisce about old times and end up saying, 'Least they didn't slice off Buster's dick, and they left his eyes.'

10

Mamie believed that I owed *her* everything for my success because I couldn't credit the white men who made me bend over or lay down before they would provide a few yards of the sticky tarmac that led me to stardom. Acting schools should offer a course in how best to be degraded by the studio bigwigs. It would be way more useful than Shakespeare. But if Mamie were alive, she'd chastize me for suggesting that anything more than luck and talent helps girls get ahead. She's owed, but less for her music than for lending Mother the fare that got us to California that August of 1930.

Our trip from Mississippi took days longer than Mother had expected, because we kept missing connections, and although I can't recall our eight-day journey or name the states that we passed through, I'm positive it was in Texas Mother, Lil and me huddled together like three hobos waiting for a bus that didn't come until dawn. When we finally reached Los Angle-less as Mamie pronounced it, it was a Saturday night and the slim crescent moon didn't light our way from the bus station to downtown. Before the Koreans and the Mexicans took over that part of town, anybody not white was welcome. Mamie had warned Mother that the city was as segregated as any below the Mason-Dixon line, so we arrived fully aware that our 'place' in the scheme of things was going to be 'no place'. When we couldn't find a 'Coloureds Only' sign on any of the toilet doors in the train depot, Mother made us pee behind a bush outside.

My only memory of our evening arrival is that my sister and I were about to squat behind a bush with its dark leaves and pink flowers, and just as I untied the string on my bloomers to pull them down, a man's voice suddenly boomed from nowhere, 'What are you darkies doing over there?' Mother and Lilian both deny this ever happened, but I will never forget that deep voice with its southern twist calling us darkies, which was half-way polite back then.

Darkies. The three of us had been scorched blue-black by the Mississippi sun, with grains of the Delta grime still caked between our toes. Of course, there would come a time when I would believe I was above toe jam, but those delusions were twenty years down the road. In fact, in 1930 I can't claim that any of us bathed every week. We probably smelled, but then so did a lot of other people back then.

Only God can really explain why Mother had brought her two little coloured girls to the city that Miss Hortense had called 'the palace of endless dreams'.

A heatwave was warming up for Sunday but that Saturday night a desert chill had settled in and Mother's teeth were chattering by the time we found a rooming house which had a small women's dormitory that was empty but for us.

My mother loved to remind me that she had arrived with two mouths to feed in addition to her own, but no contacts, no job, and only fifteen dollars saved from giving recitations. But for all her complaints about this period in our lives, we were never so hungry that we grew weak. In fact, as soon as I started caring about my figure, I was glad that an empty stomach felt normal to me.

Mamie said that church was the only safe place to begin in a new city, so it was as well that we arrived on a Saturday night with Sunday morning just an arm's length away.

The next morning while Lil and Mother snored, I ran to the only window to see what surprises the dawn had brought. Like a kid heading for a stocking at Christmas, I expected bliss. I expected to see oranges growing on trees and the big cactus plants that Hortense had described. I expected a great open range, but our dormitory overlooked the back wall of the next bungalow where an overturned trash can was surrounded by garbage. We had slept in a rabbit warren with walls that had never been painted and warped floorboards rife with splinters. A Salvation Army hostel would offer far better these days. But I was young and everything was new and exciting.

Mother was either brave or crazy to face that Sunday in a strange metropolis with two children and no prospects. Maybe that's why Mamie had said, 'Ruthie, go straight to church, 'cause Los Angle-less is teeming with okies and thieves, syphilitics and who knows what. And see how they did poor Mabel Normand.' She was Mamie's favourite biograph star who clowned with the Keystone Cops and had reputedly died from morphine addiction earlier that year. Mamie had said, 'Find you some honest church folk and you can't go too far wrong.' And mother never challenged Mamie's word.

Lilian and I sat in that women's dormitory on those old slats nailed together to make a bed, watching Mother dress carefully for church. As she took her time adjusting her slip and stepping into her brown chemise, I couldn't resist asking, 'Can't I come too?' Those churches were my stage and I needed to perform, to drink in those stares and be bathed in compliments.

'Who'll stay with Lil if you don't?'

On the journey from Mississippi, my sister had suffered boils under both arms accompanied by a low-grade fever. It annoyed me when she got sick, because I was expected to treat her extra nice, and if playing nursemaid to her meant missing the first church meeting in what was a strange, new place, I didn't want to. In fact I was temporarily wary of her because she said that the Pope hated Methodists.

While Mother arranged her hat, I was brimming with questions and was still young enough to believe that my mother had every answer. But she was feeling her way in the dark and lacked the cunning of a truly devious woman. However, with us to feed she ploughed on and combined her naïveté with plain old fashioned ignorance to potent means; to know nothing can be more powerful than knowing something. If I had to classify her as a cat, a Persian or Siamese wouldn't do. No, Ruthie Mae Matthews was a barn cat with kittens.

When Mother returned from church hours later with a long face, Lilian was sleeping.

I knew better than to ask what Mother had seen and done now, because, on the journey to Los Angeles Lilian had burdened her with, 'What's going to happen?' 'What are we gonna do?' and I was the one who got it for asking the when-where-and-how of Mother's plans. She had finally hissed in a dangerously low voice that nobody else could have deciphered, 'Irene, you put your mouth in all my business! Mamie's right! I need to take a switch to you and Lilian more often . . . See kids in Sippy with rags on their back and hands raw from picking cotton. I can't be messin' with you, this here's the Depression!'

This was the reply I had got for asking, 'How will you find a church when we get to California?'

I hated getting told off more than I hated cod liver oil or going to bed while it was light. Mother's scolding made me feel small and humiliated, whereas I liked to think that I mattered, that I was important in the scheme of things.

Anyway, when Mother unpinned her hat and threw it on a bed in that dormitory, after a good deal of moping and sighing, she produced an envelope with three names on it. When she said that the minister she met didn't think there was a Catholic church in the vicinity, I sensed that my sister was awake.

Lilian turned her face to the wall and gave no indication that she heard Mother say, 'That minister say his niece gives tap dancing to little girls on Sat'days. Her name's Louise Taylor . . . He thinks she don't charge but a nickel a lesson.'

My sister pretended to be asleep and Mother knew as well as I did that she was having one of her moods.

11

That summer we moved to Los Angeles, Lilian made sure that Mother never forgot that she wanted to go back to Camden. Like a pitbull, my sister could grip the past between clenched teeth. She daydreamed about the nuns and Camden's changing seasons; the conkers in spring and the june bugs of summer. She even harped on about the scrapple Mother used to buy. Just about everything we'd left behind was deemed irreplaceable.

Admittedly, she was ten that summer of '30 and had more of a past to cling to than I did, but for some reason she seemed to have pasted all her hopes on a Camden life. Like a toddler clinging to a worn-out teddy. And further to provoke me, she pretended that every shadow was Miss Hortense with the police, coming to drag Mother to prison.

So Lilian didn't want to adjust and nabbed every chance to question or whine, throwing the thorny head of Christ and the Virgin Mary into every conversation. Even when Mother mentioned tap again.

'We can't afford tap *and* school uniforms,' Lilian said.

But me? Irene Matthews? I had delusions and had an image of myself writing Miss Hortense a letter to inform her that I was in Hollywood studying tap. I was the same little girl who only ten months earlier had slept on a pile of newspapers, and despite Mother being KO'd every round by poverty and fear, I sensed there was hope in dancing and some victory in the fact that she was even thinking about it. I'd seen the famous Bill Robinson tapping in a film short and watched some big boys on Buchanan Street try to imitate his moves, and the thought of tap excited me more than church recitals. So when my sister told Mother, 'I don't want to dance,' they were both startled when I suddenly laid into Lil, pounding her with both fists.

The nuns had made me think that anger was wicked and Mother had passed her impoverished notion on to me that tempers were the luxury of the rich, so I don't know where my sudden eruption had come from, but I was seething. 'You do wanna tap, Lili, and don't ever say you don't!'

My mother was more taken off guard than my sister and although I got slapped by them both, I was glad that I'd made my point.

What followed two days later is what I sometimes imagine is the day my career began.

We had been in Los Angeles for under a week and when the heat in that dormitory became intolerable, Mother took us for walks. One blistering afternoon she pointed to a shopfront on the opposite side of the street. 'I betcha that's where Reverend Walters from my new church say his niece works.'

The costume store was unlike the familiar brick buildings in Camden and different from the little wood-framed shotgun houses that I'd seen in Mississippi. It had smooth adobe walls and a roof of red clay tiles and was sandwiched between identical buildings on either side.

Sun baked the sidewalk and burned the back of my neck as I stood with my hand in Mother's, afraid that she wouldn't suggest that we cross the street where only a few old Model Ts were rattling up and down.

Together we ambled over to peek into the small display window. Pressing my nose against the glass, I strained on tiptoe to see the masks, feather head-dresses, pink toe shoes with satin ties and stiff white tutus.

I must have been salivating like an old sheep dog when we entered the small shop. It smelled like a second-hand clothes store, packed as it was with slightly musty old costumes for rent.

As I prayed that my sister wouldn't mention uniforms or ask Mother any impertinent questions, my heart started to play leapfrog.

I felt like a rich kid in a toystore, because my Mother assumed a self-important air, when she told the elderly male assistant that she wanted to see two pairs of tap shoes. I didn't dare smile, because there was something sobering about the moment. Mother didn't look nervous and didn't seem embarrassed to ask for assistance which she normally was in stores, and I guess Lil sensed that something radical was happening, because even she kept her mouth shut.

The shoes that I was given to try on were black with round toes. I can't recall if I sat to try them on or stood up while somebody helped me slip my foot into them, all I know is that when I walked across the costume store in them anybody would have thought that I'd tried on some wings. My whole body responded to those shoes and it was like I was a mummer in the Thanksgiving parade. I seemed to lean back and strut. The ease of the leather and the comfort – I was like a grown woman appreciating the caress of French glove leather . . .

When I went bankrupt thirty-five years later and one of my creditors accused me of having a shoe fetish, I told the judge about my experience with Mother in 1930, during the Depression, when I was fitted for the first time with shoes, the cheapest tap shoes, which hadn't been shaped first by Mabel Herzfeld's feet. Or by my sister's.

Pretty shoes always helped me look other people in the eye.

As Lil and I left that store with our new shoes in a bag, my face must have ached from smiling. Those shoes were a rebirth.

When the whole country was littered with the jobless and home-less, Mother, a baby-faced coloured girl from the backwoods with two kids to feed and no prospects, must have sensed that she had accomplished something momentous.

Even my sister became putty in Mother's hands and did all she could to be helpful.

That's how we ended up in that crowded public school near Reverend Walters's church.

One night in '63 when it suddenly hit me that Mother was the reason I could dance but couldn't spell, I tried to stab her.

Those were the days when mothers were getting blamed for everybody's neuroses, but that wasn't the only reason that I suddenly saw her as Satan. She thought I had gone crazy.

One of the most humiliating things about my supposed suicide wasn't just the photo of me naked, ten pounds overweight, it was the suicide note that I'd supposedly written, which made me sound like a pea brain. Somebody had mastered my handwriting, which I'd hidden from fans after my husband had made fun of it: 'Irene writes worse than my granny, who never finished fourth grade.'

Neither did I really.

Sure I made it back and forth to school for a day here and a day there, but I was always behind and grew shrewd at hiding that I knew less than the other kids, whereas Lilian . . . her extra years with the nuns stood her in good stead for life.

I told Charlie that only she would have gone to all that trouble with my suicide note but he couldn't figure out her motive.

In Hollywood to be forty-two, unbankable and bankrupt was a reason for suicide, so somebody guessed that I was a suitable case, and I guess I was sort of addicted to sleepers, like most stars I knew in the 60s. If we didn't want to deal with life, it was natural to want to sleep for fourteen, fifteen hours at a stretch. But Charlie refused to bring sleepers into the house.

Marijuana, yes. LSD, yes. Morphine, even. But sleeping pills, no.

12

Louise Taylor's Saturday-morning tap-dancing class was held in the room behind her father's bar and grill, sadly bulldozed after the war in a rezoning scheme. Mr Taylor's brother, Derville, also had his shoeshine stand there, so it was a busy corner. Sociable. Where people who didn't go to church could meet. Laugh and gossip and show off their week's pay in some loud Saturday-night togs.

Louise, who we all called Miss Taylor, had been a chorine at the Cotton Club in Harlem the year before, but I didn't know that was something for her students to brag about. I didn't know that the Cotton Club was the night spot where New York's arty set, like Carl van Vechten and F. Scott Fitzgerald, went to rub shoulders with what they called the Darktown Strutters, and it would be years before I discovered that real Harlemites turned their noses up at the Cotton Club . . .

Miss Taylor was all of eighteen, though her flapper's bob made her look older, especially the first time I saw her in that deep-rose sack dress. Her pockmarked skin, a pale olive colour, wasn't the sole reason she could have passed for white; she also had straggly light brown hair and a completely flat backside.

Inching my way into the shabby back room for my first tap lesson, my head was as full of fantasies as the other eight girls. Including Lil. I'm sure we all imagined that we would emerge from day one like the sophisticate that Miss Taylor was. (I didn't think she was gawky like my sister claimed. In fact, I saw Louise as stylish and graceful. Her flat chest and boyish hips suited the Jazz-Age clothes she wore, and her long, sure stride was sort of elegant. Although it's true that in those days it was considered unfortunate for a girl to be so tall.)

I loved Miss Taylor for having such lean, muscular calves, because for the first time my own seemed less pitiful. They were the thinnest in her class but she'd remind us all, 'Bless the Lord for your legs, and oil those feet!'

She couldn't afford a pianist so she produced rhythms for us to dance to with a long baton that she beat against a wooden mallet. Class lasted forty minutes and we knew it was nearly over when she clapped her hands and wiped the moustache of perspiration from her top lip. That was the signal for us to close our eyes and listen to her dance, before we put on our street shoes for home. To have us hear the rhythm of her feet rather than watch them move was her own progressive idea . . . Her steps were as rhythmic as a typist reeling off sixty words a minute. Clack-clack-clickety-clack-clack. Clack-click-clackety-clack-click. The syncopation was like fireworks and got under my skin so, I couldn't wait to imitate the sound with my own feet.

I didn't have what they call a natural talent, but I tried to make up for it in sheer determination. It was during Miss Taylor's fourth session that I discovered that by concentrating on my rhythm, I could manipulate her smile. To get her to glance at me was like eating Mack's caramels at the bottom of the stairs. I didn't want to share her attention . . . Had Mother known, she would have whipped me without my understanding why. She would have said that I had to share everything with Lil, but that's not quite how the showing-off thing works. So I kept the admiration that I'd spotted in Miss Taylor's eyes to myself.

I've since seen men study me with that glance, those starry eyes that soon go hand-in-glove with infatuation. Whereas Louise's seemed to say something like, 'When you try, I find you adorable.'

I did everything to get her undivided attention, and what started as a game became a compulsion. Some of her girls wanted to be dancers, but little Irene wanted to be noticed. So, wherever and whenever I could, I'd slip on my tap dancing shoes to practise . . .

Clack-clack-clickety, clack-clack-clack. It's a wonder that Mother didn't go mad.

Los Angeles erased my vaguest need to return to Camden. Especially after Mother got us a ride to Venice Beach to celebrate my eighth birthday. I smelled the ocean before I heard it, and heard it before I saw it; the Pacific gets credit for being my first glimpse of what other people refer to as 'Nature'. The waves. The vastness. I squealed louder than a baby gull when I saw the way that water spread out to meet the sky. It was a clear November day and I threw my arms out to spin 'round and 'round.

Like this display of stars tonight, the ocean made me feel that I was everything and nothing.

The day I turned eight, had anybody told Mother that twenty-six years on she'd be waiting backstage with me at the Oscars to hear if my name was called for best supporting actress, she would never have believed it. Because in 1930 all I seemed destined to be was another little nappy-headed child; Negroes had as much hope of taking on Hollywood as a roach. In fact, on my eighth birthday, Mother couldn't believe that we were allowed to take our shoes off and walk the beach that Armistice Day. So we didn't.

After Lil and I had been taking tap for several weeks, it was the Saturday before Thanksgiving, Miss Taylor brought a short but imposing-looking friend to watch our class. I noticed the woman eyeing me, so I sensed that something was up, and sure enough, after class, Louise called me aside and said, 'Would you and your big sister like to split a sweet potato in Daddy's place?'

Not a slice of cake or pie.

A sweet potato. And how lucky we were to get the offer.

We may have been taking tap, but food was still a treat and hard to come by.

That occasion marked the first time Lil and I went to an eating place, and as Louise led us to the booth which her father had motioned her to take, I couldn't have been more nervous had I been asked to take communion at a high mass. I dared not look at Lilian for fear of giggling. I was giddy with self-importance. Anybody would have thought I was about to dine at the Ritz.

It was so hot that Saturday that two men, perched on stools at the counter, were in undershirts. With pots of collards and potatoes simmering on the stove it was hotter inside than out.

Lil and I each got half of a bright, orange sweet potato smeared with butter and, as we nibbled timidly, afraid to look up, Louise passed me a slip of paper with joined-up writing scribbled on it and said, 'I'll be going back East at Christmas and my friend who came to class today said to give y'all's mama this.'

I couldn't yet read joined-up writing anyway, but Lil and I didn't consider inspecting it until Miss Taylor had waved us goodbye. I feared it was about money, because money was always the worse thing that I could think of – owing it. Needing it. The word money seemed to be on grown-up lips all the time and it had a harrowing effect on me.

When I tried to goad my sister into reading the contents to me, she said, 'This is Mother's and you know it's a sin to read her mail.'

I wonder what would have happened had I listened to her?

It's possible that had we not known what those few words had said the course of our lives might have been different.

The sun was glorious that afternoon and we had a lot to be thankful for by all accounts. It was a Saturday. No school, a tap class, that warm feeling of tummies satisfied with a sugary sweet potato. And we'd just been sitting like grown-ups in Taylor's Café and Grill. With our tap shoes under our arms, it should have been enough for us two to hold hands and dawdle to the room that was temporarily home.

But that note had tickled my curiosity.

'If I could read joined-up writing, I'd read it to you. Suppose it's about money?'

My sister put her tap shoes on the ground and opened the note reluctantly. It went against her nature to do anything sinful. We could have been in the middle of an orange grove and she wouldn't have picked fruit off the ground even if we were starving.

Nonetheless, that afternoon she read that note from Bessie Lovell to our mother: 'I give classes for a dime per session and can offer Irene a place.'

Refolding it along the creases, Lil said, 'I'll get in trouble for reading this, so we have to act surprised when Mother tells us what it says.'

Although I denied it until I had more than she did, I guess as kids I was as jealous of Lilian as she became of me. I'm ashamed to say it, but hair and skin colour mattered so much to me that I envied her braids being an inch longer than mine and her skin being a couple of shades fairer. It's strange, because I was jealous and yet proud of her at the same time. She always seemed to get the best of everything, whether it was the socks handed down to us by Mrs Herzfeld or the compliments Mother received about us when we did our church recitals. But tap had been different.

Although Mother got the note, she just looked at it and tucked it in her bra with, 'Y'all go out and play.'

Every day I waited for the glory of hearing that I had been singled out for tap lessons, but the glory never came, because Mother never mentioned it. After two more sessions with Miss Taylor, dancing was to end for me for a couple years.

Is it that Mother couldn't afford the dime or decided that if both Lil and I couldn't receive tap lessons from Bessie Lovell, neither of us would have them?

I wish I had the answer.

What I know is that I blamed Lil. First I shunned her and by the time I was ready to make up, she wouldn't play with me. If we walked down the street together, I would lag behind so that I didn't have to speak to her or vice versa. In time I couldn't remember what our feud was about, but we were enemies.

Overnight, she stopped playing big sister, never taking my side when she normally would with Mother or other children in the street. A chasm grew between us which became too great to bridge.

She would mention Camden and I would tease her for it. I would talk about Miss Taylor, and Lil would laugh about Louise's slightly bowed legs.

Tap dancing had started a family feud.

13

During the past two days, when I least expect it, faces that I hardly recognize float through my mind. A disturbing number have appeared. People who were of no consequence. Some I can't identify. Yesterday, while I was having my lunch, for no reason I recalled the face of the Mexican kid who manned the cash register at the late-night drugstore on Hollywood Boulevard where I used to get my tranquillizers. That was thirty-odd years ago and he was irrelevant even back then, but his image came to me so sharply, I wonder if it means something.

Then last night, while I was trying to read my book, in comes the face of that old woman who used to clean the toilets at St Anthony's. I don't think I ever said two words to her when I was at school there, so why, nearly seventy years later, should her face come to me out of the blue? Crystal clear, it was.

I've heard that this sort of thing happens to people before they go.

Dammit, I hope I'm not dying.

Who'd look after the dog . . .

This morning, when I took her for her walk, I was watching her do her business and in came the face of that Japanese butler who gave Mother her first full-time job after we got to Los Angeles. I couldn't decide whether I was glad to be reminded of him or not, because there were times, back before the war, when I used to wonder if, in the short time she'd known him, he hadn't had a worse affect on Mother than Mamie.

Having met him only once when I was eight, it's eerie that I could envision him so precisely. I actually saw the fine black hairs which he had missed shaving on his Adam's apple. Had they been there when I'd met him in 1931?

He appeared in my mind as a complete figure, not just a face. Bowing from the waist he was and smiling, without showing his teeth. His white jacket had a high collar and looked very stiff, somehow formal, although the cut was sort of sporty. He could have been a waiter in a Chinese restaurant . . .

I think his full name was Ben Toguri but Toguri was all Mother called him. His boss was a German architect Dieter Meyerdorf, who was renting that house east of Hollywood for a year. It was beyond Griffith Park which was still a wilderness back then though a stone's throw from down town. The district that became Los Feliz, where people built big fancy houses with acres of land around them.

Mother had landed that job on the rebound, because arriving without a uniform to help serve at Meyerdorf's New Year's Eve party, the catering boss relegated her to dishwashing. She said even in the kitchen she looked out of place in her brown chemise, so it was her miracle that she was singled out for a full time job.

What really happened is that the other catering staff, refined in their fancy black uniforms, snubbed her. She got on with her work and Toguri noticed her because of it.

The guests at that party left after dawn and Mother stayed on her feet until noon, mopping up booze and scraping off food which had been mashed into the carpets. Having never seen caviar or profiteroles, lobster or mango, she couldn't put a name to half what she was scooping up.

In the large Spanish courtyard with its huge stone fireplace Meyerdorf had had a five-piece ragtime band entertain his dazzling guests. When the band broke for intervals two Mexican guitarists serenaded the couples dancing beside the swimming pool.

Mother said the noise and bustle had made her head swim. The catering staff snickered in the kitchen about the tuxedoed guests who stubbed their cigars out on the hardwood floors or flicked their cigarette butts into the floodlit fountain. Not that Meyerdorf had noticed, because early in the evening before the throngs had arrived, he'd slipped in a puddle of champagne and had had to be put to bed, where he was followed by a stream of girls who made appearances naked on his bedroom balcony which overlooked the courtyard.

Toguri ran the house but kept his gloved hands clean, noticing that Mother never took hers out of the dishwasher. When the party finally ended, he sent her to clean the tier of terraces either side of the elaborate landscaped garden. When he offered work for the following day, she didn't say that Meyerdorf's place was a three-mile walk from our room, because she was afraid that would stop him from hiring her.

Mother had never even seen pictures of a house like that. Put together with more money than sense, it was pure Hollywood.

Of course she mistook the brass for gold and couldn't understand how anybody lived with so many modern paintings. 'Look like somebody just threw the paint at them,' she said and proper antiques puzzled her. She thought everything, including the Italian marble, was to be scrubbed with Dutch Boy cleanser and thought Toguri was crazy for making her take a ladder around the house to polish the towering palms with milk. He laughed when she offered to repair the tapestry that hung in the hallway and tried to explain that being so old it was meant to look frayed.

Toguri must have had his hands full training her to clean the place and she brought home new terms at a fast rate. Ming vase. Persian rug. Victorian lace. Japanese silk. Egyptian cotton.

Every time she left for work I imagined her walking to a fairytale palace. Sometimes she'd describe how she'd perspire, polishing the dining-room table. It seated twenty-four and had a crystal chandelier hanging above it, which she was told never to touch. Every chance she got to shine Meyerdorf's two-foot-high solid silver crucifix, she prayed while she rubbed that God would protect her from breaking anything in that house.

She loved doing Meyerdorf's dressing room because she said, 'That was the safest place to work. I could drop a sock or a pair of suspenders without worrying.'

That Los Feliz job got her humming again. It was as if the richness of her surroundings gave her new confidence. She wasn't just a cleaner, she cleaned for somebody wealthy, and that helped her hold up her head. She started laughing again. It was hard to believe that she was the same Ruthie Mae Matthews who had been too timid to look Father Connolly in the eye if she passed him on the stairs. It was impossible to see her as the woman who, a year before, had sat in our L-shaped room above Mack's undoing crocheted doilies so that she'd have yarn for crocheting the next day.

I can't remember what Lilian and I used to do for the hours Mother wasn't home. All that California sunshine allowed us more street life, but I was a loner, especially after Lilian seemed to have no more time for me. I know that I had a skipping rope and used to wander the streets collecting bits that I dreamed of selling to the rag-and-bone man.

Toguri may have been in his late twenties like Mother, because he had youthful interests. He liked to Charleston and kept the radio blaring, because with Meyerdorf gone, Toguri was his own boss. He remained in the house alone when Meyerdorf was away and grew dependent on Mother to help stave off the dullness of those Southern Californian afternoons when big houses can feel like cemeteries. Places for dead people. The posse of Mexican gardeners, who spoke no English, were employed by the owners to maintain the garden three days a week, but Toguri and Mother were the only people who entered the house.

She worked every day but Sunday and came home with Toguri's copy of the newspaper to pore over every line, scrutinizing the obituaries and want ads as carefully as the front page, preparing herself for the following day, in case Toguri might want to discuss something he'd read. But when I used to see her studying the want ads, I was afraid that she had to find a new job. I stayed confused and worried about bills like I was the one paying them.

Toguri was second-generation Japanese from Toronto and filled her head with new words and bizarre notions that she wanted to impose upon us. 'I want you girls to breathe deeply when you're out walking. Fill your lungs with fresh air and take time to observe nature. Stop when you see a eucalyptus tree. Break off a leaf and smell it. The world is beautiful and you take it too much for granted.'

That was surely Toguri talking . . . Negroes in our neighbourhood were on the breadline and Mother was picking up a Japanese inflection. She was like a teenager who starts running with a fast crowd, but Lilian and I still needed her. We still needed a home but didn't have one, moving from one rooming house to the next and living out of her carpet bag.

She'd come back late with fanciful talk about some radio programme that Toguri had had her listening to which was of no interest to us. Her manner grew so stiff and detached that she thanked us for everything from scrubbing floors to making her sweet tea. 'Good evening, girls,' she'd say in a slight daze. Like a walking zombie she was some nights, but what could we say? Little girls weren't bold and never speaking until spoken to was a virtue. I thought the world was for grown-ups and knowing that people were out panhandling made my generation obedient. But Hollywood has always been wild and for all I know, Mother could have been at Meyerdorf's smoking opium every day. I've lived long enough to know that kids never know what's really going on, because more often than not, people make a point of not telling them.

Mother had described Toguri to us as handsome but on the only occasion when Lilian and I met him, I took more notice of his graceful, birdlike movements than his face. He flitted across the carpeted floors, his feet in black slippers, never making a sound.

He greeted us at the front door, giving a slight bow as though we were Meyerdorf's guests. Mother had already lectured us so long and hard that I was afraid to breathe. Tying the ribbons in my hair, she'd said, 'Don't touch nothing, don't sit on nothing, and don't dare take nothing to eat.'

I imagined that I looked beautiful because I was wearing Lilian's communion dress, but the moment we entered Meyerdorf's hallway, I was faced with a full-length mirror, and the truth stared back at me. An enormous red ribbon flopped over my brow and that dress hung on me like a teepee. My legs were pretzel sticks and I nearly cried because I felt so betrayed by my image.

Owning a pair of tap shoes, having a mother who worked for a rich man, having known a woman who was a friend of Charlie

Chaplin's, having been praised for my Bible recitations, I was a child with delusions and to discover that I looked like a little brown clown wounded my pride. But Lil and I sang for Toguri that afternoon anyway. Our *a cappella* harmonies were improved by the echo in the courtyard. 'These two are better than the Cochrane Twins on *Children's Hour*! Can't we get them an audition at RKO?'

Toguri was so excited that Mother saw dollar signs. Like Mamie, he thought that what Lilian and I had was marketable, so when Mother returned to work the next day, it seems that he was full of ideas for us. He said, 'Your girls need a catchy name . . . the Matthews Sisters sounds boring.'

I imagine she suggested the obvious, so it's lucky that Toguri didn't want to settle on Irene Meyerdorf or Lilian Herzfeld. Lilian and I could have ended up as the Alvarez Sisters or The McMichael Girls, but O'Brien won the day. No doubt at some stage Mother had told Toguri about her landlord accused of murdering his wife, because that was the sort of scandal that could have livened up a long afternoon when the sun became wearying.

Until tonight, I hadn't given a moment's thought to how upset I should have been when Mother said, 'Do y'all like The Singing O'Briens or The O'Brien Sisters?' Aged eight, the terrible irony of it missed me, because the idea of a 'stage name', never mind actually receiving one, positively thrilled me like it might any little girl even before Shirley Temple. When Mother said, 'Toguri thinks the O'Brien Sisters has a ring,' my eight-year-old imagination spun into orbit.

John Randolph Matthews had never been enough of a father for his family name to matter, and when Mother made the O'Brien suggestion, I was too young to equate that surname with Mack.

Denial.

I used it and it used me.

To think that I lugged 'O'Brien' around all those years. Fussing about how it was billed, insulted if it was misspelled on a contract, raging if I saw a poster that spelled it with an 'a' rather than an 'e'. It makes me sympathize with those crazy militants who changed their names to X. But then what's in a name?

72

I accepted O'Brien as easily as I slid my little feet into those first tap-dancing shoes. Aged ten – die cast, mould set, pattern cut.

Most roles in my life were chosen for me.

Ruthie Mae's girl.

Mrs Matthews's daughter.

Lilian Matthews's sister.

An O'Brien Sister.

Irene O'Brien.

PART II

Irene Lomax

14

From the age of ten until the day Eugene Lomax placed a little diamond ring on my engagement finger, Mother and Mamie tried to make money from Lil and I performing. Whether it was in poor men's churches which didn't have more than thirty in the congregation or in nickel dance classes taught by girls with no gift for teaching, our childhood was wasted on futile pipe dreams.

I hate to recall the times that me and my sister stood for hours in torrential rain waiting to be chosen as extras but failing to get the job. How often did we get up at dawn to go to some radio audition to be told that we were too young or too old?

Mamie was full of big ideas, but hadn't the wherewithal to execute them. So she'd rehearse us at some piano she'd get the hire of in a church hall but then accept some job of her own which forced us to cancel the audition that we'd been preparing for. She'd say, 'Ruthie Mae, them girls'll be perfect,' for every variety show that ever wanted a little coloured girl, but there weren't many that wanted two.

In my mind, I always felt that Mother cheated me out of a dancing career when she didn't let me take Bessie Lovell's dance classes, and although Lilian and I did eventually take others, I sensed that I had been deprived of a well-timed opportunity.

Mamie and Mother had me convinced that wanting to sing and dance was our duty.

We were the wrong colour to get ahead and even though there were teams like the one Sammy Davis Jr was in with his father and uncle which toured around the country, we were more in the church meeting league thanks to our repertoire of lightweight spirituals.

Lil was a Catholic and although she may have had a good voice, she became more and more detached performing at the revival meetings which Mamie claimed were our stepping stone to fame on the radio.

We had that performers' addiction. Always waiting for something to happen. Always wanting what I didn't get.

Maybe that's why my daughter Nadine was such a problem. Perhaps I could have handled her better had I not expected her to be otherwise. It was only down to Charlie I gave up expectation.

The irony is that she and he were born the same year. Spooky really.

Back in '65, I'd sit out here with him on this roof wondering if he was sent to haunt me for what I did to her. But like Charlie used to remind me, he was floating around in somebody else's womb while I was struggling with my marriage, yet all I was really doing with Eugene Lomax was setting myself up for a protracted divorce.

In 1943 during the Second World War when we tied the knot, my head was totally in the clouds.

Airy-fairy, as they call it nowadays.

What must have enticed me to accept his engagement ring was the number of brides pictured each week on the wedding page of the *Amsterdam News*, bought by Mother to keep up with the gossip in so-called Black society.

What also fooled me into thinking that I had to become Gene's wife was the imminent possibility of becoming his widow, since he'd got me to the altar by claiming that the day after the ceremony he would be heading straight for a boot camp in Georgia.

We were both twenty-one. The age Charlie was when he died.

Eugene was exceptional in many ways, and I've never known anyone more generous, but lying turned out to be his problem. I couldn't see the point in it, although I guess he must have had one.

If he said that he was slipping off to the pictures, he was liable to be going to the fights, or if he'd wired me to say he was playing New York, it was just as likely that the band was playing Boston. So

I distrusted him and was constantly on the lookout: studying his eyes, going through his pockets, searching for the truth on ticket stubs and receipts . . .

Eugene lied to everybody but his brother, although I didn't realize this when we exchanged vows. In fact I had a false sense of how well I knew him, because we'd first met in 1937 when we were fifteen . . .

I can still see us . . . Lil and Eugene with his brother Walter and me, all hovering, collars up to ward off the cold, outside that candy store next to the Lafayette Theatre in Harlem . . .

The four of us were out there with our noses running as we chomped on a bag of penny candy which my sister and I had bought as our lunch. The boys couldn't decide whether to go for ribs at the Barbeque and I was hoping that they'd invite us, because she and I could hardly afford a hot sweet potato from the street vendor.

We were about to begin a stint as chorines at a club, the Sportsman, which tried to take over from the Cotton Club when it closed. We thought we were made. But our West-Coast talent agency had loaned us the train fare to New York, and had to be repaid from our puny salaries, not to mention their agency fees, Mother to support back home and our room and board in Harlem.

But to hear Brooklyn accents and have New Jersey referred to as 'over the bridge' was exciting.

That afternoon with the four of us outside the candy store was so icy, cars crawled at a snail's pace and we saw people literally slipping and sliding down the Stroll – that block between 131st and 132nd – which in those days was Harlem's Champs Elysées and Tin Pan Alley rolled into one.

Despite the weather, the sidewalks were as busy as in springtime, with old people and kids, vendors and vagrants, workers and pimps all moving with the traffic as Gene, Walter, Lil and I blocked the door of the store, rubbing our hands and stamping our feet to keep them from going numb.

Lilian was sucking a jawbreaker and clutching the collar of her fancy red coat which was too lightweight for the below-zero weather.

Obviously, she was both freezing and overly impressed with the two brothers who greeted every other person passing with a 'Hey Gizz,' or a 'What'cha know, Poppa?'

She was seventeen. Like Walter. Yet she was as green as Mother must have been when Daddy scooped her off the train from Mississippi and plopped her at his aunt's.

Around strangers, my sister wasn't much of a talker, but she loved street-corner gatherings and was a socializer at heart, gravitating towards anybody who knew people worth knowing. In another life, maybe she can come back as one of those Capitol Hill hostesses.

That afternoon on the Stroll, she didn't want to miss any of the famous faces that Gene claimed to know, so every time he called to someone walking on the opposite side, her head would spin round to check across the street. But as Walter said, the Fats Wallers and Louis Armstrongs were either tucked up in warm beds or out of town touring, since December was a busy month for dance bands.

Gene and Walter were local boys who, like us, had been performing together since elementary school. But we were hicks by comparison, although I wouldn't have admitted it at the time.

Although both Lomax brothers still danced, by the time we met them, they were also playing instruments – Walter on clarinet and Eugene on trumpet. So that afternoon, they were full of talk about scores and sheets and riffs that I wanted to know about but didn't. Lil and I could sing but we didn't read music and Mamie had put us both off learning the piano.

At that age I worried that somebody would notice that I knew less than I was supposed to. Our education had been so sporadic and I never mixed much, whereas Gene and Walter were reachers and climbers, even as teenagers. Ambition was as much my husband's talent as his dancing and playing.

In the doorway of the candy store, the two brothers gossiped about grown musicians, respected players like Zutty Singleton and Tommy Ladnier. Name dropped like they were friends, though Gene seemed phoney and childish. With his hands thrust deeply into his tweed coat pockets, he'd cocked his Jeff to the side of his head trying to come across as smooth and tough.

In an effort to sound sophisticated, he barely spoke above a whisper, so I kept losing interest in what he had to say.

Wearing two-inch heels, I was a head taller than Gene and looked down at him as he tried to impress us with who he knew. Suddenly it struck me that Lil and I would be seen talking on the street like prostitutes. I was pathological about appearing to be lady-like and knew nothing of the local 'vipers' that he kept referring to. I thought that the marijuana they sold was for opium smokers.

When Gene came up with the line, 'Doesn't your name rhyme with mine?', I decided that he was not only short and conceited, but dismissed him as a lame brain.

He kept slipping in the fact that they were Harlem born as though it was superior to everywhere else, and even five years later, when we were man and wife, he would snub anybody who wasn't from Harlem, apart from musicians.

Aged fifteen, I was a dry prune and can see how Lil and I must have seemed like misfits to boys like him, because neither of us had dated since Mamie McMichael had escorted us as accompanist and chaperone, wearing the sour face of a prison warden whenever men or boys sniffed round.

It was still the Depression in '37 and there was no sign of it letting up. Especially for kids like us who worked, life was a struggle, and I woke up every day expecting to end up in a breadline. At fifteen it was a prayer answered when a recommendation from Miss Taylor, our first dance teacher, led to that six-month Harlem engagement after Mamie developed a frozen shoulder and had to lay off playing piano for a year. (A lasting regret is that by the time I got around to writing a thank-you to Miss Taylor, she had died of TB and the letter came back marked 'return to sender'.)

I was a serious girl, and though less religious than Lilian, I was quieter and more reserved, hoping that with luck I might attract a decent husband. Lilian still said her rosary each night and attended mass several times a week to please the Pope as well as Christ, but she went a bit wild in Harlem. And had I let her, she would have run off with a Catholic kid from New Orleans who blew his wages lindy-hopping at the Savoy. People mistook me for the eldest, as she was two inches shorter . . . Nearly Eugene's exact height. Even in those days he was small for his age and had a big chip on his shoulder because of it.

Gene and Walter, like Lilian and me, were seen everywhere together, but whereas my sister and I were a twosome due to work, the boys seemed really to like each other and be together by choice.

Lilian went to great lengths to find out information about them and when she discovered that their musician father had run around with Nancy Cunard's set during the Twenties, I said, 'I knew there was something wrong with the Lomaxes.' Nancy was an English heiress which didn't lift the stigma of her being what we all referred to as 'ofey', meaning white.

When we first met the Lomax Brothers, Gene was running around with a red-headed girl named Peggy Brown whose claim to fame was that she had danced in the floor show at a club on Broadway called The Harlem Uproar House when the Disciples of Swing made their debut as the first all-star mixed band in America. It consisted of fifteen musicians – seven whites and eight blacks – including Dolly Armendra, the female trumpeter. They made the headlines, but after somebody had repeatedly smeared their billboard with a swastika, the club closed down long before talk about them did.

Gene claimed that Peggy was Dolly's second cousin, but Walter, who was always joking, said, 'Don't listen to him. Peggy works part-time washing dishes in a soup kitchen.' Still, she was light skinned with long wavy hair, so I envied her, which in those days put her stations above the rest of us.

Both brothers were notorious playboys although still in their teens, and I couldn't understand what Lil saw in Gene with his pencil thin moustache and his hair slicked back in a greasy conk. I had warned her, 'Even if you get him, you won't keep him, because every girl in Harlem gets giddy around Eugene.'

Anytime I saw him, he was standing on a street corner jive talking about known opium smokers and reefer peddlers like Mezz

Mezzrow . . . (Charlie's eyes always lit up with interest when I told him about the old days). I used to chastise Lil. 'How can you like somebody as vain as Eugene? He sits in a tonsorial parlour for hours getting the kinks pressed out of his hair?' In truth, as he said, a lot of entertainers blew all their earnings on their hair and clothes, but he'd rushed back to the tonsorial parlour as soon as an inch of his kinky roots grew out.

When Gene and Walter went off touring down south during our first month dancing in Harlem, Lilian never stopped talking about Gene, although he was two years her junior. So the afternoon we spotted them milling amongst the crowd under the Tree of Hope, to get the news about what had been going on in town during their absence, I wasn't surprised when Lil insisted that we stop and chat to them.

The Tree of Hope was actually a tree on 131st Street that had become a popular meeting place. I was reluctant to be seen there mixing with the throng of entertainers and vipers, but stuck with Lil as she hedged over to Gene. I heard her ask him outright if he was still seeing Peggy Brown.

When he said, 'She sleeps with her glasses on', meaning that she was a prude, Lilian's loud laughter embarrassed me. She was showing off and I was ashamed when she quipped, 'Somebody says that's what you told Peggy about me.'

Before our Harlem stint was over, Eugene had become a real zoot suiter, but my sister refused to see it and even made it known in the dressing room that we shared with the sixteen other girls that Eugene Lomax was her dream man.

Those dancers were worldly and knew every ploy for trapping a man. Several believed that there were extra points for being easy, while others thought that they gained leverage from coming across as naïve. One older girl advised Lilian, 'From what I've heard Gene Lomax likes a chase but let him do the chasing.' Too many people knew that Gene had stood my sister up more than once. Lil wore a fading smile and said, 'He's just young. He'll change.'

Once he had promised to take her to a matinee of *Golden Boy* which all the girls in the dressing room were raving about. It may have been in April, because there was a downpour, so Lilian sat in our grubby room in her hat and galoshes. From noon until five-thirty when we had to leave for work, she kept wandering over to the window to check if she could see him coming up the street.

I was angry when he never showed up and suspected that both our good reputations were suffering, because every dancer gossiped as a way to pass time between shows.

It was Walter who told me that the reason Gene never appeared was that he had lost all his money in a crap shoot, but I was sorry that it gave Walter an excuse to talk to me like a loose woman in the street.

Years later, in 1940, I was surprised when the *Amsterdam News* included Walter in its list of up-and-coming eligible bachelors. The caption under his picture said, 'With talent for two', and even mentioned Eugene. When Lil saw it, she cut it out and kept the clipping in her change purse until it virtually disintegrated from her handling it so often.

Her subsequent letters to Eugene went unanswered, and I presumed, with some relief, that she'd forgotten the Lomaxes like I did. Then I bumped into Gene in '42 at a servicemen's club in LA called the Canteen, organized and run by some Hollywood stars and producers' wives.

The Canteen shows were held in a big tent, and when Lil and I weren't off singing or doing radio, I was one of the many girls who volunteered to dance and fraternize with the soldiers to boost morale.

To see Negro soldiers at the Canteen jiving side by side with white ones was a rare sight, because the service, like housing and many other things, was still segregated; but there were strict rules about soldiers of one race not dancing with girls of another. As the volunteer club leader explained: 'The house lights will go up and the music will be stopped, till the "situation" can be rectified.'

I used to tog for those servicemen's clubs, and aged twenty-one, I thought a pretty dress was more vital than oxygen. The night Eugene spotted me, I was wearing a black, box-shouldered number and frugging with a tall, dark sailor from Chicago, although he'd been my partner too often for one evening. Nonetheless, when the band played 'Shoo Shoo Baby', we were having as much fun as everybody else freezing on the chorus and yelling, 'Oh, your Papa's off to the seven seas.'

Having borrowed Lilian's fake pearls and earrings without asking, I was anxious to get home before she noticed them missing, so by ten, I was in line at the hat check to collect my moulting grey rabbit stole when a tallish guy in a tux grabbed my elbow. 'Hey sister,' he teased, 'you were always cute. But *oooweee*, when d'you get to be the finest thing walking?!'

His wasn't a voice or face that I recognized, but I didn't recoil from him when he whispered to me, because attitudes between fellas and girls had relaxed by then. Nonetheless, to have his moustache tickling my earlobe was too much of a liberty. I drew away from the liquor on his breath just as he grinned, 'How could you forget Eugene?'

I assumed he was in civilian clothes for health reasons.

He was unrecognizable as he had gone from flyweight to middleweight. He looked very fit and his face had squared and hardened. It was hard to believe that we were the same age.

His short hair formed a black skullcap against his olive complexion, and his dark brown eyes tricked mine into thinking that he was no less than an Adonis.

Like some old crow seeing a kid she hasn't seen for years, I kept remarking, 'Haven't you grown!'

He eased me out of the hat-check line and swung me around. 'Ooooweee, baby! You sure look good. Like you just stepped off the cover of *Vanity Fair*.' In those days, before I learned to take compliments in my stride, I was a terrible one for blushing. My cheeks burned.

Gene was at the Canteen standing in for a week for another trumpet player and made me swear that I wouldn't tell Lilian, but I would have told her anyway had she and Mother not been asleep when I got in and gone before I woke the following day.

That night at the Canteen, I spotted Eugene again. He was on the bandstand playing but I didn't think that he saw me. He stood to take a solo and the girl beside me twittered, 'That trumpet player. Doesn't he carry himself . . . We came in on the same bus.'

Holding his shiny horn, he was as elegant as any dancer. His head bobbed and weaved in slow motion as his sweeping notes hushed the throngs of servicemen and pretty girls.

Passing each other on the way to the toilets after the set had finished, he waved above the crowd. I didn't really want to join him, but he was forceful when he ushered me to the bar saying, 'Let's share a rum and Coke.' I'm sure he was aware of the girls eyeing him, but he was busy flirting with me, winking when he told the bartender, 'One glass, two straws.'

When I asked about Walter, he looked concerned. 'My brother wired me just today to say that he's coming to LA in two weeks. I didn't have the heart to wire back and say I'll be in boot camp by then.'

'Gosh, Eugene, you'll be going overseas?'

'I'm signing up in the morning.'

'It's going to be like World War I. There won't be any boys of our generation left.'

With war threatening his future and dimming my memory of him in Harlem, I sipped that drink with him until a Mexican combo played a set. With alcohol numbing my good sense, he got me on to the dance floor, and like everybody else that night, I was impressed. He could rhumba and samba like his joints were oiled.

I knew I had to tell Lil when I got in, but I didn't expect her to attack me. 'Hussy! How could you even speak to him after the way he treated me. What happened in Harlem was bad enough, but then I tried to forgive him and he never answered one letter.'

It was after midnight and from the living room where she slept on a pull-out bed, Mother snapped, 'Y'all don't never stop fighting. Lil, put on that nice navy suit and go to the Canteen tomorrow . . .'

He wasn't going to be there, because he was taking me to the Fremont to see Robert Taylor and Lana Turner in *Johnny Eager*.

*　　*　　*

86

Films played the major part in our courtship. Slipping off to matinees without anyone knowing, we languished in puppy love for all of three weeks while I waited for him to tell me that he'd be catching that train to a boot camp in Georgia.

We held hands but I never let him kiss me, because I believed that you could contract TB from someone else's saliva.

He said, 'You're right to save yourself for your husband,' but asked if I was a virgin.

'I can't see you any more,' I said.

'Why not?' he asked.

'Because I know the sort of girl you're interested in.' I guessed he wouldn't tolerate me resisting his lips for much longer, but then I agreed to see *Mrs Miniver* with him, because I loved Walter Pidgeon.

Gene had borrowed a car for that evening because he refused to take me out after dark on the bus, in case of a blackout, he said, but we knew that Negro boys in civvies got stopped if they were out at night.

The movie theatre was in North Hollywood, not far from the air base and as we were drifting out with the throng of people either side of us, he stopped to take something from that horn case which he carried everywhere. He produced a diamond engagement ring pinned to a ribbon dangling from a white orchid corsage.

As we stood under the blacked-out marquee as darkness fell, we saw a plane take off across the dusk and suddenly Gene's moist lips grazed my cheek. 'The first time I saw you, remember you were in one of those terrible cowgirl outfits doing that high-kick routine at that club in Harlem . . . I said to myself, "That's my wife."'

With the pink ribbon between his lips, and the horn case between his knees, he tried to pin that corsage to my blazer, making no proposal for me to accept or refuse. I was dumbstruck. Then I saw tears well in his eyes and would have done anything to keep him from crying. I even held his trumpet case so that he could slip the ring, which was slightly too big, on my finger, and imagined Gene in fatigues face down on a stormy beach while a tide rushed over him and other dead soldiers strewn to his right and left. As I stared at my ring finger, with the hundred-dollar diamond glittering, a scene from *Mrs Miniver* replayed on me ... It was of the vicar delivering his sermon in the bombed-out English country church. 'This is not only a war of soldiers in uniforms. It is a war of the people – and must be fought not only on the battlefield but in the cities and villages ...'

The skies were rarely quiet in that area. Cargo and munitions and who knows what were being airlifted, and as Gene turned the ignition of his friend's car, our motor blended with the sound of another plane taking off.

Showing Mother the ring, she agreed to keep the news from Lilian until I was sure about what I was doing. It was a relief to wrap it in a handkerchief and slip it in my pillowcase, because out of sight, out of mind meant that I didn't have to think about marrying Eugene. He was the nearest thing that I'd ever had to a boyfriend, yet I sensed that he wasn't good husband material. Nonetheless, he pressed me for an immediate wedding date by sending me a telegram which read, 'Now or Never, or Now and Forever.'

Among my anxieties about marrying was my fear that I may have had syphilis. My ignorance behind this was that Mamie had once caught me sitting on a public toilet seat and had said, 'You pick up venereal disease like that. Just don't give it to me!'

As with all things sexually related, I believed everything I heard.

Words like 'vagina' and 'penis' were medical terms that I'd seen in a nursing book that Mother kept for looking up minor ailments. Knowledge about love making didn't exist for me. I would have been happy to have remained a bride of Christ in a borrowed veil from St Anthony's, and it wouldn't surprise me if most of my generation were the same.

Anyway, believing that I was doing my share for the war effort and with a copy of the *Amsterdam News* folded open at the wedding announcements, I went nervously for my blood test.

15

Lilian was standing by the stove stirring hominy grits when I finally found the nerve to tell her that Eugene and I were getting married. I can still see her banging that spoon against the rim of the pot and grinding her teeth when I said, 'We're only having the simplest civil ceremony, otherwise I'd ask you to be my maid of honour.' She never did eat those grits but poured them in a bowl which she left on the table. When she stormed out the front door without a hat, Mother went after her.

Being naive and optimistic, I figured that she would realize that Eugene had never been hers but anybody would have thought that I'd stolen her fiancé. Within a day of finding out the news, she'd made a flimsy excuse to go to New York to work and disappeared without a goodbye.

Mother tried to be philosophical. 'You know Lilian. She holds onto things. But she'll come round.' To prove that Mother wasn't taking sides, she stayed away from the simple ceremony that Eugene and I had in Pasadena, and to be honest, with hindsight that marriage didn't warrant any fanfare.

Nonetheless, there was a beautiful azure sky that morning of 6 May when Eugene and I exchanged vows. It was a perfect southern California day with the tall palms lining the avenue to the courthouse as still as the air. It didn't seem possible that across the ocean torpedoes were flying and machine guns were peppering the atmosphere.

Everybody knew someone who'd been killed; boys who had been members of Mother's church, a kid who Lilian and I had met in Hawaii when we did that stint with the circus and even one of Mamie's teenaged godsons who was killed on a merchant ship.

So that afternoon we said 'I do' I imagined might be one of the few we'd ever share as husband and wife.

It's either pitiful or hilarious to recall that for the most part, Gene and I were strangers. After all, sitting in a movie theatre isn't the best way for two people to get acquainted. But we weren't the only kids getting married back then under those circumstances. The war had produced a marriage epidemic.

Thanks to Lil, I had never even invited Gene home for a meal when we dated.

For our honeymoon, if I dare call it that, Eugene borrowed a musician friend's duplex on South Hobart for three days. It was the nearest we could get to going away. When Mother discovered that we were to stay there, she was as giddy as anybody starstruck and said, 'Maybe I'll pop round. Willie Best's got him a bungalow over thataway . . .'

She had been getting an odd bit-part on the radio and fancied herself a bit of a star like Willie Best, who was about as big as Negro film actors got back then. It was Gene who finally said, 'Irene and I are supposed to be alone after we've tied the knot.'

When he finally carried me across the threshold of the duplex, I was a little embarrassed that his knees were buckling. It was a miracle that he didn't drop me. The word 'wedding' evokes such a romantic image it was hard to believe that getting hitched could be such a lacklustre affair. There was certainly no orchestra playing background music and no maître d' to greet us with two flutes of champagne when we entered that apartment.

Instead, there was a baby crying in either the bungalow next door or the one behind which belonged to a sax player who was loudly practising his scales when we arrived.

In Gene's arms while my own clutched his neck, my small veiled hat fell to the floor as he rushed through the sunlit living room.

Before I could take in how nicely furnished the place was or use the bathroom, Gene dropped me onto the bed, which was modern with a carved mahogany head and a plush chenille bedspread. 'Phew,' he said, wiping his brow like I weighed a ton.

I needed to get my bearings and change my sanitary towel as well as my clothes. My white wedge heels were pinching and my waist cincher was cutting into my sides. I was also sure that Gene had smudged my red lipstick on my dress because there was also some on his chin.

Mother gets the credit for my outfit. I would never have chosen the white polished-cotton sun dress with its halter top. There was far too much frill on the bodice and hem, and I resembled a country and western star. Eager to put on the satin robe which Gene had bought me, I was about to get off the bed when he hurriedly began removing my shoes and fumbling with my garters.

'Careful, Gene,' I said anxiously. 'You know how hard these nylons are to find.' He looked hot and sweaty and was yanking at his tie while I tried unsuccessfully to squeeze out of his clutches. I had considered it a bit of luck that my period had begun the night before, because I assumed that was the best excuse for postponing more than some kissing. But he was yanking off his belt, so I said sheepishly, 'Sorry, kid, but it's my time of the month.'

I would have thought it too bold to have come right out and used the word 'period' and I blushed at merely referring to it.

To draw his mind to other things, I was about to suggest that we inspect the apartment together when his hand slipped lower to stroke my inner thigh. I yelped like he'd touched me with a hot poker and tried to twist away from him, all the while embarrassed that his hand had come so close to my sanitary towel.

At twenty-one, I was ashamed of menstruating. I was disgusted by the sight of a blood-stained sheet and thought that soiling my panties accidentally was a personal disgrace. How many times did I sling out a good pair of underwear because they'd been spotted with blood?

So when Eugene tried to feel between my legs, my first instinct was to entwine them, my second was to use them to kick him back. I was frantic and resorted to slapping at him when he said, 'Your blood is my blood, baby.'

Having a few days earlier skimmed an article about vampires in a sleazy magazine, it seized my mind that I had married one. Are there coloured vampires? I was asking myself as I fought Eugene off like he was Bela Lugosi. With my dress up to my waist and that cincher rolled up to my midriff after Gene had unfastened the garters, I felt restricted but fought all the more.

He grabbed my wrists to stop my blows and was laughing, 'What the hell, Irene . . . calm down . . . it's okay . . . I'm not going to hurt you.' I never imagined that he could pry my thighs open with one knee while holding me down with his elbow on my stomach. 'Stop fighting, Irene. What are you doing!'

'No, what are you doing!' I yelled. 'You'll get blood on your good trousers and ruin this dress.' As the marriage ceremony had been delayed, I hadn't changed my towel since I'd left home that morning. I pleaded, 'I'm dirty, Gene, don't do this!'

He tugged at my panties and scraped his fingers through my pubic hair which I knew would be caked with blood.

'Please . . .' I begged.

He smeared blood on his cheek and sniffed his fingers. With his eyes half closed and his black lashes fluttering, he repeated, 'Holy mother, let's do this.'

While the springs bounced and rocked as he pumped me in slow motion, I crossed myself and said more Hail Marys and Our Fathers than I could count.

16

Eugene and I were lucky enough to find a little apartment on 77th Avenue, hardly a mile from the corner where Louise Taylor's father had his diner. It was in a two-storey building full of newlyweds, most of them up from Louisiana or Texas to cash in on all the work in the shipyards. The guy directly below was single though, a musician who Eugene forbade me to speak to because he had a reputation for cheating at cards.

It used to make me smile seeing the words 'Mr and Mrs Lomax Apt 6C' on the buzzer by our door. Although our apartment was hardly bigger than a large studio in floor space it was divided into a lounge, bedroom and kitchenette with a 8′ × 8′ breakfast room beside it which was just big enough for two. I painted it pale blue, got a canary that we called Aurora after a song that was big then and thought that we were really making it. But nothing, not even my fourteen-carat gold wedding band or my mink stole bought by Eugene on a lay-away plan, made me feel as sophisticated as our four-foot-long black and yellow bar. It stood on spindly, black metal legs in a corner of our cramped living room. I gloated over it with admiring eyes. Even without the tall stools that were meant to come with it, it was a real status symbol.

On its mirrored shelf, Eugene had posed our bottle of VAT 69 and the fifth of Four Roses, neither of which we'd opened. There was an unspoken agreement that they were there for show. When he arranged a red artificial rose between the bottles and our two crystal goblets, Mother said that he was the king of style. The goblets had been a wedding gift from his brother Walter. There had originally been four of them, but two had slipped out of Mother's hands as she'd tried to rinse them.

After Lil ran off to New York, Mother was lonely, so as soon as we were settled with a new suite in the living room, she thought she had found a second home. It was Mother whose pocketbook suffered now, because Lilian and I had always paid the rent. She popped by regularly to cook or clean, and although I could see why Eugene hated it, I was angry the evening that I heard him greet her with, 'Hi, Ruthie, back so soon?'

Although I'd been reluctant to give Mother our door key, it seemed wrong not to after she'd said, 'What if there's an air raid drill and I'm passing your door, and y'all ain't home?' After Pearl Harbour, she lived in constant fear of Los Angeles being bombed.

When Gene found out that I'd given her the key he said, 'I didn't marry Ruthie Mae, so get it back.' I assumed that he was irritable because he and Walter were booked to play the following day over at MGM. Mother having a key seemed such an inappropriate thing for him to raise his voice over, but with hindsight, I wonder if his survival instinct had provoked him.

I had to defend her. 'Walter's got a key, and all he ever does is come in here and drop ashes on the floor.'

'Get it back or get out.'

Though I had worked for years and should have had some confidence, I was still too good at taking orders and doing what I was told. I get angry now thinking about what a patsy I was for my pretty-boy husband who owned half a dozen double-breasted suits and needed more drawers for his socks than I did for my slips.

Hearing people compare Eugene to Lester Young made me tolerate more than I should have, because I thought he had a talent which I as his wife was responsible for nurturing.

For a month, Gene had let me get away with clinging to my edge of our double bed, but he had ways of letting me know that he wasn't going to tolerate being celibate for long. For instance, there was that evening when I was making cupcakes for the Veterans' Hospital bake sale. He knew that Mother had a club meeting and wouldn't be dropping by, so he had Walter in for a game of gin rummy and Boston baked beans, which Gene loved and which was one of the few casseroles I had mastered.

I was minding my business in the kitchen, blending the margarine while half listening to the radio which was crackling with dance-band music in the living room, when suddenly the two of them were standing in the doorway, grinning with a slight leer.

Just as I turned to mutter, 'What are you hipsters cooking up?' they lifted me, like it was a rehearsed dance move, by my elbows. Each to a side. They'd performed as a twosome most of their lives and it was one of those moments when Gene and Walter operated as one man controlled by the same mind. I couldn't break their tight grip as they carted me giggling, legs kicking into the bedroom.

Walter was laughing with me, his pale face flushed, but Gene sounded almost serious when he said, 'We've decided that you broads are getting uppity and it's time for us to show who's boss.'

Before I realized what they were doing, they had bound my wrists with the ties on the apron that I was wearing, tied me to the bed post and left me there.

They went off laughing as though it was just a game. I refused to give Gene the satisfaction of calling out to him, so I just sat there on the floor with steam coming out of my eyeballs, until my fury turned to tears. I could hear the two of them in the breakfast nook playing cards and jive talking.

As they spoke softer than normal, their beer bottles clinking occasionally as they were lifted and placed back upon the table, I struggled for a minute but gave up.

I don't know how long I sat there waiting for them to free me, but I tried to wipe the tears off my cheek with my knee, chastising myself: 'This is supposed to be a prank.'

I could picture them, sitting catacorner to each other like they always did when they played rummy in the breakfast nook. Gene in his undershirt with his good suspenders draping his narrow hips, and Walter with his white sleeves neatly rolled to the middle of his forearm while his striped bow tie fell from his open collar. Jacket neatly hanging on the back of his chair, because he was more meticulous than a woman about his clothes.

What upset me was that it made me feel that Gene was closer to Walter than to me. Wasn't I letting him down as a wife? Showing him up in front of his brother? Failing him like I did each night when I clung to my side of the bed with my fingertips, like a mountaineer holding back death.

When Eugene finally came and untied me, I'd probably been there for an hour. 'Irene,' he said, 'to get along in this world, you have to learn how to take a joke. Walter's not going to believe it when I tell him that you're in here crying like a white woman. *I* don't believe it.'

For weeks he held this over me, until I bought him little trinkets to try and make up.

I never told Mother, because I expected her to agree that I took things too hard, since she regularly accused me of being overly sensitive.

Even out here tonight, after fifty-five years, I feel ashamed for letting Gene and Walter overpower me.

When I told Charlie about it, he said, 'You've got to learn to protect yourself from lettin' these guys mess with you. My uncle's got a black belt in judo and the dude was your biggest fan. We'll get him to teach you some moves.'

Between waking and going to bed, Eugene and I led a double life. I'm sure the neighbours must have thought of us as the ideal couple.

I fell over myself to be what the newsreels depicted as the perfect war bride. Kept my nails painted, wore pretty aprons over my slacks whenever I cooked, never went out with my hair in pincurls, and being Catholic, I always fried fish on Fridays. I read the *Saturday Evening Post* and volunteered at the Veterans Administration Hospital.

But at night I turned off my smile as soon as Gene turned off the lights. I can't claim the problem was all down to him, because I was so resistant to every overture. Somewhere down the line, I had picked up the notion that good girls didn't enjoy sex.

Gene would say, 'I thought I married Miss "Tall, Tan and Lovely". How'd I end up with one of the Daughters of the American

Revolution?' 'Tall, Tan and Lovely' was the slogan for the Cotton Club chorines.

Was it my age or the propaganda of the daily war dramas that made me try to be as American as a Betty Grable pin-up? With my hot-pressed, upswept curls, I wanted to display that wholesome-as-apple-pie demure and am afraid that this was reflected in my Hollywood success. Off-screen, I wasn't the rebel who bucked the system, I was a brown-skinned gamine, eager to please.

So when I sat in the movie theatre holding Eugene's hand the night we watched *Mrs Miniver*, I didn't want to be her, because she was a foreigner. No, I identified with the bold, young Americans working in the munitions factories or flying the jets, with their hands on their hearts singing 'God Bless America'.

In that pale blue postage stamp of a breakfast room with its east-facing window, listening to my canary sing above the sounds of traffic below, I thought I was somebody. I thought I counted.

Mink coat and breakfast room, not to mention the bar and the whistling kettle; they made me feel I mattered in the scheme of things.

I imagined that I was straight out of the *Saturday Evening Post*, and I can still hear Walter Winchell as he broadcast to Mr and Mrs America on the radio. I felt as if he were addressing me. Like he had stepped into my living room, slipped behind the bar to pour me a whisky sour and said, 'Evening, Mrs Lomax.' His nasal New York twang, that machine-gun delivery, was patriotic and was as reassuring to me as Eugene's slow, husky voice.

Gene had taped a poster to the bathroom door which said, 'Keep Freedom in Your Future with US Savings Bonds,' but every time Mother dropped by, she would say, 'Y'all can't have that hanging up if he ain't goin' overseas.' I was twenty-one but she still expected to run my life, regardless of me being Gene's wife, and to make matters worse, he thought that he was the only one suffering.

Whenever the three of us were together, we had all the predictable mother-in-law problems which people joke about. Mother's brow seemed forever furrowed; Gene would glower and grind his teeth. They both felt that they had a right to my undivided attention, and each claimed that the other got extra. I'd strain to ease the tension and keep peace.

It doesn't seem possible that at one time, my life was so small, my realm so limited that the starched yellow-and-white-checked curtain which hung from the small square window in the breakfast room represented my security.

War blighted our future. It was one big restriction, so at night if Gene wasn't working, we'd hang around the apartment listening to the news on the Motorola radio that I had bought in a second-hand store. It was identical to the one that Mr Herzfeld had loaned Mother in Camden, and the man I bought it from said that one day it would be a collector's item.

Not that I believed him. I just liked the look of it and the fuzzy sound that it produced which reminded me of the old days. Of strudel with Miss Hortense. But it wouldn't produce as crisp a broadcast as the small one that Gene was saving to buy.

He was reasonable about most things apart from sex and Mother.

Gene always said that Mother was angling for us to get a bigger place to accommodate her which wouldn't have been extraordinary, because people were expected to take in their mothers, especially if they were widows, but Gene said, 'If we had her living under the same roof, Ruthie wouldn't rest until she came between us.' He swore she never forgave him for marrying me rather than Lilian, but it was hard to know who to trust.

Though I never went to mass, I still considered myself Catholic, fasted during Lent and considered divorce a mortal sin, so had anybody said that my mother's thirty-ninth birthday would mark the end of my marriage, I wouldn't have believed them.

Mother had arrived that morning wearing no hat which was an ominous sign. Like General Eisenhower appearing hatless at a public occasion, it was meant to signify something, because hats were as significant to Mother as shoes were to Charlie.

She wore her straw with the cluster of purple grapes stitched to the yellow band on God-fearing days when she was feeling a touch pious and holier than the rest of us. I was always relieved when she arrived with those grapes dangling over her left eye, because she was always optimistic and believed that the war would end before Christmas and a regular radio part was waiting for her just over the horizon. But when she woke up anxious with no hope for the future, she pinned on that funereal-looking black thing shaped like a flying saucer which somebody at her church had given her. It was too small for Mother's large head and black that close to her face never suited her dark complexion.

Hatless days meant that Mother woke up feeling homeless or lonely and sorry for herself. She'd hang around my kitchen making enough biscuits to feed a battalion.

17

Eugene had faults, but he was also considerate and had a loving nature. He started the day in good spirits and no other musician I've known gave as much thought to their neighbours. He never practised his horn in the apartment and though he was standoffish, he was always polite.

I had expected Mother to treat him like a son. Unfortunately, she took this to mean that I wanted her to control Gene's life, and mine as his wife.

'Reenie, you've got better things to do than stand over a hot stove,' she'd say. 'Have yourself a singing lesson, or drop by the VA Hospital and make up some bandages.' I took this as a sign of her caring, as her way of making up for the time she'd never had after she'd begun to get occasional radio work.

Mother chasing radio jobs reminded me of those obsessive Toguri days. How or why only she could have explained.

It must have been around 1939 while escorting Lilian to a casting session for 'The Colour Comedy' special at RKO Radio, Mother accidentally landed her own first small role. Offering to stand in for an actress taken ill, Mother impressed the young producer. He told her, 'We've got to have you back. Few coloured women can handle this job.'

'God bless America!' Mamie howled when she heard. 'See what democracy can do for a sharecropper's daughter.' I guess Buster was temporarily forgotten.

However, what Mamie called Mother's 'career' consisted for years of a few lines on the odd series, supplemented by occasional house-keeping and catering work. It was the income from Lilian and me that had kept us afloat.

My volunteer work at the Veterans' Administration Hospital reminded me that everybody, the best and worst of us, Mother included, are delicate threads easily broken, and for that reason I decided to make a big fuss of her birthday on 1 September 1943. It was her thirty-ninth.

I had enough ingredients to bake her favourite gingerbread cake. I also planned to buy a few little trinkets and take her to the drugstore for a malted. Gene gave me an extra twenty dollars to get her a new Sunday dress, but the day before her birthday, an electrical failure at the studio brought him home early, and spoiled my plan to visit the outsize dress shop. 'Go tomorrow,' he said, steering me into the bedroom where he had his own ideas about how I'd spend my afternoon.

So, later that night, I laid out my clothes, intending to hurry off in the morning to find my mother a dress.

Whenever he had to rise at five for a studio call, Eugene never demanded that I get up to fix his breakfast. My idea of bliss was to lounge in bed till eight. With his eyes closed, he could get the coffee percolating, shift the sofa to make room for his morning push-ups and even do them before the scent of freshly brewed came drifting into the bedroom. The morning of Mother's birthday it was a shock to hear her turning her key in our front door when he was still doing his exercises.

I didn't have to see him to know how irritated he was. Only the night latch spared her finding him half naked which, back then, would have caused untold embarrassment.

From the bedroom I heard him call, 'Wait a sec, Ruthie. Let me get the latch and run to the bathroom.'

As it turned out, Mother had arrived with no hat and with her house shoes in a string bag along with the paper, a quart bottle of buttermilk, and a slab of salt pork ... She went straight to the kitchen and started banging drawers which I knew was meant to wake me.

I appreciated her bringing food, but Gene resented anything more than the odd egg which she bought off a church member who kept a few hens in his yard. I received ample housekeeping money, and Gene claimed that we had enough canned goods to start a grocery. He considered her donations insulting.

Her motives for doing things were never clear.

In those days, if she claimed that she was down to her last dollar, it was possible that she had a crisp twenty tucked in her brassiere. After thirteen years in LA, scrambling around that lion's den for work had changed Ruthie Mae Matthews from a barncat with kittens into a tiger with claws. Mamie had helped her become a manipulator, and in my twenties, I still didn't know how to control her.

By ten to six I was in my old robe, sitting opposite her in the breakfast room with Gene parked uncomfortably in the doorway. She had made toast, complaining all the while about the order we kept in the kitchen. 'Y'all are worse than two old maids. Fussing if a knife gets in with the forks. What do it matter, with boys dying overseas like flies?'

I recall how bright the sun was that morning. It blazed through the window forcing me to shade my eyes to see Mother who was studying the *Examiner's* front page. The Bette Davis scandal had stolen the headlines and her photo looked rather strange. It had been taken the day before when she'd testified about the death of her thirty-four-year-old husband, Arthur Farnsworth. When he had mysteriously keeled over on Hollywood Boulevard his family suggested foul play, and Mother was avidly following the case. At least it kept her from thinking about all the race riots which had taken place that summer and had brought federal troops out in Detroit and Harlem, not to mention the so-called Zoot Suit Riots which had erupted when the Marines had invaded our district to beat up any Mexican in a zoot suit.

My mother had become a gossip-column fiend.

After she'd read how Bette's mother, also called Ruthie, had raised her two daughters alone back East before springing Bette on Hollywood, Mother said it was uncanny that their lives mirrored ours. I can still hear her prophecy: 'Mark my words, Irene, you're gonna be a great actress. And we can't let them stick you no head rag like Hattie neither.'

A few years earlier, Hattie McDaniel had won an Oscar playing Vivien Leigh's mammy in *Gone With the Wind*, and oddly enough, Mother had disapproved of the role because she had joined the NAACP who were trying to get the studios to improve our race's cinema profile.

Anyway, that birthday morning, I could see that Eugene's mind was on the band sequence that he was filming that day. He loved his work and imagined that he was carving out a rich future for us. I admired the way he treated even the smallest studio booking as a major role. He wasn't merely being rude when he sat preoccupied in the doorway of the breakfast room, staring into his cup of black coffee, ignoring Mother who coaxed him to read the front page.

When I said, 'Mother, Eugene Lomax no more cares about Bette Davis and Arthur Farnsworth than two Chinamen,' she begrudgingly laid that newspaper on the table.

I licked the rim of my cup and studied Bette's front-page photo. It was clear that she had abandoned her sexy screen image for her courtroom appearance. No makeup. Hair drawn back in a snood. She looked the picture of innocence.

Mother pointed to the headline. 'They say that the two of 'em hadn't been getting on ... and him with a skull fracture from a blunt instrument? No wonder that poor man's mother is kicking up a fuss. I'm glad I didn't waste my money on Bette Davis in *Jezebel*.'

Eugene shot Mother a cold glance. We were still newlyweds, it was 6 AM and he always prepared for work in silence. Though he was hardly more than an extra that day, Gene was appearing in a white film, which we all considered more prestigious than even a big role in what he called 'no-budget race movies'.

I poured him a second cup of coffee as Mother rustled the paper, ''Member ...'fore the War? My neighbour's cousin used to keep house for Bette Davis, so she'll have the facts.'

Gene flashed a mocking grin. 'The maids always do.'

His nervous finger tapping on the table was a signal of irritation. Mother noticed and purposely pressed his panic button. Her cruellest tactic for riling him was to bemoan some poor mother who'd lost a son in the War or talk about who'd signed up or had just shipped out.

Suddenly she said, 'Yesterday, I bumped into that dancer that lives below and he's off to that boot camp near Atlanta next week. Fort Benn, ain't it, Gene?'

I waited for Eugene to explode, but he rose and pushed his chair under the table. 'What's the good of getting a fancy title like quartermaster, if our boys are treated like garbage men. If I'm not good enough to hold a gun beside a white boy, they can keep their goddamn uniforms and kiss the north-west corner of my black behind.'

As it turned out, he was 4F, but I figured that he could have played in the army band even if he did have minor kidney problems. I was not quite facing the fact that he had tricked me into marriage.

Gene's jaw was set in iron and my heart pounded as the tension in the breakfast room mounted; but he pecked me on the cheek and changed the subject. 'That navy dress you laid out in the bedroom? Do you think it's right for the hospital?'

'It's Tuesday.' I buttered a piece of toast and relaxed. 'I volunteered yesterday. You know I wouldn't flounce myself around boys missing arms and legs.'

My plan to shop for Mother's gift had nearly slipped my mind. 'I was hoping you'd let me use Walter's car . . . He said I could.' Unlike most boys who knew how, Eugene hated to drive. To be fair, I think his eyesight was faulty, but he was too vain to get glasses.

It was rare for kids like us to have cars during the war, but Walter was one of those boys who always knew somebody who knew somebody who'd put their hands on what he needed. And he was more particular about that old black sedan than he was about his clothes or that clarinet. His Hudson ran well, though you had to pump the brakes sometimes, and whenever he went out of town for work he parked it at our place.

I used to love sliding into the driver's seat.

Standing to clear the table, Mother said, 'If you're dropping Gene at the studio, you can leave me on Hillhurst. It ain't that far out your way.'

*   *   *

That morning when I started up Walter's motor and felt the engine catch, a surge of power shot through me and I wanted to leap from that seat like somebody sanctified, stung by the spirit to shout, 'Thank you, Jesus!'

At the time I thought it was a good feeling, but anxiety was also at the bottom of it, because for days though suspecting that I was pregnant, I hadn't told Eugene or Mother. With him on the front seat, and her in the back, we were like the Three Stooges. There was Eugene, the irritated artistic husband fretting about his day at the studio; Ruthie, the frustrated mother, robbed by her son-in-law of her means of support; and me, the jumpy wife who thinks her husband's a vampire.

We were a time bomb waiting to explode.

I remember checking Mother's reflection in the rear-view mirror. She adored sitting in the back with her nose right up against the window like a child. Ruthie was my mother and true to the times, I believed that every mother was owed loyalty and love.

Outside the gates of MGM, when Gene said, 'It's only six-forty, and I'm not called till seven,' I waved to one of those tintype photographers who hung around taking snaps of would-be stars and their fans. It was too early for business, so I thought we'd get a bargain. 'How much for a family pose?' I asked.

'Only three bucks, and I guarantee to send it next week.'

Thanks to my rush job on my upswept curls, I stayed out of the shot and had Eugene put his arm around Mother's shoulder for a thirty-ninth birthday keepsake.

Years later, feeling distraught, I placed that picture in a silver frame and gave it pride of place on my Brentwood mantelpiece. It was a constant reminder that pictures lie: Eugene looked happy with his arm around Mother. That Clark Gable smile. Hat brim shading his eyes. Who would have guessed that he'd wanted to kill her that morning?

The black and white photograph did her wash dress no favours. Although the faded yellow suited her dark complexion, the short sleeves exposed her heavy arms. She must have weighed two hundred pounds but her plump cheeks looked so angelic that she got away with it.

After dropping Gene, I'd driven south on Cahenga and I remember slipping my sunglasses on to shield my eyes from the sun. It was a pleasure to cruise through Hollywood in those days, especially at that hour, when the street cleaners had just been out.

The lights caught me at Sunset Boulevard, and as I waited to make a left turn, Mother tried to hand me a blonde's bobby pin – pale creamy yellow – it fell onto my lap. 'Found on this back seat. Who y'all had in this car?'

First I thought about Walter who had a thing for light-skinned girls, then I thought about Gene who'd admitted that he'd once dallied with white ones.

The full skirt of my dress was hiked above my knees and that bobby pin had slipped between the folds.

For some reason I was still clutching the photographer's tiny receipt and used it to try to change the subject, as I manoeuvred the heavy steering wheel to make a turn. 'Do you believe that guy will send that picture? You and Gene were both squinting.'

'Pull on over, Reenie, we need to talk.'

I didn't want to discuss blond bobby pins. If only to spite my sister, I wanted to believe that I'd married well.

It was my fault Mother suspected that Eugene, like Daddy, kept a string of women, because after the stint Lil and I did at the Sportsman Club in '37, I had come home and painted Lilian's heartthrob as a Casanova with a bad reputation for womanizing. I had also been too forthright about telling Mother when I'd caught him in those little white lies. So she had placed Gene under what I called 'church surveillance', asking the gossips at the Sunday service if they'd heard anything about him.

My eyes stayed glued to the traffic lights, but my hand searched in my lap for the bobby pin.

Sitting out here under these clear stars tonight, I can see how I could have said, 'Mother, why were you looking down our back seat?!' I could have said, 'I'm frigid, so my husband seeks pleasure elsewhere.' I could have said a lot of things, but that was fifty-five years ago. Nobody had heard of smog, AIDS abbreviated nothing, Alaska still belonged to the Eskimos. Being dumb and twenty-one, I jumped to conclusions.

As I took the left in Walter's car, I was seeing Eugene with his head between another woman's legs. Black or white, it shouldn't have mattered, but did. I saw his head buried between pale thighs, sticky with dark menstrual blood. I could hear him murmur, 'Holy Mother.'

As he lied about small things, I assumed that he had been covering for the big one. In the blink of an eye, I saw myself deserted like Mother with little mouths to feed.

These days, for all I know that corner of Hollywood and Vine may be just as deserted as it was back then at that hour of the morning. No cars. No people. Just some fat pigeons pecking their way along the gutters.

My period was about five weeks late when I pulled into the kerb that morning. Rubbing the bobby pin between my fingers, I became a bow bending to Mother's will. Like that day she bought me the tapdancing shoes. Removing my sunglasses, I slowly turned to face her. 'I'm carrying Gene's baby,' I sighed.

Then I stuck my head out of the open window and started heaving like a cat with distemper. With a whosh, my breakfast was on Hollywood Boulevard.

Mother never could deal with vomit, so I didn't expect her to help me clean Walter's car door. She leaned on his shiny back bumper with her hand over her mouth, looking so distraught that anybody would have thought that she had been the one retching.

'Can't you stop it?' she asked.

'I think that's it,' I said, spitting twice.

'I'm talking about the baby,' she said, inching over to hand me her handkerchief. 'Wipe the corners of your mouth and there's some on the hem of that dress.'

For all its pretty palm trees and hazy sunshine, when life goes haywire, I bet Los Angeles still feels like the end of the world.

18

Whenever I felt dislocated in Los Angeles, the voice of the man who had caught Lilian and me peeing in that bush outside the train station in 1930 would echo back. 'What are you Darkies doing there?'

It came to me again that morning, locked in Walter's car with Mother on her birthday in '43. 'What are you Darkies doing . . . ?'

'Trying to get home,' I snapped aloud. Feeling Mother eye me, I kept mine on the road. 'Remember that man at the station who called us Darkies that first night . . . ?'

'Irene, your imagination always ran wild. There wasn't no man and let's concentrate on the problem at hand. You pregnant and that nigger's cheating on you.'

It was true. My mind had strayed. I was even thinking about the Zoot Suit Riots, which reminded me that we were driving through the white side of town like we owned it. In Walter's most valued possession. 'We'd better get back. Somebody could step out of one of these doorways and hurl a rock.'

'True enough. And us out here bareheaded.' In her pale yellow dress, Mother's mountainous hips spread across more than her share of the front seat. The outline of her girdle accentuated her thighs.

'It's modern days. Girls my age don't have to wear hats all the time.'

'What's okay over our way, don't hold up downtown.'

We were side by side in that shadowy interior with its small rear window and wooden dashboard. On my lap was that bobby pin. Why did I let a ten-for-a-penny, two-inch-long hair accessory as innocuous as a paperclip, tip my life into a state of emergency?

* * *

Cruising slower than usual along Hollywood Boulevard, everything was as shut down as I felt. Tonight the scene flashes back to me as a black and white still: the parking lots with their fifty-cent Saturday-night specials, the restaurants offering air conditioning with nickel cups of coffee, the drugstores and burlesque clubs and movie houses with shades drawn and doors padlocked. And that September sky telling mother that the day was going to be another scorcher.

Even a parked Pontiac with sweeping fenders and white wall tyres zooms into focus. Along with that blond bobby pin.

Had I been alone, I might have turned around and driven west to the beach, because the smell of the Pacific and the squeal of the gulls always lifted my spirits. But my mouth tasted vile and probably smelled worse. I needed to gargle with salt, brush my teeth and slip back into bed. But duty called. 'Mother, Hillhurst isn't that far,' I said, 'but won't Miss Clara be in bed?'

'This ain't no time for lollygagging with Clara.' She crossed her arms over her girdled belly. 'I got to get back and wire Mamie.'

'For what?'

'Mamie's got experience.' As our accompanist, Mamie had taken pleasure in dominating our lives. If nothing else, my marriage had served to eliminate her from mine.

The mere mention of Mamie McMichael gave me goosebumps. She was in Texas where she'd remained after hearing that Lilian had gone to New York and I had married. The Gulf climate suited her rheumatism. Eugene still hadn't met her, but when he heard that for years she had collected all my meagre earnings, giving thirty per cent to Mother and keeping the rest for herself, he said, 'Baby, Walter always knows people who can collect a debt.'

I had warned Eugene at the time, 'Mamie's too old to be pistol-whipped and, in Mother's eyes, she's the best thing since cornbread.'

Behind the wheel of Walter's Hudson, I took my eyes from the road and flashed them angrily at my mother. 'This is our secret. Nothing to do with Mamie. And if you dare tell her or Lilian . . .' I didn't finish the sentence. In those days, a veiled threat was my only weapon.

When I admitted to Mother that Gene knew nothing about my

late period she was relieved. 'I never did trust him. And to think on all them times you used to say, "Mother, Lilian can do better." Now it's your life he done messed over . . . Girl, if only I had me a rifle.'

Thinking back to that morning I'm ready to be wrong. Maybe Mother wasn't trying to destroy my marriage. But it was ludicrous that with no more evidence than that bobby pin in my brother-in-law's car, she said, 'No messin', Reenie. You end that pregnancy lickety split.'

I nosed Walter's car into the same parking place that it had occupied an hour earlier. Mother lumbered behind up to my apartment and as soon as we entered she rushed to the kitchen to prepare some gargle. 'Explain again what the woman does with the clothes hanger?' I asked for the fourth or fifth time.

Mother stirred two teaspoons of salt in the tumbler of warm tapwater. 'I'm just guessin', but I reckon you lay down with your legs open and the woman pushes the little hook bit up in you. There's easier ways, like jumping down steps. A couple hundred times can start you bleeding again.'

'How?'

'You ask too many questions,' she said, passing me the gargle before pouring herself some of the buttermilk that she'd arrived with.

'What if I break my neck?' I had seen soldiers in the VA Hospital who'd been paralysed by falls.

'Irene, why don't you listen? You not pregnant enough to throw yourself down a whole flight. That's for women already showing.'

I was married, had worked in vaudeville, the circus, and even danced in '37 at a Harlem nightclub. But I was dumb as a doorknob about female organs, pregnancy, miscarriage and abortion. Women were kept ignorant back then, and I knew less than most.

Mother suggested ways to get my period going. Drinking cough mixture or swallowing ten dollars' worth of some pills she could buy from the friend of a friend, sounded drastic. But jumping repeatedly down a few stairs sounded conceivable.

Returning to bed until everyone in the building had gone to work, Mother woke me at 10 AM. I emerged from my bedroom in some old sneakers and that navy dress. Eyeing it, she asked, 'You ain't changed? You was sick in that, and 'spose you fall and tear it?'

I'd given no thought to ruining my dress, just as I'd given no real thought to what I was about to do . . . I wasn't thinking about an unborn child, or how I could damage it. I was protecting my pride and my future.

'Ready?' Mother asked before leading me to a semi-basement of the building, where wood was stored. I followed with a sense of purpose and she promised to act as lookout so that I wouldn't be discovered. 'Two hundred jumps from the sixth step ought to do it,' she whispered.

I had stamina, resolve and the strong legs of a girl who had endured performing on bad stages in cheap shoes. But my ankles ached after I had climbed and jumped, climbed and jumped one hundred times.

Fearing that I was weakening, Mother left her lookout post outside the doorway to the stairs and joined me at the bottom while I took a short break. The light from the doorway lit her face. She was the coach, I was the quarterback. 'One step higher,' she coaxed. 'You won't break nothing.'

My ankles ached but I managed eighty-nine more leaps and climbs. Determined but breathless, I mounted the stairs for the one hundred and ninetieth time. 'Why won't it shake loose?' I asked as if referring to a pebble.

Climbing an extra two steps, I searched Mother's face for approval. It glistened. She sweated more than I did, but no matter how often she mopped her brow with the hem of her dress or the back of her hand, which she then wiped on her hip, beads of perspiration would bounce back.

Jumping from the ninth step took courage. I took a deep breath, bent my knees, leant forward, and swung my arms back. 'I'll end up with fallen arches,' I said. With her big black eyes watching me, I landed safely at the bottom, hearing my knees crack for the umpteenth time.

'Attagirl,' she said. 'You strong as an ox . . . It must be a boy, onery as Eugene.' She helped me boost myself off the floor.

'That's it. I quit,' I said.

More than slightly hysterical, she begged, 'Do another hundred ... Please, child ... You know how I struggled to get you where you are? Don't let Gene do you like your daddy did me!'

I touched my scalp to see if the roots of my straightened hair had sweated back to their original tight kinks. 'What's my hair look like?' Mother pursed her lips. The hem of my navy sundress still smelled of sick. So did my breath. 'I'm doomed. I can't do anything right.'

Every muscle ached. Even my wrists throbbed. 'I don't care if it stays up there.' Sitting on the fifth step, I watched Mother raise the hem of her dress to dab her brow again. Her rough cotton slip was exposed and my shoulder bag lay near her feet. I pointed to it. 'There's twenty bucks in there for you.'

That was a lot in those days when three pounds of yams cost twenty-five cents and chicken was thirty cents a pound. I knew better than mention that the money had come from Gene.

Standing in the shadow at the bottom of the stairs, she retrieved that crumpled note, staring at it in disbelief. I had never known her to decline my money. Not before I was pregnant nor after and certainly not once I made the big time. But as my bottom lip trembled, for one sweet moment, I imagined that she was going to stick that bill back in my bag.

'The Lord works in strange ways,' she said solemnly, tucking it in her brassiere. 'Just that second before you give me this, I had asked him to help me get you them pills. And here's just what we need, come out the blue.'

'Well, happy 39th birthday,' I snivelled. 'I was going to get you a new Sunday outfit. That yellow you're wearing suits you. Maybe you can find something that colour.'

It's hard to believe that she was three years younger than I was in '65 when my life began again.

Two days after Mother's birthday, she had me swallowing six of the ten-dollar pills which she'd bought from the friend of a friend. 'If these don't work,' she sighed, 'it's the lady with the hanger.' Gene worried when he found me in a drugged sleep. But Mother, reading the paper, claimed that I was coming down with something.

Having Gene's child seemed less fatal than visiting the lady with the coat hanger. Despite my pride, I was ready to forget Gene's cheating.

The following Saturday night, he had his last day at the studio. It was after midnight and we were heading home in Walter's car, ironically sitting at the traffic lights opposite the building on Hollywood Boulevard where Bette Davis's husband had been found dead. Gene's trumpet case was on the back seat where the bobby pin had been.

Even the side streets buzzed with young guys in uniform. Soldiers, sailors, flyers, marines. Some would be dead before winter.

With our windows rolled down, the leather seat was as cool as the night air. Gene was driving and his hairy olive fingers caressed the steering wheel. I compared them to mine. My painted maroon nails looked smart against my skirt. Our thighs were touching and we sat as silent as smoke behind a parade of red taillights. His wedding band dull, his moustache gleaming, his pressed linen suit slightly creased. My handsome, young husband, who more than a few people said would become the next Lester Young.

Traffic crept at rush-hour pace along the wide boulevard cluttered with cars and people. Walter's Hudson inched forward under the dimmed street lights while kids even younger than we were played at being grown-up: boys and girls who had snogged on the back row of a movie theatre, believing they were in love by the time the lights came up; boys with war brides whose flat stomachs hid unborn babies like mine hid Gene's. Arms entwined. Hands clutching hands. Legs propelling them faster along the sidewalk than our car wheels.

On one corner, a blowsy redhead with a two-foot-wide behind, overdressed in satin and a feathery hat was singing 'Baby Mine' from *Dumbo* at the top of her lungs while selling sausages. Some skinny-legged schoolgirls in saddle shoes, practically skipping down the street with their sailors, stopped to buy one which they stood and shared between them.

Wearing my waist cincher, I sat up straight to alleviate it pinching my side, because it left those ugly black welts.

Gene said, 'Baby, you're so solemn, tell Daddy what's wrong.'

'I'm expecting,' I whispered, afraid of his reaction.

Flashing a movie star grin, he started honking the horn and waving his straw hat out the window. 'I'm going to be a daddy!' he called to a dark skinned sailor crossing in front of us.

I was nobody, had never been anybody and pictured my future as a deserted wife with no virginity to offer. Every time I left the house, which became less frequent, every couple I saw, looked as happy as I knew my husband and I would never be. Their smiles looked more sincere and their canoodling more genuine than ours. It was as if that bobby pin had burned a hole in my soul.

These days they would call it depression.

Mother called me selfish or spiteful, depending on her mood.

She'd come to gossip about people I didn't know. Or worse, mention a few I did. Like some of the Katherine Dunham dancers filming *Stormy Weather*, starring Bill Robinson, Cab Calloway, Lena Horne and Fats Waller. I didn't want to hear about how well other people were doing.

I didn't want to hear about them.

Anytime Gene went out, I quizzed him about where he was going, and on his return I'd grill him about where he'd been. Practising at his brother's. A night at the fights. A week on tour. An afternoon rehearsal. Work, crap shoots, card games, a beer with Walter in the local saloon. I got every conceivable excuse but believed nothing.

Finally I gave up tallying his answers against his receipts. Living in a world of my own, the days came and went and I didn't bother to tick them off on the calendar. Eugene misread my resignation. 'You seem older. More settled,' he proffered as a compliment. But I felt dark and ugly, and I lost step with the war effort. I didn't know where I was heading, and hoped that the Germans would bomb us, so that I could die a newsreel type death, trapped in rubble beneath a collapsed ceiling.

The following Spring, when it became too hot to wear anything but a bathing suit in the apartment, I spent my days getting vague comfort from stunning my sensibilities with hour after hour of listening to the radio and handfuls of grapes. And sometimes I would draw, creating minute pencil images of pictures in magazines.

I used to sit around with the windows open, impatient to hear the huckster who sold grapes calling above the crackle of big bands on my Motorola. Either side of noon, he would idle up the road with his horse and rig trailed by the squadron of flies which had tagged him through East Los Angeles. His pitiful drone through his missing front teeth became the jewel of my long afternoons. 'Grapes-Matoes-Tatoes and Peas!' He usually had white sleep in his eyes. I would drag myself from the sofa and hop downstairs two at a time to reach him on the sidewalk before other customers arrived.

'Two pounds of grapes, please.'

I'd gone off vegetables and gave Eugene scrambled eggs, dried of course, most nights, because Mother stopped dropping by to cook and only came when she wanted to borrow something.

'Girl,' the huckster would drawl, 'seem to me like your ol' man oughta get you off these grapes. You gon' *look* like a grape next thing.'

'I'm expecting,' I'd sigh like my life had ended.

Mother forbade me to swallow the seeds. 'You got to start thinkin' 'bout that baby.'

Blue grapes and dance bands, dance bands and blue grapes. Memory would have me gulping them through Easter, but that wasn't possible, because in those days we could only buy grapes in season.

My twenty-one inch waistline mattered, and I was losing it faster than I thought that I was losing my husband.

That Lana Turner was pregnant at the same time left an indelible impression upon me. It made me feel we had something in common. I'm sure Eugene was trying to make me feel ugly when he said, 'I bet Lana will never lose that figure.'

I've always had great sympathy for anyone who has suffered a tragedy at Christmas. I imagine how the season becomes a painful reminder of that lover killed in a car crash or that child destroyed by fire.

The same became true for me of Mother's birthdays. Each year as September 1st approached, I used to agonize over what we did on that day in '43, until Charlie said that what happened had to happen. In that enigmatic way of his, he said, 'In your overall life, you've got to think of Nadine like my grandmother thought about her knitting. She'd discover that she'd dropped a stitch and say, "All the work I put in that doggone sweater and when I see it all I notice is the hole."'

19

She arrived on our first wedding anniversary, 6 May 1944.

Seven pounds, eight ounces. Sixteen inches long.

An hour after giving birth, I heard Gene before I opened my eyes and saw him. 'Hey, little Mommy, you've brought me a pretty angel with so much black curly hair, the nurse is threatening to cut it!' His expression told me that I'd done something right.

Eugene Lomax looked happier than a boy with his first BB gun and far too young to be a daddy. He made a declaration, but after eleven hours in labour, I was too exhausted to appreciate it. 'I'm giving up the dice,' he said, holding his cap over his heart. Crap shooting was one of his favourite indulgences, and I'd always protested that it was gambling.

Caught up in the spirit of having produced a baby with him, I temporarily imagined that I loved Gene. 'The poor thing has your feet,' I teased. She also had his hands, but Nadine didn't really resemble either of us. She hadn't my small nose nor my heart-shaped face, which were my best features, and she'd missed Eugene's lovely olive complexion. Initially, she was sort of golden, which the nurse attributed to a touch of jaundice. In truth, her big ebony eyes and broad brow were my mother's. By all accounts, Nadine was strikingly beautiful.

I can still see Gene carrying her to the ward window to examine her by daylight. Cradling her in both hands, he kissed the top of her head, and to see his black moustache disappear into her mass of curly black hair was touching.

For the entire week he would appear at the foot of my hospital bed with red roses and girls' names. Alice, Eugenia, Inez, Czarina.

Then Thelma, Dorothy, and even Eleanor, because it was Billie Holiday's real name. In a moment of weakness I settled for Nadine.

I had never been in hospital before and hated being in a four-bedded ward with three other women: two navy wives with husbands on the same submarine and Henrietta Dobson, an English woman who was older than the rest of us, and would play a role in my life.

Her clipped accent sounded snobbish to my American ears and she immediately offended me by saying that she loved coloured people and asking if I'd come to work for her. I put her right in her place: 'I'm a housewife and I entertained before the war.' Even in those days I avoided calling myself a singer and dancer, because I knew that some people considered my work unladylike.

Despite Walter rehearsing days and playing nights with a new sixteen-piece band, he kept sending little things via Gene. Booties and rattles and baby clothes that were way too big. Whereas my own sister didn't even send a telegram, although I'd written to Lil on Mother's suggestion to ask her to stand as godmother. We hadn't spoken for a year.

Of course, as expected, Mother visited too much.

The morning that I was discharged, Henrietta apologized for insulting me and insisted that I jot her particulars down on the back of the babycare pamphlet which the hospital supplied. But I had no intention of using her number or the pamphlet which I slipped into a compartment in my suitcase and didn't see it again for over twelve months.

Gene escorted me from the hospital with Nadine in his arms. Outside the emergency entrance waiting for Walter to collect us, I found the May sun so bright that it made my eyes water. Seeing a tear stream down my cheek, Gene asked if I was crying. My doctor had warned us about the post natal blues.

'My eyes are watering,' I said. 'This sun's blinding after a week in that dingy old ward, so keep that blanket over my baby's eyes.' In one short week, I had gone from taking commands to giving them. *My* baby.

At first she made me feel so strong.

When a LaSalle drew up to the entrance and Walter hopped

from the driver's seat to open the back door, I was shocked. 'At your service,' he said before explaining that he'd won the 1939 model in a crap game. It was a startling reminder that the world had carried on while I'd been in the hospital. I had never ridden in such a swanky automobile and settling in back with Nadine nestled in my arms, I was as content as a first-class passenger on an ocean liner. In years to come I developed a fair appetite for luxury, and that ride gave me my first taste.

Apart from the fact that I didn't have enough milk to breastfeed, I took to motherhood like I did to tap dancing.

At home I went from the mild depression before my pregnancy to slightly manic behaviour after it. Keeping the baby and the apartment pristine became an obsession. What added to the challenge was our building's restriction against hanging laundry from the windows. Mother considered my diaper service an indulgence, but without it the apartment would have become a wash house, with Nadine's snow-white squares drying in every room.

She'd visit and find me cleaning, or making formulas, or attending to the baby. I had an excuse not to sit and chat. Nadine was a reason to break free from Mother's shackles.

I was still eager to be the perfect wartime bride and wanted my baby to be a credit to the race, and it seemed she would be, because every time I took her out, someone would comment on her beauty, peeking into her carriage to sigh, 'Gorgeous,' or 'What a baby doll.' Even the huckster was full of praise. 'My grapes did it! You could put that baby in a beauty contest.'

Eugene was so proud that I had to make him stop rolling Nadine about the neighbourhood with the hood down on her carriage. 'That sun will blind her,' I used to say, 'and then what?'

Twice he and Walter put on little impromptu concerts for her in the neighbourhood playground. Showing off . . . Gene said that if she was going to be the world's greatest female trumpet player, she needed to catch the bug early. Some old fuddy-duddy might have complained, but Walter and Eugene, unlike most musicians back then, who relied on sheet music, were brilliant improvisers.

So they stood by the seesaw playing favourite tunes like 'It Might As Well Be Spring'. The local little shoeshine boys never stopped raving about it.

In Mother's day, men didn't change diapers or take much interest in babies, so she said it was unnatural when Gene did. She expected him to be all thumbs with a diaper pin and was always offering to babysit, but Eugene resented coming home to find her in the living room rocking Nadine while reciting bible passages to her.

I was relieved that he hadn't renewed his physical interest in me, but I suspected that he had a girlfriend after Mother had reported during my fifth or six month of pregnancy that *Stormy Weather* was filming in town with a bevy of dancers and singers in it from Harlem. It seemed likely that Gene would have some old flames among them, but I never asked who he saw or why, because I no longer cared.

One night he stumbled in before dawn, carrying a big white box tied with a huge ribbon and demanded that I wake to open it. Sprawled across our bed with his liquor breath he slurred, 'What's right for Lana, is right for my wife.' Inside was a white satin dressing gown a bit like the one Lana Turner had worn in the bedroom scene opposite Robert Taylor in *Johnny Eager*, the first movie Gene and I had seen together. It wasn't an item to wear while feeding the baby or scrubbing the bathroom, so it went into the closet with my mink and the other fancy clothes that no longer appealed to me. I'd got my figure back, but dressing up seemed a waste of time. Some trousers, some rouge, and a colourful bandana to hide my kinky edges had become my daily uniform.

Nadine was a warm bundle in my arms or sleeping between us in bed. How I loved holding her, watching her. Whereas for Eugene she became a rival. Like Mother, who still had our key but agreed to knock before entering.

My pretty-boy husband, with his fancy cufflinks and his half-dozen hats, stayed out a lot which suited me, because there was too little room in our apartment. Especially when Mother dropped by. Every inch of space mattered as more baby paraphernalia arrived. Crib, playpen, carriage, clothes, not to mention Nadine, added to the squeeze. So

Eugene stopped morning exercises and loaned our bar to his brother, although we kept the bottles of Vat 69 and Four Roses.

We needed a bigger place, but Los Angeles was overcrowded with its three million population growing as migrants flooded in looking for work. Racial discrimination was on the increase in housing and nice apartments for us outside the slums were at a premium.

For months Nadine rarely stirred, sleeping so much that Mother complained, 'It ain't natural. New babies don't sleep such long hours. Put 'em to bed at seven, you be lucky if they let you get through the night; but something ain't right. Deenie not making a peep. Wake her up.' I didn't know that my mother was right.

When Nadine was about three months old, I had a recurring dream that I was in a narrow bed, lying on my side clutching a baby which had its back to me. Mother was angling to get in with us. She was very jolly and seemed much younger, smiling in a knee-length brushed-nylon robe. Bright blue like the colour of the aprons she used to wear in Camden. 'Come on,' she kept coaxing. 'My milk's overflowing. I got enough for twins.' Her breast was huge, like a great balloon full of water, and tacked to where her nipple should have been was a rubber teat from a baby bottle. I lay there aching to say, 'Go away, I hate you,' but I was afraid the word 'hate' would damage me. So I tried to fend her off by sulking. Suddenly, Mamie appeared. When I explained what Mother wanted to do, Mamie was sympathetic.

Waking up in a state of anxiety, I at once leapt from bed, threw on my clothes and ran to the corner phone to ring Nadine's baby clinic. The French doctor that I was put through to said that it was a fallacy that all babies needed feeding every four hours.

Secretly it delighted me that I had a child who didn't behave as Mother wanted. 'She don't smile when I tickle her ... You and Lilian were quick. Quick to talk, to crawl. To get your teeth.'

'Mother, to hear you tell it,' I said, 'Lil and I were singing "The Star-Spangled Banner" before we cut our teeth.'

At Nadine's six-month hospital checkup, the regular doctor was away. The brown-skinned intern who examined her was kind, handling her gently on the scales. Shining his torch in her eyes and ears before passing her back to me, he was flirtatious. 'So many come in with rickets; I wish all our mothers kept their babies as clean and well fed, Mrs Lomax.' I was always proud that Nadine sat so still in the clinic, staring at everyone including me with those dark, penetrating eyes. I denied to myself that she was odd, not playing peek-a-boo or shaking her rattles.

But why didn't the doctors notice?

Around Thanksgiving, when she was a little more than six months old, Gene became short-tempered. Whether Aurora, our canary, sang or the kettle whistled, the slightest noise bothered him, but he couldn't blame Nadine, because she only ever whimpered quietly, even when she started cutting her first teeth.

He and I were alone one afternoon with her asleep in our bedroom. He appeared from the bathroom with only a towel around his waist and a stocking cap on his head to protect his hair from the steam. It must have been a Sunday, because the smell of our neighbours' frying chicken permeated our apartment. I don't know what prompted him to say 'You never wear that fancy robe I bought you.'

Anger took me by surprise. 'I'm not one of your floozies. I'll walk around in overalls if I want.' A woman in the apartment at the front, who worked as a riveter, did just that.

Gene's towel dropped. 'Fuck you and your hoity-toity shit, Irene!' The next thing I knew I was on the floor with his knee on my chest and his penis dangling in my face as he yanked my bandana off.

I raised my hands to protect my face. 'Nappy-headed nigger,' he hissed. 'You think I care enough to hit you? You gotta love a bitch to beat her ass, and I don't give a damn.'

His cold stare and calm breathing as he held me down scared me, but I also knew his pride was wounded. Still, I wouldn't apologize for not loving him enough. That he had me in his clutches and made no effort to force me to have sex said that our marriage was over. In truth, I guess it had never begun.

As the wet winter of 1945 unfolded, he surprised me by coming home night after night. So the quiet charade of our married life carried on as usual. Bottles, diapers, washboards, cards, war. And Mother.

It was nearly Christmas when I first noticed Nadine's strange rocking.

Having left her with Gene to pop to the grocer's, I returned to hear him in the kitchen making coffee while 'Here Comes Santa Claus' bubbled from the radio. In the living room, Nadine sat in her playpen gently rocking back and forth. I was delirious with excitement and called, 'Hurry, Eugene! Don't miss this. Come see what she's doing!' I thought she was responding to the music.

In stocking feet he rushed in with the coffee can in his hands and when he saw her swaying, he laughed. 'Your mommy won't listen to me . . . I been telling her that you're gonna to be the world's solid ace trumpet player.' Scooping her up, I watched him do a quickstep with her around the apartment. Part tango, part tapdance, with a tinge of the snake hips. Her little brown arms clung to Gene's neck, and she gazed up at him with those solemn eyes that made me think she'd come from another world and found earth a silly place.

It was just before her first birthday that Roosevelt passed away. His death on 12 April 1945 was as hard to believe as Jack Kennedy's murder almost twenty years later. And oddly, it was Mamie's reappearance which softened the blow.

Roosevelt's death hit the whole country hard, but I took it personally when the announcement came on the radio. He'd been in office for nearly as long as I'd lived in Los Angeles. From the age of ten, I'd grown up hearing Franklin Delano Roosevelt compared to Lincoln who still got credit for ending slavery. Roosevelt's speeches on the radio and his courage after he got polio gave people hope.

I was distraught until Mamie suddenly arrived with Mother trailing behind.

Mother hadn't mentioned that Mamie was returning from Texas, because she hadn't known herself. But to see those two standing in my doorway was a flashback to childhood. Mother in a cotton floral dress that she'd made from a Simplicity pattern, and Mamie dressed like she'd been to church in a hat, suit and heels recalled my youth.

Her feet looked swollen in the shoes. 'Aunt Mamie, kick them off and grab a seat,' I said.

Over black coffee and grape jelly sandwiches, we wept together in the breakfast room, recalling old times. Without Gene at home to scowl, Mamie even told stories about Buster and her old mule.

She hadn't changed from the first time I saw her in Bofield. An inch or two wider, with a few grey hairs, at fifty-odd, like women of her shape and colour, she seemed to defy age.

Nadine was already asleep on our bed, so I refused to wake her, but Mamie, insistent, snuck in for a peek, and tiptoed back to the breakfast room. I had followed and was still in the bedroom tucking Nadine under the blanket when I overheard Mother's voice. 'She look strange to you? It's hard to tell with her sleeping.'

Mamie answered, 'Like you warned me, Irene wouldn't let me take a good look . . . Sad . . . Them injuns had the right idea. They used to take babies that wasn't right up to the mountains and leave 'em for the wolves.'

I denied to myself that I knew what they were talking about.

Mamie was headed for Bakersfield, but her being back in California was a tonic for Mother, whose spirits lifted while mine were declining. With a husband that I didn't love and a baby who never laughed and whose beautiful eyes seemed vacant, I grew anxious and miserable.

VE Day fell two days after Nadine's first birthday and my second wedding anniversary. I'd no sooner recovered from the excitement, than the A-bombs were dropped, followed by Japan's surrender. It was August. Stifling. That dry, desert heat that makes my skin itch. And when the newsflash came on the radio, I was getting ready to go to the drugstore, but decided to stay in to avoid the slew of weeping and laughter that would understandably overtake people.

Not only was I too glum to get hit with homemade confetti and jitterbugging on the sidewalks, but I even shut my windows to the singing, shouting and horn blowing. Having lost step with the war effort, as the loud hurrahs seeped into our apartment, I was bracing myself to face a harsh reality; something was wrong with my child.

When we were invited to a victory party, I told Eugene to go without me. 'I'll stay with the baby.' Revellers in crepe-paper hats would have depressed me and, anxious to control what was said about her, I didn't want Nadine scrutinized.

Gene said, 'Your mother's always begging to spend the night. She can sleep in our bed and we can stay at Walter's.'

'I'm tired,' I whined. And I was. Tired of the isolation and eaten up by worry. Gene raged. 'Other girls have babies. Look at Lana Turner!' He was constantly comparing me to her.

'Lana Turner is a white woman,' I said, 'and she hasn't got Nadine . . .' It was the nearest I'd come to admitting that our baby was abnormal. But in truth, I imagined that at worst, she was just a bit slow.

Eugene ended our conversation by stomping off to our bedroom and slamming the door. 'Nadine's fine. You're the problem.'

When he stormed out that afternoon, he was carrying his trumpet case in one hand and a suitcase in the other. 'This place ain't big enough for both of us.' I think that I'd been contemplating our separation from the day we married. On the sofa with my arms crossed, I coolly asked, 'What about the rent?'

He yanked his wallet from his vest pocket and counted every dollar in it, placing them on the coffee table. 'There's a hundred and twenty-eight thanks to last night's crap game. This is your suitcase,' he said, 'my brother's got mine. I'll come back Sunday for my clothes. Be out, because I don't want you boo-hooing in front of Walter.'

His departure was so clean and swift, it was brutal.

'Dracula,' I cynically called Gene before making myself a coffee and checking Nadine. She was asleep in the bedroom where the babycare pamphlet that had remained in my case since I'd left the maternity ward now lay on my pillow. Angry that Gene had left it there, I shoved it on the floor and lay beside my baby. Unable to rest, I picked it up, flicking through the pages filled with illustrations and instructions for the new mother. There was even a short list of suggested Christian names at the back where Henrietta Dobson had scribbled her name, address and phone number in pencil.

I didn't expect my daughter's name to be listed, but it was there above Nancy.

It said that Nadine means 'hope'.

Mother was livid. 'Niggas ain't worth a damn. And don't set 'round here waitin' to go on relief. Get up and get started. When your daddy left me, there weren't chances for coloured girls like now.'

We were in my kitchen with the window open. 'Keep your voice down,' I said, 'the neighbours don't need to know my business.'

'What's the secret! Folks got eyes. Eugene walked out with that carload of clothes. Didn't nobody think he was goin' to a funeral. Niggas been leaving women since Hector was a pup.'

Expecting him back, after two weeks I still hadn't removed my engagement ring or wedding band. I also kept my hair straightened, my eyebrows plucked, Maybelline on my lashes and lipstick on my lips. I didn't want Eugene, but nor did I want anyone, Lilian in particular, saying that he'd left me. Worse than being young and stupid, I was ultimately proud.

When Eugene returned for the rest of his things, I was out. He'd placed five twenties in a jar on the ice box and scribbled three words on a scrap of paper: 'More to come', but I knew there were no free rides. If I'd blinded myself with delusions about Nadine, I had none about her father. I was the same Irene who'd seen families begging on Wells Avenue and had expected mine to be next. President Roosevelt's death renewed my feeling that nobody was safe.

By my calculation, with the $228 that Gene left plus forty that I'd stashed in a pocketbook in the closet, I had enough to pay for the gas, rent and electricity through October. I stopped the diaper service and thanks to Walter, Nadine had dresses that would fit her for another year. With canned goods stacked in the kitchen to last me until Thanksgiving, and a mink stole to sell if necessary, the greater future was my problem.

Sleep gave me no rest.

I'd think about Mother without work during the Depression and dream of a similar helplessness befalling me. Most girls with my work experience would have dumped Nadine with a sitter and rushed off to shimmy in some revue like Lilian in New York. But after two years at home, I assumed that my chances had dried up.

Alone with Nadine and the radio, Gene's claim that I was the problem repeated in my ears.

Some afternoons, with the sun turning the apartment into an oven, I'd sit on the sofa watching my baby rocking for hours on end, but I'd hear Eugene saying, 'Nadine's fine.' Once, I shook her violently, yelling 'Stop it! Stop it! Stop it!' When I grew frantic enough to choke her or run screaming into the streets, I'd control my panic by locking myself in the bedroom to read the old newspapers or magazines that Mother had left behind. Boredom even had me flip through that babycare pamphlet from the hospital. I'd see the words *Henrietta Dobson, 235 Millar Drive, Gladstone 5-1234*, and something would nudge, 'It's there for a reason. Call her.'

Gladstone 5-1234 . . . the number remains imprinted on my brain. Fifty-three years later, I still know it by heart.

20

When I told Charlie about Henrietta, we were sitting on this roof. It was a night like tonight. The stars were bright, the moon wasn't too spectacular and the night air was warmer than usual. My face was bandaged and I was sipping a soda through a straw. Before Charlie began massaging my feet, he had picked a leaf from one of the dying bushes and stuck it behind my ear.

In 1945 Henrietta, being foreign, was a curiosity. I didn't see her in quite the same way I saw white American women, and I'm not exactly sure what gave me the courage to ring her. Charlie cringed when I admitted that I was beginning to feel like my mother. I'd gone in search of a Mrs Herzfeld.

Ironically, it was the first of September and Mother was due for her birthday visit. I hadn't yet associated that date with Nadine's condition and still didn't know what was wrong. Dressing her in a starched red sunsuit with a matching bonnet, I finally headed for a stationery store to buy Mother a card.

That's when I spotted the public phone and something told me, 'Ring the Dobson woman.'

Nadine was still beautiful so it was normal for nearly everyone we passed to give approving smiles. But it was the woman standing near us at the cash register in the store whose compliments prompted me to suddenly ask, 'Ma'am, you wouldn't mind holding her for a minute while I go use the phone?'

Nadine's wide-eyed silence was sometimes a blessing, because I could disappear and she never made a sound.

Dropping a nickel into the phone slot, I covered my free ear, because a huckster was loudly hawking vegetables along the street.

'Gladstone 5-1234?' I asked when a woman answered. 'This is Irene Lomax. . .' I wanted to sound pleasant and was hoping she had a live-in position which would allow me to bring Nadine. 'We were in the maternity ward together. You put your number on the babycare pamphlet?' It struck me that nearly sixteen months had passed since then. So much had happened. Even the war had ended. I'd been so self-absorbed, it slipped my mind that she would have forgotten me.

'Pardon? I didn't catch that.' Her smooth voice was also throaty. Glancing back over my shoulder to check Nadine, I saw the old woman cooing in her face and turned my attention back to the voice in the receiver. 'Remember the Negro housewife in the maternity ward?'

Suppose she hadn't asked me to come straight over. Or suppose I hadn't gone?

Millar Drive is a steep, winding road north of Sunset Boulevard above La Cienaga. Pretty without the Beverly Hills extravagance. A B+ residential neighbourhood with houses set back behind trees, hedges and walls of bougainvillea. Henrietta's was only two blocks further from the bus stop on Sunset than she'd claimed, and by one o'clock, I was climbing the thirty steps to her door.

Henrietta Dobson was a redhead with an easy manner. She had that look of somebody pleased with the world. When she answered her door, I was surprised that she was pencil thin and a good head taller than I was. She had a spontaneous laugh and the way she fawned over Nadine took me off guard, as did the paint-splattered artist's smock she was wearing and the patch over her eye. I hadn't expected her to insist that I cross town to see her when I rang, but everything about Henrietta was unpredictable.

In hospital, her occasional visitors had all been women and at the time I didn't care why, but in her doorway, I wanted answers to everything, even the bits that were none of my business such as why her hair was dyed red.

I was too young to appreciate her subtle sophistication and judged her on my own terms. So I felt superior when I noticed the black around her fingernails and her baby, barefoot in a soiled diaper.

He was grabbing her pants leg. 'This is Jamie,' she smiled, 'and yours is prettier than you are.'

Having struggled up the hill with Nadine in my arms and wedge heels on my feet, I was sweating. Back then, flattery embarrassed me. 'I'm not pretty.' I used a finger to wipe a trickle of perspiration from my temple and hoped that the heat and sweat wasn't kinking my roots. My hair was in a bob which brushed my bare shoulders and always left a sheen of hair oil on them.

Henrietta laughed, 'I guess pretty's a rather measly compliment if one is absolutely gorgeous.' Expecting to be led through to the kitchen, I hesitated when she offered a seat on the sofa.

It was ninety degrees out, but the spacious room led to a patio which sheltered it from the afternoon sun. It felt chilly. I suspected that Nadine's diaper was dirty but didn't dare ask to change her, and tried not to gawk about the room.

I didn't realize that the scarcity of furniture was a matter of style rather than a lack of money.

Jamie's loose diaper was off white like the linen slip-cover on the sofa facing the stone fireplace. He was so tanned, his platinum curls looked fake. On the polished parquet floor, amidst wooden alphabet blocks, he'd strewn a dozen unripe lemons from a massive clay bowl on the glass coffee table. His soiled blue baby blanket was in a heap under the grand piano, white and impressive. Ripping half the cover off *Time* magazine with General Eisenhower on the cover, he handed me the piece with a mouth and chin and tried to force Nadine to accept Eisenhower's bald head and eyes with the words *TIME* MAGAZINE MAN OF THE YEAR. A weather-beaten teddy lay face-down on the sideboard beside a tall Chinese vase full of fresh flowers. I took it that Jamie ran free.

Henrietta pointed to a bronze head on a wooden stand and said, 'My first husband was a sculptor. He would have loved your face. But then again . . .' She stared hard at me. 'Maybe you're more me.' Embarrassed again, I fiddled with Nadine.

'Why blush? Beauty is a fact of life. Maybe I should paint both of you.'

From the glass doors to the patio, I could see over the rooftops south of Sunset Boulevard to the outer reaches of west Hollywood. I still had no sense of my future in it. In fact, I was so nervous in Henrietta's, I recalled being back in Dieter Meyerdorf's Los Feliz house when Toguri led us through to the courtyard.

In my starched blue and white sailor's dress, with Nadine on my lap, I didn't know what to say to a forty-year-old Englishwoman. Shielding Nadine by clutching her to my breast, I watched Jamie spout jibberish which only his mother understood. She left the room with her barefoot son trailing behind. 'My coffee's good,' she was saying, 'but my gin is superior. And why waste all those lemons!' Her English was initially hard to understand.

Kissing Nadine's cheek, I couldn't help comparing her to Jamie who was two days younger.

When Henrietta returned with a jug sweating on a tray, her babble was constant, her voice warm yet somehow brittle. 'Undo her bonnet. Gracious, so much hair! No quinine water? Isn't it great that the damned war's over . . . And need I say no ice . . . I can go home. Back to Kent and my mother-in-law's watercress sandwiches . . . I haven't seen a kipper since . . .'

I had been half smiling politely but 'back to Kent' made my expression drop. She stopped pouring the lemonade and gave me a sympathetic glance with her good eye. 'We're here for another six months. But what about the baby? . . . Bring Mummy a lemon . . . lem-mon, darling . . . there's a clever boy.' She rubbed her hands on her smock, and I wondered how the white slip-cover stayed clean. 'Doctors warned me when I got pregnant that at my age there was a good chance of me having a Mongolian idiot. So I was prepared for the worst. But you!' She looked directly at Nadine. 'Sorry . . . I didn't mean "worst" . . . I meant . . .'

That was going to be a factor in our relationship. Henrietta Dobson would speak before thinking. Without malicious intent, she would clobber my sensibilities and I would hide my offence.

Jamie sat on the floor and started banging a block. The soles of his pudgy feet were black. 'Nadine's fine,' I said. 'Some babies are sort of slow starters. She'll catch up.'

'Why does nature do it? Scoot over,' Henrietta sighed.

I'd been in her house for only fifteen minutes and she already knew what I had to hide. 'I said on the phone that it's Mother's birthday. She'll be wondering where we are. So is it all right if we talk about the job? You said you had work for me.'

'But you've come all this way. And I've done you a little lunch.' She handed me a tall glass. 'I was in love with a coloured bartender once. In Barbados. He taught me to make these. Have you ever been to Barbados? Paradise. Not stuffy like the Bahamas . . . I've done egg salad sandwiches and apple sauce for the babies. All from fresh . . . Does she need changing? Pop into Jamie's room.'

Sandwiches? Henrietta lived in a different world. Her house was a cool idyll only ten miles from my place, but as I sipped my drink I was feeling anxious in the unfamiliar.

'Will you want a full day every day?' I asked, staring at the blocks scattered on the floor.

'It depends on what you charge.'

I knew that Mother had charged five dollars a day and bus fare for housework, so I said, 'Six dollars a day, bus fare and lunch.'

Henrietta laughed. 'Six? I can't pay that. It's not fair.' Jamie was tugging at his mother's smock as I laid Nadine on her back and drew her legs up by the ankles. As she still wasn't walking yet, I kept soft booties on her feet.

The gin was taking effect. I felt lightheaded. 'What are you offering?' I asked defeatedly.

'Life models usually get two dollars an hour. I can't imagine you'll be able to sit for more than two hours a day. Especially in this heat. Maybe in October you could manage longer.'

'Modelling and housekeeping combined?' I asked incredulously.

Henrietta giggled and picked Jamie up. 'Gladys wouldn't stand anybody else in the house . . . No, a few of us paint, and as soon as I spotted you in the hospital, I thought, "Imagine the canvas you could fill with this one."'

Being hopeless at basic arithmetic, I was not only confused about the job but the rate of pay. 'There's nothing complicated about two dollars an hour and let me assure you that lunch won't be laid on and nobody'll agree to your bus fare.' Her brisk manner annoyed me and my mind flashed back to us in hospital. Two first-time mothers recovering from childbirth. In the mornings, the intense smell of disinfectant had been intolerable, and I recalled Henrietta complaining to the nurses. 'We're not amputees, for God's sake. Why all the disinfectant!' I was still gung-ho about the war and thought that civilians had to tolerate everything.

But I wasn't going to hold that against her, because six dollars for three hours of sitting around was more than Lilian and I had received some nights for performing. I accepted the job, which is how I became an artist's model for a couple of years, ekeing out a life and beginning my forays into the wider world.

For three days a week, I sat in silent repose in a studio on La Cienaga Boulevard where Henrietta gave life drawing classes. A sixteen-year-old unwed mother in my neighbourhood who'd been jilted by a sailor was glad to babysit and had more patience with Nadine than I did. Immediately those breaks from home helped more than the money, because the bus journey across town to West Hollywood and hours in the environment of artists restored me. I would sit on the bus studying the faces of pedestrians in the street or other passengers just as the artists did me in their life drawing classes.

Mother didn't know that I worked in the nude, because I assumed that she would neither understand nor approve.

I found modelling easy and did my best to please, Henrietta in particular. Lying, sitting, standing, bending, posing as I was asked to and only missing work when my period was on, which Henrietta said was only to be expected.

I never looked at their studies of me, the oils and pencil drawings. It was hard enough offering up my naked self without seeing what they made of it. But Henrietta let me know that she was pleased with me.

She sailed back to England before the Easter of '46 and I continued to work for her replacement, Jeff Menzies, who thought my name was Arlene and I never corrected him. Unlike Henrietta, he made no attempts to know me and I preferred it. His formal hello before classes and his dismissive wave afterwards suited my wish to keep to myself. I considered it a way to earn a living, and Mother gave up complaining that I was wasting my talents. I was relieved that she slipped off regularly to Texas with Mamie doing church recitals.

Henrietta was shocked to find me still on the books when she returned to LA during the spring of '48. The first thing she asked about was Nadine, and I managed to tell the ugly truth. 'My daughter walks, Mrs Dobson, but I've given up trying to get her to talk.' I was twenty-five. Not much younger than Mother when we were in Camden.

'What does her doctor say?' Henrietta asked while we were walking up La Cienaga after her first session back. The sky was clouding over as we approached Fountain and she pulled me back at the corner, because I didn't see the car turning left. By '65 I would know that corner well. I was living six blocks away when that ambulance came for my body. But it wasn't as busy in '45. Fewer apartment buildings. Less traffic. Less noise.

Henrietta pressed me further about Nadine.

'I know better than to give my money to Dr Watkins,' I sighed. 'When I'm doubled up with cramps, he prescribes aspirin, and the last time I took my little girl for an examination, he charged ten dollars to say that she was neither deaf, dumb, nor blind. Well, I knew that, because although she can't do much else, she sometimes comes when I call.' I didn't mention that I'd removed the floor of the playpen and kept Nadine caged in it when I left her in the living room to cook. She was four and her rocking made me frantic, but it was her biting her forearms that made me deranged and leaving the room didn't help.

As we marched slowly up the steep hill, Henrietta, who was carrying her old wooden paint box, was panting. By the time we reached Sunset where La Cienaga ended, she'd caught her breath. 'When I was here during the war, I used to take that hill like Jesse Owens. My heart's positively racing.' It was hard to believe she was in her forties, because even though I noticed the grey roots of her red hair, she had an energetic stride. I'd practically had to run to keep up.

At the corner, she seemed suddenly irritated. 'What have you been doing for the past two years?'

'Cooking, cleaning. Minding my child, and sleeping. And modelling, of course, thanks to you.' I also played a lot of solitaire but that wasn't her business.

Without the patch that she'd worn when we first remet, she had two very intense eyes. They were grey. 'Why not treat yourself to a game of solitaire?'

Cars whizzed up and down Sunset past the palm trees and new buildings that were rising everywhere. After a sleek new Dodge convertible shifted down La Cienaga, I saw my bus approaching but I was still half a block from the stop. 'Gotta run,' I said.

But Henrietta held my arm. 'Haven't you done enough running, Irene Lomax?'

My bus zoomed past and I knew there wouldn't be another for twenty minutes. Henrietta looked at her watch. 'Half past three,' she said. 'I know a Viennese doctor. She's a Freudian, specializing in children's medicine. Let's go call her.'

I felt that I owed her good manners but went only to be polite.

Her house on Millar Drive hadn't changed since my first visit, although Jamie was still in England, so the living room was devoid of toys. The lid on the grand piano was open as if someone had been playing it, and propped against the wall opposite the doors to the patio was a huge canvas, hidden by a sheet. After Henrietta said, 'That's my secret weapon,' she had me help her gently lift the sheet. 'It's tamer than I intended, but the whole project seemed to have a strange will of its own.'

Reclining on one elbow against a creamy background was a slim naked girl, sort of nutmeg brown. Her large, childlike eyes were black marbles in snow. With her back gently arched, the dark nipples on her cone-shaped breasts were too dominant. I looked away from her open thighs, because it seemed such a sinful pose and paintings of naked women embarrassed me. Henrietta asked if I liked it.

135

'The eyes draw you to them,' I said, to avoid telling her that I thought that a painting which exposed a woman's privates was horrible.

'But do you like it?' she pressed.

I wanted to sound intelligent. 'It reminds me of those pictures of native girls in *National Geographic* Magazine. But this one's trying to look ... I guess the word is sassy.'

'Sassy or sensual ... dear, that doesn't sound good. I couldn't get your forehead right, but my husband says I should bequeath it to Jamie before I'm tempted to sell it. I always seem to go off my work after six months. But I finished this just in time for us to sail.'

An eight-foot-long painting of me with my legs open.

'Can I use your toilet, Mrs Dobson?' I was already heading for it, because anxiety shoots straight to my stomach, and I was on the verge of being sick. What would the nuns at St Anthony's say!

'You look ... Irene? ... Are you all right?' she called as I made it to the toilet in time to lift the lid and put my head over the bowl. How many of those artists had been painting me to look like a prostitute? I broke out into a sweat and checked my face in the mirror before putting my hands in cold water and pressing them to my brow. Bending to put my mouth over the running tap, I took a mouthful and gargled a few times as quietly as I could before returning to the living room.

Henrietta sat on the sofa and looked pleased with herself. 'I just rang Dr Strauss. She can see Nadine in your apartment right away. I begged her to come immediately. She's only on Kings Road and says she can drive us. It means that you won't have to catch a bus home.' As she took a few steps back to examine that painting again, I felt so weak I took the liberty of plopping down beside her.

Ten years later I would have been capable of saying, 'What gives you the right to call some doctor and stick your nose in my family affairs and who said you could paint me with my legs wide open!' But it was 1948 and I was still poor little coloured Irene Lomax from 77th Avenue, while she was Mrs Henrietta Dobson of Millar Drive, recently returned to Los Angeles from a rambling estate on the Kent coast.

Henrietta looked at her wristwatch. 'Straussie says she'll be outside in half an hour, so we have time for a quick one.'

I showed no indication of my anger or distress as she led me into the kitchen. Beside a jug of wild flowers on her red and white checkerboard cloth was the half-empty gin bottle. So eager was she for that drink, she didn't offer me a chair but immediately proceeded to organize two glasses. 'I won't have one,' I said as she sat both tumblers on the modern Formica work surface next to the gas cooker. One of those old three-burners like mine.

It was apparent that the kitchen had had a fresh coat of white paint. With its pre-War ice box it was cheerful, especially with the three framed art exhibition posters hanging on the walls. They picked up the colours of the pink and red geraniums in the window boxes. A strong afternoon light flooded the room, casting a glow upon Henrietta's hair which was being kept in place by large tortoiseshell combs. She had gained some weight since '46, but was easily as slim as I was.

As she took a long sip of her freshly-made drink laced with sugar, lemons and a sprig of mint, we heard someone open the front door. Her eyes darted from me to the gin bottle and she leaned towards the door. 'Laurie?' she called, then under her breath she swore. 'Damn.'

A clear male voice, also English, responded, 'Hi darling,' as she poured her tumbler of gin and lemonade down the sink. Quickly putting the stopper back on the bottle, she slipped it in a cupboard over the ice box as a tall, white-haired man with a blond moustache greeted her from the kitchen doorway. 'Am I interrupting something?'

He was wearing a pale linen suit and twirling a straw boater on one finger. I had never met Laurence Dobson and was surprised that he was so handsome, since Henrietta had once described him as old enough to be her father.

I stood but he told me to sit. 'I bet I know who you are,' he said, before turning to his wife. 'Henri, you got her mouth wrong. She doesn't have the Negroid lips at all; and . . .'

Henrietta cut him off. I would discover that she hated all forms of criticism, but I imagined that she was irritated with her husband because he'd ruined her afternoon drink. 'Irene,' she said, directing her smile to him, 'meet Laurence Dobson. He doesn't normally skive off work in the middle of the afternoon, so I presume he's about to report some extraordinary circumstance which brings him home at tea time.'

As Laurie removed his jacket before opening the back door, I slid my hand over the ring which the gin bottle had left on the tablecloth. Although I had been hating Henrietta for the previous fifteen minutes, like I told Charlie, I sensed she was that well meaning sort who needed cultivating.

Laurie took a deep breath: 'My God, how I love this air. After three years, my lungs are still recovering from the stench of war.' During the final year of the First World War, he'd been an eighteen-year-old officer, then served as a war correspondent during the Second. But by profession, Laurence Dobson was a theatrical agent and a gentleman.

Henrietta's smile seemed forced. 'Why *are* you home?'

'None of your business, darling. But if you must know, I've been invited for a game of tennis at Johnny Stone's.'

Her eyes suddenly sparkled and she rubbed her hands together. 'Excellent! Tell him that my canvases are stored in Silver Lake if he wants to see anything.'

I had left home that morning looking forward to the peace and tranquillity of a normal working day. To discover Henrietta back at the head of the class had initially pleased me, but sitting in her kitchen, I became miserable. My naked image translated by her eyes had repulsed me, her arrangement for Nadine to be visited by a strange doctor had infuriated me and I longed for the bus ride home to collect myself.

It became apparent that she'd discussed me with her husband and my fury pounded in my ears.

She said, 'Remember, I mentioned that Irene has a daughter with problems? Well, Straussie has agreed to look at the girl and she'll be here any moment to drive us down town.' Leaning back against the stove Henrietta glanced at me. 'Living with that canvas every day, I feel I know you so well, yet I haven't a clue where you live.'

'Seventy-seventh Avenue.'

Laurie piped in. 'Henri, how you do get involved. Does Straussie know that she's driving to the coloured district?'

'I explained that Irene's coloured, so where else would she expect her to live?'

Laurie was exasperated. 'Take our car. Straussie drives like a Parisian. We haven't survived the War so that you can be killed in that clapped-out Ford of hers in a Los Angeles slum no less.'

21

Laurence Dobson was right. Gertrude Strauss was a terrible driver. Each time we came to a red light, Henrietta and I were thrown forward in our seats. Huddled in the back, I felt like a bronco buster but didn't dare complain. Whereas Henrietta, who was up front, gripping the dashboard said, 'Straussie, there's no rush, darling. Do slow down.'

Since my babysitter, employed at twenty-five cents an hour, did no more than listen to the radio while making sure that Nadine made regular trips to the toilet, I sat in Dr Strauss's car grinding my teeth and worrying about the state that my apartment and my child would be in when we arrived.

Henrietta looked back at me. 'I have no idea where we are once we leave Sunset Boulevard. So the good doctor will have to depend on your directions.'

'Fine, but when we get to my place, I'd like to pop upstairs first to tell my daughter why you're coming.'

'You speak with her?' Those were the first words which Dr Strauss had addressed to me, having only extended a silent handshake when she collected us from Henrietta's, where she'd hooted her horn repeatedly to avoid climbing the front stairs. As America had fought the Germans in two World Wars, her heavy Austrian accent made me mistrust her, although her insistence on examining Nadine at no charge was charitable.

I assumed that Dr Strauss was in her fifties. It was rare back then for a woman to be in medicine. Her pallid skin was lined and her salt and pepper hair, cropped short, was flattened by a hairnet. She struck me as a disgruntled old man in a woman's tailored suit. As it turned out, the most feminine thing about her were the seams in her thick nylons. Crouched in the driver's seat, with both hands planted firmly on the large steering wheel, she looked more determined than Mamie.

For the remainder of our journey, as Dr Strauss jerked at red lights and bolted forward at green ones, I plotted how I'd rush around my apartment restoring order while she and Henrietta parked the car. So, as she pulled into the forecourt of our building, I leapt out.

I took the stairs two at a time, cramming a dollar into the baby-sitter's hand, begging her to leave immediately. With Nadine in my arms I ran to the bedroom where I tore off her dress, replacing it with a fresh one. Twisting, turning, yanking, and pulling, I furiously attacked both apartment and child.

Before Dr Strauss's motor had a chance to cool, I had brushed Nadine's hair, cleaned her ears, changed her diaper and thrown the living room into a semblance of order. By the time Henrietta pushed my buzzer, I had erased all evidence of the chaos that I normally came home to.

I apologized for the stained sofa, but she looked pleasantly surprised. 'What a good little housekeeper you are, Irene. Some man will be lucky to get you ... And look at Nadine!' She bent to hug her. 'Such a pretty little thing. Should I have bought you some ice cream?' Nadine's brown face was buried in the folds of Henrietta's blouse.

'She gets ice cream every Sunday,' I said defensively, before offering seats.

Dr Strauss was only interested in my daughter. 'I need privacy,' she muttered brusquely, pushing Henrietta out of the way to draw Nadine's chin up and stare into her eyes. 'Hello, my darling', sounded like 'Halo, mein dahlinck.' When she snapped, 'Give me the history,' she was studying Nadine's bitten forearms. Due to the years of her self-mutilation they were covered in hard callouses.

Henrietta nosed in. 'Nadine and Jamie were born two days apart at the same hospital. That's how I came to meet Irene ...'

I took a deep breath. 'She clamps some flesh between her teeth and then pulls her arm away,' I demonstrated. Henrietta had the good grace to leave the room.

The words 'Nadine's history' made me baulk. I had never told anyone that on 1 September 1943 I'd tried to miscarry by jumping downstairs two hundred times before drinking half a bottle of cough mixture and swallowing the quinine tablets that Mother had bought for ten dollars from a friend. Instead I told the doctor, 'I certainly never dropped my baby. I know that's what people think. She gets milk three times a day. During the War, I gave her fruit and vegetables and did what the baby book said.'

Aurora's birdcage was hanging in the breakfast nook and when she suddenly began tweeting like she'd been disturbed, I took it to mean that Henrietta was examining my apartment.

The doctor's small, piercing eyes would look from Nadine to me, from me to Nadine. Back and forth. Back and forth until I wanted to scream, 'What are you looking at!'

The Jewish doctor and the English painter had invaded my world, yet I felt the outsider. 'I'm a Catholic,' I suddenly injected as if that could affiliate me to their exclusive club. Although I had never had a chip on my shoulder about white people, that afternoon I temporarily agreed with Mamie that each one was out to belittle me.

Henrietta suddenly appeared in the doorway with some eight-by-twelve O'Brien Sisters handbills which Mother had recently brought around to remind me that Lil and I had not always been enemies. But Henrietta introduced them for another reason. 'You've never said a word about the O'Brien Sisters ... and who's Mamie McMichael who was accompanying you? She has a nice, bright smile.'

Dr Strauss had Nadine seated on the edge of the sofa. She looked so tiny with her brown legs dangling over the side. But I was proud of how pretty she was in her pink dress with the white starched collar, which Mother had bought secondhand.

The window was open a crack, but not enough air was coming in to kill the heavy smell of disinfectant which hung over the apartment. Remembering Henrietta's complaint to the nurses in our ward, I explained to Dr Strauss, 'No matter how often I take her to the toilet at night, Nadine usually has accidents.'

'She sleeps with you?'

'She used to, but for the last couple years I've been on the sofa.'

The doctor's accent was so pronounced I hardly understood when she said, 'Pack a bag for her. Pyjamas. Sweaters. And any of her favourite toys.'

'What for?' Henrietta asked excitedly over my shoulder.

'I would like to keep her under observation for a week. Maybe two. The mother could use a rest.'

I wanted to yell, 'Yes, please, yes!' but felt compelled to say no. So Dr Strauss rose and placed a strong, sympathetic hand on my shoulder. Her brusque tone softened and for the first time I noticed that her eyes were a blue-grey. 'We have a special children's clinic near the San Fernando Valley. Near Encino.'

Nadine had been my sole preoccupation for nearly four years. In that time I'd protected her from scrutiny and cruel tongues.

'Must you consult her father?' the doctor asked.

Over the years, Eugene's forty-five dollars a month came regularly, postmarked from various cities. But I hadn't seen him since he walked out and knew I wouldn't after Mother told me, 'Nadine ain't normal.' Discovering that she'd written about this to Lilian, I assumed that Eugene had heard about Nadine from every chorus girl in New York.

Henrietta put her arm around me and studied my face which she knew too well. 'Irene, dear, we all need help sometimes.' In her free hand were the handbills spread like a fan. 'And when did you last sing?'

'A long, long, time ago,' I whispered, sliding away.

As Aurora whistled happily in the breakfast room, the loud cries of little girls jumping double dutch filtered up from outside. 'It's my turn!' screamed one southern voice. 'No it's *not!*' a northern one sang back. 'Stop cheating.'

Nadine stood up and began shifting her weight from foot to foot like a drowsy marathon dancer. Once she started, she could slowly rock for hours. I went to lift her and wipe the perspiration from her brow. In my arms, the sugar starch in her dress smelled sweet, but her eyes told me nothing. To stay? To go? She stiffened and I sought answers in her black velvet eyes. But as always they remained silent. Dense. Impenetrable.

Down in the street, when a little girl shouted, 'That ain't fair', I felt she was speaking to me, as I allowed Gertrude Strauss to guide my daughter to her car.

'I'd like to pack her things alone,' I told Henrietta, who had followed me to the bedroom. I harboured enough rage to stab her. Until that canvas of hers had stared back at me, I had been Irene, the invisible life model. Until her doctor had inspected my child, I was Irene, the struggling mother. In a few hours that painting, and the doctor's questions had destroyed all my delusions.

Gene had never returned my case. In the bedroom, as I placed Nadine's clothes in a box, when Henrietta opened her mouth to speak, I wanted to bash her with the crucifix hanging above my bed.

'You should see what the light is doing to your hair ... the loveliest red highlights ...' She touched my bob. 'It's so straight!' How could someone intelligent be so stupid? 'I press it with a hot comb,' I said pulling away.

At the edge of the bed she waved those handbills. 'I think I'll call my painting, "My Canvas Sings". Laurie promised that we'd have a few chums over to view it. Only Sunday brunch ... But I want you there, looking stunning. I have the perfect dress for you. It's a creamy tulle. Like something frothy from *Swan Lake*. You'll be Cinderella and everyone will say how clever I was to find you. You were a torch singer, yes?'

'Not really,' I said.

As I tucked three pairs of Nadine's socks down the side of the box, she kept talking. 'If Laurie hears you were a jazz singer ... He's got every record Ella Fitzgerald's done.'

I'd read horror stories about Hitler exterminating mental patients along with the Jews, and thought about Dr Strauss.

It was as if Henrietta had read my mind. 'Straussie's renowned. A miracle worker,' she said.

Walter had bought Nadine a brown doll in a fancy dress. It had never been out of its box. I placed it on top of her things.

Of course, my daughter didn't even look at me when I stuck the box on the back seat and kissed her. I was tempted to tell the doctor to drive carefully, but I was also hoping that the three of them would die in a collision. Behind the placid smile, I was demented.

How quickly time had corrupted the Irene who used to dress up to go dancing at the Canteen.

After waving Nadine goodbye, I didn't think that I could face a night alone in 6C. But as I opened my front door I heard myself say, 'Remember Dresden.'

I'd once saved a newspaper photograph taken of the city after 130,000 people had died there during heavy bombing. It looked like a stone quarry rather than a city and I imagined the survivors having to clear the rubble and rebuild. I stuck the clipping in my 'anything goes' drawer with other bits which I couldn't throw out. Whenever I'd sift through that drawer searching for something, that picture reminded me of people surmounting the insurmountable. 'Remember Dresden' became my catchphrase.

Alone in the apartment with Nadine gone, I said 'Remember Dresden,' as I folded her playpen to slide it behind the sofa.

I said it again when dipping the brown stained underpants that she'd been wearing into a sink of bleachy water.

I said it again when I decided to shut the living room window and allow Aurora to fly about. 'Go on. Don't just stand on the table, bird-brain. Fly.'

It took us both time to realize we were free.

As the tick of my alarm clock marked the minutes, and the hours became days, I lounged on the sofa with magazines and funny papers, imagining that the Virgin Mary was shaking her head in despair. Especially when I got drunk listening to the Friday-night fights. To be honest, during the twelve weeks that Nadine was away, there was more guilt than relief.

I attended mass regularly, but didn't take confession. However many rosaries I said, I believed I was the unforgiven.

It was only years later when success drove me to another kind of madness that my psychotherapist said I had a right to be happy while Nadine was away. 'She was safe and you got a night's sleep. You went window shopping and listened to the radio. Was there sin?'

Aged twenty-six, I had gone from working, to Eugene, to

Nadine – with no breaks. Paradise to me was to dawdle home after life modelling and find the apartment as clean and sweet-smelling as I'd left it.

Heaven was an unbroken sleep.

But initially, it was Henrietta's brunch which put joy into my life, because Laurie wanted to rehearse the numbers his wife had planned for us to do together. There were several pokey little English tunes that didn't suit my voice. 'One-Zy-Two-Zy, I Love You-Zy' wasn't as bad as 'We'll Gather Lilacs' which I tried in falsetto.

As opposed to Mamie, Laurie was so easy to work with and a far better pianist than he imagined, though he lacked her rhythm and attack. I've sung with others who couldn't read music as well. To hit a bum note and have him giggle about it was fun.

Their piano had a rich sound which echoed in the sparsely furnished living room.

The first time we sailed through 'Sentimental Journey' and 'I Should Care', he was ecstatic. 'You're no Ella Fitzgerald, but with your looks you could be a Josephine Baker.' During the 40s in America, her star had faded, so that seemed a backhanded compliment.

Laurie's cravats and stories about game hunting in India made me feel that I was in sophisticated company. When he told me that I was one of the prettiest girls he'd ever seen, he added, 'Name a coloured girl with your face.'

'But I've got bad hair.'

'It looks stylish to me.'

Unfortunately, the afternoon of our last rehearsal was marred, because Henrietta went to the hospital for an eye check-up. Five minutes after she'd left slamming the front door, Laurie smacked my behind as I was turning over the *Summertime* sheet music for him. 'Now there, girlie, how's about we make that other kind of music?' I pretended that I misunderstood him and suddenly needed to rush home.

He knew that I'd never tell Henrietta, but he wasn't the only reason I missed the brunch two days later. I never intended wearing her tulle gown. To be there while fifty of her friends milled about that painting of me would have been more humiliating than parading naked at a slave auction. As Charlie put it, 'And the subtext of "My Canvas Sings" was "My Black Pussy Sings".'

It was rude of me to cancel *after* guests had arrived, but I purposefully waited until the last minute to claim that I was doubled up with cramps.

I owed Henrietta, but not every ounce of my dignity.

What I didn't know is that soon enough I'd relinquish it to somebody else.

When Mother returned unexpectedly from Texas after months away with Mamie, she was surprised to hear that Nadine had been at a clinic for three weeks. 'Girl, I'd given you up. I was so sick of that long face, and now look! Hair's pressed, eyes sparklin' and skin just glowin'.'

I agreed to join her at the drugstore for an ice-cream soda, but no sooner did we take our stools at the counter, than I regretted being out with her.

Six feet from us stood a hefty, brown-skinned soda jerk in a white short-sleeved shirt and bow tie. He was explaining to another customer that he was studying engineering on the GI Bill and was only working at the drugstore part time. As he squirted syrup into a glass to make a soda, Mother asked me about Nadine. She had a *Pittsburgh Courier* which I held in front of us to stop him overhearing. Paranoid that the whole neighbourhood speculated about what had happened to Nadine, I whispered, 'Dr Strauss first offered to keep her for two weeks, but extended it to twelve.'

'They can't keep Nadine in no private clinic forever. And Mamie heard about this lady in Memphis that might take her . . .'

'Mother, Memphis is on the other side of the country. How on earth would I be able to visit?'

In that sly way Mother had of planting seeds, she dwelled on every syllable. 'Well, you don't have to say yes or no today. But think. Decent church women ain't a dime a dozen. Specially with someplace big enough for a child. And one Christian enough to take a child like yours.' She ordered a strawberry shake and added, 'That-a-way you and Lilian can go back working together.'

Despite the boom in entertainment after the war, like a lot of other talent in Harlem who could sing and dance, my sister lived a hand to mouth existence. Mother said, 'Supposin' something happens to me? All y'all got is each other. Blood is blood.'

I hadn't seen my sister for five years. It annoyed me to even hear her name mentioned. As Mother once predicted, Lilian would eventually forgive me for marrying Gene only after finding a husband for herself. But that hadn't happened by '48 and with her being thirty, I suspected it never would.

'Mother, you spread my business to Lil and it gets right back to Eugene. If he hears about the clinic, he could stop my money. Talk's cheap on Seventh Avenue.'

I didn't know how lucky I was to be in Los Angeles. When I'd seen pictures of Manhattan during the Christmas blizzard of '47, I didn't envy my sister in twenty-five inches of snow. And although people raved about Chicago, girls like me were a dime a dozen there, huddled in dilapidated slums on the South Side.

In Los Angeles, I could take the bus to Venice Beach and, like the song says, 'Gaze at the palm trees, touch the sand, and smile at the lovers hand in hand'. I was happy to sit with my bag of peanuts and spot the beauties looking for stardom and the gold diggers strolling the boardwalk in search of a rich man.

I was almost glad to get Nadine back that September, because at least it kept Mother at bay. And while I continued as a life model for three days a week, the incident over Henrietta's painting made me anxious to find other work.

After her three months at the clinic, my daughter continued to rock silently and bite her forearms. So Mother faded out of the picture again until nearly Christmas when Henrietta took me aside after a class to ask me to serve at her New Year's Eve party to bring in '49.

'Laurie can't spend the night stuck behind the piano, so I was wondering about that friend of your mother's.'

148

'Mamie?' I said incredulously. Mamie and Henrietta together were a cheap mix for an atomic explosion.

Henrietta enthused, 'You and your mother serving with Aunt Mamie at the grand piano. What a glorious picture that'd make. Some chum of Laurie's is bound to bring a camera.'

I was wearing the robe which I kept in the studio closet to cover myself when the students took their breaks, a faded satin thing which I sometimes posed in. I drew the belt tighter around my waist while I tried to think of a way to say 'no' politely. The thought of them seeing that painting made my mouth dry. But there was no point in pulling punches.

'Mrs Dobson, my mother would kill me, you and herself if she ever saw that painting.'

'But you look sumptuous and it's a credit to her.'

'Our race . . . she . . . well . . .' I didn't know what to say. Words like conservative weren't in my vocabulary then. So I said, 'Mother's a Methodist. She doesn't know that I take off my clothes. Neither does Mamie.'

'Well, you may as well know that I sold it. I imagined that you'd be upset I wasn't going to keep it, but a friend of Laurie's made an offer which I couldn't resist.'

With the painting or without it, there was no way that I was serving at her party. 'Nadine's home, so I never go out nights, but Mother and Mamie might help if they're not already working. Aside from church work, Mother gets jobs on radio. And Mamie stays busy.' That feeble excuse encouraged Henrietta to try a catering agency.

I bought the puniest Christmas tree that I could find and hardly bothered to decorate it. My gift to myself was removing 'Mr and Mrs Lomax' from beside the buzzer and replacing it with 'Irene O'Brien'. Mother was delighted when she saw it.

The close of another year made her reminiscent. '1949 . . . It don't seem possible. 'Member '30 when we first come here? You, me, Lilian and that old carpetbag? I was the same age you are. Twenty-six. Didn't know nobody. Worrying myself to death about finding work. And the next thing I'm over there in Los Feliz with

Toguri . . .' She shook her head and laughed. 'The Lord works in mysterious ways. That's the great thing about life, ain't no telling when your number's comin' up.'

Mine was about to, because 'My Canvas Sings' was hung in the entrance hall of the Beverly Hills home of movie producer, Samuel Gottlieb.

It was a coincidence that his wife Miriam, a fund-raiser for the new state of Israel had invited Gertrude Strauss to speak about her work with Jewish refugee children at a ladies' luncheon at the Gottlieb home. When Dr Strauss was greeted with that canvas, she told Mrs Gottlieb, 'I know this girl. She should be very pleased that she has pride of place in your illustrious home.'

Years later Gottlieb admitted, 'Miriam hated that painting. I hung it there to spite the greedy old bitch.'

Visibility is hard cash in Hollywood. That canvas in the Gottlieb's on San Ysidro Drive was as good as money in the bank.

PART III

Irene O'Brien

22

Yesterday when I was browsing in that Berkeley bookstore and overheard somebody ask about Irene O'Brien, I had just put down a biography of Marilyn which I might have bought had my name been in the index. Then I thought, 'Why waste your money, biographies are riddled with distortions and lies.' They should carry a public warning: semi-fiction.

Biographers paint a life to be an orderly sequence of events, but how and why things happen is very complex. What Marilyn and I had in common is that we wanted to be looked at. And see where it got us?

I didn't notice who'd taken her cover photograph, but it was the usual head-and-shoulders come-and-get-me pose. Lips parted. Dreamy expression. Chin lifted like she was waiting to be kissed. Her face was unlined and her platinum hair so full that I guess the shot was taken in our fifties' heyday.

After my 'suicide' in '65, I stopped believing she was dead. After all, I never saw the body, nor did anyone else I knew, so I like to think that she's out there still enjoying life like I am.

When I heard the name 'Irene O'Brien' I blushed like usual. I can't pretend that I don't enjoy the fact that occasionally somebody still remembers. Otherwise that whole period seems no more than a figment of my imagination. That's why I like coming across an old picture of me occasionally.

Right from Camden days, I'd believe in a snapshot before I'd believe what was in front of me. Photo images are so persuasive. Take the dogfood I buy Luna. It's the picture of the happy sheepdog on the label I'm reaching for rather than what's in the can.

Whenever I come across old Hollywood images of me, I laugh. How they fooled the world. 'Irene O'Brien' was somebody else's merry-go-round and I got trapped on the ride.

It all began to happen very quickly. That Christmas, when I was twenty-six, was lousy, and by Easter of '49 I was Aurora with her wings clipped, back in her cage. Trapped like a wounded bird in that apartment with Nadine, I barely hung onto my sanity. I was sharing that small living space with a kid beyond my control, a four-year-old who filled every corner with her incessant rocking and arm-biting, not to mention the bed-wetting or her ferocious silences. She couldn't feed herself and I had a hard time helping her eat because I couldn't stand to see her let the food, mixed with saliva, dribble from her chin onto her clothes. Maybe I could have coped with all of it had she shown any signs of recognition or affection, but I got none. Not a hug, not a smile, not an utterance of 'Mama'. She looked past me and through me and when I looked at her, I was filled with horror, because I saw no get-out clause.

Nadine was all mine forever, and there was no hope of relief. Our little bathroom looked more like a wash-house than the one above Mack's had in '29 when Mother took to washing clothes all the time. But in my case, there was no choice. Nadine wet the bed every night without fail and my hands were always raw from rubbing her clothes on the washboard.

And the little joys that make the hardship of motherhood worthwhile? She had no curiosity and didn't want to imitate anything. I think I hated her, and worse, my Catholic guilt made me hate myself for hating her. I woke up tired and anxiety ridden, thinking, 'Why me?'

Our home was a hiding place, a prison, a dry lock-up from the world.

During her rare visits, Mother always hinted that my freedom lay in a call to Mamie, asking her to contact the 'good Christian woman' in Memphis who would take Nadine. But I saw this as Mother's ploy to team me with Lil and Mamie again. Yet, on hearing via Henrietta that Dr Strauss had returned to Vienna to assist preschool survivors of the concentration camps, I regularly began to check the price of bus tickets to Memphis. Although bus transportation had improved considerably since 1930 when Mother, Lil and I had made that cross-country trip, in 1949 I couldn't imagine travelling four days with a child who needed to be taken to the toilet every hour to avoid accidents. Not to mention one that people had begun to shudder away from.

Nights that I didn't curse God, I got down on my knees and begged for his help. But He knew how often I considered putting a pillow over my daughter's head while she was sleeping ... He knew that what restrained me from bashing her skull in with the iron skillet one morning was my fear that earth is just a testing ground for heaven and hell.

I had been driven to distraction by my ignorance of Nadine's condition, but I also lacked the love and patience to cope with her abnormal behaviour. Mother accused me more than once of being born selfish, and assuming that she was correct, what was God thinking when he gave Nadine to me?

Some day her blank gaze would suddenly strike me as evil and I'd be overcome by fear that she was possessed by a demon. As I grew more certain of it, her beautiful ebony eyes terrified me. Once I even went to the church and filled a jar with holy water, to splash upon her hoping to exorcise her evil. But I also took her to be the punishment for my sins: the sin of having tried to abort her, the sin of detesting her helplessness, and the sin of hating my own mother which intensified each day.

My weekly routine is what saved me from the loony-bin during that first half of '49. I lived for Monday, Wednesday and Friday when I rode the bus into the clean air of West Hollywood and ambled down La Cienaga from the bus stop to the painting studio. That hour's journey refreshed me.

Whether it was her excitement about Jamie's arrival with his nanny on an ocean liner, or preparing for the stream of social affairs she attended with Laurie, Henrietta was a font of enthusiasm.

Believing that celebration raised the spirits, I used Nadine's upcoming birthday as my reason to have a party. I planned to bake a layer cake with icing and candles and invite the babysitter to bring her little boy, but then remembered that 6 May also marked my sixth wedding anniversary. That afternoon when Gene had carried me over the threshold.

As the day grew near, I wanted to remove it from my '49 calendar, but since Nadine loved sweet things, on the 6th I baked that cake anyway and blew her five candles out for her. She would have gobbled the whole thing had I left her . . . Faster than I could wipe her mouth, faster than I could mop the floor, she rocked non-stop while yellow cake crumbs and brown icing dribbled from her mouth.

The following day, on my way to work, I bought a birthday gift for Henrietta's Jamie. A little red fire engine. She gave me such a smile when I handed her the parcel, I warned her, 'It's just a bit of nothing.' She had cut her hair short and dyed it a carrot colour to hide the grey, but before I could say how much it suited her, she said, 'And have I got a surprise for you! Samuel Gottlieb? He wants you dropped at his house on Friday. I'm giving you the day off and I've bought you this.'

Like a magician, she whipped a chiffon neck scarf from the sleeve of her paint-splattered smock. 'Fuchsia, Irene. God made fuchsia for that tawny skin of yours.' Despite calling me names like 'my adorable little jungle bunny', sometimes she treated me like a little sister.

I didn't want to meet the man who owned that painting of me, but I had disappointed Henrietta too many times to fail her again. 'Why aren't you screaming with excitement?' she asked. 'Any other girl would be falling over herself. Your heart should be skipping beats!' My faint smile was unconvincing.

Two days later when she drove me to the producer's front door, all that I really felt I could thank her for was the ride and the scarf.

There wasn't a cloud in the sky when Henrietta's new station wagon with me in the passenger seat took a right after the Beverly Hills Hotel. Shifting into third, she rambled on and on. 'Mary Pickford's place is near the Gottliebs' . . . "Pickfair" it's called. Clever . . . Pick-ford and Fair-banks . . . Aren't you longing to see what's behind those hedges and that white picket fence? One can't but admire Mary for starting United Artists with Chaplin and the others . . . Oh, look. Somebody's installed a fountain . . . These Americans . . . are so self-indulgent.'

San Ysidro Drive forks off Benedict Canyon Boulevard. There wasn't a soul out walking. Yet I imagined some woman on hands and knees had been scouring the sidewalk with a scrubbing brush.

Although the modern ranch-style houses weren't as palatial as the mansions we'd passed on Sunset after the Beverly Hills sign, the manicured lawns with their glamorous borders looked postcard pretty that afternoon. Being spring, flowers bloomed on the trees and the bluest desert sky protected the quiet street. Either side, a parade of sturdy palm trees brought to mind memories of working in Hawaii at fourteen.

Each house was individually designed and great expertise had gone into the landscaping and architecture. They were showcases for their owners, and whereas a few houses and lawns whispered, 'Money,' most shouted it, competing to be best.

Back then I cared nothing for flowers. Couldn't have named the azalea bushes heavy with blooms. But anyone can appreciate that rainbow of colours against rich green leaves. Arrays of deep reds and hot pinks, soft purples all drew my attention. And every shade of yellow made San Ysidro Drive look as pretty as a private park.

When Henrietta dropped me off she gave final orders from the driver's seat with her motor still idling. From the kerb, I peered at her through the passenger window. 'Where's the tradesmen's entrance?' I asked. 'Irene, Mr Gottlieb paid a fortune for "My Canvas Sings" and surely other coloured people have crossed his doorstep. Samuel Gottlieb can't ask Ethel Waters to use the tradesmen's entrance. Fix your collar.'

'But she's a star.'

'Don't dispute me. And use the knocker, not the bell.'

'The knocker?'

Henrietta pointed to the house, a large ranch-style with elegant white pillars gracing a classical front door painted a deep yellow like the trellis of roses to one side. 'Above the letterbox, see the brass lion's head with the ring hanging from it? Lift the ring and bang it sharply a few times. It's much more dignified than ringing these cheap new bells. And don't look so petrified. I told you not to wear white, but it certainly gives you a childlike quality.'

Apart from the fuchsia neck scarf she'd given me, I was wearing no colour. Only my hair-do was sort of fashionable and I had brushed it off my face to show off the shell earrings. 'I'm glad I gave you those,' said Henrietta. 'I never wore them after they got chipped.'

She waved and suddenly I was alone, discreetly trying to adjust my slip. Although my flatties were slightly run down at the heel, I had taken ages to polish them and was proud of their high shine in the afternoon sun. In retrospect, I realize that what I wore was irrelevant to the great Samuel Gottlieb, because it was my naked image which had got me my invitation. My cheap clothes must have disappointed him.

The maid who answered the door so resembled a stocky member of Mother's church that I nearly turned and ran. I was timid. 'Good afternoon, Mr Gottlieb's expecting me.' In those days, we still watched out for each other, so she gave me a befriending nod and admitted, 'Child, I don't know whether to be sad or glad. You'll be our first coloured girl and I been with Mr Sam fifteen years. He wants you to wait on the patio. I'll bring a cold drink.'

At first glance I was disappointed that the house lacked movie star splendour. It seemed almost ordinary. No grand staircase. No walls of mirrors. It lacked the exotic decor of Dieter Meyerdorf's in Los Feliz or the artistic starkness of Henrietta's. A huge canvas with washes of bold colour on it greeted me in the hall and I was relieved that Henrietta's painting had obviously been replaced.

Following the maid through a long passage to the kitchen and out to a small patio, I was more impressed by the brocade and lace and the vases of silk lilies dotted about. Miriam Gottlieb had littered their long hallway with gold lamps, elaborate gilt frames and heavy velvet. So much silver was on show in the dining room, anyone would have imagined that an auction was about to take place.

In the hallway we passed a large painting of a heavy-set woman in a blue gown, wearing a tiara. 'Mrs Gottlieb,' the maid whispered,

as if the portrait was her boss in person. 'She's away . . . Crater Lake
. . . Washington State.'

I would later discover, in Hollywood's inner circle, that the Gottliebs' friends joked about Miriam's bad taste but accepted her as a
permanent fixture because she owned half of Sam's business. Her
Russian immigrant father who had established a successful belt fac-
tory at the turn of the century outside Providence, Rhode Island,
had financed Sam's silent film productions before his move with
Miriam to the West Coast.

When their maid offered me a patio chair on a back porch off
the kitchen, through the bushes I saw a butler serving four white
men, who lounged at a round poolside table.

From twenty yards away, it was obvious that the tall butler was
slightly hunchbacked. Otherwise, his silver hair was the only thing
which gave his age away. In a white porter's jacket over black tuxedo
trousers, he added some glamour. Having seen private pools in
films, I had never been so near one, and a rush of nerves made me
sweat and hiccup.

When I accepted a glass of what I thought was lemonade from
the maid, my hand shook so that the ice clinked. She put her
motherly hand on my shoulder, 'With what our people been through,
you ain't allowed to shake. This ain't nothing but a test of will. I
guarantee Mr Sam ain't never kilt nobody.' She had a huge gap
between her top front teeth and although many would have
described her as extremely homely, some would have noticed how
the direct look in her tiny almond eyes cast a gentle calm over the
rest of her. Despite the few white whiskers under her chin, her hair
was dark like her blemished skin.

She looked down at me in the chair. 'How old are you?'

'Twenty-six.'

Her mouth dropped open. 'Girl, don't be crazy. You can't tell
that to Mr Sam, 'cause he only interested in young girls. Say you
sixteen or seventeen most. My people, my people . . . Will we ever
learn?' She shook her head disapprovingly and released an exhausted
sigh, like she considered our race a dead loss. 'Sometimes you got
to lie to get ahead.'

Before I dared ask for an explanation, the butler was at her side. His eyes were unfriendly. I imagined that he had seen Henrietta's painting as contempt dripped from his tone. 'Irene O'Brien?' I felt deep shame. Faced with one of my own, it hurt not to be able to say, 'An English woman did that. I swear, I've never posed with my legs open.'

But I disclaimed nothing and marched behind him into the blinding sunlight as the heat of the wooden deck burned through my shoes. I felt totally exposed as I walked towards the round table of men.

None of them rose when the butler announced my name. It was 1949 and although the world had been to war, certain habits remained unchanged. I was coloured, so they didn't have to be polite. And it wasn't my place to address them or stare. I stood smiling with my head down to cut the sun's glare, wondering why I was there. I recalled why I had grown to resent auditions. I was familiar with how it felt to be observed as though I was blind, deaf and devoid of feelings. I had been in the house ten minutes and, though eager to leave, could only be dismissed.

From the patio three of the men had appeared the same: slightly tanned, middle-aged, overweight. The other one was a good deal younger, small, with a full head of dark, wavy hair. Samuel Gottlieb, I assumed, was the broad-faced man whom the butler had taken orders from.

Before eight eyes hidden by sunglasses, I shrank.

No smiles, no welcome, and a loud belch as the butler led me past the men to a deck chair which placed me in full view of them as well as the sun.

Two Hawaiian shirts. One bare hairy chest, leading to a bloated dark pink stomach. Three semi-bald heads.

Their conversation was clear, but I didn't risk trying to see who said what. They were discussing the famous Joe Louis/Billy Conn fight that took place after the war. I'd heard it on the radio but the four men recalled it as though three years earlier they had been ringside together at Yankee Stadium.

'Louis took Conn out with an overhand right.'

'Merv, how much did you lose on that one?'

'Max Schmelling beat him ten years before.'

'How much did you lose is what I asked you.'

'You always ask the same damn question. The German KO'd that nigger, and as far as I'm concerned that proves my point.'

The man in a robe rose from his seat and strolled towards me. 'Boxing . . . broads don't understand it.'

Like a kid again at my umpteenth audition, I tried to shine the moment I was addressed. On Gottlieb's pool deck, it was adrenalin that hurtled me to attention. I surprised myself by saying, 'I love boxing, and Henry Armstrong was better than Joe Louis. He's the only fighter who held three titles at the same time. Featherweight, welterweight and lightweight. Ninety-eight knockouts.' I was only mimicking the things I'd heard Mamie say for years. As Armstrong was a Mississippi boy, Mamie had been his number-one fan in the late 30s and raved about him like other women raved over Ronald Colman.

That little boxing speech was a landmark in my career.

Gottlieb asked too many questions and I was scared not to answer, but I don't know what I said while my heart beat in my mouth.

It was his domain, his game, and though I wasn't sure why I'd been asked, something urged me to play along.

The Forties had been another hard decade. It ended the Depression, but produced some strange men. If a man has to face too much danger or exercise too much courage, does it make him an animal, a bully? Sam and his three buddies, they were a tough little regiment . . .

When he asked, 'Kid, can you sing or dance?' he removed his sunglasses. His heavy, dark eyebrows came together above the bridge of his nose. He scratched them, then scratched his behind and called the butler waiting discreetly by the French doors. 'Tell Mercy to help this kid find some music.'

Mercy.

Her name was actually Mercedes. 'Mer-sa-*deez*', she pronounced it for me while unlocking the padlock on a door at the opposite end of the house from the kitchen.

To leave the harsh sun and find myself in a bedroom with no natural light was disconcerting. Momentarily, I was in blackness until Mercy flicked on a lamp.

'Gosh,' I uttered without meaning to as a corner of the room came into view. My eyes took in the gold piano, the green velvet chaise, the heavy brocade spread on a gilt bed, all at once.

Actually the bed turned out to be brass, but I didn't realize that until my eyes had adjusted to the darkness. 'Welcome to the Inner Sanctum,' Mercy laughed.

It would have been just as appropriate had she said, 'Welcome to the Arabian Nights.' Unlike the rest of the house, there was nothing traditional about the huge bedroom with its navy blue walls. The smell of jasmine was so strong, it was as if a heavily perfumed woman loitered unseen in a far corner. As in the Meyerdorf house, my eyes spotted items which I couldn't name. A fresco covered the ceiling, and the bedspread was more elaborate than a St Anthony's altar cloth.

In one corner, I saw my first television, a console set in a fancy lacquered cabinet. The screen was dark and anyway broadcasts were limited to evening back in those days. A miniature saloon bar occupied a second corner and in a third was a table with a fancy old kerosene lamp on it beside a typewriter. The room was a mishmash of periods and styles but I was impressed.

Mercy sucked at the gap between her front teeth and kicked off one of her wedge heels to massage her foot. 'Bunions. I wouldn't wish 'em on a dog . . . I know these feet must stink after me sweating in shoes all morning, but I could tell right off that you'd be one of the nice ones.' Adjusting the strap of her slip, she stared at me. 'What you gonna sing?'

'Am I singing?' I asked at the same moment as I noticed Henrietta's painting of me on my left.

Mercy's glance followed mine. 'You way better looking than that,' she said. 'How 'bout that song "Black Coffee"? By Sara Somebody-or-T'other. I hear it regular when Mr Sam's listening to the Hit Parade.' Sarah Vaughan wasn't as famous then as she was going to get but her first hit was being played on the major stations.

'I know the one, but not all the lyrics. Mr Gottlieb expects me to sing?' I asked incredulously.

'Maybe. Maybe not. Don't let me put my mouth in it.'

'I don't really sing any more,' I said as she turned the porcelain handle of a pale green door and disappeared behind it.

'Well, if you got any sense, you'll say you're sixteen and sing your little backside off today.' Her cautious whisper became difficult to decipher after she got the bath running. 'Just in case you worried, I can swear they won't scar you. Mr Sam ain't got all his marbles, but he know that Miss Miriam won't put up with too much nonsense.'

I had already fathomed that either Gottlieb had been taken by the notion of the girl on his canvas actually singing or Henrietta had suggested it to him. Either way, I guessed that if I tried to slip away, there might be embarrassing consequences for her.

Afraid to budge, I was still where Mercy had left me when she reappeared, drying her hands on her frilly white apron. 'My girl . . . you bring her to mind. She would have been just your age if TB hadn't taken her in '38. Then I lost my eldest to polio the day 'fore Roosevelt passed. And my baby died in Anzio. They sent us his dog tag and one of these days, I'd love to get over there to Italy to see where he's buried. It ain't Anzio Beach itself. But it's near there.

'Three kids and what to show for working all hours God gave to send money to Mama to raise and school 'em . . . My baby boy never made twenty-five . . . That bath's ready for you . . . Mr Sam's strict on y'all bathing, but you girls picks your own perfume.' She put her hand on my shoulder, and whispered as if sharing a state secret. 'I'll let you in on somethin'. Mr Gottlieb prefers whatever's in the thin blue bottle.' Bending to remove her other shoe, she said, 'You'll be peckish after, and I got some nice tater salad, but the Gottliebs being Jews, ain't no ham to go with it.'

Guiding me by the elbow to a closet, she yanked an overhead string and the sudden glare of a lightbulb blinded me again as the warm smell of lavender from the bath drifted into the room. 'Lord, don't let that tub run over!' Mercy rushed back into the bathroom. 'Not enough bubbles.' I heard before she called me to her.

The bathroom had that voluptuous film-set glamour which I'd

expected to greet me when I'd entered the house. But I was too concerned about why I had to bathe, fully to appreciate the Turkish decor. Two tall vases filled with flowers, a mirrored wall catacorner to a sunken bath with gold taps, beautiful bottles of perfume and various candelabra, tall and short. 'Gargle 'fore you get in,' Mercy said, 'then do your teeth. That toothbrush is brand new, and there's every kind of costume made on God's earth in that closet where I left the light on.'

Bolstered by her motherly tone, I asked, 'I smell bad, huh?' It concerned me that I carried with me the slightly musty stench of Nadine's urine which permeated the apartment. 'Is that how come I'm taking a bath?'

'Sugar, Miss Mercy minds her own business. My husband do the same. That's how come we been working here so long. I seen white trash in this tub one minute and they smiling on the front of *Photoplay* the next. And I don't begrudge 'em. Tell the truth, if I had the chance, I'd probably do them nasty things myself. And like I say, Mr Sam ain't never killed nobody: if this is his idea of relaxing, that's his nevermind. N'erey one of you come here with a gun at your head.'

In the bathroom thick cream carpet covered the floor and cream tiles surrounded the tub. To be honest, I had to resist a grin, because the thought that I was about to slide into that luxurious bubble bath delighted me. Compared to my puny claw-footed tub, Sam's was a wade in the frothy Gulf of Mexico.

Mercy said, 'You our first coloured girl. We've had I-talians, Germans, Swedes, Russians. Some couldn't speak a word of English. And not one of them that could really sing. So you'd be a credit to the race if you showed these old peckerwoods what we can do.'

I still owe her for my stardom.

Charlie used to love my Mercy impersonations, but I was careful to tell him only the nice bits about that afternoon, because the whole truth would have ignited him.

As Mercy watched me undress to bathe, I listened to her monologue. 'I'm sixty on Independence Day. Born 1889. Writ down in the family bible. 1889. My daddy taught hisself to write, and not just his name neither. I'm the baby. The first was born two years after the Emancipation. If Mama could see me now! Me and Louis living high off the hog. That's him carted you to Mr Sam. Lou and me been together nigh on forty-three years. And I can't complain 'bout n'ery one of 'em.

'We from Arkansas, right there at the Tennessee border, so Memphis was the nearest town to us. We left Christmas Eve of 1905, heading for San Francisco. Louis figured there be a lot of work going what with all them goldminers rolling in dough. And sure 'nuff we both got us a good job working for Miss Miriam's brother, Asa. I was seventeen and figured I was made for life, but we wasn't in 'Frisco but three months and here comes that quake to mess things up. So Mr Asa headed back for his people in Providence and we followed, 'cause we didn't have a scratch and he seemed fair enough.

'Louis's older than me, so whereas I didn't mind them snowy winters, he couldn't take 'em. Miserable he was from November through March, 'cause he was still hankering for California.'

Mercy had that ease that people imagined my mother to have, but whereas Mother usually had a motive for being sweet, Mercy struck me as somebody who was content with her lot.

Sam's round sunken tub was deep. Being immersed in the warm, scented water nearly lulled me to sleep as Mercy, happy to have a sympathetic audience, shared her history.

'Providence. That was where we lived and that's what Louis called it when Miss Miriam decided to move here with Mr Sam. Wasn't even no bad feeling between her and her brother about us coming. They was that kind of family.' Mercy overlapped two fingers. 'Jews, see. They just like that.'

As she polished and rearranged the score of pretty perfume bottles near the sink, I thought about Miss Hortense saying that I could be a maid to the stars. Mercy's life sounded stress free and I wondered if Hortense had given me some sound advice.

'We got it so good. Mr Sam ain't strict about nothing and don't never raise his voice, although I hear he raises Cain over at them studios. But it's a dog-eat-dog place this. 'Specially in his business, he wouldn't get nowhere playing the lamb . . . Him and Miss Miriam both lost people in them concentrate camps, and I reckon they grateful . . . My day off, I don't leave this house less I can help it. We got everything we need. Radio. A record player plays the new 45s. And we can even turn on that television in the living room when the Gottliebs head off on holiday.

'The only thing I hanker for is pork now and then, so me and Lou take off for a ribs place downtown. But what I need that Miss Miriam don't give me? Quality stuff too.'

I hardly moved a toe; the steamy bathroom and the warm water relieved such stress and I silently thanked Henrietta for the unlikely introduction.

'Pretty girl like you,' Mercy said, passing me a pin for my hair. 'You can't get no husband?'

I'd said nothing about myself but wondered if due to Henrietta, Samuel Gottlieb and his household knew too much. I offered no information and only had to ask a simple question to get Mercy talking again.

'Why not do some race music: Mr Sam favours it and can cut a rug, too. He used to go up Harlem way everytime he had business in New York. And he can get to singing the blues in that shower and have me laughing till tears run down my cheeks.'

I lingered between fear and fantasy, one minute thinking about Nadine, the next letting Mercy's voice flow over me.

'We should have tied that head in a rag,' she said touching my hair. 'You don't want them naps to start creeping . . . You got it nice, whereas mine,' she sighed, turning to examine herself in the mirror, 'I meant to press the edges this morning but couldn't be bothered with Miss Miriam away.'

Charlie loved me telling him the way Mercy decided what I'd wear after my bath. She had selected size eights from the closet and I said, 'Maybe I'll go with the green, because people say Negroes only wear red.'

She pushed me aside. 'You girls all the same. No 'magination. Whereas Mr Sam got a heap. That's how come he's a big-shot in Hollywood. Now, if it was me? I'd choose that coppery thing, 'cause ain't one of them ofey girls worn it. Been hanging in that closet two years, and it's brand spanking new. The fabric's far too shiny for their skin, but on you ... I can see how it don't look nothin' on the hanger, but go 'head and try it. For one thing, it's got a built-in brassiere and comes with panties 'cause the fabric's see-through. But if it don't suit, you being an eight, we got loads to choose from, 'though we ain't got all day. After Mr Mario been in to do your make-up, we gotta try and fix the back of that hair. I don't know what I was thinking 'bout. But I guess I got excited having a coloured girl here.'

She was right.

Of all the beautiful things in the closet, I would have picked a frilly Dior-type gown or a Spanish señorita dress, rather than that two-piece bronze harem outfit. But she was sure that it was for me. Struggling to get into it, I resisted being helped though she said it was her job. I was ashamed for Mercy to see me naked, because our race used to be modest about such things.

Without asking, I presumed that I was auditioning for something but didn't think it appropriate to ask what. I knew my rights and accepted that I had none. But I could hear Mother coaxing, 'Even Bette Davis needed a push.' And nothing would have made me happier than to tell Mother that I had a decent part in one of the race musicals that were occasionally financed in Hollywood.

From behind the bathroom door, Mercy said, 'No point in you being shy with this painting of you on the wall. Come out here and let me fasten you into that mess. Must be twenty hooks and eyes on that halter top. How you gonna reach all of 'em?'

Emerging into the shadowy bedroom with the halter top covering my breasts, she helped me figure out how the studded straps criss-crossed at the back and bloused the yards of silky fabric in the full-length skirt.

'Lemme see,' she ordered, and suddenly broke into laughter. I couldn't decide if she was pleasantly surprised or thought that I looked ridiculous. Head back, chunky body shaking, mouth open, Mercy had a good guffaw. But I didn't want the laugh to be on me, because while I had been in the bath, it had suddenly dawned on me that I was in the home of a big producer being pampered by his maid. At fourteen, I'd given up hoping that opportunity would find me, but it struck home that Gottlieb was my chance. I'd become involved in the game and wanted to dress up. Wanted to be looked at. Wanted to impress.

I said, 'Miss Mercy' – plain Mercy would have sounded disrespectful from somebody my age – 'Miss Mercy, I don't want to mess up. Maybe I should wear that green gown you first showed me.'

As she wiped her eyes with the corner of her apron, my own drifted to the huge canvas of me which dominated the far wall. 'Don't worry, precious ... I'm laughing 'cause I outdid my crazy self. I'd tell you to go in the bathroom and see, but we can't let you back in that steam, or your hair will nap up.'

My forefinger traced my hairline. 'Lord, I'm run ragged trying to keep up with these naps,' I said. 'If you have a rubber band, I can tie it back and wrap a scarf around it.'

'You'd look like Aunt Hagar,' Mercy said. 'We can't be wrapping that head up. I'll think of something, but first let me get Mr Mario. And don't say nothin' to him 'bout nothin', cause he worse than an old woman for carrying tales. Puts the bad mouth on every little thing, so don't trust him no further than you can throw him. Whereas Mr Mervin and Mr Fred, they harmless.'

No sooner than those unforgettable words were spoken, the door-knob turned. Mercy winked at me before the youngest of the men who had been seated by the pool entered.

'Mr Mario, she all yours. But if you don't mind me saying, sir, I would keep her out that bathroom, 'cause the steam is messin' up her hair.'

'Mr Mario' was Mario Angelli, who won an Academy Award in 1960 for make-up on some film that I never bothered to see. But in '49, he was just starting out, having failed at acting. Even though George Raft and Jimmy Cagney got away with it, being under 5′ 7″ was a problem for male actors.

His first words to me were 'Sit down.' Or 'siddown' as he actually said, pointing to a chair by the table where the lamp and typewriter sat. In his hand was a toolbox in which he carried every conceivable item for making up a face.

Barefoot, I headed across the floor and, tripping on the skirt, I heard some fabric tear. Had I ruined that skirt? Would that ruin my chance?

Under his lamp I could see the cleft in Mario's chin. Square jaw, sparkling green eyes. He had the swarthy good looks of a Rory Calhoun, and his tanned Sicilian skin was as coppery as my costume.

Mercy left the room and we were alone when he swung a white towel around my bare shoulders and silently set about his task, treating my face like outlines which he had to fill in and breathing his garlic breath on me.

My eyes avoided his, because his avoided mine. 'Don't move 'less I say so. If I say "eyes closed", do just that.' His contempt was a firebrand.

'Close eyes.' I was aware of his watch ticking and him breathing through his nose. The edge of his right palm rested upon my cheek and I smelled nicotine on his fingertips as he applied each brush to my face. 'Head down . . . Swing to the left. Not your body, stupid, just your Goddamn head.'

His fine mink brush caressed my skin. Brow. Eyelid. Lips. I know how it feels to be a canvas.

Mario Angelli's brush strokes were gentle. His New York accent was tough.

'Part your lips.'

'Eyes open. Chin down but look at the ceiling.'

His disdain to be honest was no greater than Louis's when he stuck his head in the door. 'How soon I should come back, Mr Mario? Mr Sam wants that I should run through a few tunes with her.'

Mario cleared his throat. 'Shit. Tell Sam I'll be a couple more minutes. I'm not a magician.'

I inhaled his bad breath and avoided the temptation to speak.

I heard him dropping brushes into his case before he snapped it shut. 'Touch that face before Gottlieb sees it, and I'll tar and feather you.'

Hearing him leave I imagined that I was then alone in the large room, but Louis's voice said, 'What you setting over there for, when we got work to do?' Removing his white serving jacket, in his shirt-sleeves he sat on the piano bench. If I had fooled myself into thinking that it was racism which made Mario talk to me like I was a roach, Louis convinced me otherwise. 'Come stand here and run through a few tunes. I hope you know more than Christmas carols,' he sulked.

When he opened the piano, and settled himself to play the keys, I was longing to run to a mirror to see myself but I knew to wait.

I had lost my sense of time but my thirst told me that I had been in that room a while. 'Mr Louis, do you think I could go in the bathroom and get a drink?'

Refusing to look at me, he went to the door and pressed a button. 'Mercedes'll see to that. I been working for this man since before you was born, and I hope you ain't gonna shame me.'

He seemed an unsuitable partner for Mercy. A real grouch. That she'd said he treated her kindly is all that spoke well for him. As I stood by the piano with the towel around my shoulders he gave me no reason to like him.

Louis Patterson could have been my mother's father. Despite having respect for my elders, I was tempted to be rude.

'Your wife thinks I should do "Black Coffee", but I don't know all the words.'

'You ever sung with a piana before?' he asked as Mercy rushed in, her sunny smile immediately easing my growing tension. She clapped her hands, and her expression told me that I was dazzling. 'Lord, Louis, I told you, this child looks like a movie star. Lena Horne wish she looked this good. And this girl got her some colour.'

'Woman, get her a drink. Next, Mr Sam gonna be in that door. And bring a straw so she don't mess up them lips.' Mario had painted them a warm red and highlighted them with the small beauty mark which would become my trademark.

Mercy said, 'Lou, don't you snap at me.'

'We got fifteen minutes to get this show on the road. Mr Sam got a meetin' at five sharp and I want to be pulling out that garage no later than 4:15. That gives us two hours and he got to dress . . .'

Louis didn't expect me to say, 'I'm an alto. How about "Again" in B flat and "Sentimental Journey" in C?' I was as surprised by his piano playing as he was by my singing. With the spread of his long brown fingers, he gave breath to the songs. We sailed into the languid rhythms.

'Again' was a big band tune but Louis played it like a dark, doomy blues number, which gave it the sad ring of Billie Holiday's 'Strange Fruit'. I injected it with all the romance I could muster, and Louis's icy expression gradually melted. As the piano's resonance faded into the silence of those dark blue walls, I held my final note and patted the perspiration from my brow. 'Girl, if you can sing like that, what you doin' here? Your voice brings to mind Lucille Hegamin. Hell, you and ol' Louis, we could walk out of here and get us a job tonight! Mow 'em down like Capone did the Moran gang!' He was beaming. Charged.

Mamie had always said that Lilian was the one with the voice, so I told Louis, 'My sister's the singer, it's the harmonies I do.'

Mercy suddenly rushed back in without the water. 'What's happenin'! Mr Sam'll be here in five minutes and that child needs jewellery . . . And don't think I'm letting him catch you with your hair nappy.'

Opening a drawer, she grabbed a fistful of baubles and dragged me towards the closet where a small mirror allowed me to at last inspect my face. I wasn't sure that the heavy black around my eyes suited me. I resembled Theda Bara in Salome. 'Miss Mercy, Mr Mario has made my skin up a shade too light.'

'Don't nobody see you like you see yourself,' she said, drenching me in costume jewellery. Ears, neck, fingers, wrists and waist, I was laden. Bronze and copper clusters hung heavy from my lobes. 'That bodice with them little coins looks like money, so Mr Sam is bound to like it.' Checking me front and back she called out, 'Lou, switch off the lights and do the candles . . .'

I checked my lipstick and she whispered, 'You looking too close. Plus, them three been drinkin'. It's the overall that matters.'

The way the sun lit the bronze metallic threads of my skirt, they looked bright orange, and Mercy stood on tiptoe to tie a jewelled band around my head. 'Child, I thought we'd have a minute to run the hot comb through that hair, but there ain't time, so let's go in the bathroom and pin it up.'

With the window half open, I could see the patch of green lawn and flowers beyond the Gottliebs' pool. There was a serenity, a quietude which was churchlike.

Mercy said, 'Main thing for you to remember is that Mr Sam is Mr Fix-it. He snap them fingers, and miracles happen. Now that's the honest-to-God's-truth. He done turned more okies into movie stars than I can shake a stick at, and although he can't do the same for you, he might do something else.'

Her beady eyes surveyed every inch of me. 'I can read people, and I see you got determination. Like me. I'm gonna be out in that kitchen praying for you. So grit them teeth and do whatever you got to.'

When Samuel Gottlieb snickered, 'We're gonna stick in our nozzles, kid, and change your oil,' I thought it was a movie mogul's expression. I had just finished doing my songs for them and I thought he was talking about my career. Two dozen flickering candles gave the room a romantic glow and I gushed 'Thank you, sir,' at him, Fred and Merv who were in identical robes lounging in chairs in the shadows.

I had felt those six pale eyes on me while I was singing, and although I lacked Mamie's uncanny feel for an audience, I could sense when people liked what they saw. Nonetheless, the three men said nothing between songs and I wondered what they were thinking.

Mervin Singer and Fred Koch could have passed for brothers. Except Fred had a Brooklyn accent and Merv's was foreign. When he addressed the other two, I couldn't decide if it was German or not.

'Who does she remind you of?'

'That wop I had over on Valentine's Day.'

'You don't see a bit of Mary Astor?'

Stretched across his chaise longue, it was Samuel Gottlieb's small feet which caught my attention while I avoided his charming smile. But when he had led his two hefty friends into the room, it had been his build that I noticed. He had broad shoulders and his hairy chest was exposed in the robe. Being a head taller than the other two, he looked extra imposing, but smiled at me a lot, although he said little.

I imagined him to be older than he was because at twenty-six, someone in their forties seemed ancient. And I considered Merv and Fred to be decrepit, because I guessed they were in their fifties. They carried on a conversation between themselves as Sam, a yard away said, 'I'm gonna have Mercy dress you in something else. What the hell was she thinking about, sticking you in that thing.' His mild voice sounded reasonable. 'You've got a swell voice, but you gotta sign a contract before we can do anything with you. But you don't do anything against your will.'

My heart pounded as I stood there, overwhelmed by huge expectations. My entire apartment would have fitted into that room, and I was dreaming that he could help me make enough to afford two bedrooms and a regular babysitter. An older woman maybe, like Mercy. I was thinking, they'll love a bit of bowing and scraping. 'I would like that very much, Mr Gottlieb, sir.'

'How old are you, kid?'

Remembering Mercy's advice, I assumed God would forgive a little white lie. 'Eighteen, sir.'

With a chuckle, he turned to Merv who had the largest, hairiest belly. He could have been eight months pregnant and looked ready to explode. 'Fellas, she's getting old, but she could have some good years ahead? Agree?'

Merv said, 'Zanuck wouldn't be doing a nigger movie unless . . .'

Sam interrupted. '*Pinky* . . . who wrote the script?'

'Can you believe he had a jigaboo working on it. Some wannabe actress. Her old man's head of that NAACP bullshit.'

Fred said, 'John Ford is directing.'

'Why don't you keep up with the news? They put Elia Kazan on it. A goddam Turk.'

Sam said, 'They'll never get it out before *Home of the Brave.*'

Merv had a coughing fit as Fred added, 'Don't care what you say, these coon pictures won't make dough. The KKK won't stand for it.'

Sam sipped his Bloody Mary. 'I smell a turnaround. Think about it. Last year Truman integrates the Armed Forces. Bound to have a market effect.'

I clung to their every word, because I knew that my future hung in the balance.

'Integration, schmintegration. Who cares why it's happening, it's happening. Hitler with his bullshit threw everybody in a love-thy-neighbour frenzy. But do we bank on it? Is it box office?'

'Look, you guys,' said Fred with his Brooklyn twang. 'Three nigger movies on the boil . . . *Pinky, Home Of The Brave*, and they've been working on a script for *Native Son* since '47. Now Clarence Brown's shooting that Faulkner thing in Mississippi.' He was smoking a cigar. The scent was overpowering. 'It's the year of the message movie. What's the big surprise? The question is do we hop on the bandwagon.'

'This town's been operating on the star system since Charlie Chaplin. Nigger movies need a nig star. Simple as that,' said Sam, putting down his drink to pick his toes.

It was Merv who asked me, 'Where do you live?' My address had hardly left my lips when he followed with, '. . . What's the world coming to? Sam, can't you dig up foreign imports no more?' I stood thinking about candle light and gritting my teeth. I was in no position to protest, although nobody likes to remember that these days.

The three men were laughing before Mercy knocked on the door. Her attitude had changed. Ignoring me, she was pleasant to her boss, as she collected his empty glass. I'd seen him down a Bloody Mary and assumed that he'd had a few more by the pool. But he looked as sober as he sounded. 'Haven't we got a plantation thing?' he asked Mercy. 'Something that would have looked right in *Gone With the Wind.*'

To this day I can see the boils on Sam's back and the hair on Fred's.

When Fred spat on me and said, 'You stupid nigger wench,' I was on my knees and he was standing naked above me, the robe beside his feet. For years I'd been dangling, connected to nothing. So the humiliation didn't paralyse me like it could have had I belonged to something.

I was thinking about Nadine when I put his soft penis in my mouth. The musty odour of the room, of their sweating bodies, of Merv's semen caked between my thighs, was so intense vomit kept rising in the back of my throat.

Sniffing occasionally and sipping another drink, Sam observed silently from the chaise and once he said, 'Don't bruise her. 'Cause I've got a hunch.'

Merv had fallen asleep by the side of a chair. He looked and snored like a hog and had drawn his robe up to hide his belly. 'Suck me, bitch,' Fred was saying, his hips jutting in my face as I prayed that Mercy and Louis would stay in the kitchen.

I didn't mind so much that they knew, but I didn't want them to see. I kept imagining Mercy at the stove, cooking.

When Fred didn't get hard after five minutes, I thought I would suffocate and Sam laughed, 'I don't know why he bothers. Have another cigar, Fred. This is man's work.'

'Fuck you, Gottlieb. How's a decent upstanding citizen s'pose to get a hard on with a coon. It ain't natural. And she ain't even got enough ass or tits.'

I'm glad I never told Charlie. He was angry enough and too young to have understood.

I can see the grey satin sheet and the pale brocade spread, but my mind refuses to recollect what happened to me on that bed. It was forty-nine years ago. 1949. A hundred years after the gold rush.

I was empty. Suspended. Feeling of no more consequence than a loose speck of dust in a ray of light. So it hurt . . . but not as much as it would have if I'd had a life. And I wanted to live so much that when Sam had said, 'We could do a movie with you. Maybe get Louis Armstrong or those dancers. Whatchamacallem . . .' I was braced to endure everything and did, allowing him to lead me into the bathroom and rip my skirt off before he sprayed his urine over my body. In the same tub where I had been earlier immersed in the sweet smelling water with Mercy's monologue raining over me, I closed my eyes and said a Hail Mary as his warm, putrid fluid ran down my navel to my toes.

He became conversational. 'We can't have you living in Nigger-town. I've got a building in Hollywood. We'll stick you there with a telephone, and get you some clothes. But no money. I hate free-loaders. You've got to sing.'

I know why I did what I did. But what about them?

When Sam's bedside phone rang, he went to answer it. From the bathroom I heard, 'You're worse than Miriam. I know the time, Louis. Ring the office and tell Harriet that I want a phone put into one of the furnished apartments on Wilton. And tonight, have Mercy go over and clean it. The last bitch in there was a pig.'

I was standing in the bathtub clenching my jaws as I heard the men leave and Mercy enter. She walked in with my clothes freshly pressed and neatly arranged on a satin hanger and I couldn't look her in the eye. She had changed her apron and shoes. Without pausing, she removed the hand sprayer from its cradle and hosed me down with warm water. I could tell, as she spoke, that she was blocking her nose. 'I said they wouldn't kill you. Mr Sam just spoilt and got to have his way.' She handed me a towel. 'Stand on that till I can run you a nice hot bath, and how 'bout I wash that head of yours? My eldest sister did hair. Worked from home. With women traipsing in and out all day, putting up with their nonsense.'

Every tear I wiped away, another slid down my cheek in its place.

Mercy said, 'I don't 'member Louis ever saying that he enjoyed playing for any of these girls, but he told me to tell you to sing and don't fool with these white folks and their mess. But you go 'head and do what you gotta do.'

What you can't forgive, Forget. That's just what I did at the time. Buried the shock and humiliation because I had to keep going and forward was the only direction open to me.

On the buses home, I sank my teeth into the belief that Samuel Gottlieb would get me a Hollywood apartment and a new lease of life. Although I didn't admit it to myself, I knew that Nadine wouldn't be allowed to join me; what I didn't know was how I'd get rid of her.

23

When I last went to model for Henrietta Dobson I took that long walk down La Cienaga praying that it would be the final time. It was the Monday after she'd dropped me at Sam's, and while I hadn't yet received the keys to that apartment, a telegram from Gottlieb Productions told me that there was hope of it coming.

It was apparent from her questions that she knew nothing about what had taken place at his 'audition', and she seemed her enthusiastic self, eager to hear about Gottlieb's home, as if she had never been. 'Did you see the swimming pool, did he offer you a drink?'

Before her students began trickling in, I related as little as I could, concentrating on such meaningless details as Mrs Gottlieb's portrait and my glass of lemonade. Apart from anything else, I didn't want her to think that I was nosy.

It seemed safe to talk about the Gottliebs' domestics and well within my place. I said, 'Mercedes was very nice and she and her husband weren't at all stuck-up. Not like I'd imagine a couple would be who are working in Beverly Hills.'

Our small talk built up my confidence to tell Henrietta that I had decided to move and quit modelling, for Nadine's sake. I thought she'd be angry, so her kindly hug enhanced my guilt, although I noticed that she'd angled herself in such a way as to avoid touching my hair. Offended, I withdrew, heading for the closet to get my robe. She knew I liked to be prepared before the earliest students arrived, but she followed me to the toilet where I changed. She hovered at the door, still eager to hear how I'd got on with Gottlieb.

As I was pulling my sundress over my head, I called out, 'He thinks I'm eighteen and of course I didn't mention Nadine.'

Henrietta's sudden fury was out of character. 'Are you mad, child! Did you lie! How foolish . . . Don't you know this could ruin everything?' I was unnerved. To compose myself I slowly finished undressing.

When I re-emerged, naked under the robe, I was relieved to find that she had moved away from the door and calmed down slightly.

The smell of the oil paints and turps was always strong in the studio, but it was extremely warm that day, so the scent had grown oppressive. Normally, Henrietta opened the skylight, but being preoccupied with me, she hadn't got around to it. I was afraid that she'd still be grilling me about Gottlieb when her nine students arrived. Suddenly in a more casual tone she asked, 'What were you doing when you heard that the war had ended?'

Just as most people can say where they were when they heard the news about Jack Kennedy's murder, I didn't have to think. It was easy to picture the exact moment. 'I was in my place, ironing and listening to the radio. Why?'

'There! You see!' she'd flared again. 'If you're only eighteen, you would have been fifteen and couldn't have had an apartment. In fact, depending on your birthdate, you could have still been at school . . . When were you born?'

'11 November 1922.'

'Christ,' she muttered, throwing her eyes to heaven. '11 November. Armistice Day, 1945 means that you would have only been fourteen. Irene, you'll have to tell Mr Gottlieb the truth. He'll understand. I gather that he's a generous man. Fatherly. *Beg* his forgiveness.'

I was too dumb to see the irony in this and was relieved that I probably was about to spend my last day in that studio.

Standing at her easel she babbled. 'I had a friend in London who lied about her age to the American GI she was dating. When he sprang a marriage proposal on her before shipping out for D-Day, she decided not to admit that she was twenty-seven rather than twenty until after he returned. So for two weeks she kept a list in her head of the ages that she was meant to be on certain important dates. You have to do the same . . .'

I must have looked confused, because Henrietta grabbed a pencil and tore a piece of paper from a drawing tablet. 'I'm hopeless at subtraction,' she admitted scribbling numbers. '. . . 49 minus 18, no 18 minus 49 . . . No . . .'

I had already been calculating during the bus ride. 'I would have been born in 1931. And I can say that I was born in Los Angeles instead of New Jersey. Because I've been here since '30.'

'If you're so clever, how old should you have been when the Japs bombed Pearl Harbor?'

'Twelve?'

'You see! . . . Every American out of nappies can recall the age they were when that happened. Even if they didn't know the year, they'd be able to say, "I was in third grade" or "I was about so-and-so age." As she spoke, Henrietta tallied and passed me the piece of paper. 'Let's hear it aloud,' she ordered, like a nun to a school girl.

'I was born in Los Angeles in 1931 and was ten when they bombed Pearl Harbor. In 1945 when the Japanese surrendered, I was fourteen and the following year, I quit school to model for Henrietta.'

She said, 'Do as I tell you. You've proved you can. I've asked you to sit or stand in the most awkward positions for hours, and I've never heard you complain. Memorize those dates and think up others, dear.'

After class, having given her the impression that I might have to move, I said, 'I'll send my address when I get one.'

Black and white never socialized back then, so without working for her, I suspected that we'd never meet again. I have to say that I was a little sad, because despite everything, Henrietta was the nearest thing I ever had to a real mentor, until Charlie.

I had convinced myself that the best thing I could do for Nadine was to make enough money to provide more for her. Saying the rosary and praying for help, I eased my conscience by claiming that whatever was to happen would be God's will. In fact it's only out here tonight that I accept my role in what happened to my daughter.

Even before Gottlieb had signed me to a contract, I lied to Mother and implied that he'd mentioned one at the 'audition', although I was careful to reveal no other facts. Sensing the promise of success, she clapped and hooted. We were in the breakfast room and she was sipping tea.

'My baby girl! I knew you'd be the one to do it.'

For the first time in years, she cooed affection for me. Earlier that morning, she'd auditioned for a radio play, and being hopeful that she'd get the part was probably half the reason that her spirits were so high. I expected Mother to have a solution for Nadine.

'Grandma's poor little puddin' can be in the wide open spaces and not be cooped up in here no more. Play in the mud! Worry the hens! And this Bessie Robinson woman will treat her like kinfolk.'

Although I didn't yet have the means to pay, I was anxious to organize immediate travel for Nadine's journey to Tennessee. 'Won't be nothing to it,' said Mother, ''cause Mamie drives to Texas all the time. She ain't workin' this week and would be glad to help, but you know she likes her money in advance . . . The good thing is that she knows people all cross the country.'

Considering that gas was fifteen cents a gallon, and they were planning to sleep with friends, seventy-five dollars should have been more than enough. The extortionate sum of $150 which I eventually had to pay for their journey to Memphis came from the money which Sam had loaned me for clothes. The feeling that Mother and Mamie were robbing me was nothing new.

24

On 15 May 1949, only a week and a day after baking that birthday cake for Nadine, I had been summoned to Samuel Gottlieb's office hoping to collect keys for the apartment he'd promised.

Thanks to my philosophy of 'what you can't forgive, forget', I had no shame about seeing him again. Eagerly, I rode the bus to the modern office block his suite was in on Wilshire Boulevard, but my enthusiasm was dampened by the Negro elevator operator who tried to bar me getting out on the tenth floor.

'That's Gottlieb Film Productions,' he repeated twice, looking me up and down like I was a criminal. In my pert summer hat and white gloves, I lifted my chin to snub him. 'I guess you run the building?' I sniffed, but didn't really feel I had a right to be there.

Gottlieb's secretary was even more off hand with me. I was sure that I would've received a friendlier welcome had I come to clean. She sat in the outer office with a shiny brass plate on her desk: MISS RITA KEATING. I wasn't surprised that she was nobody's choice for a wife. Her Buster Brown haircut with the blunt fringe grazing her eyebrows was as formidable as her pinched lips and her thick horn-rimmed glasses. She would have looked more at home amidst some dusty library stacks. Her large polished desk was so immaculate, it appeared that she had no work, nor did any on the tall Remington sitting on the typewriter table behind her.

As there was no one else in that outer office, it was impossible for her not to notice me approaching, but she didn't bother to glance up at me until I was standing directly in front of her and clearing my throat. Despite her cold eyes, I couldn't help smiling when I said, 'I'm Irene O'Brien and Mr Gottlieb sent me a telegram.'

'I sent that.' She removed a pencil from behind her ear and jabbed the erasered end on her desk several times. A little female Napoleon she was. Pointing to a leather sofa across the spacious room, she handed me three neatly typed pages, and ordered, 'Read this.'

Miss Keating also had a habit of chewing the end of her pencils. 'Mr Gottlieb won't be seeing you today, but sign that contract so that I can take you to see our premises. There's a place for your signature on that page you're looking at.'

'Premises' didn't sound like an apartment and, sitting on the Chesterfield, pretending to peruse those three pages, I hoped that I wasn't about to go through another ordeal. Yet reading that small print was unnecessary; no matter what it said, I intended to sign. It was no time for delusions. I was a coloured girl in Hollywood and who offered us contracts back then? To be under contract to Samuel Gottlieb still struck me as a miracle and an honour.

My hand was shaking when I bent over Miss Keating's desk to put my signature to the last page, and to this day, I don't know what the small print said. When she rose, I was surprised that she was about 4' 10". Peering up at me, she adjusted her glasses. 'Our Hollywood building is whites only. Mr Gottlieb wasn't thinking. The cabin on Kirkwood will do for now. Until we make other arrangements.'

I was so excited that my knees went like jelly and my heart thundered in my ears. I managed not to shout. Was it possible? Was I about to be saved? I had prayed so hard for this moment to actually happen, but there I was inside it and even words of thanks escaped me. For years I'd been caught in the whirlwind of circumstance, or at least that's how I saw it, and suddenly I was perched on the brink of my big chance.

The strap of my shoulder bag was slipping from my shoulder, but I was afraid to move a muscle, thinking that the slightest motion could shift my luck. It felt like a dream and I didn't want to wake from it.

It was Miss Keating herself who drove me to the little house in Laurel Canyon which was to be my home. I didn't expect her to talk to me as she sat on her cushion behind the wheel looking like a gnome, while struggling to shift those Chevy gears. The house was on the long winding road above Sunset not far from Schwab's Drugstore. I stared out the window surprised at how wild it looked. It had none of the feel of the city about it. No sidewalks. No people. Only a few rustic cottages peeking from their hillside settings overlooking the road. As the car climbed higher in second gear, I wondered how I'd keep my hair straightened while getting drenched in the rainy season. But the woodsy street had all the calm of a mountain retreat and my excitement was only dampened by a few words from Miss Keating.

'The Canyon is full of bohemians. Anything goes. So I guess nobody will put a rock through your window ... The neighbours will be told that you're a servant minding the house. Don't tell anybody otherwise and don't have deliveries.'

She pulled up in front of a wooden frame house. Small and painted pale green, it was flanked by tall pines. Opening her clutch bag to find keys, Miss Keating was less grissly but she still hadn't smiled. 'Irene, if you don't know how to drive, I'll have to find somebody to teach you. That old Chevy in the drive used to be mine, but Mr Gottlieb gets me a new one every other year.'

She could have led me to a castle and a Cadillac. Delight dimmed my vision. 'This house and a car! Miss Keating, I can't take a car.' I nearly said that my brother-in-law had taught me to drive, but caught myself. 'If I got a scratch on it or had an accident ... thank you but ...' I never believed that I would drive anything after Walter's Hudson.

'Mr Gottlieb's properties are always well maintained. You're now one of them.'

The house, with its tiny bathroom and a narrow eight-by-four-foot kitchen, was an unspeakable surprise. More like a rustic chalet, it was completely furnished and hardly much bigger than my apartment had been. Windows with white venetian blinds. An old victrola in the corner with 78" records. Red-and-blue checked curtains in the kitchen. Lace on the small table in the living room where the phone sat. A bedroom with French doors leading to a small overgrown yard with a grapefruit tree. The double bed with its blue ticking mattress and two new sheets each tied with a ribbon. On the book shelf *Life* magazine and *Reader's Digest* neatly stacked upon a pile of *National Geographic* magazines with their yellow spines showing. A black kidney-shaped coffee table in front of an overstuffed, unstained sofa. And a mantelpiece above the fireplace which had been sealed off.

But nothing comes free. The price of the house and car was what Miss Keating stated in a businesslike way. 'Mr Gottlieb doesn't want you fraternizing with anybody. No guests in the house or passengers in the car. We don't want you married or pregnant.'

The only thing I dared bring from 77th Avenue was Aurora in a fancy cage which I'd spotted in a second-hand store. I sold my bits of furniture to the young couple taking my apartment. The wife was expecting and looked as thrilled when she saw the breakfast room as I'd been when Gene and I'd moved in.

Because of the canyon house being set back from the street, I heard cars passing but never saw neighbours, which I took as a small blessing, but one day I'd rearranged my shoes in the closet and driven miles to the nearest store and I came home to find that I'd had visitors.

'Nigger Baster' was in big chalk letters on the screen door and 'We Hate Nearg' was scrawled on the wooden step. Although I laughed at the misspellings and was guzzling sugar donuts later when I washed them off. I knew that this was to be expected moving into a white area.

I went to bed for a few nights with the ice pick under my pillow. But not since Mamie's in Bofield had I had crickets to lull me to sleep and Aurora whistled her best when that sun stole through the trees and hit her cage.

Little luxuries were a novelty and made me forget who I was. Nadine hardly crossed my mind, because I had deceived myself thinking that she wasn't part of me and that her future was in Tennessee with somebody I'd never met named Bessie Robinson.

The victrola sat on a cabinet and inside were some 78s, which had been popular before the war. Not really my kind of music, but they gave me something to listen to when the radio went off. One was Perry Como singing 'Goodnight, Sweet Dreams, Goodnight', and another was called 'It's a Sin to Tell a Lie'. Managing not to see how it applied to me, I failed to note that it was an all-important message.

Generally, my hands stopped shaking and I stopped grinding my teeth. The silence hardly frightened me at all. Being in that house was better than any apartment could have been, because I initially felt at liberty to be myself.

25

Arriving mid-morning about a week or so after I'd moved in, for what she called my 'grooming session', Miss Keating was surprised to find the house cleaner than it had been when she'd originally left me.

During that first week I'd been on my knees polishing the floors and had the windows as clear as spring water. Not only had I dusted the tops of the doors but I'd buffed every surface to a shine and tracked down every particle of dirt which blew in whenever I opened the French doors. I nearly warmed to Miss Keating when she complimented my work.

'Most eighteen-year-olds want to do nothing these days,' she said. When I was alone, I forgot how young I was supposed to be and I hoped that the high polish on the linoleum floor didn't make her suspicious. 'The last actress Mr Gottlieb had here threw her clothes down any-old-where and must never have seen a bathtub. She didn't seem to realize that it had to be washed . . . I wasted no time ripping up her contract the day I arrived to find mould in every coffee cup dotted around the place. This is no do-as-you-please motel.'

That Miss Keating had opened the door with her own key was a good reminder that I had no privacy, and without even acknowledging that I'd offered her a seat, she marched straight through to the bedroom and proceeded to spread a dozen eight-by-ten photographs on what I had come to think of as 'my' bed.

I timidly followed her and stood in the doorway as she said, 'Take a good look at these. The smile. The expression in the eyes. The tilt of the head. That's what I'll be expecting from you today. A sweet, wholesome look.'

Every shot on the bed was of Doris Day. Head-shots and full-length. She was top of the hit parade and Miss Keating must have been her number-one fan.

I was holding one of the photographs and trying not to laugh when Miss Keating said, 'I've left some things in the car.'

Although I wanted to please her, I didn't know what a grooming session involved and was reluctant to ask. How was I to imitate somebody else's smile?

These things seemed the least of my worries when I heard Miss Keating welcome someone into the living room. It was a man she was addressing and when I heard the sound of Mario Angelli's voice, it made my skin crawl. Was I going to be put through another audition?

As Miss Keating ushered him into the bedroom, she ushered me out and although I acknowledged Mario with a smile, he looked through me. Whether it was the Negro elevator operator in Gottlieb's building, or the kid who'd written 'nearg' on the steps outside my door, in those days almost everybody would have been against me crossing the colour line. Mario's sneers were to be expected as was his nasty tone of voice.

'Hey, scrub that make-up off and brush your teeth,' he ordered, coming into the living room. 'And I hope you've got a scarf to wrap around that head . . . Grease . . . I hate those greasy bastards . . .'

I'd risen that day at dawn to wash and straighten my hair. It glistened with Madame Walker's most expensive pomade and as usual, I'd styled it in a bob, brushed back from my face with a few waves at my temples, pressed in with my curling tongs. I can't claim that it looked like a professional job, but it had looked nice enough to me in the bathroom mirror.

The bedroom and bathroom shared a common wall and I could hear their conversation clearly. Mario sounded too friendly towards Miss Keating. Sort of fawning. 'How come you smoke Old Golds? Aren't they for World-War-I heroes?' He was the only person I ever heard tease Rita Keating, but she didn't seem to mind.

'I want that girl looking like Doris Day.'

'Fat chance, señorita,' he laughed.

'Sam's on the golf course this afternoon, but it doesn't mean that he wouldn't drop by here unannounced. I expect your best work on her.'

'I'm a make-up man, not a magician.'

'And keep your hands off the girls.'

'Who've you got in?'

'Patsy and Grace . . . and do what you can with her hair. It's that schoolgirl freshness I'm looking for. That Ivory-Soap innocence.'

'That hair. The best thing for it is to cut it off.'

Standing there in the bathroom, I imagined that he was joking but before I could get the face cream off my hands he had opened the door without knocking and come in. His attitude was salty. 'You have to wet your hair before I do it.'

It had taken all my life to grow my hair to my shoulders and I have never even considered anybody taking the scissors to it. The idea that he could, without my permission, made me want to weep, but I knew better than to protest. Having released myself to Sam's control, I accepted that I had to be putty in the hands of his minions and obey their whims. But still I said meekly, 'Negro hair should be cut when it's dry.'

He did it in the kitchen with me sitting on a stool, a towel wrapped around my shoulders. While his sharp shears made terrible 'snip, snip' noises near my ears, I watched clumps of my dark brown hair fall to the immaculate linoleum floor. I had a lump in my throat that prevented me from suggesting that we should put some newspaper down. And all the while I was telling myself, 'You can get through this. Be strong.'

When he finished, he snatched the towel from around my neck and shook it so that flecks of hair flew in my face. As I wiped them from my cheeks he snapped, 'The living room.'

Assuming that was where he wanted me, I headed there immediately, not daring to touch my hair, which I imagined to be sticking straight out since he had chopped so much of it off.

His rudeness towards me in front of Miss Keating suggested that he was sure she approved while she watched him make-up my face. The living room was always bright thanks to a small skylight and I was glad that she'd left the front door ajar, because it felt less oppressive now, being in there with the two of them, him breathing hard against my face and her close enough for me to notice her slight wheeze.

When Mario began painting my lips carmine with a small but stiff brush, Miss Keating asked, 'Would Doris Day wear that colour?' He continued making his line and I tried to keep my bottom lip stretched across my lower teeth. It must have annoyed him to have her hovering at my shoulder, because he let out an exasperated sigh which prompted her to say, 'Come into the bedroom. We shouldn't parlay in front of her.'

From there I heard her talk down to him like a child. 'Have you studied these like I told you? Innocence. That girl-next-door look is what none of them have.'

I sat listening as sombre as a patient in a doctor's office after hearing a fatal prognosis. Then there was a light pat of rain on the skylight which went from one drop or two and gradually developed into a slight sprinkle. It had been dry for weeks and my spirits brightened at the thought of a late-spring shower.

I hadn't dared drop my chin from the position Mario had left it in, so I was still staring at the ceiling when I heard a couple of car doors slam. It was a relief to hear a female voice sounding young and peppy. 'Are you bushed?' she was asking somebody. 'I am. What was I thinking about, up till 3 AM dancing at the Mocambo? And there was me trying to tiptoe in, but Daddy was sitting up waiting in the den.'

In the fastest move I'd heard her make, Miss Keating scurried to that door and threw it open. 'Twenty minutes late!'

A second girl with a slight southern lilt addressed her. 'You know what it's like over at MGM. They don't give you a minute, and we couldn't slip off before lunch like we did for you last time.'

The one who had been dancing at the Mocambo was a charmer. 'I *love* your suit, Miss Keating. Those brass military buttons really set off the navy.'

'And who's our Cinderella today?' asked the southern voice before all three of them tumbled noisily into the living room. The first girl was blonde. I don't think she noticed me sitting in the chair by the fireplace where Mario had placed me so that my face would get optimum light. The second girl, trailing Miss Keating, had so many gowns in her arms that when I turned to see what she was carrying, only her loafers and ankle socks were visible. As she plopped the dresses on the sofa to keep the ballerina nets that two of them had from touching the floor, she noticed me. The fact that I was seated beside Mario's pots of make-up informed her that I was the 'Cinderella' she'd been asking about. Her mouth dropped open and she nodded to her friend before they eyed me in a tight-lipped silence.

The blonde, who'd been carrying six shoe boxes and balancing them under her chin, looked shocked enough to drop them, and Miss Keating, who'd been carrying what looked like a half bag of groceries, set it down and sheepishly rushed into the bedroom.

Calling after her, the brunette, Patsy, sounded irritated. 'We're booked for three hours. I hope you get everything shot today, because I can't come tomorrow. Can you, Gracie?'

Gracie merely stared at me as if she'd seen a ghost, and then, twirling the row of fake pearls around her neck, she began humming nervously. Fifty years ago, these reactions were normal.

Both girls were casually dressed in pleated pants and white shirts. They were definitely girls from good homes and looked the age I was supposed to be. Eighteen or nineteen. Twenty at most. Obviously they hadn't been told that they would be dressing someone my colour.

The dresses that they'd brought had been borrowed from the studio. From across the room, I could see that they were all pale shades and very frothy. I immediately eyed the lilac one, trying to avoid thinking about the situation I was in. After all, it wasn't normal for me to be there in that room, and after all those days luxuriating in that woodside solitude, it was a shock to be surrounded by so much tension and aggression, especially from young females.

I was relieved when Mario reappeared and told me, 'Go fix that hair.' As I walked slowly from the room trying to look unfazed by the treatment that I was getting, I could feel their eyes like so many knives in my back.

In the kitchen I lit a gas burner, turning it on full before reaching in the drawer for my iron curlers. I ran my hand over my bristly hair before I dared look at it. What angered me more than the state of it was the fact that those people had seen me looking so bad. A mirror still stood on the window-sill from my hairdressing efforts early that morning. Taking a deep breath, I looked at myself and was more shocked by what Mario had done to my face than the butchering he'd given my shining page boy. My lips broke into a huge smile. The way he had shaded my nose and cheeks and shaped my eyebrows, the way he had tinted my lids and stuck a strip of false eyelashes on each one made me look like a movie star. It reminded me of why I was there.

With a lot of determination and a little skill, I managed to hot curl my hair which I had already heavily oiled after I'd washed it. But being unaccustomed to dealing with it short, I kept burning my fingers and scalp as I wound small sections around the sizzling tongs. Cursing myself, I worked at a feverish rate, praying that I wouldn't be called back to the living room until I'd finished.

From the kitchen I could hear that it was alive with cigarette smoking and movie-town gossip and, when Gracie appeared asking for a can-opener and some bowls, I realized that they were about to have refreshments.

She eyed me as I stood at the stove with the curling iron resting on the circle of blue flames. However curious she may have been about the process, she asked nothing, but returned to the others jibing, 'She could be hours! She's cooking her hair and boy, does the kitchen stink from it.'

The dresses I had to wear were gorgeous. Two were copies of the latest in high fashion and the others had been used in films. The lilac had been worn by a chorus girl in a Rita Hayworth dance sequence, or at least that's what Patsy claimed. She and Grace offered a part-time wardrobe service but I would never have recommended them.

Gracie spoke to me in an extra-loud voice as though I was dim-witted or didn't quite understand English, while Patsy jabbed me with pins and never made one apology. To have them crawling on the floor at my feet, adjusting a hem or lining was disconcerting for all of us. Each time they had to touch my bare arms or shoulders to help me in or out of a gown, Patsy in particular seemed to brace herself like a cold pitcher of water was about to be poured on her head. I'd love to hear their version of that day.

When the photographer finally turned up, I felt like a department-store dummy at the Mad Hatter's tea party. I was both the centre of attention and totally dismissed. 'Stand here', 'sit there', 'move that leg', 'stand on that foot'. Everybody was allowed to give me orders, and only the photographer, who was French, managed a please or thank you. I had worked enough for Henrietta to find the posing easy, but the flashbulbs were blinding, and by the end of the day, I saw dots before my eyes.

I felt drained that night when I fell into bed after cleaning up the cigarette butts and coffee cups, the soda bottles and candy wrappers. Not to mention the tufts of my hair on the kitchen floor. But nevertheless, I was thrilled by the peace in that house and wish I could recall the number it was on Kirkwood. I ended up living there for almost eighteen months and it hardly seems possible that it was fifty years ago.

Half a century.

Back then it was such a big deal for me to have that phone, I didn't mind that it made the place seem like an extension of Sam's office. In fact, it made me feel connected to something to imagine that I was always on call.

When I was summoned to the office, days after the session, I arrived warily. It took a long time for me to feel that I wouldn't be erased from the Gottlieb roster as easily as a pencil mark.

Miss Keating wasn't at her desk, but I heard her speaking to a man in another room. He was saying, 'The kid's got bone structure. I thought I was going to see Garbo in *Camille*.'

'If you're looking for Garbo, get yourself a Swede,' Miss Keating's voice snapped.

'Where's your imagination? I said desire. I want to see desire in those eyes. I know it starts with a "D", but I didn't want Dorothy in *The Wizard of Oz*.'

Guessing that it was Sam Miss Keating was talking to, I tapped her bell and both their heads peered from his doorway. It was impressive to think that she'd been standing up to him, because she was half his size. They were polar opposites and whereas he greeted me with a smile, she dismissed me with a frown.

The plush carpet and wood panelling in Mr Gottlieb's office was far more tasteful than anything I'd seen in his house. His desk was the size of a double bed and he looked important standing beside it. I would have other opportunities to see the view from his window, but on that occasion, Miss Keating pushed me through to another office which she grandly called the boardroom. I was easily impressed in my twenties by petty things like that and quite forgot myself when I noticed the framed picture on the wall of Sam shaking hands with Franklin Roosevelt.

'Mr Gottlieb was friends with FDR!' I was so gullible. Like little Irene, seeing Miss Hortense in a photo with Chaplin.

It was Sam himself who answered, 'I haven't seen you since you sang for me, kid, how's Rita here looking after you?'

'Just swell,' I lied, hoping that Miss Keating appreciated it.

'You take a pretty good picture, kid, but I think we better go back to the drawing board. The gowns are wrong, and who's been messing with your goddamn hair?'

I assumed that Miss Keating was in love with him. Why else would a woman devote every waking hour to somebody else's business? But Sam mustn't have agreed with my theory, because as he was showing me out of the boardroom, I'm sure it was she he muttered about under his breath: 'Goddamn bull dyke.'

Patsy and Grace may have been taken off guard being booked for my first session, but they managed never to come again. I was to have four more grooming sessions before Sam approved my image, and a Negro seamstress was booked to help me in and out of the clothes. She didn't take kindly to me living in that white neighbourhood, and while she never stuck me with pins, she was nearly as dismissive as the two girls had been. Like I said, me crossing the colour line was going to bug a whole slew of people.

And my image? Since Miss Keating was in charge of those sessions, she half got her way, and eventually somebody remarked that I looked like a mix between desire and Doris Day.

For months not much happened in that little green house.

I'd leap out of bed as soon as the sun flashed through the French doors and throw them open in anticipation of the movie career which I hoped that Sam Gottlieb was plotting for me. I'd be thinking, This could be the day, when I'd scurry barefoot to the kitchen to tick off the date on the calendar pinned to the back of the door. As if that cross through the blank box could make things happen.

Flipping over the page when a new month began was worrying. I saw June, July, August, September, October and then November pass, reducing the decade to its final days. In the meantime, I'd turned nineteen, or twenty-seven, depending on how I looked at it.

Filling my morning with a beauty regime was my idea of preparing myself for the silver screen. First I'd drain a glass of milk, although I hated the taste, because I thought it was good for my skin and bones. Then I'd head for the bathroom where I'd brush my teeth so hard to get them white, it's a wonder I didn't scrub the enamel off.

I pushed my muscles with sit-ups, deep knee-bends and various twists and twirls, figuring that if Eugene could do it, so could I. Dabbing five-and-dime beauty creams on my face, I swore I noticed big improvements, but no doubt the reason I was looking better is that I was sleeping at night with only myself to think about.

My mundane existence could have been relaxing, but Miss Keating had ways of injecting some stress. For one thing, she would arrive unannounced, calling 'Irene' only when her key was in the door. Sometimes I didn't hear her but would discover that she had entered. Whatever I was doing, I stopped and stood to attention. Hands by my side, standing tall – anyone would have thought that it was a barracks inspection. 'Coffee, Miss Keating?' I always asked, and the wave of her hand with a grumble meant that she declined.

Had she come by, hoping to discover that I had someone staying? Did she expect to find a water ring on the table and use it as her reason to tear up my contract? Did she think she'd find me stretched out in bed in the middle of the afternoon? Or was she there to make sure I hadn't gone?

I can still see the way she used to stand in the living room, looking around at the walls and ceiling, studying the furniture, those sensible black lace-ups she wore firmly planted on the floor. A Brinks guard would have smiled more. Then she'd mosey around the apartment opening cupboards and drawers as if she'd lost something inside.

Sometimes she'd arrive when I'd been playing solitaire. She'd shoot a superior glance at my cards as if I'd been shooting craps, or she'd pick up a magazine I'd been reading in the bedroom and toss it aside. If a window was open, she would close it, and if it was closed she would open it. Tactics in her war game, to remind me that I was nothing.

The place was always clean. Every blade of the Venetian blind in that bathroom sparkled and, although it's not in my nature to keep tidy closets, I'd even lined the hangers up so the hooks faced the same way.

'Don't get too comfortable,' she'd say, looking up at Aurora in her fancy cage. 'Next week you might be moving.'

The time she said, 'You'd make a very good maid.' I said 'Thank you,' in case she thought that was a compliment.

In truth, her visits gave me hope that I hadn't been forgotten, because as the days passed into months, that possibility remained. I never asked questions, because I was afraid of the answers; Irene O'Brien wouldn't have been the first to sign with a production company and have nothing happen. At least my rent was paid and I received seventeen dollars a week, which would have been more than enough to live on had I not been paying for Nadine. Having read that Bill 'Bojangles' Robinson was earning five thousand dollars a week, I tried to be patient and submissive, believing that in doing so, my turn would come.

The minute I heard Miss Keating's car drive off after the inspections I'd run to tell Aurora 'Ol' chicken head done been and gone!'

Still, if I had to give those months a colour, I'd paint them yellow, because that period wasn't all bleak. Rita Keating couldn't stop the sun shining, she couldn't deprive me of my daydreaming, and she could never have imagined how much freedom I felt turning the key in the ignition of that Chevy to cruise around the streets of Hollywood.

Almost every day, I'd slip into the driver's seat to drive down the canyon and turn east into Sunset Boulevard. Worried that I might bump into somebody I knew, I never got out. I was happy just to pull into a gas station and get a smile from the pump attendant or a wink from some fresh kid who was cleaning my windshield.

Then I'd drive back to the green house calling, 'Aurora! I'm home,' when I turned the key in the front door. But of course she never answered.

We brought in the new decade together. Her in her cage. Me in mine, clutching that dream that Samuel Gottlieb would put me in pictures.

It was late one afternoon in April 1950 that I went to the office and the unexpected happened.

I always collected my 'wages' on Thursdays at 3 PM when the traffic was slack. That afternoon, as Miss Keating handed me a small brown envelope from the pile on the desk, she beckoned to a tall fellow in a dark suit sitting on the Chesterfield. He was tall and skinny, what people used to call a long drink of water. It wasn't his pasty complexion, the trim of his pencil-thin moustache, or his slick black hair combed back Frank Sinatra fashion, which told me he was one of us, I suppose, I knew from the way Miss Keating had addressed him. Taking a few long-legged strides to her desk, he had a dark brown hat in one hand and some blank sheets of music paper in the other.

Miss Keating sneezed several times and blew her nose. Suffering from hay-fever she looked grumpier than usual. 'This is Tommy Furness,' she said flatly. Her eyes were red-rimmed behind those thick lenses. 'He'll be playing piano for you. Time to earn your keep.'

Somehow, especially after the grooming session and seeing one of my head-shots hanging amongst others on Gottlieb's outer-office wall, I believed that Sam had plans to launch me with a decent role playing anything but a maid in a 'B' movie. I didn't see my name in lights right away, but singing? Although I was surprised, I refused to let her know it. I smiled as though it was some news I was expecting, and since Miss Keating hadn't properly introduced us, I offered Tommy my gloved hand and tried to sound cheerful. 'Hi, I'm Irene.' His palm was twice the size of mine and I avoided looking up at him, but could feel his dark brown eyes studying me.

He smiled like a man who got his way with women, and held my hand so long I withdrew it. But I was still prepared to be friendly until he announced, 'I know your sister.'

Instantly, an internal siren went off in my ears, so it's a wonder that I could hear Miss Keating when she followed with, 'You never told me you had a sister.'

'I don't!'

For a year I'd dreaded the possibility of meeting somebody who knew anything about me, and to have it happen in Sam's office made me feel queasy.

I could still feel Tommy studying my face. Those days when I'd sung with my sister, people mistook us for twins, and although I hadn't seen her for years, I didn't imagine that either of us had changed that much.

He suddenly grinned. 'Yeah, I must be wrong,' he said, nodding assuredly, but I sensed that he was just covering my lie.

I tried to remain calm and not look eager to leave until I'd been dismissed, but Miss Keating was taking her time. Blowing her nose. Fiddling with the wage-packets in front of her. Then she picked up a pencil and started jabbing the rubber tip on her desk. Tommy and I stood before her like schoolkids waiting to be dismissed, but

I didn't know if I could trust him not to mention my sister again. I stood there praying, 'St Joseph get me out of here.'

Miss Keating was probably too ill to play her nosy role. 'You'll be rehearsing at the Blue Lagoon. The owner's a friend of Mr Gottlieb's and I don't want any reports about cigarette burns on the piano or either of you helping yourself to the bar.'

Tommy offered me his arm getting out of the elevator, but I stepped aside avoiding him.

'This ain't the way to start. Look.' He stuck the blank music sheets under his elbow and thrust out the back of both hands. 'Clean hands, clean heart. Why you pretending you ain't got a sister? I met her.'

We ended up sitting in his car which was parked in a lot down a side-street. I didn't want to ask his age, and couldn't explain why I had to lie about mine but said, 'It was one of those things and now I can't backtrack. But if we're going to be working together, I'll give you twenty per cent off the top of what I make for you to keep this between us.'

Tommy was wearing solid gold cufflinks and a ten-dollar tie. His two-tone shoes were a little wrong for the suit, but I liked his jazzy style. As he reached over me to open the glove compartment, I eyed a ring on his wedding finger.

'Single. I plan to stay that way,' he said.

I wondered if he knew that I'd been married to Eugene, but didn't dare ask for fear that I'd be telling him more than he knew.

Fortunately, he had a secret too. In his glove compartment was a bottle of Four Roses and some Russian Vodka. It was early in the afternoon to drink, but I didn't say so. He had various paraphernalia for drinking in a brown paper bag. 'I can't swear that this glass is all that clean, but this stuff will sterilize anything.'

'I don't drink,' I said.

'And you don't have a sister.'

'I drink beer.'

'Try gin,' he laughed. 'And by the way, can you sing?'

27

A few weeks later I was sitting in the Blue Lagoon which was a pretty decent supper-club off Sunset. At night, manned by a doorman in a red coat and middle-aged Italian waiters in dinner-jackets, it actually looked quite swanky. But it was 5 PM and the place wasn't open yet. Tommy and I were meant to be rehearsing, but he had popped out for a pint of scotch.

I was perched on the edge of the revolving piano stool wondering if I had the energy to move over to an inviting pool of light which was streaming in from a small window. All nightclubs are depressing in the afternoon, and without the candlelight and roses, the Blue Lagoon seemed grubbier than most. The bentwood chairs were upside-down upon the tables, and with no white linen tablecloths to hide their scratched legs, those round wooden tables looked like secondhand rejects. They had all been pushed up against a brick wall which gave the room a rustic feel at night, but made it look rough in the cold light of day.

Having been hit by a heavy chest cold, I was feeling sorry for myself and wondered if I dare sneak a whisky from behind the bar, which was the only expensive fixture in the place. Impressively designed to set off the mirrored wall behind it, it was lined with clean crystal glasses.

When the back door slammed, I thought it was Tommy, but heavy footsteps warned me that it was someone else. 'Hello,' I called to the shadows. 'Reenie!' echoed back, and I nearly fell off the stool.

I didn't have to guess. It was Mother who I hadn't seen for a year. So I immediately assumed she had a motive for using that nightclub for our reunion, since she was normally the first to warn, 'Don't mix business with pleasure'.

She was standing face to face with me before I could decide the best way to deal with her, but taken off guard, I let the truth slip out. I was frozen to my seat.

'Mother, I'll have hell to pay if the manager pops his head in and sees me with a stranger.'

'Stranger! You are my child and will always be my child, don't care how old you get.'

'How'd you find me?'

'You ain't seen me for a whole year and that's all you can say?' She sounded her usual strident self.

We weren't ever the sort to hug, once I became an adult, but I apologized for my bad manners as I rose and added, 'Stand back in the light and lemme see your hair . . . those bangs really suit your face.'

'Well, I can't claim I like yours short,' she said, examining me. 'You young gals go round with all these crazy styles. I seen one in Mississippi with a pompadour stacked to here.' She pointed six inches above her head.

'When did you get back?' I asked, but what I really had the urge to do was to hustle her out of the back door. In a bright floral dress, she looked well, although shorter than I remembered. When I'd last seen her, she'd been sitting in Mamie's Ford with Nadine on the back seat, and they were heading for Memphis. That was a long haul in those days with roads being what they were, so I could have predicted that they'd decide to spend some time down south. But a year was the longest she'd ever stayed away.

'Been back three days and how I'm s'posed to reach you, since you begged me never to ring your phone.'

'I've got a party line . . .'

'Trust one of my church members to be up with the news. One told Mamie how she'd seen "Irene O'Brien" advertised outside here, but being this is all white over here, the woman was claiming that somebody had stole your name.'

To avoid Mother giving me the third degree, I tried to make small talk but didn't offer her a chair. 'Last time you wrote, you and

Mamie were planning to do some revival meetings in Texas.'

'Are you getting enough to eat?' she responded. 'You too thin.'

'How are you doing for money, Mother?'

'I ain't here for money.' Pinching a lump of my upper arm between her thumb and forefinger to show what little flesh there was, she said, 'Your old clothes must just be hangin' off you.'

'I need to be slim if I want to be in the movies.'

She brightened. 'You got a movie job? Now don't forget your poor old mother, 'cause I could use some decent work . . . You got to respect Gottlieb for saving you up. Most would have stuck you in the first ol' trash that come along.'

It was after five and Sam's office was only twenty blocks away. Worried that Miss Keating might decide to check up on me, my eyes kept shifting to the back passage. 'No, I haven't got anything yet.'

Mother sidled over to the piano and lifted the lid. Running her fingers across an octave she smiled. 'That surprised you, huh? Mamie's been teaching me.'

Between dry wracking coughs, I asked, 'What if the manager walks in? You shouldn't mess with that.'

'This B flat's out and that cough sounds rough.'

I couldn't hide my exasperation. 'Can't we meet tomorrow morning, Mother? I finish late and I'm not that well.'

'You mad about somethin'? Bessie Robinson's been on to you, ain't she, and you don't want to let on? You always were one for hiding your feelings.'

Despite me sending Miss Robinson a twenty-dollar money-order every month without fail, I hadn't heard from her nor written which suited me. 'Nadine wouldn't know if I wrote that woman or not and I'd have had a wire I bet had she missed a payment.' Trying to sound friendlier, I added, 'I've never been good about letters. 'Member that time Miss Taylor recommended Lil and me for the Harlem job and by the time I finally wrote to thank her, that poor girl was in her grave?'

Mother stood wringing her hands. I didn't realize she had reason to be anxious and merely saw it as a new habit. 'Mamie's rheumatics been playin' her up, but she promises she gettin' that money back to you.'

'She doesn't owe me. She asked for a hundred and fifty dollars, and I didn't begrudge you all that. Her finding that place for Nadine saved my life.'

The lights in the club came on and from the whistling, I knew it was Tommy. So I put my finger to my lips, indicating to Mother that we weren't to talk in front of him. After he'd explained to me that he'd only met Lil at a couple of parties, I took it that he knew nothing about me having a child.

'Hey, baby,' he called from the back passage which led from the alley. 'Why were you sitting in the dark?'

I expected Mother to fawn over him. Not only did she equate his light skin with being handsome, but, with his suspenders drawing his trousers above his ankles and his white peaked cap on, he looked sporty.

I knew he'd been drinking, because his hands were steady when he reached to touch her shoulder. 'If I'd seen you in the street, I would have said, "Betcha that's Irenie's mom." How come a beautiful girl always has a beautiful mother?'

'This is Tommy, and before he charms you to death, you're leaving,' I said removing his hand from her shoulder.

'Mrs O'Brien, one of these days we'll play for y'all downtown.'

He was still giggling to himself as I led Mother out past the draught kegs and some damaged piano stools. He was banging that B-flat key when she tapped me to give him the thumbs-up. 'He looks white. Can he play?'

I was uncomfortable about Mother's surprise visit and felt doubly so when we stood whispering in the alley. We were squinting at each other as our eyes adjusted to the golden evening light. The club was down a side street off Sunset Boulevard, only a few blocks from the far more popular Mocambo. Its overspill is what kept the Blue Lagoon crowded. Rush hour traffic noise was thick. So was the smell in the alley, but it felt good to have the sun on my arms even if I couldn't breathe without coughing.

Lifting both arms to twist and stretch, I dismissed Mother saying 'Scraggy little arms. No bigger than they were when I had you at St Anthony's. You need a milkshake or a hot rum, one.'

In the politest way possible I reminded her that I was meant to be working, but she grabbed my hand and pressed it to her chest. Being that we were never physical at that stage, it was completely out of character for her to grip me in that way. 'Tommy's waiting,' I said, pulling back.

'Nadine . . .'

Not only did I need to rehearse two new tunes in our second set, but that cold had me irritable and I wanted to focus all my energy on preparing for that evening's show. A little vexed, I pleaded, 'Can't we talk tomorrow?'

'It's better,' Mother said dolefully. 'She's out of harm's way.'

When I started coughing, Mother hit me on the back a couple of times. 'You and Lilian still want to be babies.'

'Mother, I've got a song to learn and Tommy's waiting.'

'If you'd stayed in touch with Bessie Robinson, wouldn't none of this come as a surprise.'

My mind flip-flopped and I imagined Nadine somewhere nearby sitting in the back of Mamie's car. Scenes flashed through my mind of me struggling to get her from one coloured boarding house to the next with doors closing in our faces or proprietors shaking their heads at me in sympathetic despair and saying, 'We been booked for days.' I saw myself making us beds out of newspapers in case she was still bed-wetting which I presumed she was. 'My God, Mother,' I moaned forgetting myself. 'She's back?'

'That was Mamie's point. She said with your big break it wasn't fair.'

I started trembling and bit my bottom lip to keep from crying. 'Where is she?'

Mother pointed to the metal garbage cans beside her which had already been emptied. The lids were lying on the ground. 'This here ain't where I planned to tell you, but you grown and I got to stop protecting y'all.' As she spoke, an old jalopy rattled by, backfiring twice. We both jumped.

'You'll have to hang onto Nadine tonight, Mother, and I'll pick her up in the morning.'

'Girl, that baby is gone.' Mother sighed. 'She's in God's hands.'

Like a great boulder was lifted from me. Like my ears popped and my hearing cleared. Like the traffic stopped. Like I fell in a well of silence. Strange sensations rushed me and amongst them was shame. But why no remorse? I was performing for myself when I swallowed hard and shouted, 'When!'

Mother said quietly, 'Last May.'

'Almost a year ago! And nobody wired me?!!' How can Providence ever forgive me for feeling a relief that surged through me like an electric shock? Days earlier, I had posted another money order to Memphis. I thought about money. Not my child. Where was my remorse?

Mother's black eyes were glassy. She folded her heavy arms over her breasts. 'Mamie and me had more than we could handle getting Deenie to Memphis. Maybe the car motion set her off, but wouldn't nothing calm her down. She was like a cat gone wild on that back seat till I started dosing her up with whisky and hot milk with a bit of Karo. That knocked her out part the way, and when we finally reached Miss Robinson's thankfully that baby seemed calmer than she'd been the whole seven days. But she wasn't looking a hundred per cent, bless her. We had wrapped those arms in that gauze you give us, but she had chewed that to threads and wouldn't let me put a comb in her hair.

'Soon as I seen Miss Robinson eye her, I said to myself, "Trouble." And, right off, she says to Mamie, "You promised a little girl with good hair." Can you imagine? After we come half 'cross the world? Still, she showed us to the parlour, but Deenie wouldn't budge. Stood on the porch, just rocking. Back and forth. Back and forth. Poor creature.'

Something about that image brought home what I had done. With my stomach knotted and churning I reached out for that wall to brace myself. The alley closed in on me! Was my mother telling the truth? 'Lies! Don't forget I know that you stole Hortense's stuff!'

'That was Gene's child's too, Irene. Why didn't *his* mama take her!'

We had been shouting and when we fell silent, I heard Tommy

playing. The melody was too faint to identify the tune but the tinkle rippled around the alley. 'Can we keep our voices down?'

At that stage, I still didn't want to know what had happened to Nadine, but Mother was determined to unburden herself by telling her story. I guess she'd been holding it in all those months and rightly wanted me to share her guilt.

'Irene, you was hob-knobbing back here with the white folks. Like I said, we wasn't even allowed to ring . . . I notice you didn't drive that child to Tennessee. How come it was down to me.'

'What was I meant to do?'

'For *you* we drove that baby to the river's edge and let God decide if she would sink or swim.' I couldn't think straight about what she was saying. It was too much to take in. 'Sink or swim? What the . . .'

'And He showed the way. She walked on out into that Mississippi like it was her baptism. Just as calm. Didn't stop once. She walked out to meet her maker. Just as calm.'

I was seeing Nadine before she had a name, when Gene had carried her to the window in the hospital and his moustache was buried in her mass of curly hair. Breaking into another hacking cough, I cried, 'What am I supposed to say?'

'It didn't happen yesterday . . . Go on in the club and do what you been doin' all these months without a care.'

I couldn't decide whether Mother spoke out of strength or weakness when she insisted that I go back inside to sing. I couldn't bear to look at her with that hair glittering with pomade in the late afternoon light. She had Nadine's eyes and I couldn't bear to see them staring back at me.

That night I wore my silver strapless gown and sang to a grey-haired man in the front row, and every time I faltered, wondering how I'd manage the top notes, he'd nod in a fatherly way.

I can't recall his face or what he was wearing, but he must have been sitting with someone, because nobody ever sat alone at those front tables.

28

Tommy and I worked out a perfect partnership. To make sure that he didn't ask me my business, I never asked his. He'd played in Europe before drifting back to the States to land the Gottlieb gig with me and didn't know a lot of people. He was one of those musicians who was a loner at heart and would have been just as happy sitting in a quiet room playing the piano to himself.

We spent half our time together in the car getting from place to place and he'd tell the odd story about Paris or Rome or the strange gig he had in the Alps. A couple of times he asked, 'Irenie, ever think of leaving?' and I believe had I ever said yes, he would have robbed a bank to get us a couple of tickets. But anywhere I went, my conscience was going to be sitting right there on my shoulder after Mother explained about Nadine. In fact, at the end of that night after Mother's visit to the Blue Lagoon, Tommy imagined I was looking bad after the show because of my cold and insisted on buying me a couple of drinks. I let him, gulping them down so fast, he predicted that I'd grow fond of gin. Actually, it became my best friend when I discovered how it let me forget everything. But I didn't binge like Tommy. At least not at first.

How many nights during those first two years, when Sam had me out there singing, did I rush out drenched in a big, phoney smile after hearing some club manager say, 'Ladies and Gentlemen, Miss Irene O'Brien.' It was never the way they paint performing in supper-clubs in movies, smooth and professional, with everything going as planned. For one thing, so many of those club managers who introduced me thought they were performers themselves and would tell a bad joke and have the audience frozen before I came on. Others said too little; maybe they knew how to balance the books but were embarrassed speaking to a crowd. The worst were the ones who'd speak too close to the mike while they were announcing me which meant that I'd have to rush out smiling with the whistling and buzzing of the mike feeding back.

There was always the array of white faces dotted about in couples and groups waiting to be entertained while they danced or ate. Tommy would play some introduction music while I'd try sounding sultry with a 'Good evening, ladies and gentlemen'. Then I'd start with a tune that everybody knew, because back then the idea of female singers performing songs they'd written was unheard of. Musicians did it, people like Basie and Ellington who had bands, but somebody like me was meant to sing familiar tunes. Like the theme song from *Macao* starring Bob Mitchum. I'd sing 'See the pyramids along the Nile,' and before I could get to the next line, there would be a trickle of applause in recognition.

It was never easy trying to create a romantic mood while somebody was gnawing on some steak in my eyeline, but I enjoyed singing with Tommy and we must have made a nice-looking pair, with me in a strapless gown and him in a black tuxedo. He reminded me of Laurie Dobson, the way he used to get a kick out of things going wrong, and probably too often we would get the giggles in the middle of a set and I'd have to strain to look moody singing some love song.

Those gigs weren't steady . . . We'd do a week and then Miss Keating wouldn't have anything lined up for two. Or worse, she'd have us performing at some private party where people paid less attention to us than you would to piped music in a supermarket. If Sam was attending he would introduce me to somebody as his property, and Tommy would be furious. 'What's Uncle Charley doing for you?'

When Gottlieb referred to me as his property, I never took it as a racial slur. It was one of those Hollywood terms, and anybody in pictures accepted it as such. Even Mother said that, considering my colour, he gave me the best start he could.

She and I passed what I think of as my supper-club years not speaking, apart from a few grunts over the phone on Thanksgiving and at Christmas. In fact, things weren't smoothed out between us until 1952, when Tommy, who was a boxing fanatic, angled to get us a Philadelphia engagement, so that he could be there for the heavyweight title fight between Jersey Joe Walcott and Rocky Marciano.

It was late September when we made the trip, and just before I left Los Angeles, I received my first film script from Sam's office. I was ecstatic, because I had given up hope of making it to the big screen. That autumn I was to turn thirty, and although I maintained the façade that I was about to turn twenty-one, I knew that time was working against me. I was ancient by Hollywood standards.

Despite what she had done to Nadine, there was no-one who would have appreciated the news more than Mother who had been staying with Lilian in New York. I had had no contact with my sister for eight years, and wasn't even interested in seeing her.

Family feuds. They need an occasional splash of bitterness on old wounds to keep the flame red-hot, but distance is the best thing for stoking them. It's possible, that had Lilian remained in LA, our stories would have been different.

In '52 Philadelphia was still the third largest city in the country after New York and Chicago, but I was still unprepared for the towering buildings and the incessant noise downtown where I was staying: the clang of the trolley-cars rolling down their metal tracks, the teeming people and automobiles in the street, the sound of high heels, including my own, clicking along the cobblestones.

As soon as I got there, I thought of my mother as a girl of fifteen arriving with a porter that she'd met on a train. Walking around the city center being jostled by important-looking women in their citified outfits and dignified-looking men rushing to and fro, I imagined Mother, from the Deep South, being scared and overwhelmed. Provoked by nostalgia, I guess, I hurried to a Western Union office and wired her to join me for an afternoon.

She was due on the day of the big fight, and people seemed more interested in talking about that than the presidential election. I can't remember why Mother was meeting me in a restaurant near my hotel. Probably still wary of her, I picked an impersonal spot.

At lunchtime, Horn and Hardart's was probably busier than most cafeterias. I realized as soon as I chose a table for two by the window that it was possibly a little too sleek for her: the strip lighting on the high ceilings gave it a futuristic feel and the sleek Formica tables trimmed in shiny aluminium were more modern than any I'd seen.

The large, open space was a little intimidating but the atmosphere was informal and very friendly. Young busboys, dressed in white, moved up and down the broad aisles clearing away dirty cups, plates and trays and setting out clean ashtrays. It boasted a fancy new catering concept, self-service, and people were busy choosing their own food. Businessmen and secretaries. Women shoppers with children. White-collar workers from the towering office blocks that lined the streets. It was an interesting mix.

I grew anxious about seeing Mother as I sat waiting; whereas I'd been dreaming up romantic notions of taking her to see the Delaware River Bridge which we'd viewed from Hortense's window or showing her the Liberty Bell, I gradually remembered that she wasn't the sort to be taxied about the city.

What I could never have predicted is that she would have the gall to arrive with Lilian, but that's exactly what she did.

Although I resented having my sister sprung on me, I was so staggered by the change in her that sympathy numbed my fury.

Momentarily, as the two of them stood at my table looking down at me, Mother faded into the background. I could only focus upon Lil, who was pitifully thin with her face badly blemished.

'Lilian?' I must have been staring with my mouth open. Was this my big sister, the one I used to envy for being beautiful and follow to school?

The cluster of flowers on her outdated hat were slightly crushed and her white gloves were soiled. Even her voice had changed. 'Hey, girl,' she said, sounding husky. I presumed that her big smile was forced. 'Thanks for the bus ticket. I haven't been to Philly in years.'

Dumbfounded though I was, I strained to act like I was pleased to see her, yet flashed an angry glance at Mother, who looked nervous. 'You look good, girl,' I lied to my sister.

Because of their journey, the skirt of her suit was badly creased and when I reached up to kiss her cheek, I smelled a hint of liquor. Not so much on her breath but coming from her pores. Her eyes had a cloudy look.

Mother said, 'Lil had the chicken-pox a while back, and I told her to use cocoa butter on that skin, but she never listens.'

The three of us were as awkward as tin soldiers standing there, and Lil tried to make a joke of the fact that we had all chosen to wear navy blue suits. 'At least we're sporting the same damn colours, which I guess means that we're fighting for the same side.'

Mother also erased some tension. 'Unless one of y'all is sittin' on my lap, we gonna need another table. Grab your bag, Reenie.'

We must have made a picture, weaving our way to the far side of the restaurant. Mother looked as though she'd gained weight. Her dress was very tight across the midriff, and although it wasn't the season for it, she'd thrown a fox-fur stole around her shoulders. From the back she looked as rumpled as Lilian.

'This place must seat a couple hundred people,' she said loudly above the lunchtime chatter. 'That Greyhound we took was as luxurious as the *Titanic*. Comfortable seats and so spacious. But I'm still beat and can't wait to eat.'

A train journey from New York would have taken only a few hours, but I dared not ask how long they'd been on the bus.

Settling on one of the sleek metal chairs, Mother immediately kicked her shoes off, though Lil and I remained standing. I don't know if the past was flashing through their minds like it was through mine, but an avalanche of old images of the three of us together tumbled down. I saw Lil and I in the identical green dresses we used to wear as The O'Brien Sisters, waiting in line with other hopefuls outside the RKO building. And I saw us practically galloping to keep up with Mother running to the bus depot the day we left Camden.

Lil's husky voice broke my train of thought. 'Mother, this is one of those fancy new self-service joints.'

'What's that mean?'

I pointed to the far wall lined with small glass compartments each with its own small door. 'See people selecting what they want? You can see exactly what you're getting and don't have to wait to be served.'

There was an element of friendliness in the way Lilian grabbed my elbow. 'Mother, you probably can't get those heels back on anyway . . . Stay put, and let's hit it, Irene.'

As she and I made our way to the colourful selection of snacks, sandwiches and desserts in their individual, well-lit compartments, my emotions were swinging out of control. From one extreme to another. Like a metronome, swinging between anger and sorrow. Lilian had had the ninety mile journey from New York to adjust to the idea of seeing me, but I was still overcome with shock. I looked back at Mother, who gave an innocent little wave from the table, and I wanted to lambast her for landing me into a sticky predicament without consulting me first. But to see my sister looking so debauched was a heartbreak, and I was reminded that they were my sole family.

As Lilian was eyeing the food, she was also studying the prices. 'Guess I'll just have a coffee.'

'Lilian Matthews, I'm paying. Get exactly what takes your fancy. I'll grab three coffees and you take a tray and decide what we're going to eat. No cheese for me. And I hate tuna fish.'

When I returned she was all thumbs, struggling to lift open the glass door protecting a portion of strawberry shortcake. 'Why the hell not have a normal counter,' she was snarling as a young man in his early twenties with platinum blond hair and pale blue eyes came rushing over. The small badge pinned to his jacket said 'Manager'.

'Sorry, madame,' he told Lil in a Scandinavian accent. 'Some of these doors have been sticking.' As he took what looked like a penknife to slowly pry it open, Lilian turned to me, balancing the tray of sandwiches. 'I guess you know Mother's sick.' It was a statement rather than a question, and the fact that she had chosen to blurt this with a stranger standing so near was embarrassing. He obviously thought so, too. Taking Lil's tray he said, 'I'll have these brought to you.'

Without acknowledging his kindness, she pursued the issue of Mother's health. 'Notice how bloated she looked?'

Guiding her back to the table, I said, 'Mother's always been big.'

'That's why I came down here with her. She said she didn't think she should make this trip alone.'

On hearing this, I took it that Mother had tricked my sister into coming, because I had yet to learn that one could be more devious than the other.

Lilian removed her hat as she sat. Her hair was heavily oiled but she hadn't bothered to style it. It was parted on the side and held down with bobby pins. She had always been fastidious, so I took her shabby appearance to mean that she wasn't working.

'Girl,' she told Mother, 'times have really changed. Can you believe that manager just offered to serve *me*?'

Mother removed a pair of glasses from her small bag but before she could slip them on, I asked, 'When did you get those?'

'She's had those years,' said Lil pointedly to remind me that I hadn't seen my mother in some time.

'Funny,' Mother smiled, 'first time I come to Philadelphia with your daddy, if we had tried to get in the door of a fancy place like this here, the manager would've been calling the cops.'

His arrival made her sheepish. With the chicken sandwiches which Lil had chosen, his large catering tray was laden with three pieces of strawberry shortcake. They were perfect mountains, piled high with white nests of frilly whipped cream. The juicy strawberries had bled into the sponge. 'Compliments of the house,' he smiled. 'Horn and Hardart's, first in the city, and tell all your friends.'

Mother's face was a picture of joy. Her eyes sparkled. 'Ain't this a pistol . . . I said to Lil on the bus, "Pity we couldn't have waited a few weeks, 'cause this could've been Irene's birthday get-together."'

'Thirty,' Lil mocked, as the manager slipped off. 'It's all over now.'

I blew at my hot coffee. 'Actually, you'll have to keep up my lie. As far as the world knows, I'm twenty-one.'

'Don't be ridiculous!' She took a bite of her sandwich and glared at me until Mother intervened to head off a clash. 'Don't look now, but there's a coloured woman on your left just come sit down wearing an I LIKE IKE button.'

'Negro woman,' Lil corrected. 'Nobody says coloured any more.'

'Put it this way. She ain't white and ought to be voting for Adlai Stevenson. The NAACP says we got to give him our vote. Eisenhower for President,' she snickered. 'What could that poor child be thinking about!'

Lil nibbled a second bite of sandwich but obviously had no appetite. I couldn't get over how rakishly thin she was. Her brow and cheekbones were too prominent. I tried not to stare, but when she caught me, I asked, 'Still going to mass?'

'Hell, no,' she laughed. 'Remember how we used to have to go every day?'

'I was just thinking about Father Connolly hobbling up our stairs when you said that,' Mother added. 'See there, our minds are all still working alike.'

'I betcha that man's dead . . . God, St Anthony's . . . those were the days, huh, Irene?' Lil sighed. 'Remember Willie Ruttles with his home-made scooter? He used to make such a racket up and down on the sidewalk, because his old man wouldn't let him scooter in the street.'

My mind slid back to Camden. To Black Tuesday and Killer Wednesday. I could recall how Mother grinned hearing Lil describe the police car which had whisked Mack away in handcuffs, and I saw Mother dancing barefoot around the room. Mack. It was the first time in years that I'd thought about him.

Mother put a big spoonful of cake to her mouth. Before snapping her painted lips over it asked, 'What do you think happened to ol' onery Mack after they let him off?'

'Live by the sword, die by the sword,' piped Lilian.

'What's that mean?' I asked, to make polite conversation.

'They should have locked him up and thrown away the key for messing with little . . .' Lil turned to Mother, 'Stop poking my leg. That hurt! What did you do that for?'

Mother didn't look up from her plate and suddenly seemed annoyed. 'Lilian, shut up. You talk in what you don't know.'

I interrupted, 'Messing with little what, Lilian?'

'Little girls,' she said, eyeing Mother defiantly.

This was the first I'd heard of such a charge. Merely curious, I asked, 'Who said?' but failed to associate what she was saying to me.

'Mother,' quipped Lil looking at her for confirmation. All she got was one of Mother's 'do-shut-up' frowns. Lil carried on. 'What's the big secret?' Her tone was argumentative. 'You said Miss Hortense heard things through the floorboards.'

'How come nobody told me?' I was still in denial about Mack; what was irritating was that I guessed that information had been shared between them that was being kept from me. I was starting to feel flushed.

Wiping my mouth with a napkin, I studied Mother, who refused to look up. An uncomfortable feeling stirred in me. I felt trapped. It may have been bad memories trying to inch their way out of the deep caves that I'd buried them in. I did recall while I sat there, Mack whistling through Hortense's floorboards.

Mother said, 'Lilian, why not try that cake and let that ol' mess rest, 'cause we down here to enjoy ourselves.'

I thought about her keeping that newspaper article with Mack's picture in it. Then I thought about Miss Hortense. It made me feel irritable, but I didn't know why at the time. Of course, thinking about it with hindsight, I realize that I should have been worried that what happened to me in Mack's was about to be exposed. Nonetheless, I somehow persisted, because what Lil had said needed clarifying. 'He messed with kids?'

Mother took another bite of cake, but was definitely avoiding my eyes. 'It was big girls he was fooling with. The developed ones. Like that I-talian with the long braids that all the street boys used to sniff around. And what does it matter.'

Relevant questions escaped me. 'When . . . how . . .' I began and then stopped. I had repressed the memories too well.

Lilian nodded casually towards me. 'Miss Fancy Pants was always down there. Remember the smell in that store? You couldn't get me in there.' She seemed pleased with this.

Why would Mother have let me go to Mack's knowing the risk?

In those days, that wasn't the sort of thing that I could have asked. What would I have said, 'Was I the sacrificial lamb?' Like me, she could have been in denial. It was part of life back then, to never confront things. Not only for us, but for everybody.

At the time, in Horn and Hardart's, with the clamour of lunch-time noise circling us, Mother managed to swing our conversation round to Miss Hortense. 'It hurt me to my heart,' she said, trying to look pitiful, 'how you girls took Hortense's side. To tell the truth, I always wondered if it wasn't her that had a hand in killing Mack's wife. Otherwise, how come she left all her furniture with me and didn't show her face again?'

Seated opposite me in the cafeteria, she seemed to be talking to steer me away from asking questions about Mack.

I stared into my coffee cup and watched the busboys out of the corner of my eye. They almost seemed to be moving in slow motion. It was the first time that I'd seen Mother since she'd informed me about Nadine in the alley outside the Blue Lagoon. I realized what little trust I had once had in her was gone.

Lilian was happy to reminisce about our Camden days. I guess at least in that way she hadn't changed. She laughed about us sleeping under Miss Hortense's silk comforter, but Mother didn't see the humour.

'Y'all was at school, and I was the poor fool set there lookin' at her stuff day in and out. Wasn't like she was payin' me to.'

'We did have it a long time,' Lil agreed, playing with a spoon.

I wanted to scream. I was ready to throw my cup clear across the restaurant and shatter the plate-glass window. Their chatter had me grinding my teeth. And worse, they both struck me as alien. We had become strangers. The blood ties weren't enough.

Mother licked a smidgin of whipped cream from the tip of her thumb before raising ten fingers to use them for counting. 'The Crash was in October . . .' she said, bending her fat forefinger. 'Then November, December, January, February, March, April . . .'

Lil said, 'You're not supposed to count the first month. It was only six months. Not seven. You're always doing that.'

'Six or seven. What's the difference. I didn't hear n'ery word from that wench, and us eating nothing but hominy grits.'

In light of what had happened to Nadine, I considered Mother capable of heinous crimes, so it wouldn't have surprised me at that moment had she claimed that *she'd* killed Mrs O'Brien. 'What about the penny whistles?' I spouted in Hortense's defence. 'Don't you remember that Miss Hortense sent those?'

Lil belched. 'Penny whistles. Irene, don't be a fool all your life. You're missing the picture. Mother's saying that there she was on the breadline with two kids to feed, and some woman she hardly knew leaves her with furniture and doesn't come back. Mother's got a point. It *is* fishy that she never heard again from Hortense.'

As Lilian spoke, I wondered if she knew about what had happened to Nadine and wondered what I'd say if it came up.

Mother gulped some coffee. 'Back then storekeepers was Mr Kingpin. Mack sure enough ran our lives, but Hortense thought she was too good to mess with him. Kept to herself. Then, after Mack give her them chops, his wife got everybody believing that there was something between him and Hortense and ran all up and down telling people that the worse thing about it was that Hortense was passing for Mexican. Father Connolly even stopped me once in the street to ask if it was true.'

'And was it?' asked Lil. 'Even the thought tickles me.'

I was drawn out of my silence by the absurdity of what they were saying. 'What's funny about it?'

'You know how uppity she was with that picture of Charlie Chaplin and wearing that mantilla in church? Imagine, she was just a nigger puttin' on.' Lil's voice carried and people at neighbouring tables turned to look.

'Penny whistles,' said Mother. 'If she didn't do it, she had a hand in it. Them Mexicans have vengeful natures. But anyway, what do we care, it's all water under the bridge. We can't be wasting our good time together thinking about that.'

It was 1952 and we had been talking about something that had taken place more than twenty years earlier. I was nearly thirty and I couldn't have explained why it would always be relevant to me. Only tonight do I understand that what Mack did laden me with a guilt that was beyond my understanding.

Isolated me. Isolated me. If only I'd known.

Liquor and worry can scrape the soft edge from a woman and sitting beside my sister in Horn and Hardart's it was difficult to accept how hard she'd become. Yet she hadn't lost that indefinable grace which had always been as much a part of her as the way she threw her head back to laugh. I watched her talking with her hands, wrists so fluid and fingers like ten swimmers in a water ballet. I watched her lean forward to nestle her pointed chin in her upturned palms, cupping her blemished face. Can I help her, or is it too late? I was thinking until her eyes reminded me of Nadine's. I turned away.

Sipping my coffee which had gone cold, I gently kicked Lil under the table. The tip of my alligator pump tapping the heel of her shoe. Like we used to do as kids to grab each other's attention without Mother knowing.

'Are you trying to run my nylons,' she asked flatly with that spoon in her hand. There was a teasing tone in her voice. I tried to open up. 'I missed your butt after you moved.'

Did she mean to respond with a stab in the back or was she just being thoughtless? 'I guess you heard that Eugene married an interpretive dancer?'

When I bristled Mother showed that she'd lost none of her instinct to jump between sisters to prevent a catfight. She said, 'Reenie don't care a doggone about him. She's working, like I want you to. And how about it, what is happening with you, Irene? Your eyes look clear.'

Forgetting the red rag my sister had flagged at me, I remembered to tell her about the script I'd been sent. Filled with a sudden sense of pride, I gushed, 'Sam's secretary is an onery old biddy, but he's finally come up with a movie for me.'

As Mother put her hands together to clap, the table rattled, and the people behind turned around to register disapproval. She took no notice. 'Hallelujah! See! The Lord does provide for those who wait. Like I was telling Lilian the other day.'

A busboy whose mahogany skin contrasted dramatically with his white starched shirt and cap gradually shuffled towards us, as he bent and stretched, reaching for dirty items to fill his bucket. He stopped at our table in time to hear me say, 'Mr Gottlieb plans to shoot the movie with me next year.' I wanted the boy to look at me. But why? I wanted to see praise from his eyes. Charlie used to call that piece of me that was addicted to being noticed, praised and approved my Look-at-Me Monster.

Mother was more concerned about the busboy helping her to bag the leftovers. As Lilian tried to pass him her shortcake which she had merely toyed with, Mother said, 'I'll have that, and Sugar,' she said, addressing the boy, 'see if you can find me a piece of paper to cart this home in.' She was referring to Lilian's sandwich. Then she switched her attention back to me. 'What's the movie?'

'It's called *The Long Journey Home*. It's about a nightclub singer trying to break into the big time who ends up happier as a short-order cook in Las Vegas.'

'That's just the part for you. Soon as you told me Gottlieb was a Jew . . .'

'Mother, I'm not the singer. I'm somebody who does dishes in the diner where she works.'

Lilian spluttered, 'Does that sound like a head-rag rôle?'

'The girl I play is struggling to put herself through night school. No great big rôle, but it's a speaking part and all right by me.'

I was surprised when Lilian agreed to see the Liberty Bell. Mother seemed to have a lot of control over her and said, 'You American. How can you be this close to the Declaration of Independence and not see it? Reenie says it ain't far, and I'd like to tell people that I been. What else we gonna do to kill time till our bus leaves, sit around some lowdown bar somewhere?'

Independence Hall was on Chestnut, between Fifth and Sixth.

Not far from us, but thinking about what Lil had told me about Mother's health, I insisted that we take a cab, although Lil argued that it was a waste of good money.

The Liberty Bell sat in a square white foyer which had snow-white walls, but despite the flood of light in the room, I found the atmosphere depressing.

When Mother saw that the guard at the door was one of us, she poked me in the ribs, and went over to listen to him explaining to a Chinese couple that the bell had been cracked twenty-three years before the Declaration of Independence was signed.

My sister took the opportunity to pull me aside. 'I'm looking for work, but that won't pay Mother's doctor's bills.'

I didn't need more pleading than that and gave Lilian everything in my wallet apart from five dollars.

That's how it began and when it began. Twenty here, fifty there, a hundred now, two hundred later. What was consistent is that Lilian's needs rose with my earnings. She never needed less, and what ever she asked for, Mother demanded twice that.

Back in my hotel room that night, I collapsed across my bed listening to the Jersey Joe Walcott/Rocky Marciano fight on the radio.

'Incredible!' squealed the announcer above the harangue in the stadium. I laid there listening with my good suit on, hugging the *Journey Home* script which had been under my pillow. 'The crowd is on its feet giving the count with the referee. 8-7-6-5-4-3-2-1.' The roar of the thousands in Philadelphia Stadium forced the announcer to raise his voice. He was practically shouting. 'What an event! Rocky Marciano, twenty-nine years old from Brockton, Massachusetts, five foot ten and one eighty-nine pounds is the new heavy weight champeen of the world.'

There was another roar from the crowd. I was listening with my eyes closed, and when the announcer said 'twenty-nine years old', I hugged the script tighter.

'Rocky Marciano, ladies and gentlemen, has taken the title with a right-handed punch which has knocked the champ senseless. Jersey Joe Walcott appears to be out cold! In '47, we had the all-time great middleweight, Rocky "Somebody up There Likes Me" Graziano. And now for our second Rocky. It happened in Philly tonight.'

Tommy wasn't himself for weeks after that, because of a bet he'd lost on the fight, so he said, but he swore that I perked up after Philadelphia. 'Watch out, next thing you'll get a reputation for smiling.'

It was the promise of making *The Long Journey Home* which boosted my morale. That first script was so dog-eared from me studying it every day, anybody would have thought it was the Bible. I didn't know that CU stood for close-up and VO for voice-over, but I slept with those pages, which nearly felt as comforting as loving arms.

29

The Long Journey Home starred Angela Lane, another one of those blonde bombshells who looked contrary, and was.

We were meant to shoot the picture in early 1953, but thanks to a business dispute which Sam was having with one of the studios over another picture, the *Journey* start date became a moveable feast. I can't remember when it was shot, because the dates were moved forward so often, but by the time it was released it was the late summer of '54.

There had been two directors on it before the final cut, the first being Leonard Wasserman, who also co-wrote the original screenplay. He and Sam fell out in the middle of shooting schedule, because Leonard refused to distance himself from an old buddy who was hauled before the House Un-American Activities Committee.

After Monroe Goodhew, an old director who had worked in the silents, replaced him, Sam noticed that Monroe and Angela were getting on too well. He punished the two of them by insisting that a couple of extra scenes with Angela looking wasted and downtrodden were written in. His excuse was that tear-jerkers were popular and he wanted his leading lady to look like a fallen woman. Nobody expected it to do well at the box office, but something happened which increased its takes.

When *Confidential* magazine ran a piece claiming that Angela had been a call-girl in Vegas before beginning her movie career, some ladies' groups around the country tried to ban the picture. I thought they'd succeed, but Sam figured that the increase in the public's interest in Angela was good box office. He even managed to swing an early-September release.

Communism being the real blight at that time on anyone's reputation, it seemed less critical that Angela was tainted with something as straightforward as a sex scandal.

Surprisingly, Goodhew married her before *Journey* was released. When they both claimed that the *Confidential* scandal was part of a Samuel Gottlieb publicity campaign, secretly, I believed them.

A bigger drama was brewing around that time while I'd spent those months on stand-by for the film. Tommy had been to Paris pushing to get us some offers. They came and the moment which I had been dreading for years finally happened: Miss Keating asked for my birth certificate. I insisted that I could organize a passport alone, but she insisted that I wasn't reliable. So rather than drag out the inevitable, I marched into the office and said, 'I wasn't born in Los Angeles. My birthplace was Camden. 11 November 1922.'

What joy I got seeing the blood drain from her face. It was contorting when she turned her back on me to fiddle with her Remington. Clearing her throat she said, 'Mr Gottlieb will deal with you when he gets back from Cuba. Of course, *I* knew all along. When we had you in the Canyon, I smelled a rat. Thirty-two! And after all we've done for you. It's disgusting!'

A week later, when I was summoned into his office, Sam greeted me with a wry, 'Chutzpah, Irene. I like that.' When he beckoned me to his side of the desk, I guess I was visibly trembling and wondering what punishment awaited.

'Don't lose your nerve at this late stage,' he said, rising. 'Stand over here by the light.' It was floor to ceiling window behind him.

Sam always wore a suit and tie, and usually had a dark tan. I don't think that I'd been that close to him since my audition. His aftershave was sweet but when he reached to draw me near, I stepped back. 'What's the matter? Let me see you in the light,' he said. He lifted my chin and examined my face. 'Smooth as a baby's ass . . . You're not keeping any other secrets from me, are you?' He slapped me on the behind. 'Nice tight little ass. I keep meaning to drop by and get a squeeze.'

*　　*　　*

The poster for the film was a close profile of Angela looking dejected with me far off in the background looking concerned for her while I dried my hands on a dishtowel. It's from the scene towards the end of the film where she asks if I think she should return to her middle-class family, and I say, 'What's security without love?'

I didn't have that much to do in the picture, but Sam got my photo image everywhere. Newspapers. Magazines. Cinema foyers. Angela's adverse press helped. Mother and Lilian were still in New York and Mother sent clippings of me any time she spotted one. A big critic said that I had brought something so natural to the screen that it was hard to believe that I was acting. Others repeated him, but I think Sam's all-out publicity campaign blinded the public to the fact that the picture was pretty awful and the acting mediocre.

Whether it was the poster, or the still which had appeared in papers coast to coast, a little brush-fire caught to my name, and people who claimed to predict the trends in Hollywood suddenly began to mention me. The Louella Parsonses and the Hedda Hoppers didn't write me up, but Sam guaranteed me that the people whispering in their ears were saying, 'Watch out for Irene O'Brien'.

He was always finding ways to increase the value of his property. Favours owed. Money exchanging hands. Sam was in business and his real interest was the profit margin.

For their 1954 round-up, Variety pictured me with nine others as the new faces for '55. Amongst them my brown face was the most prominent. Nobody could have been more excited than Sam. He even promised to commission a screenwriter to come up with a story for me. 'With this Civil Rights movement catching fire, now may just be the time to break you.'

Repeating Variety's forecast, the Negro papers ran big features on me. In advance of even having a script to shoot, Sam announced to the press that he was having a special project developed that I would star in.

My look-at-me monster was over the moon, but another part of me wanted to creep away from the glare of the spotlight in case it flashed upon someone or something from my past which I wanted to keep hidden.

Where was Bessie Robinson?

Would Eugene come forth to berate me?

What about Henrietta Dobson?

I circled the periphery of limelight. Every moment, I was looking over my shoulder and the only thing which calmed my nerves was gin.

By the time Sam rang a couple of months later with the mind-boggling news that I had been nominated for an Oscar for my performance in *Journey*, I had constructed my own prison cell of fear. It was early in '55, and I recall the rains being heavy that season. I stayed indoors.

Mother glowed, 'Didn't I predict this? Tell the truth, I knew you had it in you to be the next Bette Davis. That's how come it used to rile me to see you sweating over that hot stove. Now I can tell the know-nothings, "My baby's a movie star."'

Even Lilian expected some credit: 'I was the one who said, "Don't let them stick you in a head-rag . . ." Bet you're glad you listened.'

Then there was Miss Keating. 'Of course I'll get no thank you from Sam, but the Doris Day innocence appeals to people.'

And always there was Nadine. Waist deep in the muddy Mississippi in her pink dress with the round collar. Mouthing 'Mommy'. No sound. Merely her lips moving.

Charlie refused to hear about the round of parties and married men who sent roses. 'I'm surprised they let you use the bathrooms.' What's it matter that for a minute people thought you were important.

One thing I'll always remember is the time after the nominations were announced when Miss Keating called me to the office to collect a pile of fan mail and congratulations. Letters and cards had come in from all over the country. In the elevator I opened the largest of the envelopes. Inside was a single sheet of paper. Somebody had smeared excrement on it and scribbled, 'More of Gottlieb's shit for you to eat. Get back to the cotton field.'

I never wanted anybody to know about the hate mail because I was afraid that Sam would use it as a publicity gimmick. The way

I eventually avoided the ugly letters was to open none of them.

Suddenly my opinion mattered but Sam assured me that I should never have one. 'Just smile and look pretty. The colour thing's too sensitive.' So I saw articles about me in which he was quoted, or Mother, or even Lilian.

Irene O'Brien said nothing.

'Oscar Nominee' was a title. It went before my name like 'Miss' or 'Princess', which got me invited to the odd ceremony, but if Sam forgot to organize the press, there was often the embarrassment of none being there for me.

For instance, in early '55, I was invited back to Philadelphia for the re-naming of the Delaware River Bridge. To commemorate the two-hundred-and-fiftieth anniversary of Benjamin Franklin's birth, they were naming it after him. Mother thought it was such a big deal that I was on the city council's guest list, but she didn't know that I'd sat at a banqueting table between two people who were obviously offended that they'd been seated beside me, because the only thing written on my place name was Irene O'Brien. While the sixty-five other guests buzzed with conversation, I sat in silence, slowly chewing every morsel of food and trying to act like it didn't matter that not one flashbulb went off in my face.

So I went shopping. Or I went to the movies.

I made sure that even my cuticles were perfect.

I had time to ensure that every centimetre of my face and hair was perfect, taking hours over my make-up even if I was only popping out to buy another pair of high heels. I was almost as bad as Mother back in '29, undoing doilies so that she could do them up again.

Sam also wanted to keep me both in the limelight and out of it. 'Got to be careful. We can't have anybody writing about your age. But don't think you're the first to lie,' he told me one night when he was zipping up his trousers and I was trying to get one of his pubic hairs off the back of my tongue. 'I've got a buddy that can get you a deal at the Waldorf.'

'Negroes can't stay there,' I reminded him.

'It's no good you being in town. We'll say you're about to shoot some tests in New York . . . Don't worry, kid, don't I always think of something?'

In the real scheme of my life, the nomination stands as hardly relevant. The Academy Awards wasn't the big television extravaganza that it is these days. Nobody thought that the TV rating was more important than the event. They weren't watching in China. There were no satellite hook ups. It was another night for dressing up.

There was a TV link-up to accommodate the actors and actresses that had to be on the East Coast. That seemed extraordinary enough. Mother was with me at the theatre in New York where it was being picked up from. Being three hours later than Los Angeles, she complained about being tired before the night got under way. I had bought her an amber gown and an orchid corsage and she was so nervous that I forgot about myself.

'And the winner is . . .' That bright male voice was at the heart of many of my nightmares after I'd lost.

I thought that Mother was going to faint when my name wasn't called. She broke out into a cold sweat and started palpitating. I was wearing a dark cream satin couturier gown which looked like something for a debutante. The shade complemented her dress. When I helped her into the ladies' room, she had leaned on me so heavily that her perspiration stained my satin.

Rocky Marciano retired in 1955. I should have joined him. Quit while ahead. But I was tied to my contract with Samuel Gottlieb productions and there was no way out. 'Irene O'Brien' was Sam's creation.

Who could have imagined that in ten years I could have touched that height to then fall so low?

I now see myself like one of those kids who scrambles up a tall slide as fast as their little legs will carry them, but when they reach the top, they immediately start the slide down without ever pausing to take in the view from up there.

In truth maybe I was always rushing to get here. To this height only a roof top distance from the ground. Not dangling up there with the stars.

Hollywood was healthier than Miami. At least we didn't need a pass to enter after dark, but why pretend it was a picnic in the Fifties when segregation was the rule?

Take the summer before James Dean died. We'd started shooting *Odile*, and Emmet Till's murder by two white men in Money, Mississippi raged in the headlines. Him being only fourteen incensed people. Everybody talked about it on the set, but all of them being white, I kept my opinions to myself.

Anyway, one morning, I was in make-up and costume rushing back to my dressing room and overheard some of the technicians discussing the Till case. An electrician with his back to me said, 'What was that little nigger doing calling a white woman "baby"? Fourteen or not, he needed . . .'

One of the others noticed me and warned, 'Here she comes . . .'

I gave a polite nod and a 'Good morning, gentleman', but the electrician obviously wanted me to hear. 'They should have tarred and feathered the little black monkey. Like they did in my day.'

'Nigger', 'coon', 'jigaboo', 'tom'. I heard them all around the set after Emmet Till's body had been found in the Tallahachie River.

Still it wasn't the racism which got under my skin and made me need sleeping pills to close my eyes, when that story dominated the front page. It was the image of my own child drowning.

Till's murder was no worse than Buster McMichael's. The difference is that the boy's made headlines, so obviously something had changed, including the fact that I could be nominated for an Oscar, but I didn't so much cross the colour line as crawl on my belly under it.

30

Despite my Oscar nomination, it was still impossible to rent in Beverly Hills in '56, so Miss Keating put me in a bungalow that Sam owned in West Los Angeles not far from UCLA.

Lilian had moved back to the West Coast and was sharing with Mother over in Compton, but I had made it clear that as the house wasn't mine, apart from emergencies, they weren't really welcome. I figured that my having two bedrooms would present too much of a temptation for them. But guilt-ridden, I still gave them keys to my back door.

The house was nothing great, a small stucco with no garage, but I thought the kitchen was something special, because it had a broom closet and a brand new refrigerator with a section in it which held a metal tray for making ice cubes. There was a decent-sized window above the sink which overlooked a side passage leading from the front lawn to the back door. Since it faced the neighbour's garage wall with a tall hedge dividing the two properties, I never bothered to close the curtains and let what light that could steal in.

Seated at the kitchen table one morning, I saw my sister's head bobbing past the window. At least it gave me a moment to prepare for her entrance, because she stormed in with one of her usual attacks. I noticed that she was wearing a dress of mine which I couldn't recall having given her. Either she or Mother had hemmed it badly, and she had gathered the extra inches at the waist with a narrow belt, because she was still pretzel-thin.

Her stance and her sour expression, not to mention the magazine she was waving at me, told me that she was going to raise her voice, so I said, 'Maria's due any minute, so don't start with me, Lilian.'

230

Maria Ruiz was the Mexican cleaner who came twice a week, because Sam said it was important for my image to look like I was earning and spending, although I had only done two pictures. He backed every decision with, 'Why worry, I'm taking care of you.'

Lil and I never discussed the important things. For instance, she never mentioned Eugene, although she reminisced about our days working in Harlem, and as for Nadine, I avoided discovering what Lilian knew. Denial about certain matters was crucial and I now realize that I probably gave her all that money to ensure her silence.

She lived high off my sudden celebrity. Being Irene O'Brien's sister gave her status with her so-called friends, and indirectly, the money I doled out to Lil benefited all of them. She thought better of herself, because she was being generous, but I never had the nerve to ask, 'Why brag, when every penny you give is my money?'

One singer Lil knew named Freda arrived from New York with big ideas about making it, and Lil so banked on her becoming the next Sarah Vaughan that she not only fed Freda but took her to auditions in my clothes. I discovered this when Freda dropped by with Lil one day. Not realizing that the blouse she was wearing was mine, I said, 'That dark pink suits your complexion. I wish it suited mine.'

'Nice of you to let me borrow it,' she said absentmindedly, reading the newspaper, but when I complained to Mother, she came to my sister's defence. 'Lilian should have been a talent scout. She really can find 'em can't she!' Why did I expect Mother's sympathy? She agreed with my sister that my success belonged to them and our people coast to coast.

'Our people'. Everything was meant to be for the race.

The morning that Lilian barged into my kitchen waving the magazine, she didn't want to sit down. 'Rosa Parks is getting arrested for refusing to give her seat to a white man and you're in *Photo Star* with your bust hanging out!'

It was too early for a confrontation, but I snatched the magazine from her and slammed it on the table. 'I'm on the *cover*, Lilian.' I stressed 'cover', 'and I'm fully clothed. What some woman is doing in Montgomery, Alabama is nothing to do with me.'

'It has something to do with all of us.'

My photograph may have been provocative, but it was hardly indecent. I was in a low-cut affair. Black. And the photographer had me standing in a fountain of water up to my mid-thighs. A classical statue of Eros carved in stone was in the centre of the fountain, slightly casting me in shadow, water cascading over both of us. The photographer had me in a few poses, but in the one printed, he'd asked me to put my hands on my hips and throw my head back laughing. When I did, I was imitating Lilian. Because I was naked under the dress and the water was cold, my nipples were protruding through the material. It was a black and white shot and *Photo Star*'s caption in blood red said, 'Gottlieb's Negro Goddess'.

Anybody would have thought that Lil was a civil rights campaigner with the way she went on about my responsibility to the race and how I couldn't let Gottlieb use me to set us back.

I said, 'Lilian, all the man is thinking about is *Odile*. He's got a picture to sell and I'm obviously the focus of the campaign.'

What I think she had really been brooding about for weeks is the framed shot of Mother and Eugene which I'd stuck on the mantelpiece.

It was that picture taken of the two of them on Mother's thirty-ninth birthday, and I felt that I was putting it there for Nadine. I guess that was the first obvious sign that my imagination and paranoia about her were getting the better of me. Nadine had begun to prey upon me from morning till night. Less her memory than the feeling that she was hovering. Watching. Sometimes I left the light on in my bedroom, because in the darkness, I could feel her presence in the room. Even in daylight, I'd suddenly become aware of that faint smell of urine that had clung to Nadine's clothes when I'd return home from an afternoon posing for Henrietta.

I'd placed the photograph in a silver frame in the hope that it would appease her spirit, but as Lil stood opposite me in the kitchen, I suspected that she imagined I had been trying to humiliate her. That's what was on my mind when I hurled my own attack. 'When

I gave birth to Nadine, you didn't even bother to send a telegram, although I wrote and asked you to stand as her grandmother!'

'Grandmother? Girl, why don't you lay off drinking,' Lil said, heading for the door. 'I've come all the way over here. Three buses . . . our people are already saying that you're uppity and running around with white men. People know why Gottlieb's keeping you.'

'I'm his property.'

'Exactly. And in case you haven't heard, we've been free since Lincoln.'

'I don't have to answer to you.'

'People talk. Everybody knows you give it up to whitey. We all could be where you are, but some of us have self-respect.'

She banged the back door so hard when she left that I expected the glass to break. I yelled, 'And I'm sick of supporting your ass!'

Maria arrived later than usual that morning but I was still in the kitchen in my robe when she stood there putting the hairnet on her head.

She was probably my age but looked in her late forties and was so small it was hard to believe that she could have given birth to the six children under ten that she was supporting in Mexico. She used to hum when she was working around the house, and although she looked nothing like Hortense Alvarez, their accents were similar. Perhaps that's why I had immediately warmed to her.

Since she was paid by Miss Keating, Maria didn't think of me as her boss and was quite familiar. Sometimes too much so. Anyway, that morning she spotted the *Photo Star* on the table. 'Lovely,' she smiled at the cover, before flicking through it. When she came to my two-page spread, she held it away to read it without her glasses. '"Irene O'Brien,"' she gloated, '"the former torch singer . . ."'

Determined not to be ridiculed again, I got up to leave, but suddenly burst into tears before I could reach the doorway leading to the front room. 'That's not me. I just do what I'm told. Now my sister's trying to claim I'm disgracing our race.'

'You're a movie star! I've met your mama.' Maria smiled trying to placate. 'She's proud. I bet your father's proud. My sister, she's

233

jealous too. When you gotta worry is when you got nothing for them to be jealous about.'

'I keep to myself. Living like a hermit. What more do they want me to do?'

'See what the magazine calls you? A goddess. Why you crying?'

Maria was the only person I could talk to, but she wasn't too smart and knew nothing about my life, neither my true age nor that I'd been married with a child. So her attempts at comforting me were always limited. 'Sit . . . I squeeze you some juice,' she said now, opening the refrigerator. 'Then I tell you about the greatest thing that happened. Happened to me today!'

As tempted as I was to run out to get the Negro papers to check if something bad had been written about me, I was in my slippers and robe. So I sat there watching Maria line up a glass, the lemon squeezer and two oranges. With her back to me and my head in my hands, I listened to her story.

'This morning,' she said, 'like usual, I went over to the church before I come here. But today I was in for a big shock. It's usually so dim. Only the natural light from the stained glass and a glow from the rows of candles in their red glasses in front of the Virgin. Not today.' She shook her head like she was talking to herself and momentarily stared out of the window. 'Today, all the benches were pushed this way and that and had the rope around them. What you call that?'

'Cordoned off.'

'Yeah, and I'm wondering what's going on. Big white sheets covering the floor. Then I notice down the other end two ladders with a board between them, and right up high, I see a man standing on the board. He's in white overalls and he's got a big brush in his one hand and a can of paint in the other. I realize he's up there painting the church. Not that I thought it needed painting, but he's up there, so I think maybe nobody's allowed in. So I call up, but not too loud, as it's church; I'm half whispering. 'It's closed?

'I can't see him good, but I can tell he's slightly bald. You know, probably middle-aged. He says, "No, come on in. Pray all you want." He says it kind of happy like, so I try to be friendly. I'm still sort of whispering, trying not to be disrespectful to God like. "How are you today?" I say, as I'm making my way up to the altar. I usually light a candle but there weren't any . . . He says, "I couldn't be better. I love my work."'

Maria turned to me. 'He wasn't being a smart aleck. He meant it and it stops me dead in my tracks. I'm thinking about how good that must be, to love your work, and it hits me like a miracle.'

She could see that I was waiting for the point of her story. 'Yes' I said, '. . . and?'

'In this day and age, who loves their work? Look you crying because you're on the magazine, and me, I put my hands in the bucket of water and I gotta hum to keep from screaming. What if I was happy? What if I could say, "I love my work", then . . .'

'But it's no good just saying that you love your work, you've got to actually mean it.'

She smiled. 'It's okay. You don't get it. Maybe you had to be in the church with me this morning to get it.'

How could I ever have loved my work when it meant that if Sam came knocking on the door, I had to let him in?

And he did, often. 'I'm in a hurry,' he'd say, which meant he'd want to come in my mouth. Even after forty-odd years, I can't bring myself to think about it.

I remember waking each morning with the shakes. It wasn't just the drink. I didn't know what it was, but I would double up and bury my head in the pillow, gritting my teeth, conscious of an agitating tingle which ran from my fingertips to my toes. Had I been required to speak, it's likely that my teeth would have chattered, and in my head there would be a voice telling me, 'No, you can't do it, stay in bed, don't get up. Down, stay down, and they won't find you'. I would hear myself letting out pathetic little moans and have to force myself on to my knees, until I found the will to thrust my legs from the bed. If I couldn't walk to the bathroom, I would crawl, slowly, slowly, with another voice egging me on. 'Go on, Irene, you can do it, because who cares if you can't . . . They want to see you fall . . . keep crawling . . .' In the bathroom, I would bend over almost double, bracing myself to face the mirror, and all I saw were the flaws, the faint smile lines.

At parties or sitting in a restaurant, only a fugitive on the run could have identified with what I was feeling, but it was my job to look like a winner. I almost relaxed in front of movie cameras, because I was sure I was alive when I felt their heat on me and when I could play at being somebody else. But when I had to be Irene O'Brien, I was a fox being pursued by hounds. I never felt that I could relax until I'd had a few sips from the bottle.

Luckily, I was never a sloppy drunk. Didn't dribble food down my clothes when I was eating or stumble into a room.

The alcohol was my prescription for dulling the fear. If I'm honest, I felt the impending doom from the moment Henrietta Dobson told me to tell Sam the truth about my age, because I knew how much I had something to lose. But even in my happier moments, that sense of foreboding gnawed at me.

Sam could be so dismissive. 'You're coloured, Irene. There just aren't the parts,' and in another breath he'd say, 'You're a star and the only way to stay one is to maintain your mystery.'

The smallest things used to set me in a spin. Like the time I was cruising along Mulholland Drive, taking the bends slowly and trying to catch an occasional glimpse of the scenery on my right. I wasn't drunk, but by today's standards I would have been well over the limit. It was a warm day, so I had the top down on my Chrysler and the push-button radio was blaring. With my head covered in a chiffon scarf, I'd stuck my sunglasses on. I liked feeling the wind brushing my face. The car was the biggest luxury that Sam had given me, although it was in his name. It had every gadget and leather tuck and roll seats.

It was almost spring and with Mulholland being so high above the city, there was that sweet smell in the clean air. I pulled over to take to a look at the view across the valley, but before I could switch off the ignition, a bulletin came on the radio. The announcer's voice was a little mournful. 'For all those Lana Turner fans, here's a sad piece of news. Her Beverly Hills home was the scene of a murder last night when her daughter, fourteen-year-old Cheryl Crane stabbed and killed Lana's lover, Johnny Stompanato.'

That was the child that Lana was carrying when I was pregnant with Nadine. Sitting in my car, I put my head on the steering wheel and recalled how angry I used to get when Eugene compared me to Lana. Somehow I felt a connection with her. Our daughters, born around the same time, were both blighted by tragedy. Switching off the engine, I stepped out of the car. I had parked on a dusty verge, and my spiked-heels sunk into the dry earth. As I closed my eyes and leaned against the open door, images of Nadine drowning flooded me.

'It wasn't my fault. I didn't do it,' I cried out, inching towards the cliff edge. I was ready to jump, but a car roared by blowing dust in my face which snapped me back to reality.

It was 1958. Nadine had been dead many years, but with each that passed, her memory claimed more of my self respect and sanity.

Sam always pretended that he was trying to set up another picture for me, but I discovered that he had refused several times to lend me out to other studios. Miss Keating said that I looked too tired to shoot. 'Age,' she remarked. 'There's no place for it in Hollywood.'

When I turned thirty-seven in 1959, I wasn't working and was living on Sam's loans. I decided to treat myself to analysis because other stars did. It gave me something to do.

Recently it occurred to me that my depression back then may have been caused by an early menopause. Whatever the source of my problem, gin was the solution.

I had too much time on my hands and nobody to spend it with. So I slept, drank and shopped until the money ran out. I lived in my empty world, having strayed from family and the possibility of friends.

Fading movie stars. For all the times I went to bed feeling suicidal, by daylight, I was still hiding behind the pursuit of success, still needing to be looked at, although the glow had long gone from my expression. There must have been a dullness in my eyes, albeit disguised by a daily application of make-up.

I could label this period into the mid-sixties my Lost Years: lost my sense of humour, lost my drive. The new decade brought my forties and I was unprepared as a woman to face the realities of not being young.

Irene O'Brien existed vicariously through sips of gin and sleeping pills. The mild stupor replaced living.

PART IV

Venus Johnson

31

Los Angeles, the afternoon of 6 September, 1965 was both my end and my beginning.

I have never been able to recall being transferred from my apartment to the ambulance. When I gradually started to regain consciousness for the second time, I was only aware of how hot I was and how loud everything sounded. My first thought was, 'Get out of bed, Irene, you're having another nightmare,' because I regularly had my share of those. I felt seasick and noticed a repugnant smell, but still didn't know it was coming from me. Those ambulance men's voices which I'd heard earlier kept going round and round in my head. 'Guilty . . . honkies . . . this can't be *the* Irene O'Brien . . . Irene had bigger titties . . . you droppin' ashes . . . that's Bobby Lee with tired assed-Charlie Adams . . .'

In fact I was by then in a moving ambulance and Charlie had agreed to drive me to the morgue, while the other three had lunch. I was lying on my back and had been strapped to a trolley and fully covered by a sheet. Head included. I could wiggle my toes but nothing else moved. In the distance I heard a sports car rev and when a truck rolled past with its freight rattling, the noise seemed deafening.

I don't recall the ambulance's siren being on. Instead Charlie was up front singing in a high falsetto and straining to hit the highest notes of a romantic rhythm and blues tune. With the sheet covering my face, I couldn't see him, but guessed that he was young. He was singing his heart out. Really belting it. Like he had no audience and was driving along completely on his own. '*She's a gooood girl, but she wants to be free . . .*' that one line he repeated over and over.

241

Although I wanted to call out, my tongue and jaw felt numb. I kept telling myself, 'Whatever you do, Irene, don't go back to sleep.' But I must have, because the next thing I remember is that the front door of the ambulance banged shut, the two back doors were flung open and the trolley I was on was being shifted. Fortunately, the sheet slipped from my head and I was suddenly peering into the upside-down face of a brown-skinned boy in wire-rimmed glasses. Blinking a few times, I managed to produce one croaky syllable, 'Hi'.

His mouth dropped open. 'What the fuck!'

'I . . . alive . . .'

'Now that's a problem, lady, 'cause this is the morgue and I'm about to log you in the black book and stick you in a refrigerator.'

'I . . .'

'Aye-y'aye-y'aye is more like it. Fucking aye-y'aye-y'aye.'

Behind him, the white stucco walls of the morgue garage.

I squint looking up at the strip lights on the ceiling.

He checked his watch. 'My last day on this shit-ass job and Bobby Lee had to go to Fat Burger. I don't need this today. My taillight's out and I better get up to Berkeley before dark.'

'Take me . . .' I intended to say 'Take me home,' but couldn't get the words out. The omission set us on a path that would change my life.

He shoved the trolley with me on it back into the ambulance and climbed in behind it and slammed the door. Then tucking the sheet around me tightly, he lowered me to the floor. Stuffing two blankets into a body bag, he slung it on the trolley to roll it into the morgue.

I heard a metal door bang and him yell, 'Hey Henry, my last day! I'm registering my last body into the big black book.'

'Ain't much room in that fridge, Charlie. Folks drop like flies in this heat and we still got two Negroes from the riots.'

Then a metal door banged again and I lost consciousness. The next time I opened my eyes he was sliding me from the ambulance into his car.

*　　*　　*

When Charlie drove me up here to northern California that September of '65, it was raining when we arrived. Not a downpour. Just a heavy drizzle to make life more depressing.

El Sarita is how he pronounced the place.

El Cerrito is how it's spelled. It has that Mexican ring to it, so when I came to in his car and he said that's where we were headed, I somehow thought we were driving to a sleepy south-of-the-border town. It was totally out of character that I was prepared to go for the ride.

On his front passenger seat, I drifted in and out of my drugged sleep, unaware that we were driving north on Highway 1.

I smelled of garbage because of the vomit in what hair I had left.

How had he coped with the stench!

Funny what humans will tolerate when they've a mind to.

He kept saying, 'Wait till my Uncle Herbie hears about this scam. He used to be your biggest fan!'

Charlie Adams drove one of those old Volkswagen Beetles that every college kid in California seemed to own. As it chugged and putt-putt-putted along at fifty miles an hour, the radio would cut out over bumps and he'd bang the pale green dashboard like we used to slap Mr Herzfeld's Motorola.

'Irene O'Brien,' he kept musing. 'My Uncle Herb always wondered whatever happened to you.'

My mind shifted from crazy dreams to the futile effort of trying to recall what *had* happened and how I ended up in that car. Covering the torn upholstery were some old army blankets, one of which he'd thrown over me. Despite the hot afternoon sun, I was freezing.

He chainsmoked Gitanes and several empty packs littered the dusty floor. I couldn't help noticing his feet in their crude sandals made of thick leather straps and tyre-tread soles. To be cruddy was becoming a fad for some college kids and his feet were a testimony to it.

Charlie asked questions which I couldn't answer, because my lips wouldn't move and my head hurt like it was being clamped.

243

His voice was pleasant enough, but sometimes he'd enunciate like an elocution teacher and others he'd slur like a hoodlum. Half the bad boys around were mumbling like Marlon, who had made his name by mumbling like them. But Charlie was obviously educated although I had yet to discover that he had dropped out of Berkeley after his junior year.

Only three weeks earlier, South Central LA had gone up in smoke and I wanted to ask, 'And where were you during the Watts Riots?' because he suddenly struck me as one of those militant agitators who would stir things up.

I wanted him to turn the radio off and shut his window and as I tried to find the wherewithal to say as much, he asked, 'Why'd you want to fuck up your hair like that! Keep my tam on that ugly mop of yours otherwise somebody might think I'm out with my mother.'

It's a miracle that I survived that eight-hour journey.

When he reached in his glove compartment to grab his sunglasses, I slumped towards him and he shifted me back towards the door. 'Boy, you smell rough. You're gonna have to keep to your side until we can get you in the tub.'

Charlie thought that those shades made him look like Malcolm X who had been assassinated earlier that year, but he merely looked like a criminal. It's no wonder I couldn't read him at first, because he was a bundle of contradictions who said things to provoke me. Or at least that's what I thought. He talked tough but his manner was middle class.

Sitting out here under these stars tonight, I can see we began like two generations at war.

The car, the french cigarettes and Charlie's feet confirmed that he was some kind of beatnik, and I was suddenly afraid that rather than being rescued, I'd been kidnapped by one of those crazy student radicals. The previous fall, there'd been a big sit-in at Berkeley and although I remembered nothing about it, being the conservative I was, I didn't approve.

Every so often, his long caramel fingers would reach across to adjust my blanket or push the tam back as it slid over my eyes. I

244

kept wanting to scratch but couldn't and was petrified that under that coarse blanket, I was picking up some kind of skin disease from his dirty car. Ringworm or impetigo. Something that would mar my skin for life.

Curled on the seat, I was thinking, 'I hope he's washed his hands.' Despite their colour, the yellow nicotine stains were obvious. He used one cigarette to light the next.

My head was swimming, but my eyes were mesmerized by his bony foot pressing the gas pedal while his other hovered over the clutch.

'Berkeley's twenty minutes from my Uncle Herbie's house. It's a perfect hideaway,' he said above the thud, thud, thud of the music. 'He's gone back to Vietnam and left me the keys. That's where I've been staying.'

There was me thinking that we were near San Diego.

My brain wasn't working and I couldn't recall if I'd ever worked in Berkeley but was sure that Lil and I had sung across the Bay in San Francisco before Pearl Harbor. I stole a peek at Charlie again, whose baby face didn't look as though it had ever been shaved. There was a hint of a girlish moustache, fine hairs at the corner of his full lips. He was twenty-one but he could have passed for eighteen and treated those cigarettes with too much importance. Like they made a man of him.

Whenever that old VW bounced over a pothole, he'd momentarily lose control of the steering and once I managed to say, 'Take me back.'

But he kept driving north.

How many times since that day have I tried to comprehend how and why the two of us ended up in that car? Total strangers. Was he thinking that by helping Irene O'Brien that he had something to gain?

It still perplexes me. Even when I try to tell myself that back in the Sixties kids did wild, impetuous things, I can't see why Charlie took me on. Maybe he was looking for adventure and sensed that he didn't have much time left.

32

Northern California is so different from Los Angeles. Dull and sub-urban by comparison. At least that was how I felt about it in 1965. Although that summer Carole Doda was dancing topless in San Francisco to the tourists spilling into the North Beach streets, I had no desire for life and was relieved to hear from Charlie that El Cerrito was housewife territory, residential and far enough from Berkeley in distance and spirit to be a safe hiding place.

Irene O'Brien was no-one and nothing. Dead, by all accounts.

When I first got here, what I really needed was a strong drink, but Herbie, being teetotal, had nothing in the house. His old tooth-brush in a Donald Duck jelly glass was the only sign of life in the bathroom apart from a ten-year-old magazine photo of me sellotaped to the back of the door. There wasn't even a hook to hang a housecoat or a rail for a towel.

Charlie said, 'See. Told you. You thought I was jiving when I said my uncle was your numero-uno fan. He'll be over there in Vietnam crying in his Kahlua when word gets to him that you're dead. Boy, would I like to be there when he gets my letter saying that you're sleeping on his crumby sheets.'

And they were crumby. I couldn't tell if they were meant to be grey or white.

Herbie's few possessions, his fishing rod and basketball, were in the garage. That a man of forty had acquired so little in life was odd. The second-hand living room suite and the Formica dinette set with the two fake leather chairs belonged in a student dive. No doubt that's why Charlie felt so much at home here eating off paper plates with wooden picnic spoons.

There wasn't even any Vaseline for my cracked and bleeding lips.

Charlie was a little defensive about it. After rummaging around in the cupboard under the kitchen sink, he produced an old can of Spry cooking fat.

'Lard!' I said.

'Don't be uppity. My grandmother used to put it on her lips.'

He liked to give me the impression that he was from a deprived background, but his attitude reeked of somebody who'd grown up with more than enough. Privileged even. His button-down shirt hadn't been ironed, but it could almost have passed for Brooks Brothers and not many of us had attended the University of California in those days. Even his beautiful teeth were a giveaway, although he was embarrassed that I could tell that he'd worn braces.

The Bermuda shorts he loaned me said, 'middle class'.

'Nobody'll find us in El Cerrito,' he assured me. 'Aside from the fact that nobody comes out this way, the house is surrounded by trees and set back from the street. Just pray the FBI don't nab me.'

Initially he gave me the front bedroom which was hardly more than a dressing room with a mattress on the floor. He nailed a madras bedspread to the window and said, 'You can worry about your funeral in here.'

I'm not clear now whether it was in the car or on my arrival at the house he admitted that he was a draft dodger, but it seemed so unimportant in comparison to my own worries. No doubt that's what he really liked about me; I wanted to escape from life as much as he did.

Who else would have hidden out in this house with him?

For days that front bedroom was my cave. Thanks to Charlie playing nursemaid, I only left it for the toilet. How many times did I wake from a coma-like sleep to find my body wringing with sweat or discover the perspiration pouring from my neck and creeping to my chest? I would lie in the dark like an injured animal. Staring into space. Curled up tightly, with my hands locked together between my knees. Trying to be invisible.

Occasionally, Charlie would tiptoe in with a Kraft cheese

sandwich. Two slices between unbuttered white bread. Never on a plate. He'd hand it to me, holding it out between his long fingers with a 'Here. You can't lie around and starve to death.'

The RC cola bottles that I had drained dry lay haphazardly about the floor with the dirty towels he'd bring me to mop up my sweat.

'Must be I'm on the change,' I managed to say once. He was kneeling at the foot of my mattress wearing those sunglasses, although only a rose-coloured light filtered across the room through the red and blue madras bedspread over the window.

He tickled the bottom of my foot which I pulled away. I didn't like him getting familiar. 'Maybe it's the gin. Or every pore crying.'

'Have I been drinking gin?' I asked, suddenly interested.

'No. But you keep begging for it in your sleep.'

In that light his skin looked a copper colour. I examined him properly for the first time. He wasn't a pretty boy, but his features balanced evenly. The nose was broad and African. The full lips more Native American. The forehead high and wide. But his smile was his crown. The two front teeth were slightly longer than the rest and, despite his chainsmoking, they were so pearly that it was hard to believe they weren't a thousand dollars' worth of caps.

With his eyes hidden by those glasses, I had no idea what he was thinking as he perched four feet away, but I suspected that he didn't approve of me. At that stage, I didn't care.

'Why'd you bring me here?' I asked, drawing the dirty sheet under my neck in a coy pose. I was used to striking a pose and even in that uncomely state I felt naked without one.

'You asked to come,' he laughed, sucking his teeth.

'But why did you bother. Why did you go to the trouble?'

'Why not? Anything to fuck up the system . . . and how can anybody charge me with stealing you from the morgue? Had I stuck you in that fridge, my uncle would never have forgiven me.'

'Have you written to him?' I hoped that he hadn't.

Charlie took off the shades and rubbed his eyes. They were red-rimmed, I thought maybe he'd been crying, but it was just a sign that he'd been smoking a joint again.

'Vietnam. Even Cassius Clay knew better. I can't believe that

248

Herbie's gone back again. Like my Mother said, the career in the army screwed him up. When he got out the last time, he sat here watching game shows and *Search for Tomorrow*. He only went back over there to kill because he couldn't think of anything better to do.' Charlie slipped his glasses back on and rose to leave. 'No, I haven't written to him. It's sort of pathetic when you think about it, a grown man being in love with an old photograph.'

When I finally emerged from that room, I avoided the mirror. It was easy enough, because back in my apartment I had developed a technique for brushing my teeth without looking at myself, since I couldn't bear the reality. In my mind, I still looked like my best publicity stills: complexion flawless, with even a faint blemish erased by make-up or retouching, lips up-turned in a near smile, eyes as bright as moons and a confident gaze.

In truth, had I ever looked like that?

Even in the days of sitting for Henrietta Dobson, she used to tease me about the bags under my eyes, and at forty-three, they were pronounced. Like the slack skin on my neck and the smile lines around my mouth.

The only mirror that we had here back in '65 was on the medicine cabinet on the wall above the sink. To avoid seeing how my hair had been butchered, I'd allowed Charlie to wrap my head in an old green paisley scarf which he'd found in the garage. 'That do-rag suits you, Mama,' he said, standing back to make sure that he got the knot in front arranged in the middle of my forehead.

'Perfect for a mammie role,' I sighed, heading back to the dim bedroom.

Twice in one day I woke to find that the scarf had slipped off, and feeling the rough stubble above my ears where my hair had been butchered, I wept. Sure, I was prone to theatrics, but far less than other movie stars. In fact, I was always conscious of representing the race, since I was usually the only one of us on the set. Playing the diplomat. I had to be as gracious and rational as Ralph Bunche at the UN. Making a point of saying good morning to the lowly focus-puller and call the electricians by name.

The second time my scarf fell off was in the evening and Charlie happened to be entering the room with a cola for me. Tangled in the crumpled sheets in Charlie's khaki bermudas and one of Herb's dingy tee-shirts, I looked like a beggar. No make-up. Scarf lopsided. Hair matted from days of perspiration. Chipped orange nail polish. Angie, the hairdresser who used to visit me at the apartment, would have been appalled. But she wasn't there and Charlie was.

He drew so close, I could smell the marijuana on his breath.

'God, let me die,' I moaned.

'You've tried that, maybe you oughta try living a little.' He offered me what was left of a small joint which he held out, pinched between forefinger and thumb. 'Have a blow. You'll feel better.'

I pushed it away. 'I never left home without my bag matching my heels. I got my nails done once a week. And Angie came to me, because she said it was wrong for somebody of my stature to be seen in a salon with rollers in my hair.' I cried like a spoilt child, wiping the tears on the end of that grubby tee-shirt that I'd slept in for days.

Charlie said, 'Die, schmie. Calm down, lady! I'm gonna have to teach you how to relax . . . You're on holiday! Take it easy. There's no phone to bug you and no alarm clocks in the house. The way you've explained it, you've got no place to go.'

Then he started singing, 'When this old world starts getting me . . .' I realized that I'd been rescued by a mere kid.

I put both hands over my ears as he took a draw on the joint. The mild expression in his eyes shifted to one of irritation. 'What's with all this prissy white shit! Nobody said life was gonna be easy. You better get your nasty ass up and figure out your next move, because nobody's studin' you!'

'Who do you think you're shouting at!' I demanded, like a school-teacher.

'Laying around here feeling sorry for yourself. Has it crossed your mind that you don't even know me, but I've been waiting on you hand and foot for five days. What problems have you got! Take your black ass home to Hollywood and make a movie.'

'Nobody wants me,' I admitted self-pityingly, before sliding down further to boo-hoo beneath the sheet.

* * *

Charlie removed my picture from behind the bathroom door. I didn't know whether he did it out of cruelty or kindness, but I decided not to ask. Without it there I could sit on the toilet worrying about nothing but the coolness of the plastic seat against my behind. I didn't realize how much seeing that early image tormented me until it was gone. It was like a bully had been expelled from my playground.

Sometimes I sat there in that bleak little wash space and felt my cheeks and chin, pressed my lids and nose, parted my lips and ran a finger over them. Like somebody blind. I think that I was trying to see myself through kinder eyes.

Charlie had been the nurse, I was his patient, and this single-storey house with its five white rooms and barely any furnishing had become my private sanatorium.

From the windows, all I could see or hear was the wind in the cluster of pines and the unkempt grass surrounding the property. Charlie had removed Herbie's TV and transistor to the hall closet, and when I asked him to get me some newspapers so that I could see what was being said about my death and disappearance, he said, 'Get on your feet before you deal with that.'

My mind was as confused as somebody who'd been restricted to weeks in a pyscho ward. Charlie was still a stranger and I never knew what he'd do next. Sometimes he made me feel as vulnerable as Red Riding Hood confronting the wolf in her granny's bed. Like the time he brought me a cup of coffee and I complimented him on being so thoughtful. He said, 'We'll have less of Irene O'Brien. She's dead, so you better figure out who that makes you.'

'More paranoid than my sister Lilian,' I said. I was tempted to add, 'thanks to you,' but I was afraid he'd ask me to leave.

After a week, I woke up feeling more myself.

My stomach was less swollen, the diarrhoea was in check, and my eyes weren't so dry. Despite a headiness, I felt stronger and thought I would cope better with his jibes and teasing . . . He could treat a conversation like a chess game, and to talk to him exhausted me, because he wanted cute, clever answers. That's why I'd made a point of keeping to myself, but lying on a mattress in that stark room without so much as a poster on the wall was debilitating. Despite my money problems I was accustomed to sun and a little luxury. The odd carnation, and spray of perfume. Not to mention gin.

But that morning I put myself in check. 'Why start another day mad at the world. Be nice. Smile. You're old enough to be that boy's mother. Take control and stop feeling sorry for yourself.' Had I walked the Berkeley campus I would have discovered that my Hollywood mentality was at odds with the social climate. Students like Charlie wanted to change the world and would have found my vanity warped.

In that stuffy, self-imposed prison of a bedroom, I tried to re-evaluate my situation. 'This strange departure from real life is exactly what you need,' I told myself. 'Away from LA, you can get things into perspective.'

It suddenly dawned on me that I had probably lost weight, due to the diarrhoea, but without scales I was only guessing. I was euphoric. At forty-three, I still believed that all my problems could be solved by shedding pounds. I was deluded enough to think that if I could hang on here and fast, I would soon look good enough to take the world by storm. Grab the cover of movie magazines again like in '55.

Sexy. Gorgeous. Exotic. 'The first Negro to . . .' To have the press praise me had become an addiction. Without that I was in purgatory.

Curled on Herbie's lumpy mattress on the floor, having used one of his socks to tie back that pink and red madras bedspread at the window, I was snug with my daydreams, spending the money that I thought Fox would offer after Harry Cohn heard the rumpus caused by my reappearance. I envisaged 'O'Brien Alive!' headlines and imagined the big-time columnists ringing for interviews. I had the William Morris office begging to represent me . . .

I imagined an exclusive TV appearance on the *Steve Allen Show*, wearing either a low-cut cocktail dress or that blue pleated evening gown which I'd been too fat for. I thought about how I'd describe Charlie, calling him by a pseudonym to tell funny anecdotes about rescue by an ambulance driver.

I fantasized about headlines in the *Herald Examiner* and wondered what Hedda Hopper would write in her column about the pixie hair cut I was going to have to get since I was totally opposed to wigs. But, I didn't think about anything real. I didn't think about Mother or Lilian and Nadine didn't come to mind.

As the bedroom grew warmer from the direct sunlight, and my private sanatorium became a hothouse, I fell into a light sleep, but was soon tossing and turning from the nightmares.

When Charlie popped his head into the bedroom and saw that I was awake, offered to read. 'Maybe some Garcia Lorca in Spanish?' He claimed that he needed the practice and that foreign words would lull me to sleep, but he also wanted to show off: it was natural for a young man to want to impress me. He was a boy of twenty-one and although he claimed he hated Hollywood and didn't bother with movies, Irene O'Brien was somebody.

Having studied Spanish since ninth grade, Barcelona and Mexico City were two of the places that Charlie boasted about moving to to dodge the draft. I didn't approve of draft dodgers unless they were conscientious objectors, but I didn't think that he was my concern any more than I felt my return to Hollywood would have been his.

His Spanish accent was laboured but he sped quickly over the words, pursing those full lips to twirl his 'R's and glide over the *siempres* and *por exemples*. Perversely, I listened and watched with a certain envy.

I was relieved that he wasn't fluent but couldn't understand why. I hardly bothered to acknowledge him when he'd finished. Feeling guilty about it later that afternoon, when Charlie knocked on the door with a cold soda, I admitted being jealous of his youth and intimidated by his education. I jabbed his arm saying, 'You'd be in trouble if I were twenty years younger.'

It surprised me when he blushed. He was so nonchalant normally.

Later, when he was preparing dinner, frying the hot dogs and chopping onions, we seemed on better terms. As I stood by the stove watching him, he made me promise to come up here to the roof garden where he hung out after dark. It didn't seem much to ask, and I was curious about what was up here.

He didn't know that I'd decided that dieting was the way forward, so I insisted that he save my share of dinner because I knew that he wouldn't agree to eat it as I slipped off to the living room to avoid the tempting food smells. I fell asleep reading a *TV Guide* from April and woke to find him standing over me.

'The night's mild,' he said, offering a hand to help me up from the sofa.

Something forced me to say, 'Maybe I should go to bed,' but Charlie was insistent and friendly. As if layers of angst had melted away. 'Ready to forgive me for not rioting in Watts?' I joked, but refused his hand.

'Come on . . . I want you to see the stars twinkling. It's not just an expression. My uncle's got these plants . . . roses and vines. In tubs. They smell like muffins baking . . . This friend from Persia, Kay, he says the scent's like his mother's garden at home.'

In those days, Herbie only had a glorified ladder leading from the kitchen to the roof. I couldn't understand why someone with an acre hadn't planted a normal garden. But there was a lot about Herbie which didn't make sense: why he'd bought a house but hadn't married, why he'd returned to Vietnam after his army retirement, and why he'd chosen a sleepy suburb for his base when Chicago had been his home.

I discovered as I struggled to climb the ladder that I had hardly enough energy to boost myself from one wooden rung to the next. Charlie was behind and I was conscious of how wide my behind must have looked in Herbie's plaid Bermudas, but apologized for something else. 'Sorry . . . I'm slower than one of those women with gammy knees.'

'Keep going. Nearly there,' Charlie said, putting his hand on my butt to boost me. A branding iron couldn't have startled me more. It jarred me out of days, maybe even decades of somnambulance. I froze and my mind rampaged. How did I get there? What was happening? What was I doing on a a makeshift ladder in a paltry little house, hundreds of miles from home?

'Don't put your hands on me!', I exploded, addressing everybody who had ever taken liberties. I was telling Mamie, Mother, and men remembered and forgotten. I was telling every fondler, fornicator and manipulator who'd demanded more than I wanted to give that I wouldn't take any more. The venom in my voice should have pierced Charlie's eardrum.

He was backing off the ladder. 'I cook, do dishes, scrub the tub after I use it, read to you, and you act like you're doing *me* the fucking favour. You haven't given me a dime for food . . .'

As I looked down at him, his head blocked the light. The outline of his short wiry hair was all that I could make out, though I could feel his eyes boring a hole through me in his Ben Franklin glasses.

He perplexed me. What did he want? Why was I there? I couldn't get a fix on him. A boy with a dirty Beetle who folded towels and lined up his shoes although he smoked reefers? He'd been a captain in the Reserve Officers Training Corps in high school, but I wouldn't discover that until long after he was dead. For a boy who threw empty cigarette packs on the car floor, the precise way he laid the table and made his bed, tucking in the corners even if he didn't wash the sheet, made me think he was a psychopath.

'You can kill me,' I yelled, 'but I'll be damned if I'm going to make it easier for you.'

He huffed. 'Solid jack.'

With the trapdoor to the roof open, I could climb up or down. The roof. Or the kitchen. Panting with anger, I suddenly felt faint and pleaded, 'Somebody tries to kill me, you snatch me from an ambulance. Don't do it! Where's your compassion!'

Charlie was so unpredictable. His casual response took me by surprise. 'Hey, I've been thinking . . . why not bleach your hair. Start again. Why tell yourself it's too late? . . .'

I was thrown. 'I'm Irene O'Brien, you imbecile!'

Turning on the ladder, I slid down two rungs before Charlie grabbed my ankle to break my fall. 'You could get fat and sing rhythm and blues,' he laughed. 'Be a sort of LaVerne Baker. Or an Etta James. She's blonde, isn't she?'

Shaking my ankle free, I said, 'How did I get stuck with a dumb-assed nigger!' and scurrying up the ladder, I found myself out here in the pitch dark under a dazzling display of stars. White specks against black velvet. Stars. Stars splashed everywhere which threw me back to childhood and Mamie's yard in Bofield. A country sky. Each star was so bright against the dense blackness.

I had been living in LA, rarely leaving the apartment after dark and had forgotten the spectacle of a night sky.

The sight and the intoxicating air made me gasp like a baby catching its first breath in the world. I almost felt that I was choking. The sudden sensation of the pure air filling my nose, mouth and lungs was such a shock that I resisted it, coughing until I took a few short sniffs. What were the scents? Was it alpine or jasmine? The mix was as delicate and subtle as two threads tightly interwoven. Separate yet bound. I never imagined that air could be as sweet but in that darkness with my eyes straining to see, I could taste it.

That night Charie's voice drew me out of that moment's reverie. He was in one of his high raucous moods and shouted up, 'Smell that air, man! I get greedy for it and have to stop myself getting high on big gulps. I say, "Take it slow, Charlie. One sip at a time. There's more where that comes from." But wait 'til you see it on acid.'

This roof garden back then was more a notion than a reality. It was created by a city dweller used to making an outdoor space from little or nothing. Unlike now, there were no fancy redwood floorboards laid. Back then my bare feet were on rough bitumen.

When Charlie's head suddenly appeared through the trapdoor at my feet, the flashlight he was holding beamed across my toes to trace the back wall. 'Wanna soda?' he asked.

What I actually needed was some of the chicken soup Mother cooked for the Herzfelds when one of them was feeling out of sorts.

Even when called for, cross words and arguments made me nauseous. 'Losing your temper and shouting is just plain niggerish,' Mother used to say, and since that had been the last thing I wanted to be accused of, Irene O'Brien normally remained calm and dignified.

With Charlie's light exposing my grimy feet, I again imagined that I was about to faint and, bracing myself on that old painted turquoise chair that used to sit up here, I said, 'I don't know what you want from me!'

Then the dog started. It was a loud whine from a distance, but Charlie claimed it was a woman. 'I'm not up for another rescue tonight,' he moaned, before suddenly leaping like Tarzan back down into the kitchen and reappearing with socks and a sweatshirt. 'Soda's all gone, put these on. They're my girlfriend's. She's not back from the summer break.'

He was like no Negro boy I had ever known: one part Andy Hardy to one part Stokeley Carmichael with a dash of H. Rap Brown. He was a Jekyll-and-Hyde character, with his sensibilities tripping to outer space. I couldn't keep up with him. I couldn't decide whether Charlie had a personality disorder or it was down to the drugs and marijuana.

There was a silver moon that night. Settling myself on the turquoise chair, I couldn't relax. Not only was I afraid it would collapse with its wobbly leg, but I feared that Charlie might flip, though he sat on his blanket gazing at the stars.

He murmured, 'Better sit by me, that chair's gonna give way.' I didn't answer and the silence between us grew louder than drums, concealing our real instinct to shout at each other.

The Big Dipper and Venus were brighter than they are tonight, and after what seemed like hours, Charlie pointed to others, calling them by name. 'Did you know that because stars are immovable, they determine our movements for us?'

I didn't answer. Either it was the lack of gin, the lack of nutrition, or my general state of personal affairs, but I suddenly imagined that he was part of a great plot to kill me. Tonight I can laugh about it, but at the time, I was serious. With my delusions I had myself believing that my being found half-dead on the floor was related to a series of assassinations which included Jack Kennedy and Malcolm X.

Charlie lit a cigarette and before he could blow out the match, it nipped his fingers. 'Ouch,' he said, suddenly giggling. And then, we both heard a strange howl. 'Hear that,' he whispered. 'One minute I think it's a hound, but then it sounds like a woman ... I'm too stoned to play Lone Ranger tonight, and Herbie hasn't got enough room for another crazy lady in peril.'

'What are you planning to do with me?' I asked, like we were in an Alfred Hitchcock thriller. 'Cut the crap, Charlie.'

'What crap?' His smile was innocent.

'What are you planning to do with me?'

'Woweee, man . . . What have you been smoking? Why make out you're my prisoner? The door's open. But leave that sweatshirt . . . It's my chick's. Karen always claims I lose her stuff, so she actually made a list of everything she stuffed in the trunk.' I wondered what girl could love this boy. That sweatshirt was over my shoulders. It had a faint detergent smell.

The bright orange tip of Charlie's Gitane appeared to hang in space above him. Its cigar-like smell overpowered the delicate perfume of Herbie's few flowers. Relaxing my shoulders, I rolled my head about my neck to release the tension. 'I can go?'

'Tell the truth. Anybody with somewhere to go would have been gone. In fact they would have never come,' he laughed.

'Truth? Who's ever interested in the truth?' I asked myself more than him. My tears came without sobs. Just tears, which he couldn't have seen in the dark.

I'd already entertained him with my 'somebody-must-have-tried-to-kill-me' scenario to explain why the ambulance had come. I didn't have the strength to tell it again. It can get cold up here in September and my arms and legs were rough with chill-bumps

'We could head off for Persia,' he said. 'I hear that's really great. Or Morocco. Once I had some hashish from Morocco. I used to hate those Foreign Legion stories, with all that desert sand shit. So corny. But there's a lot happening I hear in North Africa.'

Had I been rescued by a raving lunatic, I wondered? It struck me that he needed to be humoured. I pulled the sweatshirt tighter around my neck and shifted slightly on the chair. Despite my mouth being bone-dry, I quipped with a most convincing little titter, 'If you don't kill me first, I'll be flying home.'

'You claimed you were broke. Can you afford that?'

Money had been my prime source of humiliation for years. His straightforward question tore at my pride and pretensions. I wiped my nose and tears on the cuff of Karen's sweatshirt and said, 'Considering that I'm twice your age, I admire your talent for making me feel small.' With that, I managed to step back down the ladder.

The house was poorly lit. An overhead light in the bathroom and hallway, no lamp in the living room and a broken bulb in the hall closet. I wondered again about what sort of man called the place a home.

On Herbie's mattress that night, I drifted into a restless sleep thinking about what awaited me in Los Angeles. I thought about Lilian and Mother and Sam who had tip-toed away quietly during the winter of '64 when I was declared bankrupt. I even thought about Nadine. But mostly my mind dwelled upon what had happened that night before those ambulance men arrived. I saw myself at the head of my bed in my white Empire-line nightgown, turning back the top sheet. I remembered noticing a small stain which I hadn't seen before. Then I checked that the telephone cord hadn't become lodged again between the receiver and the cradle, because earlier Angie had arrived to complain that my line had been engaged all afternoon.

Since I refused occasional dinner invitations, which I couldn't afford to return, I'd been resigned to another night watching the *Steve Allen Show*, and after turning the channel to NBC, I had slipped into bed with some sleepers which I chased with gin and tonic. So why had I been discovered eighteen hours later naked on my kitchen floor?

Curled on Herbie's mattress in an anxious but dreamy state, I had no answers and my thoughts switched to Charlie, who had whispered just as I was leaving the roof, 'But should my voice fade in your ears, and my love vanish in your memory, then I will come again.' His tone was seductive; he was a corner-boy playing the lover.

I guess everybody has some actor in them, and he had a double dose. His character changed as easily as he changed shoes. In those sandals, he was the protester with the joint up his sleeve. When he slipped on his polished brown loafers, he was Mr Clean-Cut College Boy just missing the letterman sweater. In the smelly sneakers, he tried to act the little hoodlum and barefoot as he had been that night, he sidled into playing the pensive prophet. Kahlil Gibran had actually written those sensuous words he'd uttered, but how was I to know?

I drifted off to sleep with that whiff of poetry dulling my senses. I was alone and needed everything.

So we gradually switched roles in my mind.

Fear cuts us down to childish levels and it made me more of a child than he.

I wanted to believe that Charlie was my rainbow.

Maybe that's the night I accepted that I needed him.

33

Hollywood nipped at me in nightmares, but from the moment my eyes opened in the morning, I forgot about it. I'd come up here to pluck at weeds in the tubs and dead-head the roses or read a bit of Herbie's old paperback copy of *Peyton Place* without being embarrassed that I needed half an hour for a couple of pages. Charlie would come to join me with that book by Roland Barthes who I'd never heard of but Charlie raved about.

He'd pore over a page, mumbling to himself from time to time or running down the ladder to come back with a pencil so that he could underline something. 'Check this out,' he'd say and read me a paragraph or two of something which went completely over my head. His enthusiasm for an idea was alien to me. I could get excited about a pair of shoes or an automobile, but I didn't know that people could leap up and down about a thought until I met Charlie.

One afternoon when the rain kept us off the roof, we sat in the kitchen together reading books. I was still on *Peyton Place* which occupied all my reading time and he was reading *Bonjour Tristesse* in French. I tried not to be impressed, but occasionally I'd study his eyes as they skimmed back and forth over the page. He had the bad habit of tapping his feet sometimes when he read, and although I tried not to let it bother me, I found it impossible to concentrate with him fidgeting. Charlie was smoking a cigarette as usual, so the kitchen was a little smoky as clouds of smoke clung to the ceiling.

'What's the date?' he suddenly looked up to ask.

I didn't know what day of the week it was and had begun to get the hang of not thinking about time. I knew it was still September and gave a thought to autumn, merely hoping that we weren't in for an early rainy season. But I didn't want to know the date. It was useful forgetting how long I'd been there.

Charlie said, 'I think my mother's birthday is coming and I haven't started making anything.'

'Making? Are we that poor?' We were using his money for food and I was eating as little as possible.

'I always make her something. It's a thing I started when I was in the scouts. One year I made beaded moccasins, another I made a sort of Mexican belt. Then it got to the point when that's what she expected.'

I'd given little thought to Charlie's family other than Herbie. It was part of our denial about the world outside. I gathered that both his parents were teaching in Rockford, Illinois, but we were so busy talking about me once I started to talk about myself, there'd been no room to discuss him.

Charlie scratched his head and studied his dirty fingernails before spinning his book on the table a few times. I went back to reading until he snapped his fingers. He beamed, 'Karen's art supplies are in my trunk.'

Rushing off to the garage, he returned with a large cardboard box which had to be slit open. KAREN SEDGEWICK was printed neatly in black marker on the top and sides.

Even before he could set it on the table to begin sifting through it, the scent of the oils and turps threw me back twenty-odd years, the term of Charlie's entire life. I wasn't concentrating on what he said as he pulled out the fat white tubes with their little black caps. It was as if he'd opened a familiar old music box and the melody which tinkled out could only be heard by me. It threw me back to the war. Back to Henrietta's. Back to those early days with Nadine.

Fragments of images flushed over me like a confusing day dream with Charlie's voice twisting in and out of it. It became too apparent how much of my life I had ruined before his had really begun.

With boyish excitement, he pulled out three long paintbrushes and lined them side by side on the Formica table. The largest had been used. In general, he couldn't have been more delighted had he won a big grab-bag at a carnival.

Charlie's enthusiasm broke through the gloom of the kitchen. He examined an expensive box of watercolours and small tubes of oils, some of which had never been opened. I looked at his girl-friend's extensive collection of pastel chalks and charcoals. The bright pinks and yellows were an anathema in that kitchen with its bare walls.

'*Voilà!*' Charlie barked, when he uncovered a small pad of art paper wrapped in a stained coarse-cotton smock which he shook out, sending the paintbrushes flying which had been wrapped in it.

'The walls could use a little mural,' I laughed, rising to leave as he bent over to retrieve the brushes.

'Aren't you gonna play?' He placed the box on the floor. 'There's room on the table for both of us . . . I'd sit on the floor, but there's not enough light down there for me to see what I'm doing.'

'Charlie, don't smells ever remind you of things you want to forget?'

He didn't answer but reached over to tug at the leg of my ber-mudas just as I made it to the door. 'You sit in that shitty old room too much. Like my mom used to say, "Put your mind to work and you won't have time to think . . ." I never understood the sense of that until I met you.'

I couldn't recall ever having held a paintbrush, and I'd never held a pastel until that day.

But there the two of us sat, with elbows resting on the table, bent over our pieces of paper with bowls of water beside us. Despite the rain and the dismal daylight, the kitchen suddenly felt as cheery as a merry-go-round, with a hurdy-gurdy playing.

I didn't even mind Charlie tapping his foot as he applied brush to paper while I made a few dots on my page.

'What's that gonna be?' he asked eyeing my crude efforts.

'Does it have to be something?'

'Not exactly. Somebody has to paint polka dots, I guess.'

'What do you want me to paint?'

'Whatever you want . . .' But I sensed that he was dissatisfied with what I was painting.

'It wasn't my idea to do this. I'm just going along with the programme. You should have said that I had to paint something specific.' After so many days with Charlie, I had learned when to challenge him and when to switch off. Yet too often I felt inferior. I assumed his education made him wise and I took it for granted that anybody who could read philosophy books could decide whether I should paint polka dots or trees.

Charlie said, 'Don't get crazy on me. I just don't want you to waste Karen's paints.'

'I thought you told me she was rich?'

'You said she was rich, I said her old man was a lawyer.'

'White lawyers are always rich.'

'You have a thing about Karen, don't you?' He pushed himself back from the table and the water in both bowls jiggled.

'Does her father know that his little blonde daughter is dating a Negro?'

'I'm not a Negro. I'm Black. So are you.'

'Don't you dare call me Black, you little hincty brown nigger!'

It was 1965 and I was still resisting the new label, but more importantly, I only pretended not to mind that Charlie had interests beyond me.

In truth I can't recall how we resolved that squabble. We had so many at first, before the change. Before I got the new face and the new name.

Holding that paintbrush is what mattered that day. Discovering that to concentrate on something as simple as painting a dot, relieved me of Irene O'Brien.

34

Ice Cream.

That's what Charlie called me.

It wasn't just a nickname, it served to cut me down to size.

It was also all I could eat after his 'surgery' on my face. He claimed that it hurt him more than me, but it couldn't have. To this day I can't recall if it was his brainwave or mine to bash my face up.

Just like I told him the afternoon that I sat on the edge of the toilet while he slipped the laundry bag over my head, 'Pain is half of what film acting's about.' Him smashing my face with one of Herbie's combat boots didn't hurt nearly as much as me getting into the ice-cold Pacific when I shot *Native Drums*.

I said, 'Charlie, If Jersey Joe could take it, so can I.' He was too young to remember Jersey Joe Walcott taking the heavyweight title once from Joe Louis. Nonetheless, that morning Charlie broke my nose, split both lips and put a gash across my right brow that changed my face so that nobody would bother to look at it.

The laundry bag was my suggestion, I know that for sure. It came to me when Charlie said that he'd never hit anybody and might have to stop when he drew blood.

It was willpower and pride that let me survive the thought of the blows, but it was really the morphine which numbed the pain and helped me endure the aftermath.

That day is a bit hazy to me now, but I know Charlie and I must have made a strange picture in the bathroom. He was barefoot in a pair of faded, cut-off jeans and his hair, which hadn't been combed for some time had flecks of lint in it. We hadn't said a cross word to each other all morning, thanks to the two joints we'd smoked.

'Acapulco Gold,' he'd murmured, licking the thin paper to roll the second, 'it's worth the extra expense. Best shit in the world.'

As I perched expectantly on the edge of the toilet seat, my hands clung to either side. I had days' worth of sleep caked in the corners of both eyes, because I'd given up washing my face. My head was tied in that paisley scarf I'd been wearing twenty-four hours a day for over a week, and, in one of Herbie's torn combat shirts half knotted at the waist, I was probably unrecognizable to anyone who had known me.

Retreating from the outside world, I'd let this house become a secret encampment of half-cooked hot dogs and burnt baked beans, star-gazing and drug-tripping. But it was no longer a holiday; I wanted to abandon my past life after Charlie'd said, 'There's nothing to go back to. Now. In the here-and-now. Haven't we got everything?'

It seemed like we did when I was hallucinating on my first tab of LSD.

As good as Charlie was at make-believe, he couldn't pretend that he wasn't a coward when he saw my blood staining the laundry bag after it had splattered that shirt, my forearms and my bony knees.

For days afterwards he kindly kept me in a stupour on the mattress in that front bedroom. Unable to speak through my swollen lips, or breathe through my swollen nose or see through my closed right eye, I stayed too high to think, grateful when he'd hold me in his arms to help ward off the edges of pain which tried to slip past the doses of aspirin and morphine. He always seemed to be at the edge of my bed asking, 'How you holding up, Ice Cream?'

I drifted from one high to the next. Out of touch with any frames of reference to Irene O'Brien, I played at adolescence. Yet discarding who I'd been threw me at the most unexpected times.

Like the afternoon I'd been napping on the sofa while Charlie had taken off for Berkeley to score from Percy, his drug dealer. I was coming to from drugged somnambulance without him there for me to perform to. Lying half comatose on the sofa with not as much as a clock tick to connect me to reality, I stared at the stucco swirls on the ceiling and thought about nothing in particular, until I noticed my fingernails.

Using one thumbnail to scrape away the chipped orange nail varnish on the other, I recalled how much I had enjoyed having Angie, my hairdresser, shape the nails before painting them. Even when I could no longer afford to indulge in a full manicure, I'd been careful about my hands which had often got compliments.

Suddenly I smelled myself lying there. Where was the immaculate Irene O'Brien, doused in lotions and powders and sweet from the hint of Chanel Number 5? Who was the vagrant with the long toenails stretched out in Charlie's Y-fronts which were a muddy pale blue because he'd thrown them in a machine at the laundromat without noticing that somebody doing the previous wash had left a dark sock in the drum?

Since Charlie had bandaged my face and taped a paper bag over the mirror to reduce the temptation to examine myself, I hadn't. 'That will just blow your mind. I'll let you know when it's time,' he'd said, playing the nurse and doctor.

But lying there looking at my dirty nails, I let out a piercing scream that should have brought out the fire engines from ten blocks away. Yet it was Charlie whose head suddenly peered around the doorway. He was wearing his glasses which he pushed back on the bridge of his nose before throwing me a beguiling grin. 'I scream, you scream, we all scream for Ice Cream!'

Had I been able to see that he was wearing his sandals, I might have guessed that I was dealing with Charlie Adams, protester.

'I knew that I should have taken you out. Weather's great. Sun is shining ... But I have to be careful ... I hate going to the supermarket after I've scored, so you've got vanilla from a little corner store. There was no big cherry. No peach. No strawberry.'

Ten months earlier, I'd owned nearly a hundred pairs of shoes, rented a nice house in Brentwood with a pool and employed Velasquez and Lola, a Portuguese couple to look after the house and garden. I never even went to the liquor store because I bought by the case and had it delivered.

Like a child who had tired of a game and wanted to go home, I started crying. Placing the brown paper bag that he was carrying on the floor, Charlie came to sit beside me. His voice assumed a motherly tone. 'Look, anybody in your shoes would be dazed. Angry. Fragile.' The whites of his eyes were bloodshot and he was wearing his khaki trousers, a short-sleeved shirt and those horrible sandals.

'I want a bra,' I cried with the gauze bandage scratching against my top lip. 'And stop calling me Ice Cream.'

'So what do you want me to call you? Irene O'Brien's dead.'

At forty-three years old I had tampered with my life like a wayward teenager who'd got in with bad company.

The sofa had a loose linen cover on it. Big flowers. Still, it was the least ugly thing in the house. Yet it was also the least visible, because Charlie hated to open the blinds. We'd become night owls who rose late in the afternoon and stumbled to bed at dawn. With only daylight slipping in either side of the blinds, the living room was a cove. 'I've been keeping a surprise for you worth ten bras,' Charlie suddenly said.

'I haven't got shoes! How long have I been here?' I demanded.

'A couple weeks, maybe more,' he said going to the pile of books which either he or Herbie had stacked three feet high beside the fireplace. They tottered at an angle and it was obvious that when he slid out the dictionary all the rest would fall. 'Lemme read you something.'

'You're some kind of nut!' I grew hysterical and leapt up. 'I've got no money, no clothes and a broken nose. I don't need for you to read, I need help.'

Charlie wasn't listening. 'Come in the kitchen. I've been saving this . . . They got you wrong. You ain't no star, you're a planet.'

'Why do you say ain't and wear those stupid sandals. Goddamn college boy trying to play the nigger!' As he headed for the kitchen, I followed and when my nose started dripping, I yanked off the head-scarf to wipe it, mumbling, 'How'd I get stuck with a draft-dodging dope fiend?' At that moment I wanted somebody rich and white as my Sir Galahad. With manicured nails. Preferably old and powerful, in the movie business, who flew first class and had his Vegas gambling debts settled. It wouldn't have even worried me if he had a wife.

Charlie placed the dictionary on the table with the bag of ice cream and started flicking through the pages. The kitchen was the only room with sun coming in and I squinted against the light streaming through the window. September here can be beautiful and as he slumped onto the chair, he blocked a sunbeam. Reaching into his shirt pocket for a cigarette, he lit it and cleared his throat.

The linoleum on the kitchen floor was cold against the soles of my feet so I turned to head back into the living room, but his voice caught me by the throat. 'Bankrupt . . . here it is . . . it perfectly defines your situation. "Destitute. In utter want. Forsaken."'

'I don't have any nail-polish remover,' I sobbed, placing that nasty head scarf over my mouth.

Charlie threw me a mean glance and pushed the other chair out with his foot. Its four metal feet squeaked in unison. 'Sit down and don't dare start crying, because I can't keep changing that bandage. You're gonna eat this ice cream and then I'll run you a bath. I was planning to save the gin for tonight, but looks like you need it N-O-W.' He pulled a small bottle from his pocket.

'Gin?' Days had passed without me thinking about it. How many years had it been since Tommy Furness introduced me to the taste? How much secret drinking had I done; hiding bottles in hat boxes, driving out to remote spots to toss the empty bottles so that nobody would discover how much I'd consumed.

Charlie beamed with self satisfaction, 'I left the quinine water in the car. I'll get it as soon as I've rolled myself a joint.'

'I'll have some of the joint,' I said, hoping that I was making the right decision. 'I'm off gin.'

Later that night, the stars weren't very bright. Charlie and I lay side by side up here with our arms barely touching. With my eyes closed I fingered the stubbly roof covering. Charlie inhaled a big gulp of the thin joint and spoke through clenched teeth to keep it in. 'If your ass had been white,' he said, 'somebody would have bothered looking for you. Lucky you cullid.' He giggled. The joint was taking effect. He was forever giggling when he got high. Doubling up in fits of laughter about something that wasn't that funny. 'Fuck Irene. It'll be a cinch to start over. Crooks do it all the time, and the good thing about you is that you can claim you were born down South. In my last sociology class I read how Black people of my parents' generation didn't even get birth certificates in places like West Virginia and Alabama. All you have to do is pick a name out of the sky. Like Venus.'

'Venus! What kind of name is that?'

'Irene was only a star. You're bigger than that, right? Open your eyes, girl.' He shook my shoulder and pointed towards the sky. 'See the brightest one? That's Venus. She got her own stars.'

Suddenly jumping up he ran down the ladder and returned with a book. 'Listen to this,' he said slumping back down beside me. He was wearing his cut-offs and his knee touched mine. 'Venus. Originally the Roman Goddess of spring, it says. But the best bit is that she's Mother of the Race. You check this out tomorrow,' he said, placing the book in my hand.

Having the rose vines and jasmine growing up here in barrels seemed peculiar but it was magical at night. That scent and the sound of trees fluttering in the breeze always made me feel that we were on a mountain above the world.

Charlie's voice grew dreamy. 'She's the patron of the flowers.'

'Venus,' I laughed. 'Wasn't she beautiful? I'll look like a crocodile when these bandages come off.' Everything was a game, and it was exciting that Charlie's head was crammed with terms that were totally foreign to me. Like Oriental philosophy. Charlie wanted to talk about Roland Barthes like other people talk about film stars, and I'd never met anybody like him. He thought showbusiness was irrelevant which may be what gave him power over me.

'Venus,' he said like he was trying it out. 'Venus . . . sounds like a stone fox.'

Charlie. Even with that dirty bandage on my face, he could make me feel beautiful.

Then we had that week when we didn't speak. He was definitely play-acting that he was the prophet, because he didn't wear shoes.

We'd communicate through eye contact, gazing at each other through the smoke screens of pot and hallucinogens.

Silence is healing.

And under these stars we were not lost.

35

I'd been here for weeks and didn't care to know that the house was only a mile from the freeway or that within twenty minutes I could walk to the stores on San Pablo Avenue. It didn't matter that from a bus stop half a mile from here two dollars could have bought me a ride across the Bay Bridge to San Francisco. Charlie had informed me that we were in a middle-class district where young mothers drove their two kids to school in a station wagon, and I felt in no danger of bumping into them, because at no time did I consider going out.

The fall semester had begun on the Berkeley campus and Charlie found excuses to drive there daily. I pretended not to mind, until Karen asked him to return her cardboard box. When I saw him drive off with all our art supplies, he thought tears were welling in my eyes because he was staying out that night. I said, 'Of course I'm not jealous. It's the paints I'm down about.'

Despite Charlie's criticism, when I painted those polka dots, creating those red and blue circles with that long brush between my fingertips brought a feeling of calm, a sense that beyond the chaos was peace. I could understand how a Henrietta in her stained smock was content in her world of colour. I even thought about the story which Maria had told me about the painter in the church saying, 'I love my work'.

So Charlie came back one day with a brown bag of paints and paper for me.

'This ... didn't this cost you a fortune?' I asked, but I was so excited when he emptied the bag at the foot of my bed.

'Five-finger exercise,' he said, twiddling his right fingers at me.

'Stolen! Suppose they caught you! Then where would I be?'

'Without me.'

Less than a month after he'd driven me here from the morgue, I watched Charlie slip on his sandals to go to a political rally on campus. He was wearing a black leather jacket that I hadn't seen him in before 'That looks good. Have you got a date for this rally?'

He stood up and reached for my hand. His was soft but his clutch was firm. We were standing in the hall and he laced his fingers in mine. It was a gentle move and I felt a little rush. He could bring out the schoolgirl in me, but as usual, I had had a few tokes of a joint and was high. 'Ice Cream, I'm afraid you'll melt in this house,' he smiled when he noticed my blush. 'Put on your red dress, and let's take a ride.'

'I no longer have a dress. Red or otherwise,' I laughed.

'You haven't been out since I drove here from LA, little Mama.' He pulled me to him but stopped short of an embrace.

'What are you doing, Charlie Adams?' I asked, pulling my hand away.

'It's time to pony,' he said doing a quick dance step, 'it's time to ride. Come on, let's go to Cal.'

'The campus?'

'Where else?'

'You're kidding.'

'What do you do here alone?' Charlie asked.

He knew that I did my little paintings, but he didn't think I had any talent. Or he didn't see anything in my polka dots or my faces of a brown girl screaming. So I didn't want to admit that that's what I did when he was gone. 'I read.'

I had good reason to fear the outside world. Especially going with him to a rally to be surrounded by a lot of educated kids, who knew more than I did. 'What if you get a flat and I have to get out of the car? These bandages could draw attention.'

'Are you getting agoraphobic on me?'

He often meant to demean me when he used exotic words. 'Always trying to be smart,' I chided in my marijuana daze.

'You're scared to leave this goddamn house. I should have known this was going to happen.'

'You're the one who's wasting good food money on gas.'

'It's only Berkeley. Nothing special. We don't even have to hit Telegraph Avenue and there'll be so many people at the rally, nobody will notice you.'

'Everybody's white, for one thing,' I argued.

'And since when did you get race conscious?' he barked. He still had a grip of my hand and pushed it away.

'You ought not to be in the streets anyway,' I said. 'I thought you were supposed to be afraid of getting caught? What about all your big talk about heading for Spain or Mexico?' The longer I'd been with him, the more I'd fantasized about us going away. He had talked about it when I first arrived, and although the thought had seemed absurd then, it seemed possible that we could head off to Argentina or someplace and live by our wits. 'Karen's back and . . .' I stopped myself.

'Nobody in Berkeley is going to know who you are. Is that the problem?'

My mind was cloudy but a couple of things were clear. 'I can't go out without a name. Who am I supposed to be?' Ageing had plagued me for years, but with no identity, I felt that I was missing something more essential than limbs.

Charlie laughed. 'If I have to introduce you to somebody, I'll say your name is Ice Cream.'

It dawned on me that I had erased myself.

What face?

Whose name?

The drama of this overwhelmed me, and I saw myself as one of the dispossessed out begging on Wells Avenue after the Crash. It was my primal fear. To be out on the street, homeless, without so much as an ID. I felt as vulnerable as little Irene Matthews again and the confusion of the world took a grip of me.

Charlie was insensitive to my panic. 'Venus . . . that's what we're calling you. Venus . . . Johnson . . . Venus Johnson. Like it? My grandmother was a Johnson. It's a good ol' Smith kind of name.'

'Venus Johnson sounds like a mammy,' I cried. 'Sometimes you're a simpleton.'

Charlie snatched off his glasses and rubbed them hard on his shirt. He did that when he was exasperated. Yawning and scratching his head as if what we were talking about wasn't a matter of my life and death. 'Okay, stay,' he conceded. 'But the buzz on campus would do you good and people mind their business. Students. You know what they're like. Everybody's running around with courses to think about. Lectures. Nobody's thinking about nail polish. In fact, there's this one girl walks around with her hair standing on her head . . . Way worse than yours. You can't waste away in here. Get out there, Ice Cream! The revolution's coming.'

Revolution.

He sounded so infantile.

'Revolution?' The word dragged me back to reality. Charlie was a kid from another generation. What was he doing holing up here with me? It struck me that he was a mere boy who should have been out dribbling a ball on a court or chasing some cheerleader. How had life driven him into our dark den?

I looked at him and saw Eugene. Remembered his dreams for Nadine when he'd show her his trumpet, and suddenly there in the hall she appeared, a phantom that I tried to reach out and touch. Raising her lowered head, she smiled at me, a young lady with her hair in a ponytail and Mother's eyes.

Anytime I had had visions of Nadine, she had always been the child in the Mississippi or the toddler rocking or the beautiful baby I'd used to hold back the world. But there she was, so real that I tried to touch the girlish dress she was wearing over layers of starched crinoline. She could have been a high-school pom-pom girl out to cheer on the team at a big game, and she was standing shoulder to shoulder with Charlie. I was about to ask if he saw her too, but she whispered, 'Mom, I'm going steady. I knew you'd like Charlie.'

To see her smiling. To hear her claiming him. Somehow it added to my deflation and tears clouded my eyes. 'Go,' I said pushing at her but pushing Charlie instead. 'You two go on out and have a good time.'

275

As I turned to head towards my bedroom, Charlie blocked me. 'Hey, it's okay. Calm down. We'll find a better name . . .' He put his arms around me and the scent of his leather jacket was stronger than the smell of cigarettes and marijuana, stronger than the must of his hair as he pressed his head against mine. For a moment we stood in the dim passage dead still, but then he started guiding me in a slow drag that was almost dancing. A gentle embrace, rocking me in a circle. Had I ever been held with such innocent intent? His long arms were wrapped around me, conforting me like so many angels' wings, until the voices of those first two ambulance men crept around me. 'She had bigger titties than these . . .' I felt the flush of frustration and humiliation that used to flow through me anytime Sam stood over me unzipping his pants. Breaking away from Charlie, I yelled as if he'd accused me of something. 'I did what I had to!'

He was nonchalant. 'Lord, lady. You and your Catholic guilt,' he sighed going into the kitchen which was behind him. 'Time for a soda.'

The Pepsi generation. It was a miracle that he had any teeth.

By the time he was sitting with me on the edge of my mattress, I had already forgotten that an identity crisis had caused that sudden anxiety attack.

Incidents from my past still controlled me. As much as I longed for a new self, Irene O'Brien had a stranglehold on me.

Charlie eased himself back on the mattress and took a swig from the cola before passing it to me. I had both knees drawn up and rested my chin on them. 'Stop fucking with your head,' said Charlie, throwing a pillow at me. 'Venus Johnson in the Here-and-Now. Let Irene O'Brien stay dead. I believe in you, man . . . I know you can do it. Say it, "I'm Venus Johnson. I'm here. It's now."'

'The past can't be brushed aside like that.'

'Weren't you the one with that stupid motto, "What you can't forgive, forget"? My point is, forget it all. New life. Clean slate. You won't be the first person who's done it.'

'Nadine . . .' I placed the pillow on my knees and placed my forehead on it. I wanted to speak words that wouldn't come. 'My daughter . . .'

He reached over and grabbed the back of my neck. 'All the guilt in the world, right? Forget her. Come to Berkeley.'

'It's immoral to forget her.'

'So look at it another way. If she could forgive you, do you think she would?'

'How do I know?'

'Come to Berkeley, I'm telling you. We could go to one of those Vincent De Paul's and get you some stuff.'

'Charlie,' I said quietly, crooking my head to the side so that I could see him. 'I killed that girl.'

His arm, stretched to its full length so that he could keep his hand on the back of my neck, yanked me forward. 'Here's what happens at a rally. Probably be about a thousand people. They'll have some speakers and . . .'

'I killed my daughter. Don't make a joke of it.'

'How many times does a Catholic have to go to confession for the same sin?'

'Once.'

'So pretend that I'm the priest and you've been.'

My calm covered a truckload of desperation. Maybe I felt the way Mother did when she stood in the alley explaining what she and Mamie had done. I wanted Charlie to be shocked. Appalled. Disgusted. 'She was five and I let some people take her down to the river.'

'I'll say it again.' He bent and his mouth brushed my ear. 'Now is what matters, and here's something else that my father used to tell me: "The cavalry is not coming. That only happens at the end of cowboy movies." Living in the moment is all that can save us. Not God. Not dope. Not guilt. And I'm not the twenty-fifth cavalry.'

36

In October the weather can be at its finest. Warm days, moderate nights and little rain. Grateful for the water that I'd been giving them, Herbie's rose bushes had a sprinkle of blooms. Raucous pinks and reds. I never have been good with names of trees, and back then I didn't know that there were manzanita and bearberry trees growing around the house. I just recognized the eucalyptus and still wonder if their round leaves make a different sound when the wind blows through them.

Though I relied on him during that time we shared, each time I heard the motor of Charlie's VW rumble out of the garage, I waited on tenterhooks wondering if he'd get high and tell somebody that he was harbouring Irene O'Brien. I hadn't met Karen Sedgewick, but I suspected that Charlie was in love with her and that they talked, though he swore he never talked about me. I wanted to believe him, because he never talked about her either beyond a passing reference. It made it easier to forget that he was hers.

My deep affection for him was bound up in the common things: his childish honesty, the enthusiasm he could have for a song. I can see his smile the day he found a 45″ record player in a cardboard box in the garage. He carried it through to the kitchen, holding it in his arms like it was a big puppy and sat it on the table. It was covered in dust, but he refused to wipe it down with a rag. 'This thing needs special care,' he said, and decided that the only thing suitable for cleaning it was a toothbrush.

'That thing probably won't work,' I said, 'and we don't have any records anyhow.'

'Wrong again, woman,' he said. 'There are three forty-fives in that hall closet behind the TV set.'

Unfortunately, one turned out to be 'Maria'. '*West Side Story*,' he moaned. 'Not Ahmad Jamal. Not Fats Domino. Not Screamin' Jay Hawkins, but "Maria". I hope when I see my uncle, he can explain this. Maybe a friend of his left it.'

He had taken a tab of LSD a few days before and was still seeing patterns when he stood in the kitchen trying to plug the record player into a socket. I knew the signs. He could be moving around quite normally and suddenly stop short to stare at something as mundane as the linoleum or the wall. Having bent down with the plug in his hand now, he was motionless, staring at the skirting board.

The record player was one of those automatics that we had all marvelled over in the fifties, because you could stack ten records on it and it dispensed one at a time, with the arm managing to jerk over each record as it was about to be played.

'People don't dance enough,' said Charlie, when I'd got one of the two records playing and steered him up here.

The first on the turntable was Little Anthony and the Imperials singing 'Love is a Many Splendoured Thing'. It was slow and moody, the lead voice whining over the dark backing vocal behind it. When Charlie asked me to dance, I refused, so he put his arms out like there was a woman in them and danced by himself. Not in the least self-conscious, nor putting on a show for me, he closed his eyes and moved his feet slowly while the hypnotic melody led him further into his trance.

I admired his body. He was lean without much muscle. That young body not liable to fill out for years. He was wearing his baseball shoes which had grass stains on the rubber soles.

I was sorry that I wasn't dancing with him and thought about boys like him, perfect strangers, that I had once danced with at the Canteen because they were soldiers.

37

An envelope which I still have downstairs dated Berkeley, 12 October 1965 contains the only letter Charlie wrote to Herb about me. I don't know where the letter got to, but I remember the afternoon that we sat up here composing it. It was the day after I'd asked Charlie to buy some scissors to cut off what was left of my hair. I was sitting on that Indian blanket with some tubes of paint nearby on that old rickety turquoise chair. Charlie was perched on the parapet with a pad of paper and a pen in his hand. Of course a cigarette was dangling from his lower lip and he had his glasses stuck on top of his head. The sun was behind him and to look his way, I needed to shade my eyes.

'Shouldn't we tell Herbie what you do?' Charlie asked.

His letter had introduced me as Venus Johnson, a Catholic from Los Angeles who could look after the place for seventy dollars a month with the rent and utilities free. I didn't mind what Charlie wrote, because I assumed that I wouldn't be here without him. Sitting idly on my blanket, I was thinking that wherever he went, I would figure out a way to join him. We had already mulled over ways for me to make a living without being able to produce a Social Security card.

I was being snide. 'The thing about prostitution is that the job requirements are the same all over the world.'

'Whoring and housework are on the shit list. It's 1965, man, a Black woman doesn't have to do that. Think of something that doesn't require singing, acting, dope-smuggling, Hollywood or anything to do with the public. Otherwise, you're bound to get caught. We have to consider this logically.'

That air on my scalp. Our voices dodging back and forth amidst the birds twittering. I felt heady and young and although he didn't know, I had a terrible crush on him.

For years I had been an expert at burrowing, and there I was with a man-child in my cave. His chainsmoking had ceased to annoy me, I didn't mind his foot tapping while he read, and my ego didn't call for time-out when he'd force some Lorca or Neruda on me in Spanish. Noticing the pleasure I got from washing his underwear in the bathtub, he insisted that I not do it again. 'God,' he said, 'the next thing, you'll be asking me what I want to do with my life. It'll be like hanging out with my mother.'

Every time he warned, 'Ice Cream, you know this isn't forever,' I knew that he was being cruel to be kind and I wonder how many mothers with twenty-one-year-old sons wouldn't have been surprised by his thoughtlessness that October 12th when he dropped his pad and stuck his pen behind his ear saying, 'In case Herbie missed it, why don't I send one of your obituaries? He'll never associate Irene O'Brien with Venus Johnson and he'd probably appreciate it.'

I tried not to look stunned. Being 'cool' is what he respected. 'I thought we agreed that you weren't going to tell anybody about me. To expect him to keep the secret is . . .'

Charlie interrupted. 'He'd want me to tell him that you died. I mean, say it was the other way around and say Mary Wells died, and I was off in the boondocks, I'd want him to tell me.'

With my left hand shading my eyes, I checked his expression, because with Charlie there was always the possibility that he was teasing. Slipping his glasses on, he was about to go downstairs, and despite sounding normal, I spoke through clenched teeth. 'You never mentioned that you've been saving my obituaries.'

He was halfway down the ladder. 'You told me to when you first got here.'

What about your N-O-W? I was thinking.

With the trepidation I used to suffer before reading my film reviews, I waited, expecting him to return with a thick pile of newspaper clippings to prove that I'd existed. That I'd been important. Maybe finally presenting me with those obituaries was his way of lowering the Irene O'Brien coffin into the ground, so that we could shovel earth upon it.

Charlie and Ice Cream.

We had so little time left and so much to do.

The half page he handed me made me giddy. To hold back a rush of nauseousness, I swallowed hard. 'This is from *Confidential*?' I quipped to hide my horror. 'Even the paper it's printed on looks cheap and nasty.' As my eyes scanned the page, Charlie was hanging over my shoulders. I twisted away. 'Boy, will you sit down and let me read this in peace.' I had broken out in sweat and wiped my brow with the tip of the old tee-shirt I had on.

Somebody had photographed me nude on the kitchen floor. The black censor boxes covering my privates made the picture more grotesque and titillating. The thick headline running across the page said, NEGRO MOVIE STAR IN SUICIDE DRAMA. My body was curled like a foetus but one shoulder was back, so a bit of my breast would have been exposed had it not been for the black box. My mouth was open and bits of my hair surrounded me on the floor. I could have been a rape victim or murdered corpse.

Hovering inches away from me on the roof, Charlie said, 'You have to laugh. First off, you ain't dead, and second, why are those papers so trashy? Look how they blew up your suicide note and stuck it in that black box. What about copyright!'

The note was almost as big as the picture, and the writing was as crude as what it said. 'To whoever finds my body, Could you please phone my mother, Ruthie Mae Matthews, and tell her that she mustn't talk to the newspapers. She may keep the TV and I wish to be cremated.'

'Who wrote this. God, I should get a lawyer! I wouldn't put it past Sam. He probably saw how he could re-sell my old pictures.'

'Oh-oh,' laughed Charlie, lighting a cigarette and slipping the matches in his pocket. 'I'm leaving if you're about to go on one of your paranoid rampages. I thought you were over them. Next you'll say I'm trying to kill you. Naw, naw, naw,' he said waving his hands in the air and backing back. 'That looks like *your* handwriting.'

The picture jarred me. I felt like I'd been sleepwalking and it was my wake-up call. 'Bastards. After all I did!'

'What did you do?' Charlie asked turning his face to the sun and blowing smoke rings.

I paused for a moment. My achievements escaped me.

'See, you *do* have to think about it.'

'I was nominated for an Oscar.'

'Ten years ago. And you said yourself that you thought Sam pulled the wool . . .'

I was so enraged by Charlie that an image flashed through my mind of me running over and pushing him off the roof. 'How can you say that! I had my picture on magazine covers. I made movies. People . . . take your uncle with my picture in his bathroom . . . I helped uplift the race,' I huffed.

Charlie said, 'Wait now. Let's tell it like it is. I know splibs in Watts that would put me down for hanging with you.'

'Why?' I asked disbelieving.

'Could be said that you were just a token nigger,' Charlie ridiculed in a sing-song voice.

'What is it with you!' I leapt up, but my right leg had gone to sleep, so I started thumping my calf as Charlie came over holding out his matches. 'One minute you say fuck the race,' I told him, 'and the next thing you're calling me a token nigger?'

Turning away I rubbed my hand over my ear, and was reminded that my hair was gone and with my eyebrow still bandaged, it was all I could do to keep from screaming. Charlie snatched the obituary from my other hand, and I stood there overwhelmed by despair. Traumatized and having to balance my weight on one foot.

He held the clipping up and was still trying to pass me the matches. 'Remember what you told me about that picture you used to keep of Dresden. How it was all rubble and had to be rebuilt? Think. This is a piece of paper I'm holding. And this woman in it. Her past? Her future? What exactly is it you're holding onto?'

I thought about what he was saying. We were out here with that delicious smell. No breeze. Only socks on my feet. I accepted the

283

matches reluctantly, as Charlie put his arms around me. 'That's my girl.'

'I didn't try to kill myself,' I told him quietly.

'Do we have to start that again?'

'I didn't try to kill myself, but maybe I have an answer for the hair, because I vaguely remember having a dream that night. It keeps coming back in flashes . . . Marilyn . . . Monroe . . . you know? She and I were in a hotel room together. One of those sort of New York hotels. Fancy. Neither of us were wearing make-up. We were young and had called room service but couldn't get a reply. It was one of those dreams, time and space were out of synch and we were both floating across the room when she said "It's time." And what I next remember is me with a straightening comb, a gleaming new brass one, but I was wiping it on my clothes as Marilyn sat on the edge of the bed offering me some silver wave-clips. "You'd be pretty," I told her, "if you didn't have bad hair." Then I started dividing her hair into sections. I don't remember heating the comb, but it was smoking and each section I tried to straighten burnt off, broke off from the dark roots. Her platinum hair came out in my hand but she said, "It's gorgeous, Irene. Let's do yours." Sometimes when I sit alone thinking, fragments of the dream come back.'

Charlie still had his arms around me, but mine were at my side. Matches in one hand. He kissed the top of my head. Gentle but not fatherly. An absent-minded kiss.

'Forget it,' he said, waiving the issue of the suicide note. Which was the way my handwriting looked when I was hitting the bottle. Laboured, unsure letters that resembled a ten-year-old's. 'I never made out that you tried to kill yourself. That was the papers. Drink and pills can lead to accidental death,' he said, to placate me, I think. 'Strike a match.'

'Why?'

He smiled and slid the obituary back in my hand. Placing his fingers on the top of my head like he'd hold a basketball he said, 'Last night when I came up here and found you hunched on that blanket painting the stars, I said to myself, "Charlie, this was not in vain. This old chick's got heart."'

'That's a lie. You mocked me and asked if I was painting polka dots again, and then you accused me of running the battery down on your flashlight.'

He dropped his hand. 'You're worse than my mom for taking *everything* I say so hard.'

As I held a match to the obituary, I kept myself from saying that I didn't want to be called an 'old chick'.

Charlie batted at the little grey bits of newspapers that drifted into flight as that half-page flared into flame and became ashes. 'Dust to dust. Burn, motherfucker,' he said before settling onto my blanket with the pen and pad and removing a second obituary from his pants pocket. 'I had three. Herb would like this one from *Ebony*, because it's got a nice colour picture. But burn this other one,' he said, passing it back to me as he turned on his stomach. 'Let's tell Herbie you're a painter. You're even starting to look like one with your hair cropped short like that. Where's that little picture that you were working on last night.'

Charlie was a landmine one minute and a goldmine the next.

38

Four days later, we stayed up till dawn, because Charlie was driving down to Mexico that morning to make a big score with his friend Percy. They were going in Percy's car and the arrangement was that Charlie would drive over to Berkeley and meet him.

He told me, 'Calm down. I'll only be gone for a few days,' but with all the food he'd stuck in the refrigerator, it looked like he was planning not to return. I said, 'It would take me a year to get through all that ice cream.'

Just as he was meant to leave, he discovered that he had a flat tyre, so by the time he changed it and got to Berkeley, Percy had gone without him. To hear Charlie's car puttering into the garage a couple of hours later was a thrill, but I knew better than to run to greet him, because there would have been nothing worse than me gloating over his disappointment.

That afternoon when he said that he was going to an anti-Vietnam rally, I even helped him paint his peace sign. He had that record player going in the kitchen, and I didn't even complain about him listening to 'Love is a Many Splendoured Thing' a zillion times.

After nailing a piece of two-by-four timber to his placard, he stuck those sandals on and asked if I wanted to join him. 'Come on,' he said, sticking me in the ribs, 'you look good with your hair that short. I can tell everybody you're my big brother.'

I didn't bother to wave him off and figured that he wouldn't get back home that night. But I was annoyed when it became two nights and angry when he'd been away for three. I pretended that I wasn't jealous, but I must have been, because when Charlie hadn't returned by the fourth day, I was thinking about all the spiteful things I could do. Like pouring all the sodas he'd bought down the sink and throwing out his Kraft slices. I couldn't put his shoes in a tub of water, because they were in the bag he'd packed for Mexico which he'd never taken out of the car. Finally, I snipped the little rubber band that secured a lever in the record player to make the arm go back and forth.

Some days after that when I'd decided that he'd probably abandoned me and gone off to Spain or Morocco or someplace, a telegram arrived addressed to Venus Johnson. I was so angry and excited that I didn't even thank the delivery boy.

The message was simple. On October 17th Charlie's Beetle was in a collision with an ambulance. He died instantly. At least that's what the authorities told his parents who had informed Herbie who had wired to ask me to stay on. I have since found out that it had happened about twenty minutes after he left here.

The grief.

I was on my knees and seemed to go grey overnight. But the certainty that Charlie wanted me to survive protected me from the gin bottle.

'Don't look back,' I could hear him saying. 'Venus Johnson in the here and now.'

I got through the days believing that for me to be Venus Johnson made sense of his life . . . That first time I went out, I did it because I expected the walking to soothe me. It made me stand on my feet. Forced me to keep my head upright to see what was in front of me, so that I didn't cross on the red.

And when I wasn't walking, I held a paintbrush in my hand and made circles by day or painted stars by night. Moon and stars. The nightscape always moving and changing.

The walking and the painting. I knew that he'd forgive me for doing it for him. Forgive me remembering his voice, saying, 'Hey, Ice Cream, let's go on the roof and watch the stars fade.' We used to wrap up together in that crummy old Indian blanket and sit here watching them disappear as the dawn crept in.

* * *

If I'd been watching a movie about my life, that's where I'd want it to fade to black. Then a card could come up saying:

> Irene O'Brien, Alias Venus Johnson, remained in the little house in El Cerrito even after Herbie Goins returned home from the war in 1968.

I don't know what I was expecting, but I recall becoming anxious at the idea of Herb coming back and me having to leave. I had grown accustomed to my quiet life and had begun to educate myself. I used to sit here reading and even practised handwriting until I improved my penmanship. So often I was tempted to write to Charlie's parents to say, 'I am who I am, because of him.'

Anyway, Herbie appeared two days before he was meant to. A tall middle-aged man with greying temples, but otherwise average-looking. Not that I was anything to brag about. I'd put on a few pounds and kept my hair short. A natural, as they called it back then.

I asked if I could rent the back bedroom until I could save enough to find something bigger, but he said, 'How about we strike a deal? Cook and clean, and you can have the room for free.'

I needed money for paints, because I had this plan in my mind that if I could afford to keep doing my little nightscapes, I might eventually be able to sell a few in some of the coffee shops and restaurants in Berkeley that hung people's work with a price-tag. So I told Herbie, 'That sounds like a live-in position. Thirty dollars on top would be fair, and it's not so much more than you were paying while I was here alone.'

We made an agreement that I wouldn't ask him about the war if he didn't talk about Charlie, because I was afraid that that would become the common ground between us. 'People die,' Herbie said, 'you can't let it get to you.' He was too quiet and mannerly. Shoulders back. A real soldier. But I didn't let it bother me. His silence bent towards smouldering, but I had been prepared for the fact that Vietnam and the growing opposition to it would make him a bit of a wreck.

Still, I was never afraid to be in the house with him. I no longer looked like the woman he might have drooled over from across the room, so I didn't even bother to lock my bedroom door at night.

It was easy to stay out of his way and make myself indispensable. Never letting dishes pile up in the sink and even ironing the sheets. I'm not sure he thought much of my cooking, because in those days he still ate a lot of pork and wanted everything fried. It kept this house alive to have smells coming from the kitchen and he admitted that he liked the sound of somebody else padding about, although he was as quiet as a mouse.

We didn't so much live together as side by side. That's probably how we managed to be housemates for seventeen years, and when people mistook us as related it was always as brother and sister rather than husband and wife.

Our swords only crossed once. It was after Reagan had been elected and I bought a star for Charlie. They were selling them with an accompanying deed in a fancy craft shop in Berkeley that also sold my little paintings. I used to get thirty or forty dollars back then, so paying fifty dollars to have a star named after Charlie struck me as a dividend. The deed was lovely. Gold leaf calligraphy on parchment paper showing the location of 'Charles Paul Adams' near Orion and stating that the name had been logged with some official-sounding body that dealt with the stars. But when I showed it to Herbie, he said, 'Why waste my pension money on some mess like that?'

I had to remind him that I made contributions to the house. We had made several improvements to the kitchen and bathroom which some of the money I'd made from my work helped to pay for.

Otherwise we never argued.

We even sat up here in shifts. He did days, I did nights, which suited me. Herbie would ask, 'How can you sit up there in the dark?' when he'd watch me head up here like a shepherd about to watch its flock by night, tam pulled down over my ears, my big plaid poncho on and my hands protected by those fur-lined gloves with the fingertips cut out. With the two lanterns I'd bought from the camping store, I could sit out here like tonight and feel like I owned the world, and I'd tell Herbie, 'I'm not just up there twiddling my thumbs, I'm painting the stars.'

I had altered my speaking voice. Rather than sounding as prim as Irene O'Brien, I tried to sound a little flat. A bit more like Mother, but I couldn't disguise my singing, so I stopped that altogether.

Once I thought he was out, and I was down there singing in the bath. Not just a hum, but projecting. Really enjoying myself, crooning some old ballad and the next thing, there's a tap at the door.

'Hello?' I called, my heart was really pounding, because I never gave up feeling that he might have figured out who I was.

'Just checking,' said Herbie. He sounded like a sergeant on duty. 'That didn't sound like you.'

'Who else could it be?' I laughed rather nervously.

'I guess you could have let somebody in the house.'

He had the odd woman in, but I never made them feel welcome. Seventeen years we were here together. Before prostate cancer took him, it almost hurt me not to tell Herb that the woman who'd been leaving the toilet seat down all those years was the girl of his dreams. But then, it wasn't me that he wanted, it was the magazine shot of that nymphet in a sarong in *Native Drums*.

He lived for the TV and sometimes he'd pack his fishing gear and head for some beach. I was afraid to ask what was going on in his head for fear that he'd wonder what was going on in mine.

The greatest shock I got was when he died and left this house to me thirteen years ago. And the truth is that I missed him so much, I used to say good morning to the fridge. Then I got some goldfish, and finally I got the dog from the pound. Trust me to find a chow that barks at the full moon. That first year I called her Mitzy but then I changed it to Luna.

The only time I considered moving was because of her.

It was after Clinton's inauguration and a Black family moved in next door. I suspected that I was in for neighbour pains as soon as they piled out of their fancy four-wheel drive. Music just blaring.

Father was more pumped up than Mike Tyson and Mother, with the psychotic eyes of a drive-by shooter, had her jeri-curl glistening with a spray shine. Her two-inch fingernails were painted bright yellow and she had both their little girls rigged out in spandex pedal-pushers. With the heavy beaded extensions the children had in their hair, it's no wonder that they couldn't sleep, although Mother put it down to my dog barking.

The creases must have still been in their kitchen curtains when Mother, in her Dacron track-suit, came to complain about Luna.

After thirty-five years of protecting my identity, I'm a pro at backing out of confrontations. Venus Johnson is a certified wimp. But that woman meant to provoke me with her hand on her hip.

So I muzzled Luna to stop her night howl, and for the ten months they lived over there, I rarely came out here.

What good's a chow muzzled at night? Not that she had much to bark about until they moved in. Luna's so meek, she used to run from robins. When she was a puppy, I used to say, 'Shame on you. What will people think about a big dog running from a bird.'

I never could understand why she barked up here, but then I heard a woman on the radio explain that a lot of dogs bark at the moon.

Daylight Saving Time won't start for an hour and here I am already yawning.

Old age.

At least tomorrow I won't be one of the ones griping about missing an hour's sleep, because Luna is my alarm clock and her bowels tell her what time it is. Like clockwork, she'll be scratching on my bedroom door for her walk at the same time she did yesterday.

It's also Palm Sunday. The start of Holy Week. I remember how Lilian and I used to be given a palm from the church. I couldn't understand why, and then Miss Hortense explained that it had something to do with the people who had used the palms originally to line the path of Christ when he entered Jerusalem and that the following year they are used to make the ashes for Ash Wednesday.

When I sit here thinking about what Charlie did for me and how I was determined to survive for his sake, I wonder if that was the whole thing about Christ. Maybe he'd been so good to some people that they kept going, kept his name alive so it didn't seem like he'd lived in vain.

I've put all this energy into recalling what I managed to forget and somehow I feel a little lighter. Maybe even ready to forgive everybody. Lilian and Mother included.

Last week when I took Luna to the vet for her shots, I picked up an old magazine in the waiting room. There was an article about screen sirens and suicide and I was pictured alongside Marilyn, Bardot, Lupe Velez and Rita Hayworth. But Lupe and I were the only ones cited as being responsible for our own deaths since the current consensus is that Marilyn was bumped off.

When I die, the truth about my experience dies too. That's all that we can take with us. But in my back room, I've kept years of work which I've bequeathed to the National Association for Autism, because I think that's what was wrong with Nadine. The nightscapes are signed Venus Johnson, but I've put the initials IOB on the back, explaining why in a sealed envelope which is in a box at the bank. It should increase their value.

Whatever happens, I can never stop some people from reducing my life to some forgettable movies.

The film buffs will sift through the press clippings and publicity stills orchestrated by Samuel Gottlieb Productions and the journalists writing about the old days may quote Lilian who believed she knew me best, because we shared a mother and a past, but doesn't every life amount to more than a few paragraphs and time-worn images?

In my case, like Ethel Waters used to sing, 'Nobody knows the trouble I've seen.'

Not Ruthie Mae Matthews.

Not Henrietta Dobson.

Not Mercy or Sam Gottlieb.

Not even Charlie.

Because no-one knows us like we know ourselves.

Alan Gilsenan was a tireless critic who believed that I could write this and endured me with patience, love and good humour through each stage.

David Godwin's early enthusiasm was encouraging, and Stuart Prebble gave more than I deserved of his time.

Simon Albury, Moira Reilly, Susan Sandon, Steve Lovi, Tony Garnett, Bassam Alghanim, Michael Ratledge, Caroline Coon, Kathy Gilfillan, Patricia Van Der Leun and Miss Karis, I am grateful to all of you.

I thank my agent Alexandra Pringle and the editorial team at Flamingo including Philip, Mandy and Jon. I also thank Geoff and Adrian at HarperCollins and mustn't forget the photocopiers at SNAP in Sandyford as well as Nigel O'Leary at Sam McCauley's.

Finally, I thank the indomitable generation which includes my mother Inez, my aunt Thelma (1923–1998), my uncle Henry, Allison Hennix and the inspiring actress and singer, Miss Dorothy Dandridge whose life fired my imagination to create this story.